I Want Mommy

WHERE DID SHE COME FROM ? WHY IS SHE ALONE ?

A KAREN BLACKSTONE THRILLER - VOLUME 2

NINO S. THEVENY

SÉBASTIEN THEVENY

SELF-PUBLISHED

Translated from French to English

By Jacquie Bridonneau

Original Title : *Je veux maman*

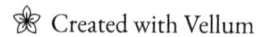

❉ Created with Vellum

For Maria, my mom, of course!

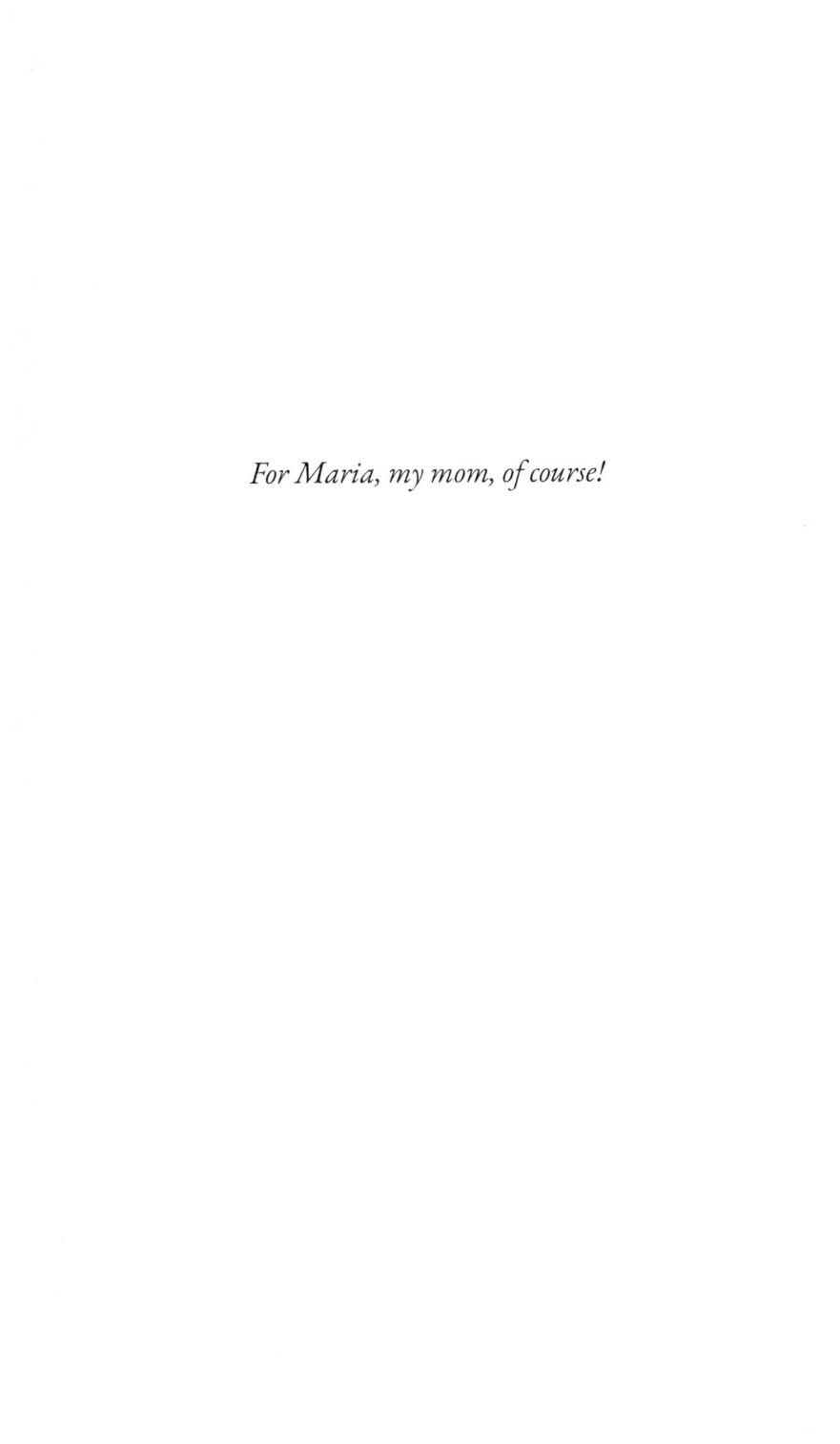

Prologue
LIKE A PHANTOM

"SHOOT! I'm going to be late with this lousy weather," grumbled Rebecca, her hands gripping the steering wheel of her old Ford Taurus. Its tires were having trouble finding purchase on that snowy road in the countryside, weaving through two soft wood forests.

The young lady had been complaining ever since she left Village of Four Seasons, when after having done her hair and makeup at home, she saw that it had started to snow again. There were already a couple of inches of immaculate white snowflakes on her doorstep and she knew that the snow would just make things more complicated. She was on the brink of phoning Gavin to cancel their date, but she wanted to see him so badly that her stomach was twisting with desire. She'd been waiting for this date for days now and it wasn't four inches of light snow that would come between her and a good time! She'd even thought of phoning him to ask him to come and pick her up, but a bit of Jewish prudishness had stopped her. She couldn't have one of her office colleagues in her house for a formal first date! Things like that just weren't kosher! Rebecca knew herself well: should she let him in, she would be the one dragging him to her bedroom to keep him there until daybreak. Meeting up in a neutral venue was the best idea for their first love date.

She thus braved the freezing cold, snow and mist, and put her key in the car to start it up. She carefully put her foot on the accelerator to see how her Ford reacted in the snow and slid down her driveway about thirty feet before reaching the road, that luckily had been plowed not too long ago.

Right after that though she began to swear like a soldier.

Night had fallen on Morgan County over two hours ago and the cold weather had morphed into frigid weather, making it difficult to drive. Rebecca encouraged herself by thinking that Gavin would be waiting for her. She turned the radio on. Creedence Clearwater Revival was asking *"Have you ever seen the rain?"*.

"The rain?" Rebecca answered. "No rain, but too much damn snow, for sure!"

She glanced at the clock on the dashboard. Already fifteen minutes late. Better to arrive late than not at all, she thought to herself.

The snow was falling harder now and large white snowflakes were making it difficult for her to see more than ten feet ahead of the Ford and its windshield wipers barely helped. She was afraid to go over fifteen miles an hour.

And luckily so.

Otherwise the accident would have been inevitable.

Though she wouldn't have been judged as guilty, Rebecca would never have been able to forget the death of that little girl all alone on the side of the road who appeared suddenly, like a phantom, in her headlights...

CHAPTER 1
Red mush on the immaculate snow

SHE SLAMMED ON HER BRAKES.

Not a good idea when it's snowing!

In the pallid light of her Ford's headlights, though the windshield with its starry frost the tired windshield wipers were trying to wipe away, the dark silhouette of the little girl was getting closer and closer.

The tires were squealing on the snow and ice-capped road as the vehicle kept on moving, with no possibility of stopping it, towards the paralyzed little girl standing on the side of the road.

Rebecca screamed as she squeezed the steering wheel with both hands, her articulations white with effort.

The collision now seemed inevitable. The young lady was already apprehensive just thinking of the muffled noise the collision between her bumpers and the little girl would make, reducing her to red mush on the immaculate snow.

Driven by an idiotic reflex, Rebecca closed her eyes so she wouldn't see that. Then she turned her steering wheel in the opposite direction the vehicle was heading.

Second error someone not used to driving on the snow made. The Ford swerved towards the little girl, who didn't budge, just like a petrified hare in a bright light.

But perhaps God was looking down on the little girl that night?

No one would ever know, but the car finally bypassed the child in an unreal ballet between metal and flesh, just like a bull aiming at a bullfighter, who nimbly would take a step aside, with an arabesque of his red muleta.

The front of the car stopped in the snow on the side of the road, just a foot or two from the little girl. Rebecca's forehead hit the steering wheel, and she opened her eyes, screaming. Blood was running down from her forehead, making it hard to see.

There was a sudden silence after the fury.

The young lady turned her head and saw the little face, still paralyzed, just two feet from her on the passenger side, her eyes wide open, but empty, not showing any emotions.

She tried with all her strength to open the car door and panicked. The door, crumpled by the shock, wouldn't budge. The other door, nearer the child, was half buried in the snow drift and wouldn't open either, despite Rebecca's frenetic gestures pushing on the handle.

"Shit, shit and reshit," she swore, gritting her teeth. "I'm stuck."

Bug-eyed with fear, she tried to talk to the little girl, whose long brown hair hanging down to her shoulders was covered with snowflakes and who wasn't even wearing a winter coat. She seemed to be three or four at the most. Nearly a baby, her brown eyes wide open like two glazed marbles.

"Hey, little girl! Can you hear me? Can you try to pull the door open?"

The little girl didn't budge though and kept on sucking her thumb.

Rebecca was getting claustrophobic, and she forced herself to take deep and slow breaths so she wouldn't panic. She tried to get into the backseat. She hoped she'd be able to get out through one of the back doors or by the trunk, as the car's hood was the only thing stuck in the snow and the back of the vehicle was free. A minute later, relieved, she was out and rushed to the little girl, covering her with her arms to try to protect her from the cold.

"Are you okay, honey? You're not hurt?"

The young lady discovered with dismay traces of blood on the little girl's neck, chin and lips. Despite – or notwithstanding – that apparent wound, all the little girl did was continue to suck her thumb.

"Are you injured? Where are your parents? What

are you doing here, all alone? Are you lost? Did you fall? Did you have a car accident?"

The little girl didn't answer any of those questions. Had something recently happened to her, and she was still shocked by it or was she frightened by Rebecca's car that nearly ran into her? So terrified that she was scared stiff and couldn't open her mouth? Or maybe she couldn't talk, the young lady briefly thought. She suddenly wanted to shake her by her shoulders to wake her up, so that she'd finally open up, so she'd say what she was doing there, in the middle of the forest, in a snowstorm, miles from the nearest town.

"What's your name, sweetie?"

No response either. Rebecca had hoped that by asking her what her name was, an easy question with an easy answer, she'd finally speak. Nothing at all though, the little girl remained silent.

She hadn't pronounced a single word, she hadn't moved, but... she was shivering and quaking.

Rebecca took her coat off and wrapped it around the tiny feverish body. She looked up and down the road in the hope of seeing a car, but quickly realized that up till now, on that little road, she hadn't yet seen anyone, and no one had followed her. She waited a few minutes, hoping to see some headlights in the distance, hugging the little girl to keep her warm, her nose buried in her long hair. But was forced to give up.

"Come on. We'll go in the car and wait for a rescue squad."

She dragged her into the car and the child allowed herself to be pushed and pulled, without complaining, just like a marionette. They sat next to each other on the back seat, then Rebecca got up and squirmed around to reach her purse, which had fallen to the floor in the front seat. She grabbed her cell phone and looked for the first contact that came to her mind, though she'd completely forgotten about him during the past ten or so minutes.

The phone rang five times before reaching voicemail, where she gave him a message with a shaky voice.

"Gavin, it's Rebecca. Please call me back as soon as you can. I had an accident, it's no big deal, a fender-bender, I'm okay."

When she hung up, she suddenly realized what had happened and Rebecca burst into tears.

The little girl, sitting next to her on the lopsided backseat, still seemed to be absent, not at all bothered by her tears. Her eyes were as dry as a bone.

What trauma could she have had that she'd lost her voice and wasn't even bothered by her near accident?

Rebecca turned the volume of her ringtone up so she wouldn't miss Gavin's call. After that she moved to the front seat, behind the wheel, hoping to start the car up again and especially turn the heat on. The temperature inside was nearly as cold as it was outside, and they could see their breath forming crystals on the inside of the windows. It's nearly freezing, she thought to herself, shivering.

She turned the key, imploring God. The motor was just as mute as was the little girl in the back seat.

"Shit!" Rebecca swore, trying to turn the key again, but to no avail.

She energetically rubbed her shoulders, freezing, despite her thick sweater ever since she gave her coat to the little girl. She leaned over on her seat and opened the glove compartment, rummaging around until she put her hand on what she had been hoping to find there: an aluminum or poly-something or other survival blanket. She could never remember its exact name. That wasn't important though and she ripped the package open and crawled into the back seat again.

"I'm going to take my coat back honey," she said to the little girl who allowed herself to be manipulated without batting an eye.

Then she wrapped her up in the survival blanket, going around her twice, and put her coat back on. That way both of them could wait for a while in the car until Gavin came and got them... who wasn't picking up, damn it!

"What the heck is he doing?"

Call emergency services, call them as her date hadn't answered, she thought. Why hadn't she done that earlier, she wondered.

She dialed 911, described her accident as well as how she'd discovered a little girl who was alone, who wouldn't say a word, with blood on the bottom of her face, sucking her thumb and holding a little stuffed lion in her other hand.

Help would come within half an hour, they reassured her. She shouldn't panic and shouldn't let the little girl out of sight. She could hang up now, they'd noted her number.

Rebecca turned to talk to the little girl.

"So, they're going to come and get us. Everything's fine, now. You're not too cold?"

The little girl didn't answer and unrelentingly kept on sucking her thumb. But at least she was no longer shaking, Rebecca noticed.

"Are you thirsty? I've got water. You want some?"

No reaction.

"Can you tell me what happened to you? And what your name is? You can tell me. I'm your friend... Did someone hurt you?"

The little girl's eyes suddenly popped wide open, her nostrils quivered, and her breathing accelerated. She shook her head slowly, haggardly.

Then suddenly there was a miracle.

"I want mommy!" she moaned.

"Sure," Rebecca jumped. "But where's your mommy?"

"I want mommy," she repeated.

"We'll find her sweetie. Don't worry. Who's your mommy? What's her name? You can tell me."

"I want mommy!"

"I know," said the young lady, rubbing the little girl's arm. "The policemen will find her you know. Come on, tell me your name. A pretty little girl like you must have a pretty name, I'm sure. You can whisper it to me if you want. It'll be our secret."

Rebecca leaned towards the little girl.

"I... want... mommy..."

A yellow light coming from a pair of headlights suddenly shown through the Ford's back window, inundating the interior.

CHAPTER 2
Unclear thoughts

THE FLASHING LIGHTS of the police car danced through the sky. The car carefully stopped behind Rebecca's. They could see two heads in the back seat.

Sergent Pete Gallister got out of the passenger side and officer Myra Stonehenge got out from behind the wheel. About a hundred feet behind them another police car was slowly approaching.

Gallister walked up to the window of the Ford stuck in the ditch and softly knocked, lighting up the inside with his flashlight.

"Miss Stern? I'm Sergent Gallister from Morgan County. Can you get out?"

Rebecca nodded and opened the door, relieved that her problems were now over with the arrival of the policemen.

She gently pulled the little girl out after her.

"Is that your daughter?" the officer asked.

"Not at all. This is the little girl I almost hit... Good Lord!" the young lady suddenly realized, bursting into tears.

"It'll be alright," Gallister consoled her while Stonehenge took care of the child.

"I want mommy..."

"That's all she's said," Rebecca told them. "Ever since I brought her into the car, she hasn't said anything else."

The young lady told the police officers how she'd run across the little girl.

"You can come with us to the police station, Miss Stern. That way both you and the little girl, you'll be able to warm up and you'll be safe. You shouldn't be out on the road in this weather," added Gallister. "My colleagues will comb the surrounding area to try to find out where this little girl came from. No way could she have appeared like that in your headlights, like a miracle... She didn't descend from heaven!"

Right then Rebecca's phone rang, and she rushed into the car to get her purse.

"Gavin, finally," she whispered.

"Reb, you okay? I was scared silly when I heard your message. Where are you?"

"Don't worry, Gavin. I'm safe and sound. The police just arrived, and they'll take me to the station. I'm sorry about our date..."

"Hey! Don't worry, what's important is that you're in one piece. We'll take a raincheck. I'll join you. Where are you going?"

"To Versailles," Rebecca answered. "But don't come, you could end up in the ditch just like me."

"Someone will have to bring you back."

The young lady looked at Sergent Gallister.

"I don't know how long this will take. I'll call you, Gavin. Thanks. And you take care now."

Then she turned to the policeman.

"What about my car, Sergent?"

"Don't worry, my colleagues will have it towed away as soon as the weather clears. But in the meanwhile, let's go."

He gently escorted her to the patrol car in which the little girl was already seated. Rebecca gazed at her, contemplating her haggard features, wondering what could be going on in her unclear thoughts.

Officer Stonehenge put the car into drive and the wheels spun for a moment in the snow before the car found purchase and slowly drove away in the freezing night. The snow was still coming down and the windshield wipers were working overtime to chase away the powdery snowflakes on the nearly frozen windshield.

"What terrible weather!" the driver said. "Luckily that poor kid found you where she was, otherwise, she would quickly have frozen to death in the ditch."

Rebecca turned around, looking at her car that was beached liked a powerless steel whale. Then she looked straight into the surrounding forest where the little speechless girl had appeared from nowhere.

Where had she come from?

Who was she? Where were her parents? Where was

she going like that, alone, her little stuffed lion in one hand and sucking her thumb?

"I want mommy..." she murmured next to her, chanting those three words as if they were a protective mantra.

* * *

It took them over half an hour to reach the police station in Versailles County. For the whole way there, in the back seat, the little girl nodded, repeating time and time again the same words that the other passengers had trouble understanding, as she no longer articulated them and continued to suck her thumb. With the other hand she firmly held her little stuffed lion against her cheek, as if rocking it. Where it touched the child's chin, the dark yellowish fur on the animal was tinted with a few drops of red blood.

While Officer Stonehenge was driving on the snow-filled roads, Sergeant Gallister had the office call a doctor.

"Tell him to come as soon as we arrive," he told his colleague with the car's private phone. "We have to get this little girl checked. She's freezing, she's covered with blood on her neck and seems very confused. I want her taken care of immediately."

And that was what happened as soon as they reached the police station. Officer Stonehenge took the little girl to see Doctor Aloys Johnson, a seventy or so-old doctor who now only worked part-time, but who was always on call when the cops needed him. All three of them went into an adjacent room and Pete Gallister and Rebecca Stern sat down in another.

"Sit down, Miss Stern. Would you like a cup of coffee, something to eat?"

Rebecca was still shivering, from the cold or from the emotions.

"A coffee would be great, thanks."

"Sugar?"

"No, thanks."

Two minutes later, the sergeant came back with two steaming mugs that he put down on the desk.

"So, Miss Stern, could you tell me about this evening that wasn't like any other? I'd like to know how all of this happened. To start with, can I ask you where you were going at this time of the night in a snowstorm like this?"

"I was going out to dinner."

"A business dinner you couldn't cancel? What could have been so important that you decided to go out in a snowstorm like this?"

"I was meeting a friend."

"A boyfriend?" Gallister insinuated.

"What does that change?" responded Rebecca without missing a beat.

The sergeant smiled and shook his head.

"You're right, that doesn't change a thing. You left from your house then? Where do you live?"

"Sunrise Beach."

"And you were going to...?"

"Right here, in Versailles. Paloma Restaurant."

"Nice place," Gallister approved. "I went there a couple of weeks ago with my wife. But that doesn't have anything to do with the investigation, sorry, let's get back on track. Did you see any other cars on the road?"

"Not a one. I was completely alone. But you're right, I shouldn't have gone out."

"True. But just think that at least that allowed you to find that little abandoned girl in the middle of nowhere wearing next to nothing in this huge snowstorm. Without you, who knows where she'd be now. You know you probably saved her life."

When she heard these words Rebecca once again shivered and couldn't control herself, despite the relative heat of the coffee in the mug she was holding with both hands.

"Unless..." the sergeant continued.

"Unless what?" the young lady asked.

"Unless you really didn't *save* this child, literally speaking. Let's look at the hypothesis – and I'm really sorry but I do have to ask you this question – that you already knew that little girl that you *said* you picked up on the side of the road..."

Rebecca nearly spilled her steaming coffee on her knees.

"Jesus Christ, Sergeant, what are you insinuating there? That's nuts! Your whole story is completely crazy! Like pretty soon you'll be suspecting me of who knows what when I didn't do anything reprehensible at all. If I hadn't *picked up* this little girl, like you said crudely, I would have been accused of failure to assist a person in danger, that's something I can understand. But here, this is completely cockeyed. No, Sergeant, I can assure you that I never saw that little girl before I nearly ran into her on that road."

"I understand your reaction, Miss Stern. But you know, in our line of work, we see all kinds. You cannot even imagine how black human souls can be when on the outside they're as white as snow."

"So you're also poets in the police force?" asked Rebecca ironically.

Gallister took a sip of his already cool coffee.

"Let's just say that sometimes we have to relativize, so we don't go crazy too. So, let's go over this once again. You're driving to meet a friend at a restaurant, you didn't see any other cars on the road, when suddenly you see a little girl, who jumped out of nowhere, in your headlights. You slam on your brakes, losing control of your car, and you nearly run her over. You get out, go get her and you bring her back into your car while waiting for us to arrive. Is that all correct?"

"Like I said, yes."

"Did you try to see if another car had gotten stuck on the road not too far from you? Maybe her parents had an accident, and she was the only one who was able to get out of the car."

The young lady shook her head.

"I instinctively tried to get the little girl in the car and warm her up so she wouldn't freeze. After that, and in all due respect, Sergeant, it's your job to search and investigate. Not mine."

Pete Gallister laughed.

"You're right. And that's what my colleagues are doing right now. While we're waiting for the results of the on-site investigations, I'd like to ask you one more question. Do you have any children, Miss Stern?"

"What does that have to do with anything?"

"Please answer my question."

"No, I don't."

Right then, Doctor Johnson walked in, frowning and worried.

"Sergeant, may I see you for a second?"

"Excuse me, Miss Stern," said the cop following the doctor into the adjacent room.

The little girl was sitting on the desk, looking at the door, still holding her little stuffed lion.

"I checked her out," Johnson began, "and didn't see anything serious, except for some frostbite on the tips of her fingers and especially on her toes, which makes me think that she'd been walking in the snow for quite a while, poor kid."

Gallister, horrified, only noticed then that the little girl was only wearing a pair of bedroom slippers that the doctor had taken off and put on the floor. Slippers decorated with white fur and a purple pompom on the top of them.

"She was luckily discovered before her toes were completely frostbitten. I'd say another half an hour in the snow, and we would have had to amputate them," the doctor continued.

The sergeant put his hand on his mouth, appalled.

"Jesus, what happened then with this kid? Where did she come from? A flying saucer didn't drop her off on the side of the road! There must be a rational explanation."

"There's something else, Sergeant."

"Yeah? Don't tell me that she was..."

"No, no, nothing sexual, thank God. Just something strange when I examined her face and her neck. She had lots of coagulated blood on her chin."

"Probably due to the accident, or maybe she fell. Or she was scratched by some branches or brambles?"

"I can affirm without any possibilities of an error, that none of that was the case, Serge. I cleaned her up and she didn't have the tiniest wound at all, not on her lips, not on her chin, not even on her neck."

"Whose blood was it then?"

"I don't know, but it wasn't hers, anyway..."

CHAPTER 3
Blood on your face

TAKEN ABACK, Pete Gallister looked at Dr. Johnson and then back at the little girl, who was still sucking her thumb.

"You mean it's not her blood?"

"Affirmative. At least this blood didn't come from a wound on her."

"Crazier and crazier," Gallister sighed. "What did you use to clean her face up with Doc?"

"Ordinary hydrophilic gauze, why?"

"What did you do with it?"

"I tossed it in the bin, why?"

"I'd like to have it analyzed. Myra," he said, looking at his colleague. "Can you bag it and send it to the Jefferson lab*?

"Consider it done."

---

* Jefferson City, the capital of Missouri. Morgan County reports to Jefferson City.

"She still hasn't said anything?"

"Not anything else than what she keeps repeating: 'I want mommy.' I'll keep on asking her questions as calmly as possible, but I don't have much hope here. I think we should call Frances in, don't you?"

"Who's Frances?" the doctor asked.

"A child psychiatrist from Jefferson who we work with when we have to ask children questions. Often, us cops, we're not really trained for stuff like that, and we know it. Everyone's got their own work, right Doc?"

"Totally! Can I go now?"

"If you can just write up a certificate that'll allow us to quickly put her into a specialized structure, while we find out where her parents are... that would be great. And in the meanwhile then, we'll take her to the hospital so they can take care of her frostbitten members."

"Poor kid," Myra added, tenderly running her hand through her hair, "she's so tired she can't even stand up anymore. Come on honey. You still don't want to tell me your name?"

All four of them left the room, Officer Stonehenge to take the little girl to the hospital, Dr. Johnson to go back home and Sergeant Gallister to return to Rebecca, who was still sitting on a chair in his office.

"Miss Stern? Thanks for waiting. Just a couple more questions and you can go home."

"Let me remind you that I don't have a car..."

"One of my colleagues will drive you home, don't worry," said Gallister, sitting down.

He mechanically grabbed the cup of coffee and took a sip. He immediately spit it back out.

"Shit, this coffee is completely cold. Yuck! Tough luck... Miss Stern, you've got blood on your face. What happened to you?"

"What can I say... You perhaps know, Sergeant, that I sort of ran off the road a while ago. And when my car finally stopped spinning on the snow and ran into the ditch, my head hit the steering wheel. My eyebrow opened up. And let me thank you again for having thought of me when the doctor was still here..."

Pete Gallister pursed his lips.

"Oops, sorry. We were just thinking about the little girl, I'm sure you can understand. Do you want me to call Dr. Johnson back?"

"No, that's okay," replied Rebecca, touching her forehead. "It's not bleeding anymore."

"So, it is your blood then on your face..."

"Excuse me?"

"It's your blood?"

"Of course it is! What a question! Whose blood do you think it is? Seriously!" the young lady suddenly said, now more annoyed. "Are you almost finished with all these ridiculous insinuations that you keep on repeating ever since I've been sitting on this fucking uncomfortable chair? That's enough! I'd like this damn evening to be over once and for all. I was calmly driving to a restaurant, I saved the life of a little girl who showed up from nowhere, I had an accident, I busted open my eyebrow, I called you for help and here now you're treating me like I'm guilty of something. I am sick and..."

"Calm down, please. Listen, let me be clear here, I'm not accusing you of anything. I just have to ask you some questions so I can understand what, for me too, is a totally crazy event. Ever since I've been a cop I've never seen a case like this. If I insist – maybe too much, I agree – on this story about the blood, it's because I just learned that the blood on the little girl's face wasn't hers. She wasn't wounded at all. So I said to myself, that maybe, when you got out of the car to help her and you hugged her tightly to warm her up, maybe then some of your blood got on her face. Could that be the case, Miss Stern?"

Rebecca lowered her head, exhausted. Now she was nearly crying.

"I have no idea, Sergeant. Everything went so fast, and it was so crazy that I don't know any more exactly what I did. But I don't remember having put my head on her neck. Maybe she put hers on mine, that's more probable, don't you think?"

"Of course. To allow me to discard this hypothesis, I'd like a sample of some of your blood to analyze it with the child's. Will you consent to this, Miss Stern?"

"Do what you have to do, Sergeant, and let's get it over with. I just want to go home."

The policeman got up and walked to the medicine cabinet and took a package of hydrophilic cotton out.

"Here, clean yourself up with this, and then give it to me. That'll be enough to analyze it. I'll print out your declaration, and then you can read and sign it. After that Office Patterson will drive you back home."

Gallister picked up his cell phone and walked out of the office before suddenly turning around.

"Miss Stern?"

"Yes?"

"Thank you. Thank you for that little girl."

* * *

Sergeant Gallister left the room and went outside to call his colleague who was on-site at the accident scene. It was still snowing, and the parking lot was a thick blanket of white. Pete pulled the collar of his jacket up to protect himself from the wind and lit up a cigarette. He took a long drag, his eyes closed, enjoying this short break from such a curious evening.

"Hey guys, it's Pete. So, whatcha got for me?"

"Hey Pete," his colleague answered, "let me tell you, you're the lucky one here. We're freezing our butts off here. And all that for *nada*."

"Meaning?"

"To sum it up, we didn't find a thing around here. Too much snow. Even the kid's footsteps were blown away or covered. In about a thirty-foot radius around the accident site, we didn't get anything, or it was polluted by tire tracks, or footprints that could have belonged to anyone: the lady, the little girls, all of us, etc. I don't have to spell it out for you."

"Fuck!" grumbled Gallister putting his half-smoked cigarette out. "That's not going to lead us anywhere. I'd imagine that you investigated the surrounding area?"

"Affirmative, Chief! And you know what? Well, we didn't find nothing. Not a single car that was stopped or had an accident for miles around. We'll keep on looking tomorrow when it's light. We all think that the kid appeared by a miracle, like Virgin Mary, get it?"

"Yeah, Our Lady of Fatima, Our Lady of Guadalupe, all that shit. All that Catholic bull! Hey, we're cops man, not priests! So what are your logical conclusions then?"

"Listen, I've been thinking about that, and I only see two possible explanations."

"Which are?" Gallister encouraged him.

"So, either the kid walked for a couple of miles in the snow and her footprints were snowed over or blown away."

"Or?"

"Or someone let her out of a car, sort of like a dog you abandon in the forest before you go on summer vacation, on the side of the road..."

CHAPTER 4
Almost like a noise an animal would make

THE SSM HEALTH ST. Mary's Hospital in Jefferson City was a modern, human-sized facility where the little girl who had been found in the snow the night before was taken, allowing her a few precious hours of sleep.

Yet, lying down in her bed in the pediatric ward, her hands and feet bound in hydrophilic gauze, and arms linked to a serum filled IV tube, the child seemed to be floating in an artificial and medically induced fog.

When a shadow appeared behind the door of her room, she didn't even turn her head to look at it. Her eyes only slid open imperceptibly in their orbits to discover the lady slowly walking up to her bed. She smiled warmly at the little girl and sat down so their faces were at the same level.

"Hello. My name is Frances. What's your name?"

The little girl's pupils didn't move.

"See my lab coat? I'm Dr. Frances Cagliari, and I'm

a specialist in children, like you. They told me your feet and your hands got really cold. I can see they've been taking good care of you, don't you think? You've got nice bandages around your fingers. Can you move them?"

If the little girl could move them, she didn't show it.

"I introduced myself to you. Now it's your turn, can you tell me what your name is? That'll make it easier for us, don't you agree? I'm sure your parents gave you a nice name..."

The little girl winced, her mouth twisting itself as if it was holding back a sudden pain. Right after that she closed her eyelids and pretended to sleep. But she only kept them closed for a minute before turning her head towards her bedside table.

Then she made a noise, without saying a word, just like a prehistoric child would have when they'd not yet invented a real language. A muted protest came from the bottom of her throat, almost like a noise an animal would make.

"What's wrong, sweetie? Do you hurt someplace?" Frances said, following the movement of her eyes.

There, on the floor next to the bedside table, she saw the stuffed animal that the little girl couldn't reach. She bent over to pick it up and handed it to the little girl lying in the hospital bed with its clean white sheets.

"Oh. So that's what you wanted, right?"

The child psychiatrist laid the little stuffed lion

down on the girl's chest, where she immediately put her arms around it, tenderly.

"You like your little friend? He does too. He loves you even. I'm sure that he missed you and that he's happy to be with you again. What's his name?"

Hoping to hit a raw nerve, the professional in child psychology believed, for a fleeting moment, that her technique would bear fruit, as the little girl's eyes twinkled. This hope though was quickly quelched by an oppressive silence.

"Okay. Let's play a game then. I'm going to try to guess his name. If I'm wrong, you shake your head, and if I'm right, you blink, is that okay with you? So, I'm going to start now. Umm... a nice baby lion like you, I'd say his name is... Roar!"

No reaction. Frances thus continued her enumeration without trying to obtain a yes or a no, just now hoping to establish a tie with her.

"Okay, so that's not his name... How about Misty? No?... Oscar? Not Oscar either... I'm not very good at this apparently. Let me try Tommy... Willie?... Winnie? Pooky? Sugar? Simba?... Can't you give me a little hint? Just the first letter? No?"

Suddenly Dr. Cagliari thought of something else. What if the child didn't understand English? There was no guarantee that she was American. After all, no one knew a thing about her. Neither her name nor even her age. She didn't have any papers on her, or anything that would have allowed them to determine her origins. Where she was born, where she was going, who her parents were. She'd been picked up on the side of the road, her feet in the snow, and up until now, when Frances was at her bedside, the police had not been able to find any car accidents in the surrounding area.

In a nutshell, the child had appeared from nowhere... from no one... as nobody had reported a missing child. Why? Because her parents had died in an accident? Because they'd abandoned her?

Frances Cagliari put her hand on the stuffed animal, then gently took it, standing it on its little feet at the end of the bed.

"Let's try another game! As you don't want, or maybe you can't talk to me, let's say that your baby lion, whatever his name is, will talk for you. It'll be fun! He'll be your ears and your mouth. If you want, you can put him in front of your face, and he'll answer me..."

The doctor did this, handing the stuffed animal to the little girl, who hugged it.

"So, Little-Stuffed-Animal-Without-A-Name, do you know the name of your friend?"

The stuffed animal wasn't more cooperative than its owner. Frances didn't give up though, after all, it was her job. She'd been contacted to communicate with the child, and she would do it, whatever method worked, to free that child from a weight which, undoubtedly, must weigh down her soul. What had happened to her? What was she the survivor of to mentally regress like that?

"Pretty-Lion-Without-A-Name, you don't want to talk to me either? You don't have a tongue? And the big girl who's holding you in her arms, does she have a tongue?"

Her reaction astonished Dr. Cagliari.

The little girl interacted for the first time: she stuck her tongue out.

"That's great!" Frances said enthusiastically. "This big girl who loves you so much does have a tongue. And she understands me. So, my little stuffed lion, can you tell me her name?"

The little girl continued and said the only few words she'd pronounced up till now, with an accent that Frances didn't immediately recognize. She perhaps was trying to imitate the voice of a baby lion.

"I want mommy..."

THE PROBLEM WAS that the opposite didn't seem to be true: up till now, no mommy had come to get her daughter who'd vanished...

CHAPTER 5
Little~Stuffed~Lion~Without~A~Name

I THINK *I like this lady who said she's used to children like me.*

But I can't talk to strangers. That's what they always kept telling me.

So I don't say anything. When I see a stranger, I keep my mouth shut even if my tongue, in my mouth, it wants to move and talk in my place.

But I don't have the right to speak. They told me not to.

I won't say anything even if I understood what the lady she was trying to do. She wants to make me think that my stuffed animal can understand and answer her questions. Come on! I know that toys can't talk! My little lion is just some cloth with yellow fur like the hair on a horse and buttons for his big eyes. Before, I liked to make him dance, jump, and run.

I believed a little bit though... But my little lion, he only talks to me, and he only listens to me. I'm his mommy! He's my baby. He's the only one who really understands me.

So even though the lady she looks like she's nice, I don't want to talk to her about me, or about my baby lion, ... or about the other people...

I didn't want to talk to the others either.

First the lady who almost ran over me on the road. I was afraid that I'd be hurt, but she didn't hit me. She scared me at first when she got out of the car. Her hair was a mess, her eyes were strange, and I think she was afraid and maybe angry too. I know what anger looks like in people's eyes; I've seen it enough.

Then there was the lady wearing the police uniform. That lady looked nice too, not like the other big policeman who was with her, the one who really scared me with his big muscles, his big face and his eyes. Maybe he was the boss. So I couldn't talk to them either because I didn't know them.

You never talk to strangers, that's it. Never.

Then there was that doctor who looked at me all over to see if I was hurt, that old man with white hair on his head and none at all on the top. Nice too, but... but I don't like old men, they scare me with their bushy hair that they have all over their face and that come together above their eyes. And sometimes even, like this old man, they have hair that comes out of their ears, it's ugly, like it looks like a bunch of dried parsley that even guinea pigs wouldn't eat.

So, I didn't say nothing to nobody except 'I want mommy.'

And my little stuffed lion won't talk to nobody either.

Because I'm his mommy and him, he's my baby, and I learned him the lesson: you never talk to strangers! Not a word! Never!

CHAPTER 6
Like open wounds

THE NEXT MORNING, after a few hours of sleep, the Morgan County police force set off once again to investigate the area around Rebecca Stern's accident. It had finally stopped snowing, and the immaculate white landscape gave Sergeant Pete Gallister the impression he was a character in one of Jack London's novels, one he'd certainly read, like many other American kids, when he was in school. The long straight line linking Gravois Mills to Versailles was white, cold, and silent. The tow-truck had removed the young lady's car and all that was left in the ditch were traces of tires and crumpled metal, like open wounds in the thick powdery white snow.

Open being the key word, like the investigation that had been *open* since the day before. An investigation that didn't smell good at all, thought Gallister, walking up to his deputies who were already there and would give him a verbal report.

"Hey, Chief, hope you slept well," Bauer, mocking him.

"One more crack like that Mike, and I'll give you a disciplinary sanction for libel against your boss," mumbled Gallister, giving a friendly tap on his young colleague's shoulder. "Okay kids, recess is over. I brought you some coffee to warm your buns up."

"Pete, what would we do without you?" his subordinated joked. "The way I see it, little attentions like that deserve a promotion. At least a promotion to captain, or why not even sheriff!"

"Okay, I get it, you're trying to butter me up. You didn't find anything at all since yesterday, is that it?"

Taking a cup of steaming coffee into his gloved hands, Deputy Bauer answered his boss's question.

"We patrolled up and down Route 5 once again from Gravois Mills up to Versailles and didn't find any vehicles in the ditch or that had had an accident. And after that we took the secondary routes and paths from Route 5, you know the ones that go into the forest, and *nada*. We crisscrossed a mile and a half radius around the place where we picked the kid up and zilch. We need more men, Pete. You know how it is around here - forests all over, streams running through them, fields right and left. Plus with all that, hard to find anything with all the snow that fell last night."

"There must be some farms or houses where a handful of country bumkins live? Did you have time to knock on any doors?"

"Only the closest ones, Sergeant. We need more

men on the ground to go to all these houses. But you gotta understand with the lousy weather we had last night, all the people living around here preferred to stay nice and warm in front of their fireplaces rather than sitting on their front porch to see what was happening outside. I'm sure you would have done the same thing."

"If I could have, I would have accompanied you in front of the fireplace with a beer, or even better, a rum grog. Anyway, I'm going to launch an official call for witnesses, or else we won't get anywhere with this story. What did you learn in the interviews?"

"Like you can imagine, Pete, not much. Everyone living around here didn't see a thing and didn't hear anything either. That little girl could have cut across their lot, and they wouldn't have noticed her. At least that's what they told us. On the other hand though, some of the inhabitants were really moved by her story."

Gallister's eyes sparkled when he heard this.

"Meaning?"

"Yeah, here I'm thinking about the old farmers who live about a quarter of a mile from here. When they answered my questions and they knew a little girl was involved, that did something to them, especially an old lady who even started crying. I asked her what was wrong, and she told me, between two sobs, that a couple of months ago, their neighbors, also farmers, had lost their daughter and they would have been about the same age as the one we found last night."

"What do you mean, 'lost?' Their kid went missing?"

"For sure! She died, the poor little angel, apparently some uncurable condition. So you understand that my questions brought back bad memories, and the old lady broke down. She calmed down though after a couple of minutes, joined her hands together and said a silent prayer so that our little girl from yesterday would quickly find her parents. And she added that if we had a picture of her, she'd probably be able to identity her, if she was from around here."

"You're right, we'll launch a call for witnesses with a photo of her. Hopefully we'll get some tips."

"An AMBER* alert?" asked Deputy Bauer.

Sergeant Gallister twisted his mouth, annoyed at that question.

"We won't be able to use something like that, Mike."

"How come? That way it would be broadcast at a nationwide level."

"You're right, Mike, but this is only used when a child goes missing. Not when one appears..."

---

* An ***AMBER Alert*** is a system used in the United States and in Canada when a child is missing.

AMBER means American's Missing Broadcast Emergency Response. This alert was named in honor of Amber Hagerman, a child who was kidnapped and killed in Texas in 1996.

CHAPTER 7
An angel who burned her wings

THE NEXT DAY, Sergeant Pete Gallister received permission, not for an AMBER alert, but to issue a call for witnesses, at a federal level. To do that he needed a good photo of the little girl and went to St. Mary's Hospital in Jefferson.

When he entered her room, the little girl was sleeping, her arms hooked up to saline bags and tubes coming out of her nose. *Poor kid*, thought the cop, looking at the bandages covering the child's fingers.

He didn't want to wake her up. She made him think of an angel who'd broken her wings and who had been tossed down to Earth by some evil divinity. Maybe that was how this all happened? An angel who had tumbled down from heaven? A fallen angel? Like Satan…

Gallister pushed that ludicrous and absurd idea out of his head.

Paranormal nonsense.

No, he said to himself, *there must be a logical and cartesian explanation*. And it was his job to find it. And sooner rather than later.

He tiptoed out of the room and asked where Dr. Frances Cagliari's office was. The nurse at the office told him which floor she was on, and he went up, hoping the child's psychiatrist would be able to give him some good news.

"I HAVEN'T BEEN able to get a word out of her yet," said Frances regretfully when he asked. "I'm sorry, Sergeant. I have no idea what happened to this kid, but it must not be something nice. She is completely blocked, locked in. I've already had similar cases when kids were victims of violence within their own families, or were kidnapped, or taken hostage, or sequestrated. But never to this degree. This little girl only says the same three words."

"'I want mommy'" the policeman confirmed, having already heard it too. "She said the same thing to us and to Rebecca Stern. Like a robot who only had those three words on its hard disk."

"That's sort of the same effect she has on me too," confirmed Dr. Cagliari. "A formatted human being, repeating over and over again that simple sentence, with a monotone voice, no expression in it, as if she were disembodied."

"When you say it like that, it's almost as if she were brainwashed, don't you think so?"

"Could be. You know, kids are like sponges. You have no idea what they're capable of absorbing, whether it's at school, for example, or in a situation of data erasure."

"Data erasure?" Gallister asked, astonished. "What do you mean, Doctor?"

"I was thinking of the processes used by gurus in some sects. That's the principle of a sect: indoctrination. They tweak the plasticity the human brain has in assimilating precepts hammered into them as unwavering truths. Are you familiar with how formatting works in a computer?"

"Basically, yes. Why?"

"Because that's what this little girl's case makes me think of. At her age, the brain is malleable. An influential person, or an evil adult is perfectly able to psychologically erase data, if I can compare this to a computer, data contained in the neurons of a child. A reset, if I can put it like that. The default format. When that's done, on ground that's now empty and fertile, on that electronic chip you could say, a person could reprint as much data as they want. Like those three words she keeps repeating: 'I want mommy.'"

Gallister slowly digested this information, nodding.

"You think she's been influenced then?"

"It's the hypothesis I'm working on for now. But I'm not really worried, because this type of memory phenomenon is not irreversible. When specialists or experts treat a formatting case, there are always traces behind it that can be reactivated. It just requires time and a lot of patience. So I've got an ounce of hope."

When Gallister went back into the little girl's room, her eyes were open, though they remained fixed in the same position, inert, lifeless, showing no emotions.

"Hi! Do you recognize me?"

The sergeant wasn't really expecting a joyful answer and his feeling proved itself to be true faced with the child's characteristic aphonia.

"Are you feeling better? They're taking good care of you here? And your stuffed animal, I sure hope it's not cold anymore. Hmm, I see that you're not more talkative than you were yesterday, sweetie pie. So, can I take a nice picture of you and your stuffed animal? I guess than means I can," concluded Gallister, as she still hadn't said a word.

He called one of the nurses to ask her if it would be possible, without risking anything for the little girl, to take the tubes out of her nose for the picture. As the nurse said it would be okay, the sergeant took pictures of the little girl, sitting up against a big pillow, her stuffed animal next to her.

They were good pictures and would be perfect for the call for witnesses. No one could be indifferent to that child with her vacant eyes, her absence of a smile, her curly hair and her little stuffed lion propped up next to her. The sergeant hoped with all his heart that someone, somewhere, would give him a tip so this investigation could quickly progress.

"An angel," he repeated to himself, looking at the digital photo he was about to broadcast all over the United States. An angel who'd burned her wings.

Praying that all the gods in heaven would be looking down at that little angel, Gallister was far from imagining the flood that would soon descend on his... far from finished case.

CHAPTER 8
All the darkness of the human soul

CONTRARY TO WHAT Sergeant Gallister had thought, the impromptu switchboard set up to receive any eventual calls from witnesses was hopping. The officers assigned to that ungrateful task were drowning in phone calls about the little girl who had suddenly appeared in the countryside in the middle of nowhere in Missouri on a dark and cold winter's night.

They nonetheless had, as each time something like that took place, to know how to sort the wheat from the chaff amongst the hundreds of phone calls coming in, some crazier than the others.

It's hard to imagine the number of nitwits making calls, attracted like vultures by the opportunity of approaching a child, who, in appearance, didn't seem to have a family to love. There were all sorts of psychological profiles. There was the old lady living alone, who wanted company, ready to adopt that poor little girl like a grandma would, to sterile couples hoping for the chance of a lifetime to avoid the interminable way of the cross that legal adoption procedures constituted, up to perverted pedophiles thinking they'd enjoy a bit of fresh flesh without lifting a finger... The cops would have liked to have arrested those guys.

A wanted notice like that revealed all the darkness a human soul was capable of.

Policemen from Versailles and Jefferson were exhausted from spending countless hours on the phone and listening to this and then its opposite, good and bad, the most moving as well as the most despicable.

The team working the phones, made up of nearly equal parts of men and women, recorded those calls and emails coming from all over the United States, from Florida to Alaska. Some even came from Canada and Mexico where the notice had also been broadcast. Men, women, teens, adults, grand-parents, uncles and aunts. Farmers from Nebraska, a lawyer from New York, an architect from Houston, a teacher from Greenville, Maine, and a folksinger from Texas, were just a few examples of testimonials that deserved a more thorough investigation compared to the myriads of unbelievable statements. So-and-so thought he recognized his neighbor's daughter, another one thought it was one of his students who hadn't turned up at school for a couple of days. Someone else saw a child who would have been as old as she was, had she not died a few months ago.

"Jeez Louise, Sergeant, this is getting ridiculous," regretted one of the deputies after he'd hung up.

"What was it this time?"

"The craziest explanation I've received up till now. Listen. This guy said that the little girl was the reincarnation of an ancient bonze who died in Tibet seven years ago. Can you believe it?"

"There are loonies all over," signed Gallister. "I wonder if we're making any progress with this call for witnesses. I don't know if it was a good idea I had here."

"Gotta keep on hoping, Sergeant. There will certainly be something positive in all of this. In the middle of the desert, sometimes you stumble upon an oasis," the deputy said philosophically.

"Great image, John. Let's keep our fingers crossed then."

Two hours later they had another call, one that the investigators took more seriously. It was from someone employed at a gas station in Gravois Mills.

"Versailles police? I'm phoning about the announcement for the little girl, the one no one knows who she is."

"Yes, it is. This is Agent Fitzpatrick, I'm listening. What's your name?"

"Do I have to give it to you?"

"If you want, your call can remain anonymous. But it would be easier for us if you gave us your name. Unless you've got something to hide?"

"No, no, no, not at all," the person replied, stuttering. "My name is Rubens Pereira, and I work at Happy Jack gas station in Gravois Mills, you know where it is?"

"Yes, I do, Mr. Pereira. Can you continue please?"

"So, I think that little girl, I think I saw her two days ago at the gas station."

"Two days ago? You're sure?"

"For the day, I can't be mistaken because I was working the day before yesterday when the snowstorm began. Heavy snow like that isn't that frequent around here, so I do remember it, and as we didn't have a lot of traffic on the roads, it's easy for me to remember when the few clients we had came."

"And can you affirm that it's the child we're talking about in our alert?"

There was a brief silence on the line, and then he cleared his throat.

"Well, what I could say is that if it's not her, it's her sister, like people say."

"And did you see the little girl from afar? Did she stay in the car while the driver was filling up and when he came to pay you? Or did you clearly see her across from you?"

"She went into the shop, that's for sure. With her dad, they both went to the bathroom and then a couple of minutes later they came out to pay for their gas."

"How do you know it's her dad?"

"Because she called him daddy," the gas station attendant said hesitantly.

"Did the man pronounce his daughter's name?" the policeman instantly asked.

"If he did, I don't remember. I think he said something like 'honey" or 'sweetie,' something like that."

Sergeant Gallister frowned. His colleague had gestured for him to come closer and had put the conversation on speakerphone.

"Shit," Gallister grumbled.

"Mr. Pereira," the policeman continued, "did you note the car's license plate number?"

"No, I didn't. Why? There was no reason to do that. But if you want, it should be on our CCTV outside camera."

"How long do you keep the recordings for?"

"Seven days, I think. You'll have to ask the boss; he knows more than I do about that."

"Could I speak with him?"

"He's not here right now but he'll be back in an hour or so, after his lunch break."

"Perfect. We'll send one of our colleagues over to look at the footage. Thank you so much for calling, Mr. Pereira."

"I hope it helps," the gas station employee said.

AGENT FITZPATRICK and Sergeant Gallister had a quick meeting about all the calls received. Over a hundred and twenty calls had been logged in, most of them too nonsensical to be taken seriously. Some said they had recognized the little girl the day before yesterday, which was plausible, whereas others affirmed having seen her yesterday, when she was already hospitalized in Jefferson. No use following up on those. However, others swore they'd seen the child in the days or weeks before she was discovered, either in the country, or in neighboring cities such as Gravois Mills, Jefferson, or Versailles. Nonetheless, when all that info was cross-referenced, most were improbable. At the same time the little girl was spotted in Los Angeles, Miami, in Nebraska and Idaho, in Long Island and in Denver...

"Either this kid is ubiquitous, which I seriously doubt," Gallister protested, "or she's come back from the grave, which I also don't believe, or she looks like a lot of little girls of the same age, and it's that's true, we've got our work cut out for us. And what a job I think this will be. Come on guys," he said to his team, "let's get down to business!"

CHAPTER 9
Digging up secrets

PORTLAND, Maine

Here, at *True Crime Mysteries*, we're usually the ones who trigger investigations. Myrtille Fairbanks, at the top of the list, the first one – of course, because she's our dear boss – to rummage around in the local stories of a host of papers from many states, either in their hard copies or digital formats. She also spends a lot of time going through specialized web sites and trolling on forums for cold cases. Anonymous but impassioned individuals, who, using pseudonyms, love to index crimes, disappearances or kidnappings, tragic events that occur each and every day all over America and abroad. Digging and picking through this wealth of information, Myrtille then chooses the cases that seem the most exciting to her, and lets us loose on them, just like a pack of enraged dogs, thirsting for truth. So that's how my colleagues and I find ourselves spread out all over the United States, investigating in one of the country's large cities or in the tiniest holes in the ground where you wonder if you're even in the 21St century.

But this time, and for the very first time in my career, *True Crime Mysteries* didn't go hunting for a cold case to solve.

This time, the cold case came a-knocking right on our door, no middlemen, from the farm to the table, I could say.

Or in other words, it was delivered to us on a silver platter.

My dear boss had just hung up, the way she usually does and that's something that's always bothered me, with her inimitable: "Get cracking hun!"

And I knew that I was going to have my work cut out for me with this new and twisted affair.

My phone had rung just a few minutes ago and the first "hun" had landed in my ear, as soon as I'd picked up.

"Karen hun, you're going to thank me," began Myrtille with her shrill voice and her machine gun output.

"Myrtille, you know I always tremble when I hear your premature enthusiasm. Spit it out first and then I'll tell you if I should be overjoyed and thank you. I'm listening."

"Let me start out by telling you that this time, I'm not sending you to a hole-in-the-wall in Maine"*.

"True, you tricked me once with your trip to Greenville in rainy fall weather. So where are you sending me now?"

"To New York, my sweetie pie!"

"The Big Apple?"

"Well, almost. The State of New York, but not just anywhere, you'll see. You, my lucky girl, are going to the seaside in the Hamptons!"

"You're sure it's not a town named Hampton hidden someplace in Nebraska or Ohio? You are talking about the Hamptons at the end of the Long Island Peninsula?"

"Those Hamptons, my little hun! See? This time I'm not making fun of you. A dream trip to one of the most up-market and high-class places in the country, all expenses paid. And even better than that, you'll be staying at the Montauk, right on the tip of the peninsula, the Hamptons' cherry on the cake! So who do you want to thank?"

"Okay, thank you, Princess Myrtille. So now, what's the hitch? What wretched affair are you going to assign me?"

"Something completely over-the-top, you'll see... So this morning, I got a phone call from a granny, who initially seemed to have lost her marbles, but a little

---

* cf. *Sugar Island* that takes place in Greenville, a little town of 1,500.

birdie whispered into my ear that she wasn't as crazy as she seemed. Well, that's what she said anyway. She stumbled upon a call for witnesses about a little girl who was found in a tiny town in Missouri, and she recognized her as being her grand-daughter."

"So? What's the problem? If they found the little girl, everything is hunky dory."

"Yes, when you see it like that, like Aldous Huxley said, 'everything is for the best in the best of all possible worlds,' right?"

"Voltaire!"

"What, Voltaire? Who the heck is he?"

"A very famous French author and philosopher, my dear Lady. He was the one who wrote this sentence, in *Candide*, not Aldous Huxley. But that's not important, keep on, I'm hooked."

"Hey, listen up hun, and please be polite when you're talking to the boss! I'll let it slide this time. So, where was I? Yup, everything would be for the best if the discovery of this little girl in the Midwest had closed the investigation about her, for example, like the granny's grand-daughter had been kidnapped, or something. Except that, and hang on to your seat here, the little girl in question reappeared, she *rose from the dead*..."

"What? What kind of tale are you spinning here?"

"Just like I told you. She told me several times, apologizing each time, that her grand-daughter had died and was buried several months ago. Yet, unless she's completely crazy, there's something that intrigues me here. She's sure that it was her dead grand-daughter in the call for witnesses. And that's where you'll come in, my little chickadee."

"My little chickadee? That's a new one. Even if you persist in using poultry allusions. But anyway. So what would be my role in this, Myrtille? You want me to pack my shovel and pickaxe to dig the little girl up and see if she's still breathing?"

Myrtille Fairbanks burst out laughing.

"You're getting creepy now. Karen, I didn't know you were so ironic. But at the same time, it's something I like, you can well imagine."

True, it is something I could well imagine. My dear boss has the gift of loving dark stories, and she quickly thought of eye-catching titles for them to put them on the cover of our magazine. I already thought of one that you couldn't miss, "*The Walking Dead of Long Island,*" or "*A Little Girl Escapes from her Tomb...*" Nothing could surprise me anymore with her in shocking our readers and making them believe her stories each week.

"Specifically, what do you want me to do?"

Myrtille gave me the crazy granny's contact details before concluding.

"You hightail it off to Montauk, you sit your butt down and your suitcases at the Montauk Manor where I reserved a room for you, you'll love it... And then you go meet this old granny full of greenbacks and you question her the way you know how to see if she's nuts or not. So hun, I already got the ball rolling for you:

the little lady is expecting you at her place tomorrow, I'll send you her email too. And of course, you'll write me a hell of an article on the subject, like you always do."

"Hell, you chose your word well, talking about the walking dead…"

"Enough of those rotten puns! Prepare your shovel and go and dig up… secrets."

CHAPTER 10
The biggest enigma of my life

MONTAUK, Long Island.

As soon as I'd hung up with Myrtille, I started to pack my bags for New York. A mission on Long Island, though we were in December, and I wouldn't be swimming or working on my tan, was something that I'd always wanted to do without having set foot there. Though I'm not much of a swimmer, deserted beaches in winter, when the wind's blowing, and sand is flying into your face are something that doesn't bother me at all. I'm a quite solitary person and like long hikes, alone listening to the waves rolling in rather than interminable sessions of tanning on a beach where you have nine square feet to put your towel down.

I made sure I didn't forget to pack my medication, that daily dose of pills that I can't miss, something I've done for years and can't seem to find an end to it. I live with it; you could say it's my cross to bear.

I also packed that special file that I never go anyplace without, recorded both on my computer's hard disk as well as on a paper copy. Tips for my personal research, connecting me more and more with my own past, my eternal demons. Since I'd returned from Greenville, Maine, I'd made a bit of progress, though I hadn't had enough time to devote to it because of my various journalistic investigations. But now I was hoping to finally solve the biggest enigma of my own life…

In the meantime though, it was time for that difficult investigation. I threw my bags into the back seat of my old, beige, and invincible Ford Ranchero 1967 pickup, the one that my late father drove everywhere for years and that he left me. That timeless vehicle always got the job done, meaning that it took me from point A to point B without costing me an arm and a leg in repair work.

That was how I drove smoothly from Portland to New London, where I embarked on the Cross Sound Ferry linking the continent to Long Island. Night was falling over the ocean. The twenty nautical miles of the crossing relieved me from my six-hour trip. My Ranchero's hood was still steaming in the entrails of the ferry when, well covered by my coat, I went up to the deck, my arms crossed over the rails, admiring the illuminated coastline with its thousands of Christmas lights.

When a handful of other passengers and I got off at Orient Point, I knew that Montauk was over an hour's drive, though as the crow flies, it was a mere few miles away. In this part of New York filled with islands and peninsulas, the road was far from being a straight one. In summer, the New London ferry would take me directly to Montauk, saving me a couple of hours, but it was now December, and the route was closed for the winter.

I made the best of it though, and about nine I finally pulled into Montauk Manor's parking lot, which was already lit up for the upcoming holiday season. What a beautiful hotel! Myrtille had put her money where her mouth was this time. Should I consider this as a Christmas present she'd gifted to one of her best investigators?

A few minutes later, I closed the door to my room, which was just as luxurious as the rest of the hotel. But I was exhausted! I swallowed my daily dose of three pills, took a long, hot shower, brushed my teeth, wrapped the soft bathrobe the hotel had given me and hopped into bed.

My eyes wide open, I looked up at the white ceiling, which reminded me of a piece of paper inserted into a printer, the symbol of a new investigation to write about and new truths to unearth.

At that instant though, I had a very bad feeling. I feared falling once again into a very painful headache. Each time I have to unravel an affair concerning children, my heart races, I fear seeing hidden events from the past emerge, events that make me sick to my stomach.

I hate violence and especially violence towards innocent beings.

Right before my eyelids shut and my brain switched from the "on" to "off" button, I had one more thought. *I just hope that it won't be the case, this time...*

CHAPTER 11
A heartbreak

I WILL NEVER UNDERSTAND PEOPLE, too many of them in my humble opinion, who put a pool in their yard that's as big as my apartment in Portland, when they live right next to the sea. This was exactly what Melinda Vaughan did, that old lady with curly white hair who I went to see at her home on Surfside Avenue.

It was just as if you were in the country here. A narrow road with hedges on each side composed of softwood and deciduous trees who'd successively lost their leaves in fall and with the winter frosts now, reminded me that Montauk had been able to retain a fisherman's village spirit, which is what it originally was, despite the hype that the little village had enjoyed for the past couple of decades.

Behind a simple wooden fence, Mrs. Vaughan's house was original, far from the standards in the village. It was a two-story building with white walls and a tile roof with a wooden colonial style balcony surrounding it, a house that would not have been out of place in the French Quarter in New Orleans. Beyond the house, I could make out waves that seemed so close that they were breaking on the limits of her property.

I rang and an old lady opened the door, after I'd heard several clicks of locks and bolts. Though the scenery made me think of life in a little village, the old lady seemed to think that she was living in one of the worst neighborhoods of Brooklyn or Queen's.

"Mrs. Vaughan? My name is Karen Blackstone, and I'm the journalist at *True Crime Mysteries*, you know the magazine that you called yesterday about the little girl."

"You think I'm so senile that I can't even remember what I did yesterday?" the old lady said cutting me off brusquely.

Her welcome, like the weather, was frigid.

"I'm sorry, Mrs. Vaughan, but you spoke to my boss on the phone, not me, so I don't really know what you two said. I just wanted to introduce myself."

"Come in," she said, opening the door and moving away so I could. "I'm no longer used to having people over anymore, and this story has really stirred me up, I'm sure you can understand."

"Of course."

"And I don't really appreciate it when people doubt I can remember things, in spite of my age," she added, so I'd understand that she hadn't lost her marbles. "Let's go into the living room. It's got the nicest ocean view. Would you like a cup of tea or coffee to warm up? It's so cold outside."

I nodded, taking my coat off that I had been holding around my chest up till now. Here, in the old lady's luxurious villa, it must have been at least seventy-five, which though a bit warm, was still appreciated. While my hostess was busy in the kitchen, where I could hear a kettle whistling, I realized that yes, the ocean view was truly spectacular here. I got up and walked to the huge picture window that went wall-to-wall and looked out. Her lawn was perfectly mown – unless it was a synthetic one – and there was a bean shaped pool in the middle of it. At the end of the rectangular yard, there was a wooden railing with stairs leading directly to the shore, to a sandy beach that was easy to make out. And after that the ocean, as far as the eye could see, a breathtaking view. One that, at this time of the year, was agitated and turbulent.

I jumped.

"You see everything that goes on at the beach from here," Mrs. Vaughan said behind me, surprising me. "Yet, I didn't see anything."

"You didn't see anything? What didn't you see?"

The lady with the prematurely white hair – now that I looked at her closely she must not have been that much over sixty, – sat down on the other side of the angled couch and asked me to do the same.

"I'm talking about the tragedy! Why do you think

you're here? To talk about now much snow there is and the cold weather?"

Still quite aggressive, this granny. Or at least defensive whereas I was here to help her, not the opposite.

"Mrs. Vaughan, please understand me. I'm not here to judge you, just to listen to what you have to say to me. From what I understood, you have quite an extraordinary story to tell me, and I mean 'extraordinary' in the literal sense."

The old lady sighed, blowing on her cup of tea.

"Ever since I saw that call for witnesses about that little girl they found in Missouri, I haven't slept a wink. I think it's making me go crazy. All of that is still so fresh in my memory, in my heart. Excuse me if I'm a little agitated..."

The grand-mother's voice suddenly broke, expressing all the painful memories she seemed to have gone through. Her eyes became veiled and troubled, and a few tears trickled down onto her red cheekbones.

"Mrs. Vaughan, I really can understand," I said, trying to be reassuring. "Take your time and tell me. Is it alright with you if I record our conversation?"

She nodded and dried her tears with a shaky hand.

"I'll be alright," she continued, "I can do this. The only thing though is that I'm afraid you'll think I'm crazy. Which I probably am after all. I don't know how I couldn't be with all this; you'll see for yourself."

"You know, in my job, I think I've seen it all, even

completely improbable things. '*Plausibility is a trap for the truth laid by lies.*' I read that someplace."*

"I don't understand a thing here, all that's too complicated for me. Just like I don't understand what's going on in my head. I wasn't raised to believe in ghosts, in ghouls or the undead, in Jesus who rose three days later or in Lazarus who he resuscitated. So no, I don't believe in any of that nonsense, and I don't believe either that my grand-daughter rose from her grave to reappear magically in Missouri. My poor little grand-daughter, my adorable Katheline, so pretty with her curly brown hair and her pouting little lips."

Once again, the grieving grand-mother began to sob. She didn't even try to hide it this time as it escaped from her throat and heartbroken soul. She took her head between her hands and her eyes.

"I'm sorry to be so fragile," said Mrs. Vaughan sadly.

"I understand, don't worry," I said, trying to reassure her. "Please don't worry, I'm not here to judge you."

She finally got up from the couch, and walked to the large bay window through which the cold, gray and bright winter light was streaming in. She put one of her hands on the window, as if trying to catch the grains of sand on the beach below.

"It was there, at the bottom on these stairs, that I

---

* Yvan Audouard

saw my little grand-daughter alive for the very last time…"

CHAPTER 12
These prints of life

"THERE ARE some images that you will never forget, that remain engraved in your memory just like hieroglyphs that were chiseled in stone. Except that here we're talking about my heart and the chisel that left an indelible mark on me."

That was how Melinda Vaughan continued the story of the last day of her grand-daughter's life. I let her elaborate without interrupting her. I know how much easier it is to relate secrets and memories when the person speaking to you tell you them as if they were happening right now, under the narrator's eyes.

"She was right here, her little baby face looking out this bay window, her chubby little hands leaving fingerprints all over it. You know, those fingerprints where you see the furrows in your skin, the ones that, at least that's what the experts say, are unique to each human being on earth. Do you think that's true? That there can be that many combinations? That no one else has the same fingerprints as someone else?"

"That's what I've always heard anyway," I confirmed. "Mother Nature and biology are well designed."

"At that time I was obsessive about cleaning, and as soon as my grand-daughter had turned around, I quickly grabbed a rag and my window cleaning spray and cleaned those marks away. Good Lord! You can't believe how much I regret that gesture, that obsession! How much I would have liked to have kept them forever, those fingerprints, these prints of the life of my princess. That would be all that remains of her today."

"Mrs. Vaughan, the souvenir that you're telling me about. When did it take place?"

"How could I ever forget it? It was last summer, not this year, but the year before. That would be nearly eighteen months, and the exact date was…"

∼

<u>… July 13, 2022, Montauk.</u>

That summer in Long Island was unseasonably hot. Tourists were flocking into Montauk by train, fleeing the scorching heat in New York. The beach below was packed. Melinda Vaughan hated that time of year when those darn New Yorkers invaded her beach, clumped together like sardines on the sand, nearly right below her windows. Such indecency! In the summer, the widow never went down to the seaside, and only used her pool to refresh herself. But her grand-daughter, who she was babysitting that day, didn't agree with her. She was attracted by the kids running around and having fun on the shoreline and all she wanted to do was join them on the beach.

Katheline glued her face and hands to the window in the living room, leaving her sempiternal traces. She kept on jumping up and down, always repeating the same thing.

"Granny... sea. Granny...sea."

"Honey, wouldn't it be more fun in the swimming pool? There won't be anyone to bother us. But not right now, it's still much too hot to be in the sun. We'll wait until mommy comes back, okay?"

"Mommy... sea."

And the little girl with her curly brown hair put her lips to the window once again, drooling on it, to her grandmother's despair.

Though the little girl wanted to go to the beach, she still was quite an obedient child. Her grandmother was able to have her forget the sand by taking her to her playroom in this large and too often empty villa and both played for over an hour with her dolls and many stuffed animals.

When her mother finally got back, the little girl

jumped with joy and her obsession immediately returned.

"Mommy... sea!"

"Come here sweetie and give mommy a kiss. You want to go down to the beach? Do you have your swimsuit?"

"Swimsuit, Granny?"

"I'll go get it honey."

When Melinda came down with her granddaughter's suit, she watched her daughter help her get dressed, but still wasn't happy.

"How can you stand being with all those people when you can swim in the ocean after the peak season? And our pool isn't good enough for you anymore? Let me remind you that its upkeep costs a pretty penny, and I pay just so you can use it when you want!"

"I know, Mom, but it's not the same thing. Come on hun, put your leg through here."

"I certainly agree that it's not the same thing", Melinda, peeved, grumbled. "You know that your father agreed with me. He hated crowded beaches, all those low-class people cooking on the sand, lying right next to each other, half nude."

"Mom, you're just jaded. You seem to have forgotten that you weren't born with a silver spoon in your mouth. If you hadn't married dad... Ready honey? Maybe we'll even see that little friend you made the other day, remember, you made sandcastles with her."

"Friend... sand?"

"Oost! Here we go my little pirate. Can we go out this way mom?" asked the young lady, pointing at the picture window.

"Go ahead, you ungrateful kid. And don't come back too late, I'm making pancakes for supper. And don't forget to take the buoy at the pool while you're there."

Melinda Vaughan watched her daughter and grand-daughter walk through the yard, going down the little private path through a natural hedge of cane leading to the beach.

∾

"And they never came back up to eat their pancakes," Mrs. Vaughan sobbed, putting her forehead against the window.

Then I thought about the traces her skin would certainly leave on the glass and wondered if she'd bother to clean them up.

"So, both of them disappeared on July 13, last year?"

As soon as I'd said the word *disappeared*, my brain began to speed up like a V12 motor. I tried to express myself clearly.

"If they disappeared, maybe your grand-daughter didn't die. In that case, maybe it really is her, that little girl they found in Missouri."

Mrs. Vaughan shook her head, a sad smile on her face.

"No, Miss Blackstone, that's not possible. Believe me, I'm sure she'd dead. And so is my only daughter, Laura, her mother. Go down to Amagansett Cemetery. I won't be able to accompany you though, it's too hard for me. You'll be able to see their graves. They're resting in peace together there, forever…"

CHAPTER 13
Revealing useful secrets

GRAVOIS MILLS, Missouri

CONGREGATED IN FRONT of an old screen that seemed to date back to the Cold War, the Versailles police investigators were looking at the CCTV footage from the camera located outside the gas station that was supposed to film license plates should any of the customers decide to leave without paying. Happy Jack's manager had given the policemen the footage, and Sergeant Gallister was sitting in the front row of his tiny office. And *tiny* was the key word here, as between two boxes of cookies, piles of paper on the desk, packages of unsold magazines tied together by a piece of string and other unidentifiable objects, there was hardly any place for them to sit. The heat given off by so many bodies plus the heat given off by the radiators turned to their max made the officers sweat uncomfortably in their uniforms.

"Can you jump to the time when your employee thought he saw the little girl with her father?" asked Pete.

"Easy, Sergeant." Then he turned to his employee. "Rubens, what time did you see those two?"

"I'd say that it must have been around four at the latest, because I remember it had already begun to snow, and it was getting dark."

The manager fiddled with the keys on his computer and went back to the day and time in question.

"Shit," Gallister grumbled, leaning towards the screen. "We can't see too much."

"Hey, I'm not the one behind the camera," said Jack O'Connor, the manager, an unlit cigarette hanging sadly from his lips, as if it were glued on.

"There!" shouted Rubens Pereira. "I think it's them in front of the fuel pump."

Sergeant Gallister and Myra Stonehenge, his deputy, were paying close attention to the screen. The vehicle, a dark green Dodge pickup, at least that was the color they thought it was, had stopped in front of the pump. A tallish man with large shoulders – though with his heavy winter coat it was hard to be sure, – got out and took the fuel pump, opened the gas tank, and began to fill up, his back to the car and his face looking at the price display.

"It's as if the guy doesn't want to be recognized,"

Myra said. "Plus with his hat pulled down nearly to his eyes, that's not helping us."

"And another thing that's not helping is the lack of sunlight."

"Can we zoom in?"

"No, sorry, not directly on the film," said O'Connor. "We can zoom in when we're filming live and the camera films like that, but here, we didn't have any reason to."

"Okay. It's not a big deal. We'll be taking the files with us to analyze them," Sergeant Gallister warned him.

He stretched his neck and squinted his eyes a bit more to try to make out the letters and numbers on the license plate.

"Jesus Christ, the gods just aren't with us today. Their plate is completely covered with snow. Shit!"

A few minutes later, the man holding the fuel pump hung it up, and went around the car, opening the passenger door. A child came out, also warmly dressed in a winter coat with a hood on it that masked her face. Yet a few curly strands of hair hung out of the hood and the size of the child seemed to match the size of the little girl who had been found two days before. But it was too early to be sure. The man took the little child's hand, and both went inside the gas station, disappearing from the unforgiving eye of the outside CCTV camera.

"You got a camera inside?" asked Gallister, though he was pretty sure of the answer. He was hoping to have been able to follow the two of them, with a better angle on the faces of the man and child.

"All that costs big bucks," replied the manager. "I'm not a movie producer, I manage a gas station!"

The sergeant turned to Rubens.

"Mr. Pereira, can you confirm that these two people that we just saw on the footage correspond to the ones you remembered? That they went to the restrooms before paying for their gas?"

"Yes, I can. It was the right time, and I remember that the little girl had a hood. Plus when she came back from the bathroom, she still had it up. The man had his hat on too. But if you asked me, I wouldn't be able to tell you if he had hair, or if he'd shaved his head."

"What can you tell me about him?"

"I don't know, he had a beard and dark eyes, that's about all I can say for sure. You know I really wasn't paying attention to them."

"And the little girl?"

"Brown hair, with eyes that seemed... empty."

"How old do you think she was?"

"Three or four at the max."

"Fine. And it couldn't have been a little boy? At that age and with a hood and curly hair, it's hard to be sure of anything."

"I agree with you, Sergeant. Even with the voice, at that age you can't tell the difference between a boy and a girl sometimes. But the guy referred to her as 'sweetie' or 'my little honey,' things like that."

"I understand. Can we see the rest of the film?"

The manager started up the video again and after a few minutes without any movement in front of the gas pumps, as there weren't any other customers, they saw the man and little girl leaving the gas station. He opened the passenger door and helped her climb in, then closed it. Then he hopped into the driver's seat, and they drove away. It was impossible to make out anything on the license plate."

"Myra, do you have a USB flash drive?"

She handed it to the manager.

"Can you copy this file, please?"

"I don't know how that stuff works. You'd be better off doing it yourself."

Myra Stonehenge sat down in front of the computer and transferred the footage. It would be given to the IT experts in the police department who, Sergeant Gallister dearly hoped, would be able to reveal useful secrets.

CHAPTER 14
Amongst the living

MONTAUK, Long Island, December 2023

As is the case with most of the cemeteries in the region, this was a peaceful final resting place. There was a white door leading into Amagansett Cemetery. A name that resembled many of them in this part of Long Island – Montauk, Sagaponack, Mattituck, Cutchogue, Patchogue, and so on, – proving that back in the day, this peninsula was the home to native Americans. When the first settlers moved here, they discovered the Algonquians as well as the Shinnecock and the languages spoken by these tribes became the names of the towns.

A lush green lawn, one that had been well watered, surrounded the many tombstones, some which dated back several decades, and other more recent ones, such as the one where Laura Parker, née

Vaughan, and her daughter Katheline Parker, now rested.

Looking at that granitic headstone, I didn't know what to say when I saw the date of birth and the date of death. Katheline hadn't had time to enjoy life. Only a bit over two years amongst the living, enough time to learn how to walk, talk, love and be loved. Was she loved?

Melinda Vaughan was hanging onto my arm, sobbing. She'd finally decided to go with me to the cemetery where her daughter and grand-daughter rested.

"This is the first time I've been here since..."

She didn't have to finish her sentence, I knew what she was alluding to, as she'd begun to tell me the details a few hours before in her living room in Montauk.

* * *

Katheline's grandmother turned her back to the picture window overlooking the beach and sat down next to me on the large corner sofa in her huge living room. The harsh winter light shone into the room, gray like the morale of the lady submerged by her memories.

"That day in July, I rushed into my kitchen to prepare the pancakes I'd promised to Katheline. That was her very favorite meal, served with orange marmalade on top and either maple syrup or peanut butter. My little Kathy, she loved to eat! When I'd finished cooking them, I covered them with aluminum foil and left them cool slowly on my countertop. Then when I was waiting for the girls to come back, I did a couple of crossword puzzles by the pool. I try to do a few every day, that's something that relaxes me. Even from there I could hear kids yelling on the beach, as well as the noise that jet-skis or motorboats make. Talk about a relaxing atmosphere! About six, I thought it was strange that they hadn't come back up yet, but it was really hot out on July 13th, so I said to myself they were making the most of their afternoon. I did two more crossword puzzles and when I raised my head to look at the clock inside, it was nearly seven. That's when I started to get worried. I got my phone out to call Laura, hoping that she'd taken hers down to the beach. It rang a couple of times but then went directly to voicemail. I hung up and didn't leave a message, but I phoned back a few minutes later. She still didn't pick up and that time I left a message. I must have called her six or seven times in half an hour. But no one ever answered. So I decided to go down to the beach and bring them back, whether they liked it or not. I don't like to eat too late, otherwise I don't digest well and can't sleep. Laura knew that. I put my sarong on and went down the little path. They were often there, right at the end of the path. No use going any farther! When you've got the sea right at your footsteps. But when I got there, I didn't see their towels or even the bag that Laura was carrying when she left. Or Katheline's buoy. I wondered where they'd gone and why she hadn't answered when I'd called. At that time of the evening, a lot of people had already left, so it should have been much easier to find them. Most of the tourists had already gone home, as the sun was no longer shining directly on the beach. There were just a few groups of teens who'd be spending the evening, or even the night there. Sometimes I could see them from my window. They'd build campfires to warm up and grill hot dogs and marshmallows. And of course they drank a lot, they listened to loud music and made a lot of noise. I often had to put earplugs in so I could sleep. Anyway, I didn't see Laura nor my little Kathy. Karen, believe me, I was mad. I know I grumbled when I was looking for them on the beach and coastline, between the ocean and sand dunes. But I had to decide on a direction before leaving. East or West? I decided to go east, heading for Montauk Point, you know, where the lighthouse is, the one that lights up the ocean as soon as it gets dark, and that Laura loved when she was a little girl. I thought that maybe she'd taken her daughter there to see it closeup. Even if nowadays, there aren't any more lighthouse guardians because everything is automatic, and the lighthouse itself has become a museum. So much good stuff gets lost, in my opinion. So while I was walking on the beach, I tried to call her again, but she still didn't pick up. I finally didn't walk all the way to the lighthouse, because that would have been a good three miles one-way from my house and at the same time, I wasn't sure of finding them there, so I didn't want to walk over six miles for nothing, if you get what I mean, Karen.

"Of course," I reassured her. "So you turned around then? And you didn't see them?"

"No, I didn't. Neither on the beach, nowhere. And not back at home either, as I was hoping to find them there if they'd gone walking in the other direction. No, I never saw my daughter or my grand-daughter again. Not that evening, never. Except three weeks later when they called me to identify their bodies at the morgue…"

CHAPTER 15
An out of the body experience

LONG ISLAND, August 2022

THE TERRIBLE HEATWAVE continued in New York, that summer of 2022. When Melinda Vaughan, wearing black clothing, went into the morgue, the air-conditioning was like a benediction for her. It actually could have been a real pleasure in different circumstances.

Except there, Melinda was preparing to live a few minutes that would forever be a nightmare for her, cursed minutes that you wouldn't even want your worst enemy to experience. Lieutenant Garrett, from the New York criminal investigation department, had phoned her a few hours ago, with a compassionate voice, a true professional who was used to giving people bad news. After having done his due diligence, Melinda Vaughan was the only close family member who could formally identify the bodies in the forensic medical department.

"The bodies..." repeated Melinda, terrified by this plural.

The policeman had to repeat what he'd previously said, but Melinda didn't seem to have heard it. Her mind, her intellect, both seemed to be floating above her, like an out of the body experience. She remembered having read someplace that people often had that sensation in the case of an NDE, a near death experience*. Though she wasn't the one who was experiencing that this time, it was the same thing for her. She thought she'd understood that someone had discovered the cadavers of her daughter and grand-daughter, the two only people that were left in her family since her husband passed away. Why keep on living in that case? Why continue alone, so terribly alone? So while she was dying and floating above her own body, that she actually saw when talking to Lieutenant Garrett, what difference did that make? It would even be better that way, after all.

But she unfortunately was alive.

And it was her duty to lean over those two stainless steel tables in the morgue. As she no longer had anyone close to her, she'd asked Mrs. Nollington to come with her to New York to help her through that trying experience. She didn't even feel like she would be capable of

---

* An occurrence in which a person comes very close to dying and has memories of a spiritual experience.

taking the train in Montauk Station, the train which nonetheless would have taken her right to Grand Central in New York. Her neighbor, also retired, had of course immediately agreed to help her through that, especially as she'd known Laura when she was a little girl, then Katheline, whom she often talked to above the hedge separating the two yards. It was also a shock for her, but a small one compared with the cataclysm submerging Melinda.

The morgue was just as she'd imagined it while they were on the train. A cold and sanitized hospital, though one without life, one with aggravated pain. And that smell, a terrible one she associated with ether or formol. She walked slowly, her head hanging down, holding on to Mrs. Nollington, who supported her the best she could down those endless halls of the facility, until they reached the forensic medical department door. Why were those departments always in the entrails of hospitals? Because they didn't require any light anymore? Because it was better to hide dead people, who were shameful, or unacceptable? Because they were afraid that the souls of the deceased would escape through the windows? Instead of sunlight, there were one-way and impersonal rooms, only lit up by cruel and relentless neon lights.

Lieutenant Garrett was waiting for them outside the door.

"I'm so sorry for your loss, Mrs. Vaughan. Please follow me."

The policeman was a tall and affable man with greying hair, whose shoulders, just as large as his abdomen, were imposing, yet contrasting with a soft voice and youthful twinkling eyes. He led them to the autopsy room where two bodies were awaiting their legal identification.

Behind that door, horror would affront Melinda.

"Do you want me to go with you?" her neighbor asked. "Do I have the right?" she added, looking at Lieutenant Garrett.

He nodded and Melinda also gladly accepted her neighbor's help, squeezing her arm with a gesture of gratitude.

The door opened.

They saw two stainless steel tables.

A body lying on each, both completely dissimulated beneath a white sheet with the hospital's name on it.

On the right table, the sheet only covered a small mass, just a bit larger than a dog that someone could have run over. There was a tiny two-year-old girl beneath it.

"I know that what I'm now going to ask you to do, Mrs. Vaughan, is something very difficult, but I don't have the choice. It's the legal procedure, do you understand?"

"Of course," replied Melinda, sniffing. "I understand, Lieutenant."

"I'd also like you to know that we found identity papers in a beach bag, not too far from where the bodies were found. The name of your daughter, Laura Parker, née Vaughan, was on them, but we didn't find anything for the little girl. And when we went through her cell phone, we saw that you'd called her several times. This is why we called you to identify them. Will you be okay? And I know it's a little strange, but which body would you like to start with, Mrs. Vaughan?"

Melinda instinctively pointed with her chin to the table where the sheet was covering the biggest cadaver. She undoubtedly wanted to retard the moment as long as possible when she'd see the mortal remains of her beloved granddaughter, her little Kathy.

The medical examiner, who back in the day was called a coroner, came up to them with a compassionate and very professional air about him, walking to the stainless-steel table where Melinda reluctantly noticed a little runlet around it, those channels where body fluids run off during autopsies, as she'd seen on TV in those police series she was fond of. But today this wasn't fiction, and she immediately gagged, trying to suppress it while tittering to the table.

The medical examiner took the sheet, and with a respectful gesture, slowly unveiled the face of the deceased person.

Melinda's hand rushed to her mouth to smother a scream. She squeezed Carmela Nollington's arm so hard her fingers were white.

"My daughter... Good Lord..."

"Can you certify that this is Laura Parker, your daughter?"

"It is."

Melinda closed her eyes as if she wanted to delete the expression on her only daughter's face. Tears slowly spilled from the corner of her eyelids and rolled down her hollow cheeks.

She then opened them again, for a few interminable moments, giving her the luxury of scrutinizing the new immobile features of her daughter, her Laura. She finally realized that they'd never again move, never again speak, and she turned away, implying that the examiner could now lower the sheet.

They all then focused on the second table.

The tiny sheet.

The tiny dead person.

The one she didn't want to see.

But she had to, Lieutenant Garrett had said it was the procedure.

The medical examiner stepped forward, took ahold of the sheet and lowered it, uncovering the unspeakable.

CHAPTER 16
A black soul and a black heart

MONTAUK, December 2023

We were both sitting on the couch in the living room. While Melinda Vaughan told me about those atrocious minutes when she had to identify Laura and Katheline's bodies, I saw her break down once again, as if she was reliving those moments that no mother should have to experience.

She trembled, she cried, she gulped, before overcoming her emotions.

"When the examiner lifted the sheet, I thought I would faint right there on the white tiles in that horrible room that stank of 90° alcohol or some other cleaning product. I felt my legs start to give away under me, my ears began to ring, I couldn't hear a word because of the humming in my head. Then Lieutenant Garrett pulled me out of this state. I heard him pronounce my name in a deep voice, one that came from beyond the grave or from an echo in a dark cavern. I opened my eyes, and I saw my Kathy's beautiful princess face. Holy Jesus, what a shock!"

"What was on her face?" I asked.

The grieving grand-mother burst into tears once again, this time with wincing hiccups.

"My little Kathy. Later they assured me that the thanatopractitioner had done a really professional job on her so I wouldn't be shocked, so that she'd look more like my darling Kathy, but he couldn't do miracles either. Katheline's face was covered with hematomas, as if she was beaten to death. Barely recognizable. Karen, can you imagine something like that? And can you imagine the pain a grandmother has when she sees the flesh of her own flesh martyred like that? A child of that age, she was only two! Still a baby! Who? Who would commit a sacrilege like that? Who could have such a black soul and a black heart for such an ignominy? Attacking innocence itself..."

Melinda quit speaking with that litany of questions that had haunted her for months now, ever since that day that marked her heart, the heart of a mother and grandmother, with a red-hot iron. A terrible silence reigned in the room. I looked out the window and saw waves with whitecaps on, announcing the approach of a winter storm.

"Did you ever find out what happened, Mrs. Vaughan?" I asked when she seemed to be less tormented.

She blew her nose noisily before answering.

"You can well imagine, that despite my reluctance, I wanted to understand how that double tragedy could have taken place. I heard, more than listened to, the explanations the coroner gave me. I didn't want to accept those words that he was throwing at me, as if he were throwing stones into a pond, if I can put it like that."

"Meaning?"

"Meaning that the bodies of my little Kathy and my daughter Laura had washed up on the shore of Oyster Pond, which is almost at Montauk Point. It's a relatively large brackish pond and has big waves when it's windy. Waves from the ocean come in through a type of natural passageway. A couple of hikers found the bodies when they were on the trail going around the lake. They were walking their dog who had started to bark and run to the pond.

"Did they drown?" I asked, with a lump in my throat.

"That's what the medical examiner said. No doubt about that. But what is the most terrible is not knowing how and why that could have happened. And I'm not buying into his explanation. I don't want to believe it; I can't imagine it."

"Explain it to me, maybe I can."

"You really think that a loving mother is capable of beating her own daughter and then drowning her?" said Melinda Vaughan with a voice that this time was not broken, but completely destroyed.

"Was that the conclusion of the medical examiner?"

"Exactly. I can still hear the coroner explaining that Katheline had been hit on the face several times, probably powerful smacks administered by a woman's hand."

"How could he conclude that?"

"Because there were scratches on her face that were allegedly caused by a ring. Like the ring my daughter had. That's what caused the hematomas. The coroner tried to explain the facts in their chronology, supposing that Kathy had been beaten in the face when she was still alive, then after that Laura had taken her between her arms before jumping into the lake… to drown with her, both reunited and inseparable in death. Can you imagine that? It's ghastly!"

And it certainly was. I cannot believe that a mother could find the mental strength to kill her child before committing suicide herself. And when I heard the grandmother tell me this story, I was overwhelmed and now it was my turn to shed tears that dripped down my cheeks. I swallowed and tried to make sense of what I'd heard.

"To sum it up then, your daughter killed herself and beat her own little daughter to death, holding her under the water while they both drowned in the pond."

"That's the conclusion of the medical examiner and Lieutenant Garrett, yes. The only point that's vague in their investigations is to know if Kathy died because of the beating or if she was still alive when Laura and she drowned. But that's not important is it?" Melinda Vaughan suddenly shouted out.

Outside the wind had picked up and there were raindrops on the huge picture window. Were they salt spray that the north wind had blown up to here or raindrops? In the house, in spite of the heat that I'd found a bit too high before, I now was freezing inside, sick to my stomach from the story Katheline's grandmother had told me. Yet, I kept on asking for more.

"And did you accept those conclusions? I mean, intimately? You were a mother, then a grandmother, you should know if that type of behavior would have been possible for Laura."

Melinda shook her head.

"What do you want me to say? Of course I didn't believe it, how could I believe something like that? I had never, and I mean never, seen my daughter act violently, not when she was a child, not when she was a teenager, nor after that. So for me to imagine her hitting Katheline, for me that's impossible. But still, the marks were there on her little face, they were palpable and visible. How could I contest something like that?"

"Have you got another theory deep inside you?"

"I don't know. I don't know anymore. I'm completely lost. How can I refute proof?"

"Sometimes, and I've often seen this in my investigations, facts can be quite deceiving. What we think of as reality is merely a mirage, an image that is distorted by the mirror of our fantasies."

"Excuse me, but I don't understand a word of that, Miss Blackstone. Could you rephrase?"

"What I meant was that you can't always trust what you see, the facade, but you should try to see what's hiding behind the walls. Your psychological walls. And then understand how things happen because they have a *precise reason to happen* and *not just the way we see them*. I'm going to ask you a simple question and I'd like you to answer without thinking about it, give me the first answer that comes to your mind."

"Okay. Go ahead."

"Close your eyes and listen to my voice, only to my voice. Your daughter and your grand-daughter were discovered dead. Why?"

Melinda Vaughan answered with a broken voice after having hesitated for two seconds.

"Simon."

CHAPTER 17
Juggling with secrets

HER ANSWER STUNNED ME. But it was her heart that had spoken, her heart that had said that first name. I still had a few questions.

"Who is Simon?"

"Laura's ex. Katheline's father."

I suddenly realized that up till now, no one had said a word about Katheline's genitor. Even myself, caught up in Melinda Vaughan's tale, I'd completely occulted that nonetheless necessary character. A child must have a mother and a father. At least from a genetic point of view, or a family point of view. I do understand that today, the term "family" covers a huge range of acceptations and variations. A traditional or nuclear family, or even binuclear, a single parent, gay parents, a stepfamily, an adoptive family. Where should I place Laura... Parker then?

Parker, the last name of the child.

"Simon Parker, then," I said to her.

"That's right. His name was the only thing he gave to my poor grand-daughter, that bastard."

I could tell that there was no love lost between Melinda and her former son-in-law. To the point that he could have been suspected of having played a part in Laura's and Katheline's death? I asked her for more info.

"Why do you say he's a bastard?"

She expressed her contempt by blowing through her nose.

"Because he is, that's why. That guy, as soon as I saw him, I knew there was something sleazy about him, as frank as a donkey backing up. When Laura introduced me to him –I think she was sixteen at the time and he was nineteen – I immediately loathed that guy. I don't know why, maybe because he never looked you straight in the eye, or his forced smiles. I never understood how she could have been attracted by someone like that. He wasn't even good-looking. I suppose that looks, taste, all that's subjective, right? Plus, nowadays, parents can no longer choose a husband for their daughter. Nothing to say about that. That's today's world. So anyway, we couldn't tell her what we thought about him and even less so when Laura told us she was engaged to him. I'm saying 'we' because at that time my dear husband was still alive and Karen, believe me, he couldn't stand that Simon either."

"So love won out in the end then... And it flourished when they had Katheline, their child, the fruit of their union."

"Poor kid, with a father like that. When I saw her, so beautiful, so sweet, I often wondered if she actually was his daughter."

That reflection instantly triggered my curiosity, like a mental flash, as I was so used to juggling with secrets of families during my numerous journalistic investigations. How many tragedies were simply the consequence of secrets that had been jealously preserved for ages before they suddenly came to light?

"She doesn't look like him at all then?" I continued.

"Oh. For sure. Neither physically nor morally. She was as brunette as her father was blond, her brown eyes thousands of miles away from Simon's blue ones. Kathy was actually the spitting image of her mother, a mini-Laura, and you can believe me I loved her even more because of that, Karen."

"That's easy to understand," I admitted with a twinge of sorrow. "Your daughter's daughter. Also a small part of yourself, I imagine."

"That's exactly right."

"So this Simon was separated for Laura at that time? How long had it been since they broke up? That's astonishing because Katheline was still a little baby if my calculations are correct. Why did they split up?"

Melinda put her palms up in the air on both sides of her, while nodding her head, in a gesture of complete helplessness, as if she was apologizing for not having sensed that tragedy.

"Because of his violent behavior, that's why."

"He was violent with your daughter? Or with Kathy?"

"To tell you the truth, my husband and I knew nothing about that for a long time. We didn't notice anything. When all three of them came to our house, they completely pulled the wool over our eyes. Even though I'd always felt he was a hypocrite."

"You never remarked any traces of violence on either of them?"

"Once. Laura came with a black and blue mark on her cheek, but she assured me that she'd slipped on the ice coming out of work. You know, that is something that often happens."

I knew what she was alluding to. The shame that victims of domestic violence have though they are never responsible for it. I nodded and Melinda continued. I needed to understand the circumstances and the people in their story, one that already seemed quite dark.

"I think that Simon's behavior got worse after Katheline was born. He didn't want the responsibility of being a father, added to that of being a husband. Some people aren't built for things like that. They'd be much better off being single, at least that way they wouldn't be a burden on their families. Simon was like that. So, anyway, one day Laura came here, crying, with Katheline who was sleeping in her arms. She must have been two or three months old at the most. But that evening, when I saw the marks on Laura's face, I was horrified.

∼

Montauk, summer of 2020

"Laura, Good Lord! What happened to you? Is Kathy alright? Is she sleeping?"

Laura Vaughan, now Laura Parker, as she and Simon, Katheline's father, had gotten married about six months ago, put the sleeping child down on the couch and burst into tears at her side.

"Kathy's fine, Mom, don't worry."

"And you? Your face…"

"It's Simon, Mom. I can't take it anymore," the young lady said sadly.

"He beat you? That was already the case, last time when you had that black and blue mark on your cheek?"

"Yeah," Laura finally admitted. "I didn't want to worry you with that, I said to myself that he was just having a bad day, and I happened to be in the wrong place at the wrong time, that it wouldn't happen again. So I lied to you. But now, it's happening more and more often. Ever since Kathy was born, Simon's not the same person. I don't even recognize him anymore."

"Thank God. Ah! If your father were still here with us, believe me, Simon would have regretted having been born. Robert would have smashed his ugly face in..."

"Mother!" said Laura, astonished to hear language like that coming from Melinda.

But, driven by her anger, she couldn't control herself. She went to the phone.

"You have to call the cops, you have to file a complaint, honey. Nowadays, it's a crime for a husband to beat his wife."

Laura sighed, closing her eyes.

"Stop, Mom. Please. Anyway, Simon's left me. He won't be coming back. He stuffed some clothes into a suitcase, grabbed our car keys and ran out. Elegantly, saying 'Adieu, you filthy bitch!'"

Melinda's hand flew up to her mouth, astounded by what her daughter had just said. Katheline began to squirm on the couch, opened her eyes, and began to cry.

"Time to eat," concluded Laura, unbuttoning her blouse, freeing her breast for her little girl.

As she hadn't been able to be a good wife, she thought, at least she'd be a good mother.

∽

Montauk, December 2023.

"And she never filed a complaint against Simon Parker?" I asked Melinda.

"Laura didn't want to. I wanted her at least to report that to the police. But anyway, ever since that day we never heard anything else about Simon. He'd vanished. Disappeared. And of course, he never wrote or called or even tried to see his daughter again. We don't even know if he's dead or alive now."

CHAPTER 18
Like a tacky liquid

SOME PLACE IN AMERICA...

His skin was freezing.
His teeth were biting the cloth.
His body was covered with dust.

He was cold, he was aching.
Reduced to silence, all the man could do now was to suffer.
Undergo and suffer.
His head was killing him and had his hands not been tied behind his back, he would have been able to touch his aching shoulder, where he could feel a tacky liquid running down over his chest and arm. A damp substance clinging to his clothing.

A threatening shadow stepped towards him, a long object in its arms. It was merely a silhouette with indistinct contours, clouded by his shrunken field of vision.

His ears were ringing. He must have a fever or low blood pressure, probably both. Had he lost a lot of blood? He had no idea but wasn't feeling well at all. He had known better days, that was for sure. Despite the pounding in his ears, he was able to make out words, like a distant echo in his subconscious.

"Jesus fucking Christ! What the hell did you do with the kid, huh? You had to be an idiot again? You couldn't just let it go? No, that would have been too much to ask of you. So now what are we going to do? What am I going to do? How am I going get us out of this shithole one more time? It's always up to me to fix your stupid mistakes!"

The man, tied up and gagged, had the reflex to try to respond to that logorrhea, but only incomprehensible sounds came out of his mouth, as the rag that had been stuffed in it made it impossible for him to speak.

"You asshole! Damn it. I don't know what I'm going to do with you now. If only you could have died this afternoon... But no, you're too solid for that. Here, I don't hold any grudges, I brought you something."

And the silhouette, leaning down over the slumped prisoner, put a plate on the ground, pushing it over to him with a foot.

"Sorry, I can't untie you. You'll have to use your teeth to eat like a dog does. Okay now, I'm going to take the gag out of your mouth, but before, you have to promise that you'll shut the fuck up, okay?"

The man's eyes squinted, but he didn't move.

"Well? I didn't understand your answer. You're gonna be a good boy?" Otherwise..."

The prisoner nodded his head slowly, only once. The other person took the rag out of his mouth. As soon as he could, the prisoner began to scream.

"You fucking..."

The silhouette immediately clocked him right in the ear, causing another buzzing that continued.

"You can it or you're not eating! And if you start, I'll use this. You already know that I can do it, right?"

The prisoner clearly saw, displayed right in front of his sour sweat covered eyes in spite of the cold, the characteristic shape of a gun.

He shut up and opened his mouth to take the meatball that his jailer stuffed inside it without any amenities. Then a second, then another one, just leaving him enough time to chew and swallow, so he didn't suffocate. No time wasted.

"You thirsty?"

He nodded. A flask of cold water was put to his dry lips and the water ran into his mouth while spilling over his chin and neck.

"You had enough now. I don't just got this to do with this clusterfuck you got us in, you son of a bitch."

Then once again, he had the rag pushed into his mouth and a sweatband around his neck.

Then the silhouette left. He was able to make out a blinding beam of powerful, cold and white light when the door opened and closed, just leaving him enough time to see the immaculate white and frozen countryside.

CHAPTER 19
The spuriousness of appearances

MONTAUK, December 2023

Upon leaving Amagansett Cemetery, walking from the Vaughan family's tombstone where Robert, the grand-father, Laura, his daughter and Katheline, his grand-daughter, had their final resting place, I thought of what Melinda Vaughan, the only survivor of this tragedy, had said to me this morning.

When I'd asked her if the official version concluding Lieutenant Garrett's investigation, stating that Laura had killed herself and taken her own daughter, Kathy, with her corresponded to what she believed, she had an ambiguous answer.

"How can I not accept it?"

"But still, deep inside, you don't believe it, do you? What about Simon Parker? Do you think he played a part in this?"

"Of course, the implication of that bastard would relieve my conscience, because, without that, how can I admit the inadmissible? But when the investigators opened Laura's purse and discovered a handwritten letter in it explaining her gesture, I couldn't doubt it anymore."

"Excuse me. You mean that Laura had left a suicide note saying that she'd also killed her daughter?"

"It was written black on white," Mrs. Vaughan said, sobbing loudly. "I know the words by heart now."

Then she told me about when she met with the policemen.

∽

Long Island, August 2022

Sitting across from Lieutenant Garrett, Melinda Vaughan felt like she was floating in a horrible mental fog. She didn't dare believe what the policeman had just put on the table in front of her. Yet, she could not deny it. She would have recognized her daughter's handwriting anywhere, that cursive script where you could tell that there were still remainders of when she was at school. Nonetheless, it was easy to tell that the text had been written in a state of stress or despondency, as several letters were shaky and hesitant. As if Laura's hand was refusing to obey those thoughts about... suicide.

Melinda drew upon the tiny rest of courage she still possessed to read those few sentences written by Laura before killing herself and explaining the reasons for it.

I'M SO sorry it had to come to this, she read. *For a long time I thought I could resist, get through this. I thought I was strong, that's what people always told me. "You're a fighter, Laura. My daughter, you're the salt of the earth." The spuriousness of appearances. The facade, the shell, like a walnut shell. But inside that shell, the fruit was rotten, flawed. Flawed? Just like the circle in which I've been spinning around for year now, that vortex that inexorably sucks me into its heart. Sitting on the banks of Oyster Pond, I'm looking out into the middle of the lake, this body of water linked to the turbulent ocean. I'm attracted by its waves, I'm tempted by the backwash, the eddies seduce me. Is the solution there, at the bottom of the lake? It wouldn't require much to find out.*

In my arms, I'm carrying the epitome of innocence. Just in appearance though, once again. My darling little Kathy. I'm troubled by the way she looks at me, so young, so diabolic...

What can I do? Leave an orphan behind me? Her father has disappeared, there won't be anyone to take care of her.

Mom, this would be too much work for you. I can't impose this on you. You're not the one who has to pay the price for the errors I made when I was young.

I believe it's better to die together, both of us, hand in hand, or even better, holding my little Kathy tightly against my heart.

I just have to find the strength of hopelessness inside me.

Laura.

∼

Montauk, December 2023.

"I remember each and every word she wrote in that letter," Melinda Vaughan insisted with a dry voice.

Tears were shining on her pale cheeks.

"I'm so sorry," was all I found as an answer, overwhelmed and distraught by what the grieving grandmother had just told me.

She nodded several times, got up and went back to the large picture window in her living room, the one you can see the ocean from, about ninety feet below, where the waves were now gently rolling in on the cold sand. That ocean that, a few months ago, had taken the only two loves of her present life from her. I wasn't surprised at her conclusion.

"Now that I told you everything, Karen, I'm sure you understand why I think I'm going crazy when I told you that I was sure I'd recognized my little Katheline in the portrait the Missouri policemen broadcast on TV. You can see it's completely impossible."

"It's irrational, that's true. So, Melinda, tell me

why you decided to contact *True Crime Mysteries* then, as you knew full well that the little girl who was found in Missouri couldn't be your Katheline?"

"I don't know. Maybe because I couldn't see myself calling the cops about this. They would have dismissed it, saying I was crazy. If I contacted you, it's especially because I'm still hoping to find out what happened to my daughter and my grand-daughter. How Laura could have come to this, as the only solution. Karen, I know that you're capable of achieving incredible results when you try to untwine the ropes of the past. I read about your investigation into Veronika Lake, in Maine. Your job is to unearth the truth."

"At least that's what I try to do."

"So please, do it for me, do it for the salvation of my soul. I've never believed in the hypothesis of suicide, that's impossible. There must have been something else..."

CHAPTER 20
Young tormented souls

JEFFERSON, Missouri, December 2023

She was no longer hooked up right and left anymore, though she still had her hands and feet wrapped up. The frostbite had been severe, much more than they'd believed when she was admitted. Yet that didn't stop her from holding the blood-red pen between her thumb and the rest of her fingers that were folded into a fist.

Dr. Frances Cagliari looked at her with her expert's eye, concentrating on what the little girl was drawing, sitting in her bed, her back leaning up on a pile of pillows. The child psychiatrist, still confronted by the little girl's persistent silence, had decided to propose sheets of paper and a huge box of colored markers. Sometimes, when words can't be spoken, drawings can replace them. So many messages can be decrypted in the hesitant lines of a child's pictures. You just have to know how to interpret them and that was something that Dr. Cagliari had learned early in her career. She'd counseled myriads of young, tormented souls who could only express their pain, their fears or their desires through drawings, be it using pencils, pens, chalk or markers.

"Do you like to draw?"

A slight nod of her head proved to the doctor that she had understood her. Though that was far from being sufficient to communicate, Frances had to be satisfied with it for the moment.

"You're really good!" she flattered her, encouraging her to continue.

Right now on the white sheet of paper, it was hard for the doctor to interpret what she'd drawn. The series of vertical lines could be interpreted in a thousand different ways, so Dr. Cagliari, seated on the side of the bed right next to the little girl, was waiting patiently until she understood. The little girl was concentrating on her drawing, the tip of her tongue could be seen in the corner of her mouth, her chubby little fingers were holding the red marker tightly.

Her little stuffed lion, on the other side of her, was carefully and attentively waiting also. Its brilliant eyes, like two malicious marbles, seemed to have a life of their own. As if the toy felt the emotions of the little girl, just as much as she did, mused the child psychiatrist.

"What are you drawing? Can you tell me?"

She made a little noise in her throat but didn't utter any intelligible words. However, the marker was going at full speed. Then she chose some other colors, made circles around the vertical lines, enclosing them into a square shape that perhaps could have been a window. A window with bars on it?

Now her hand was rushing around on the sheet of paper and the friction of the bandages on the cellulose fibers gave the doctor goosebumps. It was something nearly as irritating as the sound of chalk on the blackboards of her childhood. Unless that epidermic reaction had been caused by how she was interpretating the drawing?

There soon was the shape of a house. A crooked one, just like a witches' hovel in fairytales for children. Then the little girl grabbed the green marker, coloring the bottom of the sheet, undoubtedly green grass. On top of it she awkwardly made a horde of yellow circles. Her breathing had picked up, there were tears in her eyes and her gestures were now erratic. Dr. Cagliari internally congratulated herself for this idea, hoping that with this drawing the little girl would finally open up, express her emotions, and who knows, tell them her name...

But nothing like that happened.

The child was now more and more disorganized. She was putting markers down and grabbing others, at random it would seem, and began to draw shapes that perhaps were silhouettes. One. Then two. Then three. Two big ones and one small one. Her family? But the outlines weren't done well and all of a sudden, to the child psychiatrist's surprise, the little girl began to scribble in black, over everything that she'd drawn, covering their faces, mixing black with the other colors and thus producing a large black stain in the center of the piece of paper. The paper was soon covered with moist marker, running off onto the white sheet below and on the sides.

Then she threw everything into the air, her markers, the paper, her little stuffed lion.

And began to scream.

Dr. Cagliari leaned over her, blocking her arms so she wouldn't harm herself.

"Calm down sweetie, everything's fine. Calm down. Take a deep breath."

But the child's breathing began to accelerate to a point where the doctor was forced to request the assistance of a passing nurse, who had come to see what was going on in the room.

"Help me hold her down," asked Frances, tightly holding on to the little girl's arms that were strained by her nerves.

That though was not enough to calm the child down. They had to use a sedative that the intern on guard administered to her through the IV.

A few seconds later, the little girl was resting calmly on her pillows and the nurse was able to lie her down in her bed, covering her with the soiled sheets, until she could fetch some clean ones.

Frances Cagliari sighed, frustrated and irritated by

the experience she'd attempted, which finally ended up being a counter-productive one. She picked up the paper that had fallen to the floor, looked at it, puzzled, put it in her file and left.

While going to her office she wondered how she would ever be able to obtain a few words from her. Just a few. Just her name, which was no big deal. Her first and last names, whatever could help Sergeant Gallister progress even a little in his investigation that she knew was at a standstill.

Not for long though, as it was soon to take a surprising curve...

CHAPTER 21
To empty his head

VERSAILLES, Missouri, at the same time

While Dr. Cagliari was struggling with the little electric girl at Saint Mary's Hospital in Jefferson City, at the Versailles police station, the team of investigators were getting cranky and irritated. They weren't making any progress in this case and had to deal with a host of useless phone calls. And unfortunately the CCTV footage at the Happy Jack service station was not exploitable. Each time the presumed father of the little girl appeared, his face, even when it was enlarged, wasn't clear enough to be able to generate a composite drawing that could be exploited. Nor could it be used to cross reference it with their internal database.

"Once again it was all for naught," grumbled Gallister, nervously clicking away on his computer, scrolling through the images one by one, second after second, squinting his eyes with the hope of making them clearer.

But that didn't work.

Irritated by the lack of results, the sergeant was also bothered by an inordinate amount of noise coming from the front desk of the police station. Behind the walls that separated it from the door, he could hear vociferations, which were bothering his concentration. Plus, the cup of coffee that he'd poured himself half an hour ago was now cold and his electric radiators weren't working correctly, forcing him to keep his winter jacket on.

"Fuck it!" he mumbled to himself.

He closed the program and sat back in his chair, raised his head, pressed it against his hands behind his neck and sighed. Closing his eyes to better empty his head and concentrate, he was interrupted by three short knocks on the glass door of his office.

"Yeah?" he answered, disillusioned.

Myra Stonehenge, his deputy, poked her nose through the door ajar.

"Pete? You better come see this. Something that will interest you."

"All that ruckus I'm hearing? So what is it this time? Another bum who wants to warm up? That's not gonna happen here with these damn radiators on the fritz again. There's no money they keep on telling us. Jesus, how do they expect us to work in conditions like there?"

The sergeant straightened up, stretching, a good-looking policeman with a loudmouth and large shoulders, and followed his deputy out to the front. When he walked into the lobby, he discovered a picturesque spectacle that directly immersed him in the heart of the subject. Myra was right, this was indeed something that could interest him.

A middle-aged woman was yelling, sputtering spit onto the receptionist's face, though he kept trying to avoid the lady's salivary projections. She though continued, with cheeks reddened by the freezing weather or perhaps another phenomenon policemen on the beat were sadly used to, repeating the same thing over and over.

"Why the hell don't you want to believe me? I told you she's my daughter!"

"Ma'am, please keep your voice down," the agent replied. "I never said that I didn't believe you, I just wanted to make sure of a couple of details to write your deposition correctly."

"I don't care how it's written, I just want my daughter back! Where is she, huh? I'm not gonna leave her without her, got it?"

"I understand, Ma'am. But you also have to understand that I can't..."

"Damn it! You can't what? It ain't hard!"

Gallister stood in front of the woman, interposing himself between her and his colleague, who was relieved to see his boss taking over.

"Ma'am. I'm Sergeant Gallister, the head of this unit. Just follow me, I'll personally take care of you."

"You're the boss here?"

"I suppose you could say that."

"Okay, I'll follow you then."

Myra Stonehenge preceded them, escorting the lady towards Sergeant Gallister's office. The lady was walking hesitantly, swaying, and from what Gallister behind her could smell, she'd been imbibing a few alcoholic beverages that must have exceeded 40°.

"Please sit down," said the sergeant, pointing at a chair.

She plopped down more than actually sitting down. Officer Stonehenge sat down in a chair next to her and Gallister went around his desk so he could be directly across from her.

"Tell me everything, Ma'am... What's your name again?"

"Chastain. Carrie Chastain."

This name rang a distant bell with Gallister. A name he'd already heard, but he had no idea why or when.

"Where do you live, Mrs. Chastain?"

"Got a place next to Gravois Mills, chief. A farm in one of them bends around Gravois Creek. See where it is?"

"I do. But you drove all the way here in this weather. That's dangerous. Especially in your state..."

"What are you insinuating?"

"Your state of... nervousness. You should have called. We could have taken your deposition at your house."

"It's melting... anyway I'm not scared of snow. Plus you wouldn't have believed me on the phone. You woudda said 'She's got a screw loose,' but here, you see me, I can't cheat."

"Because you could have cheated on the phone? About what?" asked Gallister.

Carrie Chastain frowned, probably annoyed by what had just slipped out. She corrected herself.

"No, Sergeant, that's not what I meant. What I mean is that in flesh and blood, it's easier to talk things over and agree."

Pete looked at her, thinking she certainly had enough flesh, before continuing his questions.

"Mrs. Chastain, when you say that it's *your daughter*, you're talking about the child that was found three days ago near Gravois Mills, am I correct?"

"Yup, bullseye! The kid I saw in the announcement you guys made, you know saying she was lost, and she didn't know how to say her name or where she was from. Well, me, and you can believe me here, I can tell you where she came from *'cos she's my kid* and she ran away from me the day that she was found..."

CHAPTER 22
In shock

OFFICER GALLISTER WAS QUITE wary at what Carrie Chastain, sitting across from him, with a thick, slurred voice had just said.

"You're saying that your little four-year-old daughter ran away from home on a cold, winter's night?"

"That's it, Sergeant."

Gallister bit his lower lip, weighing the words he was about to say.

"There's something that bothers me a lot here Mrs. Chastain. I'm having a lot of trouble understanding why – or how – a mother, whose child ran away at night, and then was found after a public call for witnesses, could wait for over three days before coming to see the police. Mrs. Chastain, what did you do for those three days?"

She seemed to be disturbed by the policeman's question and seemed to be thinking it over, while fiddling with her entwined fingers, rubbing them, bending them until her articulations were white.

"Um... well... I mean... You understand Sergeant, I was in shock!"

"And when you were *in shock*, you *forgot* to alert the police to inform them that your little girl had gone missing? If I were you, I think this would have been the first thing I would have done, don't you agree?"

Carrie Chastain nodded while rocking from front to back on the chair, her elbows on her thighs, just like a naughty little girl. She though remained silent.

"Let me ask you again. What did you do for those three days when the entire county was searching for *your* daughter?"

"I was looking for her, what do you think!"

"And when you didn't find her and though it was freezing outside and the poor little girl didn't even have a coat on, you kept on looking for three whole days without ever thinking of contacting us? I can understand that you were in shock, Mrs. Chastain, no question about that. But I have to insist here, I hope you understand that losing your child isn't the same thing as losing a pair of slippers, like Cinderella. Slippers, you can replace them. Not a child."

"I'm telling you I was in shock, damn it!" shouted Carrie pounding on the desk with a fist.

Myra Stonehenge tried to calm things down.

"Ma'am! A bit of calm please. Just calm down."

Trembling, Carrie sat back in her seat.

"Why are you trembling?" asked Gallister, suspiciously. "Have you had any drugs today?"

"No! I don't take shit like that. I'm not a junkie, if that's what you wanted to know."

"I just wanted to make sure and give you a little test, that's all. And I'm also going to have ask you to blow into a breathalyzer because it seems quite evident to me that you're not in your normal state, Ma'am. Did you have anything to drink before driving here?"

Carrie sighed noisily.

"Like I told you, I was in shock. Plus it's fuckin' freezing out. So, yes, I did indulge in a little something."

"Little? That's not my impression, Ma'am. Myra, can you bring me a breathalyzer test and a salivary test, please."

"Coming up, Pete."

Gallister's young deputy left for a couple of minutes during which the sergeant tried to obtain Carrie Chastain's contact and administrative details: date and place of birth, employer, marital status, name of her daughter and her place of birth. It was hard for him to get straight answers from her as Carrie was becoming more and more confused as time went by, undoubtedly because of the alcohol she'd ingurgitated.

"Her name is Jessy. My little Jessy," Carrie finally sputtered.

Finally! Gallister thought to himself. The kid had a name, that angel face could be associated with a first name, if she really was this lady's child, something he wasn't convinced of with all her incoherent remarks.

When Myra came back into the sergeant's office, she handed the breathalyzer test to Carrie, who was slowly dozing off, numbed by the alcoholic vapors.

"Ma'am, could you please blow in here? Ma'am? That's it, keep your eyes open and blow right here, a good long breath, a nice smooth one. No, not like that, you have to keep on blowing. No, that's not right, could you please do it again?"

Gallister, disheartened, watched the sad show the drunken lady was giving.

"Now, if you don't cooperate," he said, "I'm going to have to take a blood sample, Mrs. Chastain. In the meanwhile, Myra, have her do a salivary test. Mrs. Chastain, you just have to spit onto this tab…"

She could spit, but it was a spit of wrath. In her drunken state though, this was of no importance.

Her inebriation was confirmed with a blood test in the following minutes, despite Carrie's weak protests, who, though she didn't agree with what they were doing to her, protested less and less. She did though articulate one request.

"I wanna see my kid now. Where is she? I wanna see her."

"Sorry, Ma'am, that's not going to be possible," Gallister confessed.

"How come?" Carrie immediately replied.

"For several reasons. The first one is that you're not in your normal state. The second one is that Jessy, let's call her Jessy, is currently in the hospital. And the third one is that we have to proceed with several verifications before allowing you to eventually see the child. Understand?"

Her eyelids drooping more and more, and her eyes glassy, Carrie Chastain nodded, her greasy hair falling on her forehead.

"I don't got a choice, do I? If that's all, can I leave now?"

"No, you can't," replied Gallister, walking up to her. "Not with your alcohol level that we just checked. I don't think you really understand this situation. First of all, you can't drive home."

"Hell's bells," shouted Carrie, "I wanna go home! With my kid!"

"Sorry, Ma'am, you don't understand. You'll be staying with us tonight, in the drunk tank. We'll see tomorrow morning, if you're feeling better and if so, maybe we could set up a meeting with the child. And in the meanwhile, please follow me."

CHAPTER 23
Unraveling the psychological thread

MONTAUK, December 2023

SITTING on my king-sized bed in my room in Montauk Manor, my back ensconced in the pillows and my eyes closed, I was rubbing my temples with my fingers, the index and middle finger of each hand, with slow, circular movements. Before that I'd put a drop of peppermint essential oil on the tips of my index fingers as I knew how much this simple remedy could often ease or prevent migraines when I was able to catch them early.

My first day at Long Island had been a tough one for my nerves. When I'd set foot on that peninsula, I had had no idea that I'd be swept over by such a wave of emotions. Melinda Vaughan, that grieving grandmother, had literally overturned my heart and soul. Her poignant tale, however, had left me with an aftertaste for some unexplainable reason. There was something in her that was bothering me, and I wanted to pinpoint that *something*.

First of all though, I had to know where I stood on what I'd learned and what I still had to check. My investigation was still at its infancy. I wouldn't be finding a missing person this time as I knew that Laura Parker and Katheline, her daughter, had both died. On the other hand, I wanted to understand why the mother had committed suicide, and why she'd killed her daughter at the same time, drowning her in Oyster Pond. Now I had to unravel the psychological thread the various players had in order to explain what had motivated that irreversible gesture. To accomplish that, I had my personal method which was asking questions to family members, but also to friends or local acquaintances. I wanted to meet someone who intrigued me, that Simon Parker, Laura's ex and Katheline's father, who was nowhere to be found, including and above all, since the double tragedy.

I washed my essential oil filled hands, mechanically swallowed my evening pills and opened my laptop to record a few things to check up on.

My eyes were burning, and I pulled the thick duvet over me and fell asleep within minutes.

EARLY IN THE MORNING, after a good night's sleep and a delicious breakfast of scrambled eggs, smoked salmon and slices of pineapple, I plucked up my courage and went outside, braving the freezing weather. I couldn't wait to go to the shore, the one Melinda Vaughan's villa overlooked, the place where she'd seen Laura and Katheline for the last time.

I've always needed to immerse myself in places and their specific atmospheres. Drawing on my senses one after another, I nourished my view, my sense of smell, my hearing, taste and sometimes also touched things. I picked up a handful of sand, brought it to my nose, smelling the salinity of the water; I listened to the wind as it blew over the dunes; I sat down on the wooden steps leading down to the beach.

I suddenly had a flash. Not a lightbulb idea, just a reminiscence born from this place. I'd never been to Long Island, yet it was as if I knew it. My memory was invaded with notes of music and the voice of Beck Hansen when he was singing this haunting song:

"*CHANGE your heart*
　Look around you.
　Change your heart
　It will astound you.
　I need your lovin'
　Like the sunshine."

I CLOSED MY EYES. Images of a movie that had really touched and moved me at least fifteen years ago superimposed themselves on top of those notes of music. I saw Jim Carrey, unrecognizable, his memories wiped out, with Kate Winslet, in *Eternal Sunshine of the Spotless Mind*. This very deserted beach, now covered with a thin layer of snow! Those dunes where canes were growing! Those wooden steps! The little Montauk train station! That was it, I was submerged in the decor of this emotion-filled movie.

"Look around you[*], Karen, embrace these places," I murmured to myself.

I closed my eyes and tried to visualize Laura Vaughan-Parker and her daughter Katheline, lying, or sitting here on the sand, at my feet. That summer had been a scorching one, the opposite of right now where I was wearing a winter coat with a faux fur-filled collar, a hat, and gloves. My imagination though was taking me back. I wasn't as cold now. The sun, rising on the horizon, warmed my eyelids. Tiny red then white dots sparkled in front of my eyes. The beach was deserted, yet I could hear a thousand voices. Kids having fun, teens playing beach-volley, diving in the sand, mothers running after their children, fathers shaking off water above their towels. I was there, it was summer, I was nearly hot. Was it sweat running down my forehead or pearls of frozen snow that were simply warming up?

Little Katheline seemed to be happy, she kept on asking her mom, insisting on going back swimming,

---

[*] "*Look around you,*" from Beck's song, *Everybody's got to learn sometime*.

she even wanted to go in without her little flotation device, but Laura didn't agree. The little girl obeyed, raising her arms and putting her head into the circle of plastic that was resting on her hips. Now she would be safe. Hand in hand, they ran down to the beach and went into the water, up to their waists. Kathy swayed from right to left with the waves. She was laughing, she was happy.

How long would that last?

In just a few hours, no one would know where they were. Up until the time when two people on a hike, two weeks later, would find their bodies floating on the calm surface of Oyster Pond, on the other side of the peninsula.

What happened after that?

Who had they run across?

Now I began to shiver again. I was back in the present, in the cold weather, with snowflakes falling on my hat.

I opened my eyes. They were red. Because of the freezing weather?

I was suddenly aware of someone looking at me.

About ten or fifteen feet from me, on the foot of the neighboring stairs, there was a man only wearing a technical t-shirt, shorts and a hat, who was stretching, his hands on his hips. Between two series, he turned around and looked at me with a friendly smile.

"Hi" he said to me, slightly out of breath.

I think this guy must have gone jogging early this

morning on the beach, only wearing shorts and a T-shirt. Light years from what I was capable of doing.

I smiled timidly back, still immersed in my retrospective thoughts.

"Are you one of Melinda's relatives?" he asked, surprising me.

I realized that where I was standing, at the bottom of a private path, below Mrs. Vaughan's villa, that his question was only logical.

"No, not at all. I was just thinking."

"Oh! Sorry to have bothered you then. I just thought... Well I'm Carmela Nollington's son, and we live right next to her."

With his chin he pointed at the path winding through the dunes up to the house that was right next to Melinda's, then he walked towards me with his hand out.

"Paul Nollington, at your service, Miss."

"Karen. Karen Blackstone. You must know the Vaughans then."

I mentally thanked my lucky stars for this meeting that would save time for me in my quest for testimonials from the neighbors.

"Oh. Sure do. I grew up here, so yes, I've always known them. The parents but especially Laura. We went to the same schools for quite a while. We were in the same class. Isn't that sad about her and her daughter, or maybe you didn't hear about that?"

"I did, and that's actually the reason why I'm here

in Montauk. I'm a journalist and I'm investigating that double tragedy."

I could tell he was surprised by that answer.

"What more is there to investigate? I thought the case was solved... Isn't the official version a suicide?"

"Yes, like you say, the *official* version. But Mrs. Vaughan doesn't believe it. She believes that Laura would never have killed her daughter and herself."

The jogger sighed sadly.

"That poor lady. She's completely devastated. Can you imagine something like that? In just a short lapse of time, she lost her husband, her daughter and her grand-daughter, a lot of people would have gone crazy or had a depression."

"Crazy enough to think that Kathy could still be alive?"

Paul sure hadn't been expecting that one.

"What the heck?"

I briefly explained why I was here in Montauk, as Melinda Vaughan had thought she'd identified her grand-daughter who had drowned in the portrait of another little girl who was found safe and sound in Missouri.

"You want to know what I think? It's simple. I think that the old Vaughan lady is a raving lunatic."

"Excuse me?"

"Yeah, I mean that ever since that took place, she's got a couple of loose marbles in her head! She's going crazy. But I understand her. All that plus, she's been hitting the bottle more and more since then."

"Meaning?"

"Drinking more than she should, if you prefer. Almost all day long now. It's not surprising that she's hallucinating."

CHAPTER 24
Drowning her sorrows

A FEW DETAILS came back to me that substantiated what Paul Nollington had just said. Melinda Vaughan had been drinking more than she should ever since her daughter and grand-daughter died. Nothing surprising there, in my opinion.

I could see her yesterday, up there in her villa, with sentences that were often hesitant, her absences, that strange smell in her breath when she approached me and her curiously glassy eyes, something that matched a widow who was drowning her sorrows in alcohol. A widow and ... *an orphan of a child and grandchild...* I suddenly realized that there wasn't even a word in English for this atrocious situation!

When your mother or father dies, you're an orphan.

When your spouse passes, you're a widow or widower.

But when your child dies?

There isn't a word for that...

And if there isn't a word to conceptualize that situation, how can you console yourself? From there to slipping into an excess of alcoholic beverages and insanity, there was probably just a tiny step that Melinda had undoubtedly taken.

I WENT BACK to my questions.

"Mr. Nollington, could you tell me a bit about Laura Vaughan? If you have time, that is."

I had to admit that the man was candy for the eyes with his technical t-shirt and shorts. He turned his hands towards himself and answered, with a smile.

"In this state, after a 10K early in the morning in the sand, I'd prefer that you not partake in my smelly company. But if you can give me a bit of time to finish my stretching and take a hot shower, fine with me. I'm on vacation at my parents' house until the beginning of the new year, so there's nothing to prevent me from chatting with you around a cup of hot chocolate. That would even be a pleasure. An hour from now, would that be okay with you?"

"Perfect! You know a nice place?"

"Yep! How about meeting at Joni's Kitchen, on Etna Avenue at nine sharp for breakfast?"

"Sounds great. Thank you, Paul."

He gave me a military salute with his index and middle finger joined together touching his forehead and took the stairs, two by two, up to his mother's villa. I got up, brushed the sand from my slacks, and before going into town, I looked up at Melinda's house.

I could see her standing in front of the picture window, looking at the ocean and its waves coming in, breaking on the snow-covered breach. Waves that, when they went back, pulled the snowflakes towards the sea. She seemed to be lost in her thoughts, alone and sad.

I ARRIVED at Joni's at nine sharp, before Paul. Inside it wasn't crowded at this time of the year, but the atmosphere was warm, just like the temperature in this little diner. There were dozens of little glass containers on the counter, full of cookies, cereal, dried nuts and fruit and other undefinable goodies I couldn't make out from where I was seated. I ordered a macchiato from the owner while waiting for Paul to come and so I'd stay warm. As soon as it was served, he walked into the little restaurant. He was wearing another hat but had shed his shorts and T-shirt for slacks and a wool sweater.

"Am I late?" he asked, putting his coat on the back of his chair. "I couldn't seem to get out of the shower."

"If I were in your shoes, I think I'd still be there," I replied with a smile. "Are you going to be ordering breakfast?"

"Sure am! I always go jogging without having had anything to eat, and after that I allow myself the luxury of a copious breakfast. Like here, I'm going to have an Olé-Olé."

I looked at the menu and whistled with admiration at that choice: eggs, guacamole, whole rice, black beans, Monterey Jack cheese, jalapeño, and sour cream, and all of that rolled up in a tortilla.

"Not bad, to kick off a day."

"When you go running, you get hungry. You should try it."

"Your tortilla or running?"

"Both! You don't run?"

"Only after secrets of the past..."

There was a short silence. An hour ago we didn't know each other and now here we were, having breakfast together in this cozy little café. I wasn't really at ease but thanked him for coming.

"Thanks for giving me some of your time, Paul. I must admit that I don't know how to tackle this very strange investigation. But, before I begin asking you questions, I want to tell you who I am, who I work for, all that... that's the least of things. And after that it's up to you to decide if you can trust me."

"So, tell me everything, Karen."

"Okay, to give you the short version, I'm a journalist specialized in unexplainable disappearances, cold cases and other mysterious crimes. The magazine I work for is called *True Crime Mysteries*, I don't know if you've ever heard of it?"

"Sorry to disappoint you Karen, but those kinds of magazines aren't my thing."

"Don't be sorry, everyone has different tastes and interests. It's true though that sometimes our readers are ashamed to admit that they read our publications that some people refer to as voyeurism, indecency, or solicitation. But you must admit that those who read *Playboy* don't admit it either," I said, jokingly.

Paul burst out laughing, and a mouthful of his tortilla almost went down the wrong way.

"Touché! I can't deny that there was a *Playboy* hidden beneath my mattress when I was a teenager, but that's not the subject. But what I'd like to know is how the deaths of Laura and Katheline could possibly interest you, as everything has been clearly determined?"

"Well, like I said before, I didn't come to this case, the case came to me. Melinda Vaughan contacted us after she'd seen the call for witnesses about a little girl who had been found in Missouri, and she thought it could be Kathy. So there's the mystery. And here I am."

"Karen, there's no mystery there. Believe me, you're wasting your time. I know the Vaughans. The investigation concluded that Laura had committed suicide, and she took her daughter with her to the tomb. What can I say? Except that it's something that doesn't really astonish me, unfortunately."

"Excuse me?"

"Like I said, I grew up alongside Laura Vaughan and I can say, without boasting, that I knew her well enough to conclude that her suicide didn't really surprise me that much. When she was a teenager, she had a lot of ups and especially downs."

"Downs that were really bad?"

"That's right. Melinda didn't tell you that? I'm not astonished, rich people in Montauk never want to admit that their daughter tried to kill herself when she was only fifteen or sixteen."

CHAPTER 25
Laws are laws

VERSAILLES, Missouri, December 2023

IT WAS tough waking up the following morning. Carrie Chastain opened an eye, then the second one, and she saw the bars of the drunk tank where she'd been placed the night before, waiting to sleep it off and find the lucidity required to understand the situation she now was in. You could say that the woman had thrown herself into the lion's den, showing up inebriated and psychologically fragile, at the Versailles police station. She'd told them she was the mother of that little girl who had been found three days earlier though she couldn't really explain how she'd let so much time go by between the time her little girl ran away and the time she went to the police station.

"Can I see my daughter now?" she yelled out,

sitting up on the uncomfortable bed in the cell. "Anyone home? Hey! Hello?"

She stood up, still tottering, and walked to the bars to begin tapping on them with the ring on her right hand.

"Hey, that's enough!" one of the policemen said. "You have to wait until Sergeant Gallister begins his day, got it?"

"Fuck! Can I at least have a cup of coffee? Something strong, 'cuz my head is killing me."

"I can make that happen if you calm down, okay?"

The prisoner grumbled a few incomprehensible words but went back to her bed, docile.

Five minutes later the policeman came with her coffee.

"Would you like to phone someone?"

"No. No one's home..."

"If you are the person you say you are, meaning the little girl's mother, there must be a father somewhere. You don't want to call him?"

"Ain't no daddy no more. He flew the coop."

"Whatever. You'll explain all that with the sergeant."

Carrie Chastain swallowed the coffee, an instant beverage that at least was hot enough to make her think it was real coffee and get her neurons back on track. Finally, Gallister came, and escorted her into his office.

"Mrs. Chastain, do you maintain last night's declaration?"

"Of course I do! I wanna see my kid! I'm not asking you for something that's impossible!"

"It's not that easy. First of all the doctors must agree that you can see her. This child is fragile, she was traumatized by the cold weather, the night, she was frightened. She's being followed by a child psychiatrist, and she has to agree. After all that is done, we can think of having you visit her. Is that clear?"

"What a shitty world we live in! This country is completely cockeyed. But like the old saying goes, laws are laws."

"In the meantime though, I'll have to check your papers, yours, and your *daughter's*. Do you have an ID on you?"

"You think I got all that crap on me?"

"Hmm. You should. At least your driver's license in the car."

"I got all that in my purse. But I left really quick, and I didn't take nothing with me."

"We'll accompany you home then. You'll have to take the breathalyzer test again, to see if you're in a state to drive it."

As the test was negative, Carrie Chastain was allowed to get behind the wheel again and they escorted her to her home. A patrol car driven by Officer Bauer preceded her on the still snowy road to Gravois Mills, and a second one, driven by Gallister with Myra Stonehenge in the passenger seat, followed her.

The convoy, after half an hour's drive at a very slow speed, arrived at Carrie Chastain's property, an aging farm composed of a hangar, a barn and what looked like a house. All the buildings were old and falling down, their roofs in need of replacement competing with decrepit walls.

"Looks like she's down on her dough," Myra Stonehenge said to Pete Gallister.

"Looks like she's down on her life too. And even less, the life of a four-year-old kid. There isn't a swing, no bike with its helping wheels, no toys in the driveway. Had someone told me that this place had been abandoned, it wouldn't have surprised me."

The three vehicles stopped in front of the house. Carrie got out, as did the police officers. But they didn't have any reason to go inside, and because of this were not authorized to penetrate into private property, in compliance with the fourth amendment. They had to let her go in and wait outside until she came back with the IDs they'd requested.

It was freezing outside, and the police officers waited, either stomping their feet or warming their hands in their armpits, or for the bravest of them, lighting up a smoke. Nonetheless, after ten or so minutes had gone by and Carrie still had not come back out, Gallister was starting to find the time long.

"What can she be doing? You don't need three hours to find your ID card, especially when it's in your purse, as she said."

"You want me to have a look?" asked Myra.

The sergeant nodded.

"Discreetly though."

Officer Stonehenge walked up to the window next to the front door, the one Carrie had closed when she went in. The police officer at first couldn't see anyone in the room that must have been the kitchen. Then she saw her silhouette through one of the doors, before it disappeared once again. She was walking around nervously, her hands moving in the air, her arms making large movements, as if she was talking to herself or yelling at an imaginary person.

During this time, Gallister walked around, just as much to keep warm as to inspect the surrounding buildings.

He went to the barn to try to see what was in it. But there weren't any openings. The building was closed by a double iron sliding door. Both parts of the door came together and were locked by a swinging metallic bar, with a hook on it, as well as an iron chain and a padlock. Pete tried to look in though a crack between the door and the wall, but it was too dark inside for him to make out anything. The only thing filtering out was the smell of damp straw and organic waste. Gallister backed up, not appreciating the odor, and went back to the patrol cars at the same time as Myra, escorting Carrie Chastain, who was holding her papers.

"This what you wanted? You cops are really sticklers for details."

"Mrs. Chastain let's not be aggressive. Just show me your papers."

The woman handed her the ID cards.

Hers was the first one. Carrie Leonie Chastain, date of birth: June 23, 1981, making her forty-three. She couldn't have been a young mother if her daughter was only four.

That was what Gallister wanted to check when he read the next card. Jessy Virginia Chastain, date of birth: January 14, 2020 in Jefferson City, Missouri. She soon would be four then. The photo on the plastic card dated back two years, with the picture of a rosy-cheeked little girl on the left side. To confirm that the face on the card was that of the little girl Rebecca Stern had discovered would be risky, as children change so quickly between the ages of two and four. But to say it wasn't her would have been equally risky.

"She's got your last name," Gallister remarked. "There's no father here?"

"I told your colleague that earlier on. He left."

"He didn't acknowledge the child then?"

Carrie made a vague gesture with her hand.

"Let's just say I'm an independent lady, that sums it up. So, can I go get my kid now?"

"Follow us," the sergeant simply said, walking to his car. "We'll see what we can do..."

CHAPTER 26
The limbo of dreams

THE TWO VEHICLES, Sergeant Gallister's patrol car and Carrie Chastain's car, parked next to each other in Saint Mary's parking lot. Myra Stonehenge had gone back to the station. Pete got out of the car and waited for Jessy's mother.

"I talked to Dr. Cagliari while we were coming here. She'll let you see your daughter. But she did tell me that Jessy is still quite weak, and she didn't want her to experience a big shock. So, easy does it, and Mrs. Chastain, I'm counting on you to be calm. Understand?"

"Sergeant, I'm not stupid. I know how to behave in public places."

The policeman strongly doubted that but didn't answer, busy walking slowly on the frozen and icy pavement in the parking lot. The hefty lady took poorly assured steps, swaying.

They went into the hospital and took the elevator

up to pediatrics. They found themselves face to face avec Frances Cagliari, who had been advised they were coming.

"Doctor," Gallister greeted her, "this is Mrs. Carrie Chastain, who affirms that this child is her daughter. Her name is Jessy Virginia Chastain. I've got her ID. What do you think?"

"Hello Ma'am," said the child psychiatrist while examining the document. "I'm going to have to ask you to be very delicate with your daughter. She's still in shock, probably a post-traumatic shock, without even talking about the wounds she has on her hands and feet because of the cold weather. She's still very weak and we have to be careful with her. Even though I do understand that you're anxious to see her, I'd like this meeting to be beneficial to her too. Do we agree on this?"

"Yeah," grumbled Carrie Chastain, trying to look over the doctor's shoulder to see inside the room.

"We'll accompany her," said Gallister.

"Let's go."

The trio went down the long hall before arriving at the room that was being guarded by a sentry. Ever since the little girl had arrived at the hospital, three men, in eight-hour shifts, were posted in front of her door.

Frances Cagliari went in first, followed by Carrie, then Sergeant Gallister.

The little girl, lying on the bed, seemed to be sleeping, her eyes closed, but her head was swaying slowly from left to right, as if she were having a bad dream.

When she saw her, Carrie's eyes opened wide, and she began to run to her. Gallister grabbed her arm.

"Remember, we said slowly."

"My daughter! It's my daughter!" the woman shouted, trying to free herself from the officer's grip. "I wanna hold her! You can't stop me from touching her! It's my daughter! Jessy, honey..."

The child opened her eyes, slowly emerging from the semi-artificial sleep that the painkillers nearly permanently immersed her in. She blinked several times and turned her head towards the origin of the noise.

"Mrs. Chastain," scolded Dr. Cagliari. "You have to be calm; this isn't good for her."

Gallister held on to her ever more tightly.

"If you don't calm down, I'm going to have to ask you to leave and we'll have to postpone this meeting. Or even cancel it, or we can go back to the police station, if you prefer."

The lady calmed down a bit, or at least she was silent. They were able to approach the bed, with Carrie between the child psychiatrist and the policeman.

The child had dozed back off, her face turned towards the window.

Dr. Cagliari began to speak softly to her.

"Jessy? Jessy, can you hear me? There's someone who wants to see you, sweetie. Can you look over here?"

The little girl turned her head, though her eyes were still closed. She was hugging her little stuffed lion against her chest, which seemed to be rising in an irregular rhythm that was far from being peaceful. She seemed to be awake, but incapable of opening her eyes, just like in moments of torpidity at the end of a long nap, where you know that people are around you, yet you can't find enough strength to completely emerge from the limbo of your dreams.

"Jessy, it's mommy," said Carrie with her heavy smoker's raspy voice.

When she heard these words, the little girl suddenly opened her eyes, just like those roller blinds when someone lets go of the string.

She suddenly seemed to realize what was happening in the room and her reaction stupefied both the sergeant and the doctor. She hugged her little lion cub even tighter against her chest, putting a still bandaged hand over its black eyes, as if she were preventing it from seeing the new person who'd come in.

Her eyes were wide open now and she began to scream.

"No! I want mommy!"

CHAPTER 27
Eating away at your soul

MONTAUK, December 2023

COULD someone who had already attempted to kill herself when she was a teen try again, using an identical or different way a few years later? Are people ever cured of that evil, eating away their souls, as time goes by? That was what I was wondering when listening to Paul Nollington's story while we were seated across from one another at Joni's Kitchen in Montauk.

I'd finished my drink, and he'd devoured his Olé-Olé wrap while telling me how his neighbor had attempted suicide when they were both teens.

"I'm really surprised that Melinda never mentioned it to you, because, believe me, that was something terrible for their family."

"Maybe she just didn't want to talk about that painful episode. Plus, something that also reminded her only too well of when her daughter died. As Melinda doesn't want to buy into the hypothesis of suicide, you could say she'd completely ignored this."

"But let me tell you, at the time, everyone in the neighborhood was talking about it."

"When did it happen?"

"Wait a sec, let me think," Paul said, turning his eyes towards the left, a synonym of mental research in the past. "So, if I'm counting correctly, because we were both in the same grade, Laura and me, she must have been born in 2000 and have been fifteen or sixteen then. That's right, we were both in high school. So it was in 2015 or 2016. Right, okay, got it now, it was in the summer of 2016. I remember because that was the year that I went sailing with some friends in the Caribbean. But that was after it happened, end of August."

"How did Laura try to commit suicide?"

Paul Nollington bit his lip while wincing painfully.

"Not in the most painless way, I was sort of in the front row there."

"What do you mean?"

"Because I was the one who discovered her, looking out from my bedroom window…"

∽

Montauk, July 2016

. . .

It had been another hot summer day on Long Island. Paul Nollington was sprawled on his bed, lying on his back with his hands crossed under his head, looking up at the ceiling where he was contemplating the ribbing in the wooden girders. He'd turned on his favorite radio station, WUSB, an independent station sponsored by Stony Brook University. They were playing *One Dance*, the latest hit by Drake, a Canadian rapper, who was currently in the Top Ten.

"*Baby, I like your style*
 Grips on your waist
 Front way, back way
 You know that I don't play."

That song was going to his head, and not just there incidentally. He closed his eyes and imagined himself with Laura in a horizontal dance that was as torrid as the one described by Drake. Too shy to make a move on her, Paul merely fantasied on his superb neighbor's beautiful body, Mr. and Mrs. Vaughan's daughter, with whom he went to high school every day.

When they were in middle school, they'd flirted a bit for a couple of years, but it was just kid stuff. They both wanted to know how to French kiss, so they tried it on each other. It was the easy way out for both of them, just like hands-on work when they were on the doorstep of that huge and frightening world of adolescence. They were both eleven. They'd hidden in a cranny of the hedge separating their parents' two properties. That place was an intimate cocoon in a no man's land, a place where they could flirt without any prying eyes. That year Paul – and this was something he'd never forget –, had braces and he was afraid that he'd hurt his partner, afraid to approach her mouth. But Laura, a bit more knowledgeable, took charge, pulling on Paul's neck firmly until he was next to her up until their lips touched, opened, allowing her tongue first, then Paul's, to penetrate, in a long and slightly salivated kiss that reflected their lack of experience.

With Drake's lyrics in his ears, Paul thought back about that year and dreamed of having the same complicity, now a bit rusty, with Laura. Finding her again and sublimating her. Not just settling for a simple kiss, but welcoming her, nude, consenting, and experienced into his bed. These though were just pipe dreams as ever since that one and only kiss, Laura hadn't stopped there, flirting right and left, flitting from boyfriend to boyfriend, and Paul knew this, giving her virginity to that stupid Maxwell guy she'd gone out with during the whole last summer. Though she was no longer a virgin, that wasn't a big deal, and Paul was still hoping to sleep with her, here, in his bed, overlooking the ocean.

Drake's song was over, and Paul got up and walked to the window. That was where he could always discreetly see what was going on at the Vaughan's pool.

He knew that Laura was at home, and as it was hot today, she'd surely be hanging out at the poolside. He also knew that when her parents weren't home, she often went swimming topless, her little budding breasts pointing their nipples because of the cool water. Paul had a good pair of binoculars, and he grabbed them from the shelf above his computer.

He pushed the curtain away and with the binoculars, began to look out at the neighboring pool.

He felt as if his heart would stop. He didn't believe his eyes, what he saw took his breath away.

Right there, in the middle of the Vaughan's pool, Laura's body was floating on the surface of the water. And around her, the water was turning red.

CHAPTER 28
A heart as fragile as crystal

MONTAUK, December 2023

"Laura took advantage of her parents' absence to slit her wrists with a cutter at the poolside, then she dove in, perhaps hoping to make sure it worked this time, a death either by drowning or by loss of blood. I luckily spied on her that day," Paul said, a bit ashamed, with tears in his eyes.

I was moved by the young man. I could visualize the sixteen-year-old teen in his eyes, in his voice, when he discovered his neighbor floating in the pool, surrounded by her blood.

"Paul, it was because of you that she survived, you should be proud of yourself."

"Of course I was, even though it wasn't very honorable to be staring at her like that with binoculars, fantasizing on her, nearly drooling behind my curtains in my room."

"You could say though that your unremitted love for her saved her and see things through that angle. Did you ever find out what led her to try to commit suicide?"

Around us in Joni's Kitchen, there was a handful of clients having a nice hot breakfast, not paying attention to our discussion at all. Paul and I both ordered a cup of coffee.

"Yes," he confessed, blowing on his hot coffee, "because for Laura, I was the person she had no secrets from, someone she trusted, never her boyfriend. That made me happy of course, but not as much as I would have liked. So anyway, she'd told me that she had broken up with a guy a couple of days ago and she was sad and heartbroken. She was completely crazy about a high school guy, I think his name was Rupert, but I'm not really sure of it anymore and anyway that's not important. And that guy took her for a ride. He'd promised her the sun and the moon before summer break, hinting that they'd go down to Florida together for their vacation as his parents had a place there. She'd never been to Miami and had always dreamed of going there. Laura's parents had said she could go, and they'd made all the plans required up until... until Laura discovered Rupert-or-whatever-his-name-is, making out with another girl, who he then went to Florida with. So you can imagine how she felt."

"Yes, I can. When you're a teen and someone

dumps you, it's like the whole world is caving in around you, right?"

Paul agreed.

"Exactly. And Laura was a poor sensitive person, she had a heart as fragile as crystal. And that summer it broke into a thousand pieces. And it was too much for her. She wanted to fly into the country of dashed hopes, of faded dreams."

Paul Nollington's poetic attitude surprised and attracted me. I like it when tough situations are described with sweet or tender words. I looked sweetly over the fumes from my hot coffee to that young man, who could nearly have been my son, and that moved me. I felt unsettled, either by him or by what he'd just told me. That phase of the life of a teenager reminded me of my own, one that wasn't always great either. An age where passions are exacerbated, desires powerful, and pain incommensurable. I chased that parasitic thought from my mind and got back on track.

"Was that the first time she'd tried to commit suicide?"

"I think so. But not the last."

"Really?"

"As far as I know. A couple of months later she tried again, this time by taking an overdose of paracetamol."

Why hadn't Melinda Vaughan told me about those attempted suicides? I noted in a corner of my little brain that I had to ask her that question, even if it was something she didn't want to talk about.

"So when all is said and done then, her death really wasn't a surprise nor an aberration for you?" I asked Paul Nollington.

"Absolutely not. I'd always imagined that she'd end up like that. But to want to die and her own daughter with her in that folie... That's not just a suicide, it's a crime!"

The word was out, like an H-Bomb had been dropped.

I did a quick mental calculation.

"So if my math is correct, Laura had Katheline when she was only nineteen or so. That's still pretty young. And do you know who the father was, as you two were so close?"

When I said the word "father," Paul Nollington's face fell and hardened.

"Simon? That son of a bitch? Of course I knew him. Everyone knew who he was anyway in high school. He was a good-looking guy, quite a bit of a 'bad boy' you could say, he never shied away from a fight or never refused a beer, an association that's not always a great one, if you see what I mean."

"I do. But I still don't see what Laura saw in this guy if he was really the way you describe him. And Melinda actually said about the same thing, and even added that he had already been violent with his wife."

"That doesn't astonish me at all. When you like to fight, you're more of a wolf than a sheep. Me too, I've always wondered why she fell for that guy. How could she have been attracted to someone like him? Someone so different from the other guys she went out with. Light years from…"

"From you?"

"Yes, from me, admitted Paul, blushing. "You know, Karen, I blame myself so much."

I made a face, fearing what I was about to hear.

"For what, Paul?"

"For not having protected Laura like I should have."

The young man's voice broke at the end of this sentence. He remained silent, lost in his regrets. I tried to reassure him.

"You can't and you shouldn't blame yourself. Each person is responsible for their acts and Laura is the one who made that choice, probably sparked by her mental instability and by her unhappy and unsatisfactory married life."

Paul Nollington still didn't react. I could feel he was mulling over dark thoughts. He finally decided to answer.

"I'm intimately convinced that somehow or another, Simon Parker, directly or indirectly, killed his wife and his daughter. I'd like to get my hands on that bastard…"

CHAPTER 29
Frightened and disoriented

JEFFERSON CITY, Missouri, December 2023

IN THE HOSPITAL ROOM, the commotion had now hit a peak. The little girl was screaming, Dr. Cagliari was trying to calm her down and immobilize her to avoid her getting hurt with all the medical devices she was still hooked up to. Carrie Chastain wanted to run to the hospital bed and was trying to squirm out of Sergeant Gallister's arms. The sentry on guard ran up to help him drag her outside, and both were needed to evacuate the lady who was now hysterical, hearing her daughter screaming like that. Two nurses ran to the room.

"I want mommy!" yelled the child, crying.

"I want my daughter!" shouted Carrie from the hallway where the curious visitors and patients were sticking their heads out from their rooms, trying to understand what was going on in that surrealistic scene.

The two policemen, accompanied by Dr. Cagliari, took Carrie Chastain to the doctor's office and sat her down.

"Mrs. Chastain, you didn't respect our morale contract here. I think that you and I must have a serious discussion."

"What do you want me to say? You didn't respect the contract either, did you? All I want to do is get my daughter back. I just want to stay with her for five minutes, just the two of us, in her room. I'm not asking much as a mother, am I?"

Frances walked in front of Carrie, and began to speak, using her calm and relaxing professional voice.

"Mrs. Chastain. Carrie, it seemed to me that your *daughter*, as you said, wasn't very enthusiastic about seeing you again. This perhaps was due to her recent post-traumatic shock or some other totally plausible reason, but I've got the child's medical responsibility here in this hospital and ward, and it's my duty to protect her. Against *anything* or against *anyone*. What's the most important to me is her health, and I didn't like what just happened. I didn't like that at all. Carrie, can you explain what went on?"

"Hey," the lady countered, perhaps avoiding the question, "I don't even know you. And stop using my first name!"

"Understood... Mrs. Chastain. Please answer my

question. How can you explain such a brutal reaction of your child?"

"Yeah, you just said it, 'cuz she was in shock, like me!"

"I can understand that, of course. Yet, she didn't start screaming when Sergeant Gallister or Mrs. Rebecca Stern, the person who found her on the side of the road, or even I approached her. So why, when she saw you, was she so terribly frightened and disoriented?"

"Fuck off with all your questions!"

Gallister stepped in front of Carrie who'd jumped from her chair to defy Dr. Cagliari.

"Hey! Stop it! Calm down! Mrs. Chastain, I think there are several very incoherent elements in your story. To start with, I can't admit nor understand that you left your four-year-old daughter run away and that you waited three days to try to find her. Then you show up here, inebriated, and you want to get her back. And as soon as you both are in the same room, she seems to want to escape from you. What is going on here? What happened between you two recently?"

"Jesus, Sergeant! It's finished, you're busting my balls! I'm not going to say another word, I'll wait until my lawyer comes..."

"Mrs. Chastain, we're not in a TV series here, quit your complaining. Do you even have enough money to pay for a lawyer?" Gallister asked with a smile.

"'Cuz I look like a bum, maybe?"

"I was just asking you a simple question. It doesn't

matter. Mrs. Chastain, we're going to talk about all that back at the station. I'd like to have an official declaration now. Let's go."

* * *

Back in Sergeant Gallister's office in Versailles, at the end of what had been a bad day, Carrie sat, her head down, hands clasped between her knees, her elbows on her bulging thighs. Pete, sitting across from her, read her rights, the now infamous "Miranda rights" that those who watch cop shows on TV nearly know by heart, those that American citizens can't ignore and that policemen in the US must recite *in extenso* before any official questioning begins, ever since the Miranda vs Arizona affair in 1996.

"Mrs. Carrie Chastain, you have the right to remain silent. If you give up that right, anything you say can and will be used against you in a court of law. You have the right to an attorney and to have an attorney present during questioning. If you cannot afford an attorney, one will be provided to you at no cost. During any questioning, you may decide at any time to exercise these rights, not answer any questions, or make any statements. Did you understand these rights I just read you? And considering these rights, do you want to talk to me?"

She nodded her head, resigned, now quite calm.

"Of course, I understood. Plus, you know, you're right Sergeant, I don't have enough money to pay for a lawyer and I don't even care if it's a free one, like you said. Anyway, I ain't got nothing to hide, so, let's go, what do you want me to say?"

Gallister adjusted his large body into his rocking chair and put his hands together in front of his mouth.

"Let's start at the beginning one more time…"

"What do you mean by the beginning?"

"Mrs. Chastain, I'd like to know who you are."

"I don't understand what the problem is. What are you accusing me of?"

"Don't put the cart before the horse here, for the moment, you're not accused of anything. Just suspected of falsification of identity."

"What?" shouted Carrie.

"Absolutely, Mrs. Chastain. I've got the impression that you're not the person you say you are…"

CHAPTER 30
Caught red-handed

MONTAUK, December 2023

Just like Paul Nollington, I sure would have liked to put my hand on that Simon Parker, Laura Vaughan's ex-husband and Katheline's dad. But contrary to Paul, who was driven by belligerent and aggressive intensions, all I wanted to do was ask him a few questions about his relationship with Laura.

"What you're affirming there is pretty radical, Paul. You reasonably believe that Simon could have been involved in the death – or suicide, if you believe the official version – of Laura and Katheline?"

The young man, his jaw and fists clenched above the table at Joni's Kitchen, seemed to be ready to leap up.

"*Reasonably*, Karen? What the hell is *reason* doing

here? Or in other words, what other *reason* could have pushed Laura to commit such an atrocious act? We're not talking about a simple attempted suicide for the umpteenth time here. She dragged her daughter with her into the abyss... If you had known Simon Parker, you'd understand why I'm sure he was the person who caused this."

"Tell me about him."

"Hmm, what else can I tell you? He wasn't a guy that you'd want your daughter to go out with. I never understood what Laura ever saw in him. A one-night-stand, why not? He was a good-looking guy, a tough one and all the gals turned around to ogle him, hoping he'd look back on them. In high school, I'm sure they all dreamed about him. About who would be the one to end up in bed with him. You know how it is, often girls from good families are attracted by bad boys."

"Maybe just an urban legend, I don't know if that's really true. It certainly isn't for me, anyway," I replied, looking Paul right in the eye for a couple of seconds. "I'm personally attracted by a dreamer, a poet, a tender and loving man..."

Why the heck was I blabbing on like that? *Karen, get a grip on it, old girl*! I thought to myself.

A moment of embarrassing silence hung over our cups of coffee, just enough time for Paul to assimilate what I'd awkwardly let escape about my love life or lack of it.

"So, I can understand that Laura reacted like all the other girls in high school. Sleeping with Simon, why not? But to have a relationship that lasted for weeks, then months, that's completely beyond my comprehension. Even if that guy was a stud in the bedroom, for everything else, he wasn't the sharpest knife in the drawer. Any discussions with him were basic, let me tell you. Except for football, he was the quarterback of course, you couldn't have a decent conversation with him on any other subject at all. Or to put it another way, I'd say that he was 'all muscles, and who knows, maybe well hung, but nothing upstairs.'"

"Flattery will get you nowhere," I joked ironically. "So, to sum it up, in your opinion, he and Laura weren't a match made in heaven. An unbalanced couple. How was she?"

Paul Nollington raised his eyes towards the ceiling as if he was trying to invoke his souvenirs of his neighbor and best friend.

"They were very different. Laura was a cultivated girl, very pleasant, often smiling in spite of her psychological fragility. She was always reading books, we often talked about them and when she'd read a good one, she'd tell me about it and vice-versa. Not that she was really an intellectual, but she was a hard-working student and did her best to have good grades. With her and Simon, it was like she was the brains, and he was the brawn. I really, and I mean really, can't understand why they went out together for such a long time. And why the hell she married him! When she told me that, I thought I'd die right there in front of her."

When he said the word *die*, with such fervor, something bothered me when I heard it coming from his mouth. As he was secretly in love with Laura, what had he thought when they actually got married, that improbable union with his teenage love? I had a terrible flash suddenly. And what if the worst thing wasn't what he was insinuating? What if Paul, driven crazy by jealousy, had committed the irreparable? I quickly chased this horrible thought from my head. No, not him, not that reasonable, cultivated and well-educated young man.

"How did she tell you that she and Simon were going to get married? You were her best friend, she told you everything."

Paul made a vague gesture with his arm, as if he wanted to push what he we were getting ready to say aside.

"In the usual way. She assured me she loved him, that he loved her, that they were happy together. I asked her to be sincere with me, to explain what she saw in that guy. And she answered, without looking me in the eyes – I would imagine that she didn't have to face my criticism that way, – that I couldn't understand, that she herself couldn't really explain why she loved Simon. But she'd made her decision, and she wasn't going to change her mind. They got married a couple of months later. And she got pregnant quickly."

"With Katheline ?"

"Yup, that adorable little kid who was the spitting image of her, like a mini clone."

"That's what Melinda told me yesterday too. Kathy looked just like her mom, not at all like her father, and a lot of people were relieved by that."

"You're preaching to the choir! And if that Parker bastard had left her his bad temper and his empty brain as an inheritance... Thank God though, that wasn't the case."

I suddenly had a nonsensical idea, well maybe not that nonsensical after all, because of my experience in the domain of family secrets.

"Katheline doesn't look at all like her father?"

"She was as brunette as Simon was blond. She had her mother's brown eyes, not her genitor's blue ones."

"And what if he wasn't her father after all," I insinuated.

Nodding his head, Paul thought about what I'd just said, troubled.

"That could be a hypothesis," he concluded with a smothered voice.

"One that you'd envisaged, at least for a while?"

"One that you can't exclude, that's true."

I remember Melinda telling me about the day when her daughter showed up unexpectedly, holding Kathy in her arms, her face full of black and blue marks, when she'd admitted that Simon had abused her.

"Melinda said that when Simon left after having brutalized Laura, he'd shouted out at her that she was a 'filthy bitch' before taking off. How would you interpret that, Paul? Does it ring a bell?"

When he heard those words, Paul made a fist, mulling over what I'd said. I could tell he was boiling over with hatred deep inside.

"That bastard added verbal violence to physical violence. Calling Laura a *filthy bitch*... What could she have done to deserve words like that?"

"Are you think of what I'm thinking of?"

"I'm all ears, Karen. I'd prefer if you said it yourself."

"Okay. What I understand here, and I'm not putting any gloves on, is that Simon had some suspicions that Laura was cheating on him, if I can put it like that. Maybe he caught her red-handed, found her with someone else and beat her to punish her, as his pride as the dominant male in their family was tarnished."

"Contributing to fragilizing her psychologically by beating her, insulting her, finally dumping her, up until the time when she was so exhausted of being a victim, that she killed herself and killed Kathy with her."

Then I jumped in, associating ideas.

"Let's push this line of thought up to the very end then. Imagine that Simon knew that Laura had cheated on him and at the same time learned that this had been going on for a couple of months. You see where I'm going here?"

Paul winced and concluded in my place.

"Then he understood that he wasn't Katheline's

biological father... But is that a sufficient motive to want to kill your wife as well as the fruit of an adulterous union?"

CHAPTER 31
Confrontation

VERSAILLES, Missouri, December 2023

CARRIE CHASTAIN WAS BACK at square one.

She was starting to get used to that place. Pretty soon she'd be able to apply for a job as a hostess at the Versailles police station. After a first declaration she'd volunteered, then a night spent snoozing in the drunk tank, the lady with her prematurely salt and pepper colored hair and her pathetic looking face was once again confronted with Sergeant Pete Gallister's questions. This time though she wasn't the one who had come to them; her presence was motivated by the sergeant's summons. He was assisted by Officer Myra Stonehenge, sitting on his right.

Gallister put a voice recorder on the tap in the audition room and pressed the start button.

Audition of Carrie Chastain, December 19, 2023, at 11:37 a.m. in the presence of Sergeant Pete Gallister and Officer Myra Stonehenge.

Sergeant Gallister: So, Mrs. Chastain, let's start at the beginning then. We summoned you here today in the framework of an investigation into the little girl Rebecca Stern discovered alone, on the night of December 15, 2023, near Gravois Mills. Yesterday, on December 18, 2023, you declared that she was your daughter: Jessy Victoria Chastain. Yet, after a confrontation with her, many questions arose, leading me, Sergeant Pete Gallister from Morgan County, Versailles station, in Missouri, to conduct this audition. Officer Myra Stonehenge is assisting me today. Do you agree with what I've said?

Carrie Chastain: Couldn't have said it better myself.

Sergeant Gallister: Marvelous. Can you please state your identity?

. . .

Carrie Chastain : Carrie Leonie Chastain, at your service Milord.

Officer Stonehenge: Please, stop trying to be ironic, we're not in a TV series here.

Carrie Chastain : If I can't even crack a little joke...

Sergeant Gallister: Mrs. Chastain, I'm finding your attitude quite contradictory. You don't seem to be taking this situation seriously. The life of a little four-year-old girl is at stake. Yesterday, you seemed quite worried about her, though you let three days go by before informing us of her disappearance, and now you're trying to joke about everything. Let's just concentrate please. Your date and place of birth?

Carrie Chastain : June 23, 1981, in Eldon Missouri.

Sergeant Gallister: Marital situation?

Carrie Chastain : Separated.

. . .

SERGEANT GALLISTER: Have you ever been married?

CARRIE CHASTAIN : No, never.

SERGEANT GALLISTER: The name of your partner?

CARRIE CHASTAIN : Mumin Blasharov.

SERGEANT GALLISTER: That sounds like a foreign name. Is he an American citizen?

CARRIE CHASTAIN : He's from Georgia. Not the State here, the country over there, near Russia, see where it is? He obtained his American nationality a couple of years ago.

SERGEANT GALLISTER: How did you two meet?

CARRIE CHASTAIN : He came from a family of political refugees. His parents moved here when he was just a little kid, after the fall of the Soviet Union, or something like that. I don't understand nothing 'bout that stuff. He worked on a farm near mine. We met in the fields during the corn harvest.

SERGEANT GALLISTER: Is he your daughter's father?

CARRIE CHASTAIN : Of course! What do you think? I'm not a harlot! I've only had one man in my life...

SERGEANT GALLISTER: No one insinuated anything like this Ma'am. Where is this Mr. Blasharov now? Why haven't we seen him yet?

CARRIE CHASTAIN : Because the bastard did a runner.

SERGEANT GALLISTER: Can you be more precise?

CARRIE CHASTAIN : Yeah. He took off with my little girl the other night. He took the car, and they split. He kidnapped her, that bastard! He didn't have the right to, she's my daughter!

Sergeant Gallister: His too if I understood correctly. So, you affirm that the father of your daughter Jessy left your home on December 15, taking her with him. Was this departure planned or organized? Like to visit some other family members for Christmas?

Carrie Chastain : Not at all! It was a kidnapping, I keep telling you! He deserted our home. I'm sure he'd planned this, that son of a bitch!

Officer Stonehenge: Why are you sure, Mrs. Chastain? Did you have any reasons to think that your partner wanted to leave you? Were there problems in your couple?

Carrie Chastain : No, not that I know of. What can I say? We've lived together for pretty many years now and like all married couples, even if we're not really married, we've had our ups and downs, you know how it is. But him just up and leaving like that, I don't understand.

. . .

Sergeant Gallister: The vehicle he took to leave, would it perhaps be a dark green Dodge pickup?

Carrie Chastain : Jesus fucking Christ, yeah! How do you know that?

Sergeant Gallister: Our sources told us that this vehicle was seen in the evening of December 15 at the Gravois Mills gas station, with a man and a little girl abord, whose ages seem to correspond. That night there weren't a lot of people on the roads because of the snowstorm. Do you think it could have been Jessy and...um, Mumin Blasharov?

Carrie Chastain : Sure as hell was! No doubt about that. Last time I took the pickup, it was almost out of gas. He must have filled up before leaving. It wasn't a very good idea to choose a day like that to split, was it Sergeant? A dumb idea he had there.

Sergeant Gallister: Unless he wanted to take advantage of the snowstorm so you wouldn't catch up with them. The pickup seems more adapted to the weather conditions than your own car. What time was it when they disappeared? Were you there when it happened? Did you try to prevent them from leaving?

. . .

CARRIE CHASTAIN : I don't know exactly what time it was. They hit the road when my back was turned. It was when I came back from feeding the chickens behind the barn that I realized that they'd left. Those little birdies flew away! The pickup wasn't in the yard anymore and there were tire tracks in the snow leading to the road. I'd say it must have been about four or five, anyway it was already dark outside.

SERGEANT GALLISTER: Did you try to find them? To phone your partner?

CARRIE CHASTAIN : Yeah, I called him, but he didn't pick up. I left several messages.

OFFICER STONEHENGE: Did he leave you an explanation, a letter or a note to explain what he'd done and why?

CARRIE CHASTAIN : Nothing! He left me like a dog you abandon on the roadside. And he took the kid. If you catch him, don't let him go and bring him to me, I've got two or three things to say to him. I busted my butt so much for him, and that's how he pays me back.

Sergeant Gallister: Mrs. Chastain, how can you explain the fact that we found Jessy, and we didn't have any trace of Mumin Blasharov? Nor of the Dodge?

Carrie Chastain : Got me. Plus, that's your job, not mine. Me, I told you what I know, who I am, who they are and now I'm telling you I want to get my kid back and now. I am sick and..."

Sergeant Gallister: Okay, we understood. Can you give us Mumin's phone number?

Carrie Chastain : I don't know it by heart. Look in my phone, the one you took from me when I arrived. I'll give you my permission.

Sergeant Gallister: Very nice of you. Okay, that's all for now. Mrs. Chastain, would you like to add anything?

. . .

Carrie Chastain : I wanna see my Jessy.

Sergeant Gallister: We'll talk about that later. It's now 12:15 and this interview is finished.

∽

Pete Gallister pressed the stop button on his voice recorder and put it in his pocket.

"Mrs. Chastain, I'm terribly sorry, but I can't allow you to see your daughter now. The experience this morning was enough for me. She needs to rest, and so do you. As for us, we'll have to untangle a couple of threads and do some verifications and cross-checks. In the meanwhile, we're not going to keep you here any longer, you're free to go."

"I can leave then?"

"You can, but on this condition, don't leave the county. We must be able to reach you at any time."

CHAPTER 32
That horrible lady

THAT HORRIBLE LADY *has finally left.*

You can open your eyes now, my little Leo.

My hands weren't big enough to plug your ears, but I hope you didn't hear all her nonsense.

Poor little Leo, you know, I'll always be here to protect you from the others, from the bad people. Even if me that makes me hurt. I'm used to it.

You know what? They thought I was sleeping, but I wasn't, I just had my eyes closed to rest and not see them. But I knew the lady doctor for children was there, I recognized her perfume. I like how she smells, she smells nice, like flowers. But I still mustn't talk to her. Same thing for you! Promise? Not a word!

And I know that the tall policeman was there too, the one who asked me questions when the lady found me on the road that night.

But I smelled someone else right away. A different

smell. A smell I don't like at all! It tickles your nose, makes your head spin, it scares you.

When I opened my eyes I saw her face right in front of mine and I screamed because I was too afraid of her eyes.

You know Leo, how to tell if people are nice or bad?

Don't even bother listening to them, often it's a bunch of lies. Listen to what I'm telling you, it's gonna help you later on, if one day I'm not there to protect you. So, to know what people have in their hearts, you have to look them straight in the eye. Over there, behind that thin skin covering the eyes, there's a little light that lights up just like a star when people are nice.

And when they don't have a nice heart, there's not a little light, it's all black, all dark, all sad.

And her, in her eyes, it's worse than black, it's like emptiness. Leo, you think emptiness is white or black? Or transparent? I don't know, but the horrible lady, looking into her eyes was really awful.

Plus she talked too loud, and her mouth smelled bad. 'It's mommy,' she kept repeating.

So I was really scared, and I screamed.

Because it's not true.
She's not my mommy.

CHAPTER 33
Like blades of a knife

MONTAUK, December 2023

Paul Nollington's latest revelations about Simon Parker, together with what Melinda Vaughan had told me, made both of our brains go into overload thinking mode. His theory of a direct or indirect possible implication of Simon in Laura's death left me speechless. We'd finished our coffee; Joni's Kitchen was emptying out as the morning had gone by. I honestly hadn't noticed how long we'd been there; it was so nice talking to him. Plus you had to admit that he'd told me a huge number of instructive things about the Vaughan case. One of those journalistic investigations that I was enjoying: meeting pleasant people, interesting interviews, and juicy revelations for my readers in *True Crime Mysteries*. I knew that when I'd summarize all that for Myrtille, she wouldn't regret having sent me here to Long Island, despite the outrageous price of my room in Montauk Manor.

"I think I've already got plenty of food for thought with everything I've learned in the two days I've been here," I concluded.

"Karen, if you want to talk about this some more, just give me a call. I'll be here in Montauk a couple of days with my parents for Christmas, so I'll be easy to find."

"On the bottom of the steps, at the beach?"

"For instance. And if you're not afraid of getting up at the crack of dawn and you feel like stretching your legs and breathing in some ocean air, you can come running with me!"

I smiled, nodding.

"I'll think about it. Though I might join you when you'll be on your last lap."

"Whatever, Karen. In the meanwhile, I can give you my phone number if you want. Do you have a pen on you?"

I rummaged around in my purse and handed him one, as he picked up one of the paper napkins in a distributor on the table. He wrote his number down and added a little smiley that seemed to be winking as well as a stickman who was running.

"Thanks for your time, Paul. I really appreciated it."

We left the coffee shop. Snowflakes were whirling around in the brisk sea breeze. I lowered my head to my shoulders to offset the biting cold.

"Can I drop you off somewhere?" he asked.

"That's really nice of you, but I'm going to walk a while. It helps me think."

Each of us took a different direction.

Temporarily?

* * *

Watching Paul Nollington walk away, I said to myself that this sure wasn't peak tourism season here. Yet, as in each time I'm investigating, I need to *sense* the venue, to immerse myself totally in the places where the case I was working on took place. Up until now, I'd gone into the Vaughan's house and seen, through the bay window, the pool where Laura had tried to commit suicide when she was only sixteen. I'd also sat for a while on the steps delimiting the beach below the villa, the place where she and Katheline were seen for the very last time. I'd gone to Amagansett Cemetery to see their headstones.

Doesn't the old saying go that walls have ears? That places breathe, feel and can convey their emotions to us? Just like the time when I'd spent a night on Sugar Island for the Veronika Lake investigation, here I wanted to see with my own eyes the key places where this case that the investigators had closed took place.

I opened the Maps app on my phone to go to Oyster Pond, where Laura and Katheline's bodies had been discovered by a couple walking their dog. Melinda had told me there was a trail around the body of water. I quickly found it on the digital map, and when I saw how far it was, I decided to go to my hotel first and take my car. I didn't want to catch my death with this freezing weather!

Fifteen minutes later, I parked my Ranchero in one of the clay parking lots from where the hiking trails left. The sky was overcast with grayish clouds reflecting like blades of a knife on the cold waters. I'd stopped at the southern bank, where the cadavers had been found, floating at the surface of the water, held prisoner by the canes and algae there. It was a few minutes' walk from the parking lot to the shore where one of the paths snaked through. Between the path and the shoreline, I could see half-immerged interlaced roots, canes swaying with the wind, all that in about a foot of brownish water. From what I'd read on the internet, this natural belt made boating impossible in this pond, and it wasn't even a very good place to go fishing. Oyster Pond's banks had recently been classified as being dangerous in several municipal by-laws. Going past them, it seemed evident to me. From where I was standing, which was between two trees in the sediment forming a sand-filled ramp where a small boat could be launched, I could make out the opposite side of the pond. This pond, which was actually very unique, reached the ocean by a passage that went directly to the shoreline, making it easy for people to access Oyster Pond, as well as the ocean.

That got me thinking. I tried to imagine Laura and Katheline's final hours. And I couldn't forget that the events took place in the middle of summer when it was boiling hot. Not like today.

The last place where Melinda Vaughan had seen them was right below her villa, on the beach in Montauk, where they'd laid their towels down. The opposite side of where I now was, almost on the other side of the peninsula. From there, it would have been completely possible to walk along the seaside up to the lighthouse on the end of Long Island, then take the northern littoral up to the mouth of this pass.

And from that pass, it would have been easy to sink into the pond and float and eventually go to the bottom, and all that without necessarily being seen by the myriads of people on the crowded beach.

But, as Melinda had said, it was pretty far from one point to another if you walked along the coast. On the map, I made a ballpark guess of seven or so miles and that was without taking into account all the crannies on the coast which could have easily added another mile. So let's say eight miles. Could a little girl who was only eighteen months old walk eight miles? Plus doing that in the sand where her feet would sink in?

I didn't believe that scenario at all. Or could Laura have carried her in her arms or on her back? Also difficult, in my opinion. That being, I'd learned from the past that the most unexpected situations could sometimes be the ones that were true.

But I came back to that question that was eating away at me. What had Laura and Kathy done between the moment when they went down to the beach and when they drowned in the pond? Right here, where my eyes were looking down at these troubled waters whose bottom had to be full of a thick black mire, just like a damned soul.

Speaking of which, I was still missing an essential piece of information. I knew that they disappeared on July 13th and that their bodies were found in August.

But that didn't tell me when they'd drowned…

CHAPTER 34
Plug the holes and fill the gaps

WITH ALL THOSE UNANSWERED QUESTIONS, I needed to know more. To get some answers, I knew I had to contact the authorities in charge of the investigation when it took place. Get the official version.

A cop named Garrett from the Long Island police, and the medical examiner who had carried out the two autopsies: both had spoken to Melinda Vaughan about identifying the victims.

After a bit of research, I called the police station where the lieutenant worked. Luck was on my side: the operator told me he wasn't on Christmas vacation yet. After I'd introduced myself and told her why I was calling, I asked if I could speak to Officer Garrett. He picked up a few seconds later, just as cold as the freezing weather.

"What do you want with me, Miss Blackstone? You think I got time to chat with journalists right before Christmas? I'm overloaded with files I have to close, my desk is full of papers I have to read and sign, so I don't have to paint you a picture."

"I'm sorry to inconvenience you Lieutenant Garrett, and I understand all the work you've got right now. I just wanted to speak with you a couple of minutes about the double death of Laura Vaughan and her daughter, Katheline Parker, in Montauk. It was eighteen months ago, in July last year, I'm sure you haven't forgotten it."

"Affirmative. I remember this case. Suicide and drowning in Oyster Pond. The case is closed, Miss. Just sadly commonplace events. A tragic event, but one where the investigators were sure of their conclusions. Clear as spring water, and not like the water in that damn pond. There you go. So if..."

I cut him off, fearing that he'd hang up on me.

"Wait a second, Lieutenant, please."

I quickly outlined for him what brought me to this county, why Melinda Vaughan had called *True Crime Mysteries*, what I'd learned from the grandmother and Paul Nollington. On the other end of the line I could hear groaning, like a bear when its hibernation is about to finish.

"Okay, what time is it? Stop over then. I'm going to have a sandwich break at about one. Stop at the deli and get me a pastrami bagel and a salmon one, with a soda and while I'm waiting, I'll get the file back out. You'll save me from going out with this crappy weather. You're lucky that Christmas is just around the corner with its presents."

That guy sure had nerve!

At one, after having run all over to get the lieutenant's order, I walked into the Long Island police station. The agent at the front desk picked up his phone, announced me and asked me to wait on the bench across from him. A minute or so later, a fifty something man, gray buzz cut, plump red cheeks, with a prominent gut preceding him, walked out.

"I forgot to tell you to bring me some extra ketchup," he said loudly, shaking my hand. "Lieutenant Rudolf Garrett."

"Karen Blackstone. I anticipated for the sauce," I said, handing him the bag. "Thanks for allowing me to come."

"Oh. A woman with initiative. I like that. Follow me."

He escorted me to his office through a maze of halls, greeting a few colleagues on the way. After he'd closed the door behind me and invited me to sit down across from him, he unwrapped the sandwiches without waiting.

"So the tuna salad must be for you, I'd imagine? Okay then, Miss Blackzone, what do you want to know about the Vaughan affair that hasn't been published then?"

"Blackstone! But you can just call me Karen."

"Sorry, Karen. Before I start, I have to tell you that I don't like journalists. Maybe you realized that on the phone earlier."

"You have to stick to what you know," I replied hesitantly.

"True, it takes all types to make the world go around, but I must admit that muckraking like you do in your profession completely exasperates me. Always in our way or searching through the garbage after us, dissecting each and every word in our documents, and asking, like today, if we could have another look at this or that case that we closed months or even years ago. As if we hadn't done our work well… You know, here in the police force, there are departments that check our work, we're not depending on journalists like you to do it for us. Anyway, you're here, so let's do this. By the way, before I take the file out, I'd like to make sure that you have a press card."

As I always had this magical sesame on me, I gave it to him. He looked at it, as if he were disgusted.

"Okay. Can we really call what you write in those tabloid magazines journalism?"

"Lieutenant, please, I'm not here for a sterile debate like that. You and I both know that the general public loves criminal investigations, and both of us realize this on a daily basis. So let's overlook these cliches, enjoy our meals and study the Vaughan case."

"There isn't any Vaughan case. There was a tragedy, yes, but it was explainable, explained, and now it's closed," said Garrett, taking a big bite out of his pastrami sandwich, sauce dripping down over the corners of his puffy lips.

"Nonetheless, like I told you earlier, Melinda Vaughan, Katheline Parker's grandmother, is persuaded, after she saw the call for witnesses on TV and despite any rational logic, that her grand-daughter and the little girl they found in Missouri are the very same person."

Officer Garrett nearly choked on his sandwich, bursting out laughing at what I'd said. It took him a while to swallow.

"Karen, I don't believe in ghosts."

"I must say that I agree with you, Lieutenant. But I'm trying to get some questions answered."

"Give up, that won't get you anywhere. The poor lady went completely nuts after her daughter and granddaughter died. I heard that several times already. She quickly made the bottle her best friend to plug the holes and fill the gaps in her heart."

"Guess there are poets in the police force," I joked.

"A tender heart in the body of a furniture mover! Have a look at this file and try to find the autopsy report Dr. Huan Li wrote."

With one hand, the officer pushed, between the pastrami wrapping paper and his glass of recycled card-board, the thick file on his desk with the name of Laura Vaughan and Katheline Parker on it, to me. Putting down my fork for my tuna salad, I opened it and glanced at the reports, declarations, and analyses, looking for the medical examiner's conclusions.

While flipping through all the various items in the file, spending a bit more time on some of them, such as audition reports, constatations *in situ*, reports from the technical and scientific police, my stomach began to churn.

I suddenly came across a series of color photos and froze.

I have no idea how cops can endure things like that, but I certainly shouldn't have opened that file during my lunch break...

CHAPTER 35
Cutting the wings from an angel

ALERTED BY MY glassy eyes that were rolling and the way my head began to lean to the side, Garrett dropped his sandwich, got up as quicky as his fat body would allow him to, rushed to the other side of the desk just in time to catch me before I fell from my chair. His powerful arms caught me a few inches from the floor, so my head didn't clunk against it.

"Hey! That was a close one! Miss Blackstone, can you hear me?"

I mumbled a few unintelligible words while the lieutenant helped me over to an aging leather armchair in one of the corners of his office. One he probably used for after lunch naps as you could tell it was used to being on the receiving side of a heavy body. I nonetheless appreciated its welcoming softness and slowly opened my eyes, still blinking, still taking tiny breaths.

"Here, drink this," he said, handing me my bottle of water.

Which I did. You don't discuss orders when a policeman gives them to you!

Slowly coming back to my normal state, I thanked him, rubbing my face.

"Karen, you don't eat enough. A salad! There's no calories in it!"

"I'm afraid that with two pastrami sandwiches at noon each day I'd soon be a blimp," I said with a wry smile. "But I think about anything I would have eaten today would have caused me to faint after seeing images like that..."

"True. I should have warned you, I'm sincerely sorry. Are you going to be okay?"

I don't know why, but I could feel he was being a bit ironic here. I was persuaded he wasn't unhappy to have played this little trick on me to test my resilience as a journalist specialized in crimes and cold cases.

"Thank you, I'm already feeling better. Could you please hand me the file?"

He went back to his desk and brought it to me.

"I thought you were used to looking at documents like this. Why don't you jump directly to Dr. Huan Li's summary? He's the medical examiner who performed the double autopsy and who requested additional tests."

It was true that I was unfortunately quite used to reading autopsy reports. I'd gone through loads of them during my many years as a reporter.

So I knew how they were written. Data of the investigation in a chronological order, the removal of the body, X-ray exams, external exams of the body, the autopsy itself, detailed organ by organ, samples taken, discussion, and then the conclusion. While I was leafing through the report, Garrett went back to his desk to finish off his sandwiches, seemingly not bothered by my little fainting episode.

"Karen, you're still pretty white. You should finish your salad, even if it's not enough to fill your stomach," he said with his mouth still full.

I focused on the documents, putting Katheline's and Laura's photos next to each other – they were still making me sick – with the details that the coroner had noted.

The file, which was very professionally put together by Dr. Li, was so thick that I decided to jump to the conclusions of each autopsy to have a global overview. After that I'd delve more deeply into the details.

∼

I started with Laura.

Category of death: Violent death.

Cause of death: Voluntary drowning preceded by intoxication caused by barbiturates and a massive absorption of alcohol.

Then Katheline.

Category of death: Violent death, of a criminal character.

Cause of death: Blows and wounds followed by drowning.

~

After having read the conclusions and looked at Kathy's photos, I could better understand Melinda Vaughan's pain when she had to identify the body. Her swollen, discolored, and distorted face, that little girl who wasn't even two, who'd died because of this. How could anyone bear this? It must have been hard for her to even recognize her granddaughter.

How could a human being be capable of such atrocities on a little innocent being?

How could you imagine cutting an angel's wings?

I looked up from the file, my head spinning, my gut churning. Was it hunger? Disgust? I looked over at Garrett.

"Lieutenant, what was the conclusion of the official investigation?"

He sighed loudly, massaging his head, before answering me.

"An ugly story, wasn't it? We see things, horrible things in our lives and jobs, but there, I guarantee you that this one sickened me. When you put everything together, the investigations that our services carried out plus the scientific ones, the coroner, the laboratory analyses, and the testimonials, this is the scenario that everyone agreed on. On July 13, 2022, Laura Vaughan and Katheline, her daughter, were seen at the end of the afternoon on the Surfside Avenue beach, near the Vaughan's villa. After that, they both vanished. Disappeared from the radars. Unreachable. Their cadavers were found at the beginning of August, floating near the shoreline of Oyster Pond, stuck between the canes and roots. What happened between those two dates? We can't determine it with certainty. We have no idea if they went to the pond going around Montauk Point by the lighthouse or by another itinerary, for example, by cutting through the fields, which would be quite a bit shorter, obviously. Nonetheless, when their bodies were found, they were only wearing their swimsuits."

"And? What did you conclude?"

"I didn't conclude anything, I just can't really imagine them walking through Montauk just wearing their swimsuits, even if we were in the middle of the summer. Plus there's a municipal by-law stating that tourists can't go walking through town just wearing their swimsuits."

"Maybe they drove?"

"Possibly. However, the coroner couldn't establish the exact date of their death. As their bodies had been found a couple of weeks after they'd drowned, pretty roughed up if I could use that term, Doctor Li thought that their deaths had occurred between July 13 and July 20, at the latest. A gap of seven days in which their last moments were impossible to retrace. Or at least in which no testimonials concerning any eventual apparitions of them here or there had been heard. So, that being said, the coroner thought that this may well be what happened: on the day that she died, with the toxicological readings and the study of the organs in the abdomen – liver, gallbladder, stomach, pancreas, kidneys, and bladder – it would seem that Laura Vaughan had ingurgitated a large amount of alcohol plus there were signs that she'd been taking antidepressants for quite a while."

"Okay. "Alcohol plus antidepressants, that's a cocktail that's not really recommended. She was taking that medication against her suicidal tendencies then?"

"That's right, this wouldn't have been her first try. So that was the physiological and psychological state she was in at that time. The report of the psychiatrist who testified during the investigation showed that. Could she have had an attack? Possible. And why? We have no idea. And why did she take her daughter with her? Had she disobeyed her? Had she been really naughty? Did Laura break down, as she was depressive, exhausted, and tired of raising her child alone? The psychiatrist thought that might have happened. As her husband had been violent with her, she was used to being beaten, and she produced the same type of behavior with her daughter."

The lieutenant's words really shook me up, sparking another question.

"But to actually kill her?"

Garrett scratched his chin with its three-day beard on it.

"I know that it could seem crazy to see a mother behave so desperately and violently with the fruit of her own loins, but that is something that does happen. During this investigation I learned that murders by drowning are historically a form of infanticide. In the Middle Ages, that was how you got rid of a non-desired child, sort of like you do with little kittens, putting them in a bag weighed down with a stone. Poor humanity, I feel like saying. But it must be quite easy to kill an innocent little kid who's only two. You saw how she looked in the photos... The coroner noted the presence of several scratches and lacerations, on her face and in her hair, which were caused by a blunt ring that matched the one Laura had on her right hand, and Laura was a right-hander. A ring that also had several very sharp asperities that you can also see on the photos in the file. So, to the question of whether the little girl died because of the physical violence or by drowning, once again the medical examiner had the answer, during his dissection."

"And what did he find?"

"That the child's lungs weren't filled with water."

"How come?" I said, wrinkling my brow. "I can't understand how the body of a human being that was immersed for several weeks in water can't have swallowed some."

"It's easy. The little girl was no longer breathing when she drowned, pushed to the bottom by the weight of her mother. So technically she didn't drown. She was already dead!"

CHAPTER 36
Blood ties

I REALLY WASN'T sure that I was reassured and comforted to know that Katheline had died before her mother drowned her. That she, you could say, escaped from an atrocious death. When a child dies, nothing can console you.

"Was the coroner able to determine the lapse of time between Kathy's death and her submersion in the pond?" I asked Lieutenant Garrett.

"That wasn't easy," the policeman replied, with a scratchy emotion-filled voice. "When a body is in the water for a long time, a lot of elements are inconclusive, and the analyses are always difficult to do with any exactitude. He's nonetheless categorical about how this took place. Did you ever hear the terms *white drowning* and *blue drowning*?"

Taken aback, I looked at him with eyes as around as basketballs.

"Never. What are you talking about?"

"Okay then, let me try to remember all this and I hope I don't get things mixed up," the lieutenant said, with a mimic of deep reflection on his features. "If you're really interested in this, you can read Dr. Huan Li's report, it's quite detailed. So, coroners classify people who drown into two categories according to the color on their epidermis. Some people are waxy white, hence the term *white drowning*. You could also use the term *syncopal drowning* or *false drowning*, as opposed to people who are cyanosed on their faces, fingers, or lips and who are thus referred to as having died from *blue drowning*. Those people actually died because of asphyxiation, contrary to white drowning victims who died before they were asphyxiated. But that wasn't all that pointed the coroner in that direction. Another difference between these two types of death is the presence or not of liquid in the respiratory tract. Mechanically, when a dead person is submerged in water, they're no longer breathing and so there's no respiratory movement in the water. And that was the case for Katheline Parker, as opposed to her mother, who had her lungs full of pond water. So that was how the medical examiner was able to conclude that Katheline had died *before* her mother took her into the pond."

"A suicidal and murderous woman, plus infanticide," I resumed, horrified, nearly nauseous.

"Despite her angelic appearance," Garrett sighed. "Like the old saying goes, you can't trust still waters."

"That sure was true here. But tell me Lieutenant,

are you really sure that Laura was the one who killed her daughter?"

"Unfortunately yes, Karen. There were traces of blows on the little girl's face, lacerations from the ring that Laura was wearing, the fact that she dragged her with her into the pond, all these elements converge to the same conclusion."

The policeman's arguments still puzzled me though.

"The question I can't seem to answer though is *why*? What could justify this for Laura?"

Removing his large derrière from his armchair, the policeman joined me and took the file. He went through it for a short while, took the piece of paper out, and handed it to me. Of course I didn't recognize it, because I'd never actually seen it, but Melinda had told me about that letter. It was Laura Vaughan's handwritten letter explaining her act. In the relative silence of the police station, outside of the people walking down the halls during the lunch break, I read it.

I'm so sorry it had to come to this. For a long time I thought I could resist, get through this. I thought I was strong, that's what people always told me. "You're a fighter, Laura. My daughter, you're the salt of the earth." The spuriousness of appearances. The facade, the shell, like a walnut shell. But inside that shell, the fruit was rotten, flawed. Flawed? Just like the circle in which I've been spinning around for years now, this vortex that inexorably sucks me into its heart. Sitting on the banks of Oyster Pond, I'm looking out into the middle of the lake, this body of water linked to the turbulent ocean. I'm attracted by the waves, I'm tempted by the backwash, the eddies seduce me. Is the solution there, at the bottom of the lake? It wouldn't require much to find out.

In my arms, I'm carrying the epitome of innocence. Just in appearance though, once again. My darling little Kathy. I'm troubled by the way she looks at me, so young, so diabolic...

What can I do? Leave an orphan behind me? Her father has disappeared, there won't be anyone to take care of her.

Mom, this would be too much work for you. I can't impose this on you. You're not the one who has to pay the price for the errors I made when I was young.

I believe it's better to die together, both

of us, hand in hand, or even better, my little Kathy who I'll hug tightly against my heart.

I just have to find the strength of hopelessness inside me.

Laura.

"There you go, is that clear enough for you now?"

"It is. But there's still something that bothers me. She kept talking about the *spuriousness of appearances*, a *vicious circle*, the *vortex sucking her in*, the *father who'd disappeared*, her *errors when she was young*... Lieutenant, did you ever question Simon Parker?"

"Hmm. Let's talk about that guy. He could be the object of your next journalistic investigation."

"What do you mean?"

"Because he disappeared! Isn't that your core job, people who just go missing like that?"

"You never called him in to hear his version of what happened? After all, he's the father of the little girl and Laura's ex-husband. I'm certainly not going to teach you that sometimes people go missing for years. And then one day they're found on the other side of the country or on another continent."

"Or sometimes never..."

There was a moment of silence in Lieutenant Garrett's office. I leafed through other pages in the file, hoping to stumble upon some details that could guide my own investigation.

"Okay Karen, I think that's enough now," the policeman suddenly said, putting his hand on the file.

"Could I have a copy of some of the documents?"

"Nope. These officially cannot be communicated. Maybe in twenty-five years. You were already lucky I let you look at them. And thanks for the sandwiches."

I got up and slowly began to walk out.

"You're welcome. Lieutenant, is there any chance of reopening this investigation?"

"Here? And for what? It's closed and I don't see any valid reason to reopen it. Everything seems very clear in this case, even, and I must admit it, if it's atrocious to hear. But that's life, sometimes it's good, often it's very bad."

The policeman walked with me to the door and opened it, letting me out. But there was still something holding me back. I had to say what was weighing down on my heart, that tiny little thing titillating me, preventing me from blindly accepting the official version. I stopped.

"I'm persuaded that Simon Parker played a role, either directly or indirectly, in their deaths."

"Jesus Christ, lady, stop making a mountain out of a molehill. What makes you think that?"

"It didn't seem strange to any of you that he never seemed to be bothered that his own daughter died? Where is he? Why didn't he even go to his own daughter's funeral? And why hasn't he shown up since?

Personally that's something that bothers me. He is the father after all! Blood ties are important."

"That's his right," said Garrett philosophically. "Anyway, and I'm repeating myself here, this case is now closed."

"What would I need to get it opened again?"

Lieutenant Garrett sighed loudly, showing me the door.

"You'd need a new fact, some new evidence. You got that up your sleeve?"

I grit my teeth, angry because of the policeman's resignation, walking down the hall next to him. Before leaving the police station, while he was actually holding the door open for me, I looked him straight in the eyes.

"I'll find it, Lieutenant. I'll end up finding it."

CHAPTER 37
An interminable task

VERSAILLES, Missouri, December 2023

THIS INVESTIGATION WAS MAKING Sergeant Gallister pretty darn cranky. Just a few days before Christmas, he was beginning to think that this can of worms would result in quite a few hours of overtime, or even prevent him from celebrating the Christmas holidays with his family and friends. You could say that being a cop wasn't an easy task! Like they said when he signed on, "you signed on the dotted line, you're gonna regret it."

Sitting in front of his computer, Pete was swearing at himself. Would he be able to enjoy a nice Christmas dinner with Gaby and Zia, his kids and Charlene, his wife, his parents, brothers and sisters plus all their respective offspring while knowing that the poor Jessy Chastain would be spending Christmas at the hospital or in a home for children? He couldn't stand that idea and blamed himself for not making any progress in his investigation.

He was going to have to step on it, conclude this affair quickly, untangle all the ins and outs of it before finally weaving the cloth of truth.

He called Mumin Blasharov, hoping that he'd finally pick up. His hope though was quickly dashed as his call went straight to voice-mail.

"Mumin," a deep voice said, before the beep.

Gallister dithered a couple of seconds, weighing the pros and cons, before deciding to leave a message.

"Mr. Blasharov, this is Lieutenant Pete Gallister from Morgan County, Versailles station. Wherever you are, please get back to me as soon as possible, it's extremely important. It's about your daughter, Jessy Chastain. She was found safe and sound. Please contact me immediately."

Sullen, Gallister hung up, looking at the screen of his phone, his head full of questions. Where could that man be now? Why had he left his home that night with his daughter in his pickup truck? Where was he going and why? Why had the cops found the child but why wasn't there the tiniest trace of her father nor of the vehicle? What had happened between the time when they were seen at the Happy Jack gas station and the time when Rebecca Stern ran across the little girl on the side of the road, scared stiff and nearly frozen?

Had Blasharov finally abandoned his daughter?

Had she run away, escaped from her father, probably hoping to join her mother?

That repeated "*I want mommy*" that the little girl kept on saying, with that curious accent or perhaps a type of lisp, kept on haunting Gallister. She seemed to want to see her mother, but when he took her to her bedside, she began to scream and shout instead of jumping into her arms.

What was going on in that little girl's head?

Or perhaps this was a better question: why was this family so dysfunctional?

Officer Stonehenge walked by his office at that moment.

"Myra! Can I see you a couple of minutes?"

"At your service, Chief! What can I do for you?"

He wrote Mumin's phone number on a piece of paper and gave it to her.

"I'd like you to give this hot potato to Fitzpatrick, so he can get through to Blasharov's phone operator. Have them send us a list of ingoing and outgoing calls. I want the name of all the contacts that Blasharov spoke to recently. And if he can do it, track his movements through his phone's geolocation app."

"Consider it done, Boss!" said Myra, taking the paper from him.

∽

A couple of minutes later Gallister's phone rang. He picked up right away, hoping it was Mumin Blasharov calling him back. But it was only one of his deputies, Agent Mike Bauer, who was in charge of investigating the sector where Rebecca Stern had found Jessy Chastain. Pete had asked him to go knocking on the doors of everyone who lived around there as well as those who lived close to Carrie Chastain's farm.

"Hey Mike. What's up? You still freezing your balls off in the snow?"

"I'm not laughing Sergeant! That's psychological harassment towards one of your subordinates, that could cost you! Instead of trying your hand at standup comedy, you'd better listen to what I have to say, you're going to like that my friend."

"Some juicy stuff then. So let's hear it then Mike, I got a lot of work."

When Agent Bauer finally spit it out, Gallister quickly got up from his armchair, swearing, and ran out of the police station, taking Myra with him.

They hopped into the sergeant's unmarked car, Gallister at the wheel. The tires squealed on the plowed parking lot when he stepped on the accelerator.

Direction Gravois Mills, more precisely, Donovan's house, Carrie Chastain's closest neighbors.

CHAPTER 38
Caught red-handed

GRAVOIS MILLS, Missouri, December 2023

AGENT BAUER WAS POSTED on the lookout for his boss at the end of the dirt path going to Donovan's house. He waved him down as soon as he saw the car. Slowing down when he saw him, Pete rolled down his window.

"Hey Bauer. Hop in, I'm in a good mood today."

It was roughly a quarter of a mile before arriving in the courtyard of a farm that was a bit better maintained than Chastain's. There was a couple, a good sixty years old, standing on the front porch waiting for them.

Everyone introduced themselves and the couple invited the police into their darkish kitchen where there was a strong relent of cabbage, mixed with the more pleasant odor of fresh coffee, that the hostess served to everyone.

"Mr. Donovan," Agent Bauer began, "could you please repeat to Sergeant Gallister what you told me a couple of minutes ago?"

The man, whose wrinkles betrayed his age as well as how hard the work of a farmer was, sniffled, then wiped his nose using a handkerchief he took out of his pocket.

"I really don't know where to start," he said, hesitating. "Maybe you can help me."

Bauer took out a photo that he placed on the table, between two cups of coffee. The light wasn't very good but that wasn't a big deal as they'd already seen the picture. Gallister asked the question burning his lips.

"Can you tell us if you recognize this little girl?"

"Well, I mean, I think so, but I can't guarantee it a hundred percent, see?"

"If I said that it was Carrie Chastain's and Mumin Blasharov's daughter, they're our closest neighbors, would that seem pertinent to you?"

"Pertinent?"

"I mean, would that be possible?"

"Yes, it's completely possible," Donovan admitted. "But you gotta know that we don't talk to each other that often, our neighbors and us. So I hafta say that it's been a while that I haven't seen their kid. But yes, that could be her."

"Could you tell me her name?" Gallister asked.

When she saw how dumbfounded her husband seemed by the question, Mrs. Donovan answered.

"I think it's something like Jess or Jessica. Or Jessy. Is that it?"

The sergeant nodded his head.

"Jessy, that's right. One more question, do you watch the news on TV?"

"Bah! To see wars and misery and horrors, no thanks. Why?"

"So, you never heard of a call for witnesses about the disappearance or should I say the *appearance*, of a little girl, not too far from here, a few days ago, on the side of the road? Alone and freezing? Speechless, except to demand her mother."

The two farmers looked at each other for an instant and both frowned at the same time.

"No, we're sorry," the husband answered. "If not, we would have contacted you immediately, of course!"

"Could you tell us when you saw that little girl for the last time?"

"Oh! That dates back pretty far. I wouldn't even be able to tell you if it was this year," Mrs. Donovan said.

"You haven't seen your closest neighbors for a year then? Or for months?"

The husband shook his head before answering.

"No, not at all, we saw them not too long ago."

Gallister questioned Bauer with his eyes, his eyebrows squinched together, as if wondering if these farmers weren't a bit feeble-minded. He decided to rephrase.

"Excuse me, but I'm not following you here. You just said that you hadn't seen the Chastain family for a long time and then right after, you affirmed that you recently saw them."

The man shook his head and made a tired gesture with his hand, as if apologizing for having expressed himself poorly. He started over.

"Oh! Excuse me, we're not understanding each other. What I meant is that we did see the neighbors, I'd say... around Thanksgiving. But I meant the parents, not the little girl."

"Yes, that's it, Hank, you're right. We saw them at the Thanksgiving church service, now I remember too," added his wife. "But the little girl wasn't with them, of course."

"Why 'of course?'" Gallister quickly asked.

"Um," she hesitated as if caught red-handed, "because she hadn't been living with them for months, that's why!"

CHAPTER 39
A knot in the middle

"WAIT A MINUTE THERE!" shouted Sergeant Gallister. "What are you trying to say Mrs. Donovan? That Jessy Chastain hasn't lived with her parents for months? Is that what you meant?"

"Oh"... sighed Mrs. Donovan. "Your questions are driving me crazy. Yes, of course that's what I meant. The kid hasn't lived there for ages now. I'd say... let me think... something like a year or two."

"A year or two?" Myra Stonehenge and Gallister repeated in perfect harmony.

"Yeah, about that. That's why we couldn't tell you with a hundred percent certainty that the little girl in the photo really was her, when you asked us before. Everyone knows that little kids change so quickly, even if their facial features, their eyes, hair, smile, all that, don't really change that much. It's not like us folks, for us give or take a year or two, it doesn't make a big difference. But a year-and-a-half year-old kid and a three-year old, – she must be about three now, right? – it's just a different as an apple and a pear side by side. Both of them are fruit with seeds, a stem, a skin, but they don't taste the same."

The sergeant didn't really understand the relationship with that comparison but could visualize the image. What he understood though and what was now pissing him off, was that he'd now found himself with another knot in the middle of this story, something else that had to be unraveled. Just a couple of hours ago, he thought he'd found the Chastain mother and child, even though there didn't seem to be much love lost between them. And now the neighbors were telling him that the kid hadn't lived there for months or maybe even longer. What – or who – should he believe?

He suddenly wanted to subpoena Carrie Chastain right now, to talk to her *face to face* until she spit out the truth. This truth that she had been dissimilating ever since the beginning. Gallister was boiling mad.

"Mrs. Donovan, how and when did you learn that the child no longer lived with her parents?"

"Um, I think it was at this year's harvest festival. Carrie herself told me."

∼

Harvest Festival, Morgan County, August 2023

. . .

LIKE ALL OVER in the United States that year, it had been a scorching hot summer, breaking quite a few records and the harvest was in advance. It wasn't going to be a good year though because the grain crops hadn't had enough rain. Yet nothing could have changed the date of the harvest festival in Missouri, which invariably took place the last weekend in August and was appreciated by both the young and the old. Just like the other Corn Belt States, towns in Missouri enjoyed this event where farmers, shopkeepers and breeders could get together and celebrate.

Above all a commercial festival, this was an opportunity for visitors to see tractors, combines and other technical farming equipment, but also to let their kids go on rides, shoot guns at targets, hopefully winning a prize, admire the floats decorated with wheat and corn, and appreciate country dancing. In a nutshell, something for everyone.

Tourists appreciated demonstrations of how farming was done in the pre-industrial era, such as haymaking that consisted in cutting, baling, and harvesting hay. All this done by hand, obviously, with the help of powerful and handsome draught horses.

Mr. and Mrs. Donovan, also farmers, never missed a festival. Hank, like every year, competed in the plowing contest with his antique tractor and his three-toothed plow. He'd won the contest ten years ago and had finished in the top three a couple of times since then, but as years went by, he was getting tired and he only took part in it because of the tradition, no longer hoping to win. What was most important was to participate, plus, when the sun had set, to enjoy this pleasant conviviality between farmers and visitors around a hot barbecue and a cold beer.

Hank and Marta Donovan sat down at the end of one of the long wooden tables on sawhorses, with benches on each side where people sat haphazardly next to their neighbors. That evening, the Donovan's sat next to the Chastain's. They called them the 'Chastain's though the husband was from one of the former Eastern European nations or what they used to call the USSR, something like that, because his last name had a Russian sound – a name ending in -ov: Marakov? Samsonov? Hank could never remember, and he only used his first name, easier to remember: Mumin.

Though their fields were next to each other near Gravois Mills, they hardly ever saw each other during the year. But the Donovan's didn't think the Chastain's were very outgoing. He was distant, a man of few words. She was a lady who never looked you straight in the eye, who often swore or insulted others and someone who'd never learned any manners.

So it was purely by chance that they were sitting next to each other that year and it actually was an opportunity for both to get to know their neighbors better. After all, often people remain steadfast with preconceived ideas that are erased when they know each other better.

"Anyone sitting here?" asked Hank, putting his

recyclable cardboard tray with its sandwich and large glass of foamy beer down.

Carrie mumbled something that he took as meaning 'go ahead.'

"Have a seat, neighbor," replied Mumin, with a gesture.

Mumin began to talk about Hank's plowing contest, congratulating him for an honorable result.

"It was easier for me ten years ago," the farmer said with a smile. "Now I just compete for fun. What about you? You didn't enter?"

"No."

That was it. The four of them simultaneously raised their glasses without toasting anything or anyone, ate for a few minutes silently and then began to talk about the usual trivial subjects. The weather, the crops, how hard it was to farm, the difficulty of making ends meet.

A local band began to play country music, and members of the Gravois Mills dance club all got up.

A few minutes later, probably sparked by the festive atmosphere and undoubtedly by a slight overindulgence in alcoholic beverages, Marta Donovan leaned over to talk to Carrie.

"You didn't bring your daughter with you? What's her name, already?"

Carrie, eating a chicken salad sandwich, turned towards her.

"Yeah. You know, it's not easy with kids. She's only two and a half. Her name is Jessy."

"That's right, such a pretty name. Is someone babysitting her?"

Carrie nodded without answering and took another bite of her meal.

"We haven't seen her in ages. I bet she's grown a lot."

"She has."

That was all she said. Evidently Mrs. Chastain didn't want to talk about her daughter, which was quite unusual, as mothers of young children generally can't shut up about how wonderful their offspring are. But Carrie's closed lips ended that conversation. Later on, Hank took Marta for a spin on the dance floor, while tapping his feet to a "Madison," and she wondered out loud why her neighbor wasn't more loquacious about her little girl.

~

"That's it?" asked Sergeant Gallister to Marta Donovan, sitting across from him at their kitchen table. "That wouldn't have astonished me. They must have had someone come in and babysit their daughter so they could enjoy the harvest festival."

"Just wait," replied Mrs. Donovan, pouring each of them a second cup of coffee. "That's not all. That was just the beginning of those little nothings that make big somethings. You'll see."

CHAPTER 40
With a jolt

"A FEW DAYS after the harvest festival, I was alone at home," continued Marta Donovan. "Hank had gone to the market in Sunrise Beach, leaving at five a.m. You know you can earn quite a bit sometimes at markets. We sell our good farm products there directly, that helps us butter our bread like they say, but it's not for lazy people, right Hank?"

"Marta," her husband said, cutting her off, "get to the point. These people from the police aren't here to talk about farm markets."

"Excuse me, that's true. So, anyway, that day I was making a cake, using some of our good eggs from our hens, and I was plum out of sugar, so I thought to myself, I'll go ask Carrie Chastain for some. So I walked over to their farm, and Carrie was there in the kitchen. That Russian guy wasn't there."

"Marta, he's not Russian."

"Well, what is he then? Anyway, Mumin, that's his

name, he wasn't there. She was all alone, sitting at the kitchen table, her elbows on the oilcloth, hands crossed, looking at nothing, or maybe her eyes were even closed. I knocked on the window of the door, but she must not have heard it the first time. I could see her through the window, she didn't budge. So I knocked a little harder and this time she quickly raised her head as if I'd woken her up with a jolt. She grumbled 'Who's there?' and I answered, and she let me in."

* * *

Gravois Mills, Missouri, September 2023

IN THE CHASTAIN'S KITCHEN, it smelled like rancid oil that had been used dozens of times too many. Marta walked in.

"Hi neighbor," she said, "I was wondering if I couldn't borrow a package of sugar. I'm making a cake for my Hank when he gets back from the Sunrise Beach market and I'm fresh out. I can't believe I don't even have a spare package, how dumb."

"I think I've got that, yup," said Carrie, getting up from her chair wincing with pain and holding her back.

She went to have a look in the cupboards behind her and found what she was looking for. She handed an already open package to Marta.

"Thanks, that's really nice of you, but are you sure you won't be needing it?"

"Bah! Naaa."

I WANT MOMMY

"Maybe you wanted to make your little Jessy a cake."

Carrie's eyes pivoted suddenly to glare straight into her neighbor's eyes.

"She doesn't like sugary stuff," she replied. "You don't even have to give it back, I don't need it."

"Jessy's not here? I brought her a package of candy thinking she'd like it but if she doesn't like sweet stuff... But candy, that's not the same thing, is it? Can I see her? I love little kids. And Hank and me, well you know that we couldn't have any."

"She ain't here."

Carrie escorted Marta slowly but surely to the door.

"Shoot, she must be in school at this time of day. I mean in kindergarten."

Carrie noisily blew from the side of her mouth, glaring at her neighbor.

"Marta, why do you keep asking to see my kid?"

"Just because I love children, they're all so cute. And yours, that little angel, with her curly hair just like when she was a baby. Does she still have her curls?"

"I told you, she's not here. We sent her to Florida, where we've got family there, for a while. Here, on the farm, it's not easy to take care of a kid that age. So to make things easier for all of us, we sent her to one of Mumin's aunts, who lives there in Florida, where it's always nice and sunny. Plus they've got money, and we don't have much, so she'll have everything she wants down there. So, you happy now? You know everything now! You can leave the candy here, I like candy."

* * *

Sergeant Gallister was hanging on to every word in Marta Donovan's tale.

"She was really strange that day," she concluded. "Plus, at their house, there wasn't anything to show that a little girl lived there, you know? Not a single toy, not any children's clothing, no cereal or candy, nothing. That story about Florida bothered me, because it had been ages since we'd seen that little cutie. Like I said, at least a year. So I asked one of my nieces who works in school administration in the county, and believe it or not Sergeant, there was no Jessy Chastain enrolled in any of the kindergartens in the region."

Pete Gallister's head was full of questions and assumptions, and he had her repeat.

"You're sure of what you're stating here, Mrs. Donovan?"

"I am. That is why, when your colleague questioned us earlier, about that little girl they'd found not too far from here on the roadside and you showed me her picture, I thought that maybe it could have been little Jessy. But I can't imagine her leaving their farm, because, like I said, we hadn't seen her for ages at our neighbors' farm. And if Carrie Chastain told you the opposite, she's lying to someone. Either to me, or to you, Sergeant!"

CHAPTER 41
The direct line

WHEN SERGEANT GALLISTER left the Donovan's, escorted by Deputy Myra Stonehenge and Agent Bauer, he was fuming, swearing between his teeth and scathing at Carrie Chastain.

"What the hell is going on here? That lady is driving me crazy. So, as long as we're here, let's give that neighbor a little surprise visit. Bauer, you can go back to the police station now, and I'll take Myra with me."

They jumped in his car. He started it up, stepped on it, its tire's screeching on the Donovan's' clay courtyard, and backed up so suddenly, nearly turning around, that he almost ran into Pete. If you cut through the fields, the two farms were quite close to each other. When driving though, you had to take Donovan's long driveway, go to the road and turn about half a mile farther to reach Chastain's driveway.

When they arrived, the two police officers quickly

got out of their car and ran up to the door, knocking loudly on it.

"Looks like nobody's home," said Myra.

"You think she split?"

Gallister hammered on the door window, and then tried the doorknob. It opened, creaking.

"Pete, we can't go in like this. That'll come back and bite us in the ass, you know that."

"Shit."

Furious, the sergeant turned around and began to walk around the house outside.

"She must be somewhere close," he said, noticing Carrie's car that was parked beneath a hanger next to the barn.

He suddenly heard a noise that he immediately identified: the clucking of a group of frightened chickens. Following the sound, he walked over to the chicken coop, a structure covered with metal sheeting and saw the farmer's silhouette. She was gathering the eggs that the hens had laid that day.

"Mrs. Chastain!" he called out.

She turned around.

"You scared me, Sergeant! Now what is it? You bringing my little chickee back to me?"

And she laughed, a loud guffaw interrupted by a smoker's cough. A cigarette that seemed to be out was hanging from her lips.

"Not at all Ma'am. And if that's how you're taking my visit, I could add that you seem to be quite a strange hen yourself. One of those that can't take care of its offspring. Or even one of those that eats its own eggs. Know what I'm getting at here?"

"Sergeant, I can see that you're an expert in chickens. Were you raised at a farm or what? It's true, I already had problems like that with some of my hens. Ah! Let me tell you, sometimes some of them don't deserve to be mothers. So, what can I do for you now?"

Gallister was fuming inside. Ready to jump up and clock the lady so she'd shut up. He controlled himself though.

"Mrs. Chastain, you made fun of us. You've been trying to fool us with all your stories. Now, it's time to tell us the truth, the whole truth. You're going to follow us to the police station for a new and official interview."

The farmer lady's lips smiled wryly.

"I have to?"

"Mrs. Chastain, don't make me…"

"No, because maybe I'm not the sharpest knife in the block, like they say, huh! Maybe I'm not God's gift, but I know my rights, if you see what I mean. I watch TV, those series with cops like you and I know that I don't have to come with you if you don't have a warrant. Is that the right word in your cop jargon?" asked Carrie ironically, turning around to push one of the hens away and pick up the eggs she was preciously brooding.

Gallister nodded his head, biting his lips.

"Okay. You want to play like that? No problem!

Myra, you stay here with the lady while I go back to the station. Keep an eye on her, I'm counting on you."

Sergeant Gallister hopped into his car and drove out. He connected his Bluetooth with the car's phone, and while heading for Versailles, called the direct line of the Morgan County Prosecutor.

When he finished explaining his desiderata concerning what he now called the "Chastain Case," the prosecutor said he could count on him.

"Pete, as soon as you get to Versailles, the warrant will be on your desk. Consider it done."

And as a matter of fact, the document that the agent at the front desk had received by email was already printed, signed and waiting for the sergeant in his office.

Now that he was legally covered by the judiciary administration, he hurried back to Chastain's farm. At this point, a few more miles were nothing. He would have driven all around the county to find the truth. And he was getting pretty darn tired of turning around in circles in this case. A quarter of an hour later, he'd already arrived. As Carrie Chastain had invited Myra Stonehenge to come in and warm up, the two women were sharing some coffee in the kitchen. When Pete walked in, Carrie asked him if he wanted one.

The sergeant shook his head, declining the offer and dropped the warrant on the table, in front of Carrie's eyes.

"If that's alright with you, Mrs. Chastain, this

one's on me. We've got great coffee at the police station, you'll see."

* * *

Versailles, Missouri, a bit later

BACK TO THE same place she'd been to a couple of days ago, Carrie Chastain looked stoic and untouchable, her eyes half-closed, her lips pursed. The sergeant had just explained her rights to her and reminded her that this time, he would be carrying out an official interview which would be filmed by the camera he was pointing at. He asked her if she would like to be assisted by a lawyer, but she refused, saying that she was big enough to defend herself, just like she'd always done in her life up till now.

Carrie was at one end of the table, Myra and Pete at the other, and the voice recorder was in the middle. Pete pushed the button down.

"Please give us your complete name, today's date and state that I advised you to benefit from the assistance of a lawyer, and that you refused."

"You know what date it is today, no need to make me say it," replied Carrie. All the rest is too complicated for me. I'm okay like I am."

"Please do what I asked you."

Which she did, albeit very reluctantly. Then Gallister began.

"So, this time, no more lies, you agree? You persist

in saying that the child who was found the other day is Jessy, your daughter?"

"I don't see why I'd change my mind. You don't change daughters like you change your socks."

"And you affirm that she ran away from you in company of her father, Mumin Blasharov?"

"That's what happened, Sergeant."

"And you have no idea what they did after that?"

"Of course not, remember I wasn't with them. Come on, you gotta be logical!"

"Mrs. Chastain, there's something that's bothering me. You told us that your daughter ran away on December 15th, in the evening. But some of my sources told me that Jessy hadn't lived with you for weeks, or even months. And that then you told them that you'd sent Jessy down to Florida, where one of your aunts lives. So, how can a four-year-old child, who's living in Florida, all of a sudden run away from a farm in Missouri at the same time?"

Carrie's eyes opened wide. That was something she hadn't seen coming. Her lips began to twitch.

"I don't know," she stammered.

"Let me tell you what I think. I believe that we have two possibilities here: either the little girl that was found the other night isn't yours, and in that case, I don't understand why you're affirming that she is, or the other case, that she is your child, but then you have to explain to me how she could have been in two places at the same time. So, what's the right answer to this enigma?"

"I don't know anymore…"

"What do you mean, you don't know anymore? Are you still inebriated, Mrs. Chastain? Do I have to do another breathalyzer test?"

"No, all I've had since this morning was coffee."

"All right then. As you seem to be eluding my questions, I'll tell you what I think. Personally, taking into account the little girl's reaction when she saw you in her room in the hospital, I think this little girl *isn't* your daughter. Or else, you're not a good mother, like those hens we talked about that ate their own eggs."

Carrie Chastain closed her eyes and took a deep breath.

"You're right, Sergeant," she said, her eyes still closed.

CHAPTER 42
The weight of secrets

IN THE INTERVIEW ROOM, outside of the purring from the heating, there was a deafening silence between Sergeant Gallister and the detainee. He felt that Carrie Chastain was ready to confess, though he read in her eyes an unexpected despair and distress. As if the weight of secrets hidden away now were too heavy on her shoulders, on her black soul. Pete Gallister kept on with his line of thought.

"When you said that I'm right, which affirmation were you referring to? That you're not a good mother or that you admit that she's not your daughter?"

Arms on her thighs, rocking forward and backward compulsively, she finally answered, with an emotion-filled broken voice.

"That's true, I'm not a good mother. An old and bitter hen, not even one that you could eat boiled up for soup. You're right, I abandoned my child."

"Tell me the details."

"Here's what happened, a couple of months ago. So my Jessy must have been about two and a half, and she wasn't an easy child, you know. Plus, all the work on the farm, in the fields, harvesting, all that, it's a tiring job. Both for your body and for your mind. Plus, you can see I wasn't a young mother, huh? There must be stuff that's easier for you to bear when you're twenty rather than almost forty like me. I met Mumin pretty late, and we didn't want any kids. And then one day it happened. A bun in the oven. That's Mother Nature, or what the Lord wanted, I don't know. I mean that Mumin and me, we didn't take those modern precautions, I don't gotta explain that to you. If it happened, it happened. And then I had the kid. She was there. But like I said, it was too much work. The days never seemed to end, especially during harvesttime where you work all day, and then at night I still had to make supper and take care of her. Plus it was hard to get her to eat and she kept crying all the time and we're too old for that, we couldn't stand it. And then one day, it just was too much. I did something foolish."

Carrie began to tremble, her hands agitated, twisting her fingers as if struggling against a compelling need to move them.

"What did you do?" asked Gallister, inviting her to continue.

"Like I said, something foolish, but more of an

unhappy gesture. Something I couldn't control! Sergeant, you got any kids?"

"Yes, two."

"You can understand me then."

"I'm not really sure that all parents behave in the same way with their children. Can you continue please?"

"Oh. I see. Milord is perfect, is that right? Anyway I was sick and tired of hearing her whine, cry, scream. My hand had a life of its own. Maybe I hit her a little harder than I should have. Her head spun and the red mark from my ring stayed on her cheek. She opened her big eyes and her mouth too and then she didn't make another sound. She ran into her room as fast as she could. I wasn't too proud of myself after that. Mumin neither. He looked at me without saying a word, his arms dangling like an idiot. But I understood in his eyes that he didn't blame me. That he would have done the same thing because he was like me, he couldn't stand it either. Except him, with his mitts as big as laundry beaters, one slap on the face would have killed the kid, would have unscrewed her head. So that night, while we were eating our soup and the kid had fallen asleep without even getting undressed, Mumin and me, we decided something. We'd send Jessy down to stay with one of my aunts in Florida. Just a couple of days, or a couple of weeks, we just needed time out from her. That would be best for everyone and would give us a break, things would be better after. There you go."

Attentive, Gallister nodded, writing everything down in his spiral notebook.

"So can you tell me where this aunt in Florida lives?"

Carrie's forehead wrinkled in concentration.

"Um, well she lives next to... what's that name already? Um, Tampa! Yeah, I think that's it, that's the name of the town."

"Much more of a city than a town, in my opinion," Gallister corrected her. "If you drove her there, you should know."

"Well, actually, my aunt came to pick Jessy up here. Mumin and me, we don't like to drive that far. Yeah, that's what happened, that's how she left, my Jessy."

"You seem to be hesitating Mrs. Chastain. This must have been an important date for you."

"Yeah, but it was a while. Sometimes I forget things."

"Perhaps! So what is this aunt's name?"

The policeman's question was met with a long moment of silence before Carrie put an end to it, her eyes spinning around.

"Esmeralda! Esmeralda Winter. She's one of my mother's sisters, that's why me and her we don't have the same last name."

"So this sister married a Mr. Winter then?"

"That's it."

Gallister wrote this down.

"Could you give me her address?"

"No, sorry, Sergeant."

"Sorry, but you don't know exactly where your daughter is living? And that doesn't bother you?"

"As long as I know that she's doing well where she is..."

"Like a hen that couldn't care less what happens to her eggs," commented Gallister. "A little effort, use your brain here Carrie."

"My brain? What the hell is that? Ah! Wait a sec, I got it. It came back to me like a flash. 1275 Mulholland Avenue."

"You're sure?"

"Like two and two make four, Sergeant."

Gallister got up and walked to the door in the interview room.

"Don't move, Mrs. Chastain, I'll be right back. Would you like a cup of coffee or a bottle of water?"

"Water would be great. Talking like that, it dried my throat out."

The sergeant walked out, leaving her under Myra Stonehenge's responsibility, and sat down in front of his computer. He entered several instructions and spent a few minutes consulting the answer on his screen. Then he picked up the phone and called one of his colleagues. When he was finally sure of the information, he went back into the interview room.

As the door had remained open since he'd left, he charged in and slammed the door, walking to Carrie Chastain. He held a sheet of paper up with one hand, glaring at her.

"Mrs. Chastain, you're still trying to play me…"
"Now what?"
"There are no streets named Mulholland Avenue in Tampa. And even less an Esmeralda Winter living at number 1275…"

CHAPTER 43
A Mexican showdown

IN THE ROOM, everyone was staring at everyone else. Carrie was looking at Pete Gallister, who was looking at Myra Stonehenge, who was looking at Carrie. Like in a Mexican showdown. The sergeant bit his lip.

"Sergeant, maybe I got a little mixed up with the address," Carrie whined.

"Same thing for the name of Auntie Esmeralda?" he responded bitterly. "Who by the way, was one of your husband's aunts in the explanation that you gave your neighbor a couple of weeks ago. None of this makes any sense. How do you think we can take your seriously, even for a minute?"

"My memory has always had its ups and downs..."

Gallister plopped heavily down on a chair and sighed deeply.

"No, Mrs. Chastain. What I think is that you've been pulling our legs ever since you arrived. Or even for the past couple of days. You're a pathological liar! You invented a life, didn't you?"

"What? Are you crazy Sergeant? What are you talking about? Oh! And I'm tired of all this, I'm splitting now," shouted Carrie getting up, ready to hit the road.

The policeman also got up, standing between her and the exit.

"Hey! Where do you think you're going like that? You must have forgotten that you're no longer free to leave. Do I have to show you the prosecutor's warrant again? You sit down right now, Mrs. Chastain. This isn't over yet."

But the lady only had one idea in her head, pushing the sergeant away, hoping to escape.

"Move it! Let me outta here!" she screamed, pounding on the policeman's powerful chest.

Myra Stonehenge rushed up to her boss, trying to calm Carrie down.

"Carrie, you have to be reasonable. Let's start this official interview again, calmly, is that okay with you? We'll all have a glass of water, relax a little bit, and try to unravel all of this. I'm sure there's a valid explanation."

"But I gave it to you, the explanation! I'm sick and tired of this!"

Nonetheless, they were able to sit Carrie back down again. She put her head between her hands. Began to sob.

Gallister gave her a few minutes, time for her to

calm down. When she raised her red eyes, he began once again.

"Okay, let's start at the beginning. Where is your daughter if she's not with your so-called aunt in Florida?"

"I don't know," Carrie replied, sniffing. "I don't know, Jesus Christ, I don't know... I lost her."

The two investigators looked at each other, gaping.

"Mrs. Chastain, what do you mean by 'I lost her?'" asked Myra.

"I don't know where she is. She was there, now she's not. She left, she came back, over and over again."

"Explain yourself slowly," continued Myra. "Take all the time you need."

"I thought I'd lost her. She was at our house, not in Florida, like I thought she was."

"What?" blustered Gallister. "You don't lose a child like you lose your keys or your glasses, for goodness' sake!"

"Oh! Don't scold me... You're scaring me. I need some time to think. I can't think here, these walls are closing in on me, you're stressing me. It's true, I miss my daughter. And suddenly, when I saw the call for witnesses with this kid's photo, I thought I recognized my Jessy. So I said to myself, 'it's her, my little Jessy sweetie, she's home!' and I went to see you at the police station. To get her back. And you told me she was asking for her mommy... That's why I came."

Gallister's brain was boiling was the woman's incoherencies. What should he believe amongst her various declarations, both today and the previous days? One day her daughter had disappeared, one day she lived in Florida, at her aunt's house. Then in another version, she discovered the existence of the child through the call for witnesses while continuing to complain that her father, Mumin Blasharov, who was astonishingly silent and absent, had kidnapped her. The sergeant listed all these hypotheses to Carrie, who hesitated for a long while before answering.

"Okay. Okay! I'll tell you the truth."

"Isn't that just wonderful!" said Gallister ironically, visibly exhausted by the crazy lady's versions. "We're all ears."

"Here we go. A year and a half ago, in the summer of 2022, our daughter Jessy was kidnapped."

CHAPTER 44

An interminable sleep

AUGUST 2022

Cornered in the back of the dark room, the little girl cried silently. Warm tears flowed slowly out of her red eyes. She felt lost, disoriented, desperately alone and abandoned. She didn't recognize this place. She kept on trying to force her memories to come back, but she couldn't access anything that was recent. At her age, memory was more of a question of sounds, smells and feelings. An instinctive one, almost like an animal's. One thing though was sure: this was the very first time she'd been in that place. In another place, one she recognized, she would have felt if not safe, but at least in familiar territory.

Here, no.

She didn't know if she was hungry, cold, in pain or frightened. Or all of that at the same time. She must have been extremely tired. It seemed to her that her eyelids weighed a ton, and she couldn't keep them open for over a few minutes at a time. As if emerging from an interminable sleep, just like Sleeping Beauty did.

A minute litany escaped from her thin and dry lips. The same few words: "I want mommy, want mommy, mommy…"

The room where she was locked in didn't even have a window so the light of the day could penetrate. There luckily was a lightbulb that was on most of the time, so that she didn't have to vegetate in the dark, like a sewer rat. There were no decorations on the bare walls, no wallpaper or not even a layer of paint. Just barely whitewashed walls to keep the surface dry, prevent it from dampness and moisture content. The little girl spent time gazing at the cracks in the walls, that for her turned into figures with which she tried to associate things she remembered, people that she loved. There was a single bed against one of the walls, and on the opposite side, a plastic pail so she could do what she already had learned to do alone.

And her little stuffed animal that she always held.

Sometimes the lights went out and that was horrible. Tears would roll down her face and sharp frightened sounds would come out of her mouth. When this happened, after a couple of minutes – or maybe it was a couple of hours, she had no idea how to measure time, no idea if it was day or night — she'd hear heavy footsteps above her and then some grunting from the other side of the wooden door. The lights would then come back on, and the cracks in the walls too, to keep her occupied.

At other times, her lethargy would be troubled by the muffled sound of someone walking behind the door, then it would open, squeaking on its rusty hinges and there would be another light, a more powerful one than the one coming from the nude lightbulb on the ceiling, that she could see through the opening of the door.

Behind that light that blinded her, there was a massive silhouette, like a shadow figure. Though any adult would have seemed enormous to her, such a fragile and tiny child.

That day – or was it that night? –, the silhouette came into the room. The child's instinct told her to get away, to try to hide in a corner, the farthest away from the door, where it was still dark. Scooting away on her buttocks, holding tightly onto her stuffed animal, the little girl dragged herself on the dusty concrete floor.

"Don't be afraid, honey, everything is alright. I don't want to hurt you, you know. Come here. Are you hungry? Are you thirsty? Look, I've got something for you."

"Mommy," whispered the child, pushing her back against the bed, her little stuffed animal on her chest, in which her little heart was beating faster and faster as the man approached her.

She was like a frightened guinea pig in a cage.

"Mommy's upstairs, don't worry. In the meantime

though, you have to eat something. Look, it's really good, a delicious puree of carrots and mashed potatoes with pieces of chicken in it. I made it myself. You'll love it."

The little shook her head though her stomach was growling a "feed me now, yes," message, one that was sharp and instinctive. But, as when you're as young as she was, often instinct wins over reason and she finally let the man get closer until he put the plate with a little spoon in the mashed carrots and potatoes and chicken down in front of her.

"You know how to eat all alone, don't you? Or do you want me to help you?"

The child remained silent, and he thought that he'd obtained the answer to his question.

"I'm going to go upstairs, but you don't cry, okay? No crying! If you do, I'm going to cry too."

The man took two steps over to the pail in guise of a toilet, bent down to pick it up and turned around.

"I'll be back, I'm going to clean this."

He disappeared behind the door after having locked it.

While he was gone and despite her tiredness, making her fight to stay awake, the little girl grabbed the spoon and began to calm her stomach's growling. It was just like in the fairy tale *Goldilocks and the Three Little Pigs*: "not too hot, not too cold, just right." That did her a world of good. After she'd had something to eat and drink, the little girl felt sleepy and slipped under the covers in bed. In the windowless room, where it was also "not too hot, not too cold, just right," she snuggled in and fell asleep before the man came back with the clean chamber pot.

The man fondly bent over the bed, admiring her brown curls – curls that were brunette, not gold – and ran his fingertips through her hair.

Then he left, turning around once again on the doorstep to murmur something to himself.

"Sleep tight, my little sweetie, my dear little Jessy."

CHAPTER 45
Far from suspecting

MONTAUK, December 2023

SOME NEW EVIDENCE. That would be the only thing that would allow me to reopen the investigation about Laura and Katheline's double death. At least that was what Lieutenant Garrett had told me. I'd been racking my brains ever since we spoke at noon in his office.

How could I find some tangible evidence? If the cops weren't able to find another explanation than an infanticide followed by a suicide during their whole investigation, how could I? Unless, following an intuition that neither Garrett nor his colleagues had had – or one that they had voluntarily discarded as it didn't match any logical or forensics evidence they'd obtained by the various statements they'd taken – I would be able to find something else?

Back in my Montauk Manor hotel room, I was just as impatient as the person talking to me on the phone.

Sitting cross-legged on the bed, a voice I knew only too well filled my Bluetooth earplugs, one that, as always, had forgotten to say hello.

"Listen my little chickadee, it would be about time for you to write me a juicy article, don't you think? Unless you're just on vacation in Long Island? Living the good life?"

I've always loved my boss's ironic humor. I know she loves underscoring how much I owe my fantastic working conditions to her. Well, *fantastic*, maybe not that much…

"It's a really nice place, there's snow on the beach, it's beautiful. That reminds me of a Jim Carrey movie '*Eternal Sunshine of a Spotless Mind*,' you ever see it?"

"You think I work for a movie magazine maybe? So come on, tell me, what's up with that crazy old lunatic from Montauk?"

I told her briefly about my latest interviews and my intuition that perhaps Simon Parker had played a role in the tragic fate of his ex-wife and their daughter. The man who had vanished since the events took place, in the summer of 2022.

"Okay. You keep digging in that direction. And make sure you find the trace of that man who seems sleazy, not too clean, just like your gut is telling you. I trust your flair; it's never let me down. In the meanwhile though, I'd like a juicy article that focuses on the murderous mother, see where I'm going here?"

I sighed. I'd anticipated that she would love a theme like that. Those who read *True Crime Mysteries* enjoy stuff like that, and if they enjoy it, they'll buy the magazine. And if they buy it, Myrtille will be thrilled.

"I'll do it as soon as possible," I said.

"Great! I need it for tomorrow."

And she hung up without even giving me one of her noisy air kisses. The very first time my boss had done that. Was she changing?

Then I made another call. The person picked up after three ringtones.

"Karen! What a pleasure to hear your voice!"

"The pleasure's all mine, Barry. I hope you're doing well."

"Like a retired person in the middle of winter: sitting by my fireplace. What about you? Are you in our neck of the woods? I'd love to see you again."

Barry Fenton, the former Greenville Chief of Police, had been of invaluable assistance to me in the investigation I'd carried out on Veronika Lake's disappearance. Today I was hoping to pick his brain on the Vaughan-Parker affair.

"Unfortunately no, I'm in Long Island, not in Maine. And if I'm calling, and I'm ashamed to admit it, it's because I need your help."

"Don't be ashamed, I'm always happy to help you. What can I do for you?"

I summarized what I knew about the various characters and then I got to Simon Parker.

"So that's where I am today. This guy vanished in thin air and the investigators don't really seem to care about finding him or not. The case is closed for them according to their conclusions. But there's something that's been bothering me. This guy logically should have been there to identify the bodies and go to the funerals. I'm trying to pin him down, but I'm not making any progress, no one knows where he is, and no one seems to want to go looking for him. I know that your experience will help me, Barry."

On the other side of the line I could hear the ex-cop making little "hmm, hmm," reflection noises.

"My poor Karen, I'm now only an old has-been without much of a network anymore. But I'll try to find the number of someone I used to know who might be able to help you find your missing man. A guy who really helped me in quite a few of my investigations."

"That would be great!" I said enthusiastically.

"Remember though. And I have to be clear here. I didn't say anything, and you didn't hear anything. This guy, 'coz he is a man, wants to remain anonymous."

"Fine with me. Where'd you find this pearl?"

"Well, let's just say that a long, long time ago, he might have had a few problems with the law in Maine. When he was young and crazy, he was into IT, networks, internet, and *tutti quanti*. Stuff I've always hated, personally. So, one day, he went a bit too far in the illegality of the web, and like they say, he *racked*..."

"*Hacked*!"

"Yeah, he *hacked* some governmental sites... And got caught with his hand stuck in the cookie jar. But instead of leaving him rot in some old jail for having poked his nose into other people's business and threatened to make their wheeling and dealing public, we preferred to negotiate with him, if you see what I mean. Since then, he's become, I'd say, a highly qualified resource person each time we need to non-officially delve into the lives of people who are trying to escape from us. So you think that is what your Simon Parker is trying to do?"

"I certainly do, Barry. A little bird who flew away from a nest I'm trying to find. What's your resource guy's name?"

"I won't give you his real name, just his favorite nickname. Spiderweb. You can't invent something like that!"

"A well-chosen one. A spider who spins his web in the shadows on the Web!"

"That's exactly right. You'll see, he's a little strange, but not unpleasant. I'll text you his number when I hang up. In the meanwhile though Karen, I'm glad we got to talk. How are you doing? Have you made any progress on your personal research?"

I was surprised by this question, but my investigations had pushed my own quest into the background. I remember that last year in Greenville, Barry and I had talked about that.

"Not much, unfortunately. But I'll soon have some time to take care of myself a bit more."

"And how's your health?"

"Could be worse, could be better. What about you, Barry?"

"Like I said, a retired cop sitting in front of his fireplace."

"Take care then and have a Merry Christmas. And please give my regards to your wife."

"You too Karen. And if you're ever around here, do stop in. You know where I live, and the door is always open for you."

"Roger that!"

A FEW SECONDS later I had a text message with Spiderweb's phone number, and I hoped that this strange person would help me progress in this case. But it would be progress in a direction I was far from suspecting...

CHAPTER 46
A maximum of precautions

IT SEEMED like I was talking to a teenager on the phone. Yet, Spiderweb must be in his late twenties or early thirties now, if what Barry told me was true. But spending his days in front of a computer – he officially was a professional gamer and a video game designer – perhaps made him an eternal teen?

"I'll call you back right away," he said, hanging up immediately.

I thought then he didn't care about me but just a couple of seconds later, my phone rang, but this time the screen had *Unknown Caller* on it.

"I always take a maximum of precautions, Mrs. Blackstone, hope you don't resent that. You know, Uncle Sam and his big ears, all that. So? Heard you need my services? What can I do for you?"

He religiously listened to me explaining what I was looking for concerning Simon Parker and I outlined all the dates, places and names of the various protagonists.

Every once in a while I heard a guttural sound coming from him, though he never interrupted me. While I was speaking, in the background I could hear the noise of computer keys being pressed. I finally finished.

"Is that something you could do?"

"No problemo, Mrs. Blackstone."

"Why don't you just call me Karen, I won't feel so old."

"Okay then, no problemo, Karen. I can do all of that! Nothing can resist me. I'm sure Barry told you about my past. But still, I'll need a bit more info, for example, the guy's phone number. You got it?"

I frowned.

"Nope. But I'll try to get it and hope it's still the one he uses now.

"Oki doki. When you get it, just give me a call. No more text messages. You got a piece of paper and a pen? Here's my Proton Mail account. Write to me here and create one for yourself, if you can. It's free, but best of all, it's secure and encrypted. Swiss quality. So in the meanwhile, I'll start digging around on my side with everything I already have. And we have to talk about my... fees."

"Okay. How much do I owe you?"

"For something like this, let's say two hundred."

I wondered for a moment if my boss would validate those hidden expenses, but as she leaves me *carte blanche* as long as I get results, I agreed.

"*Ciao!*"

And imitating Myrtille Fairbanks, he hung up.

I immediately called Melinda Vaughan to see if per chance, she'd still have her ex-son-in-law's phone number. And luckily for me, she was able to find it on a paper directory. I created my own Proton Mail account and sent it to Spiderweb with his phone number.

THE DAY WAS DRAWING to an end. I looked out from my window in Montauk Manor at the pinkish sky towards the west. It wouldn't be snowing tonight I thought, a bit melancholic. I suddenly was overwhelmed with sadness. I thought about Katheline, who'd never again see the sun set. I let my thoughts wander and thought about another child, who was somewhere, whose name I didn't know, who didn't know that I'd been looking for him for so many years, who I wanted to meet, even if it was just to admire the sunset together...

I PUSHED MY LAPTOP, my notebook and my phone away and laid down on top of the bed. I'd started to doze off when my phone rang. I thought it must be Spider while doubting that he'd had enough time to complete his mission so quickly. A bit surprised when I looked at the name, I still answered.

"Hi Paul."

"Hi Karen. I hope I'm not bothering you."

"No, no, not at all," I replied, relatively troubled by his call.

"As you'd asked me to contact you if I'd thought of anything else about Laura Vaughan or anything concerning people who knew her..."

"Yes?"

"Well, that's why I'm phoning. I remembered something that could interest you."

"I'm listening, Paul, tell me."

He hesitated for a moment, and then continued with a scratchy voice.

"If it's all the same to you, I'd prefer to talk about this... face to face."

"No problem. I'm available. Where do you want to meet?"

"In Manhattan."

"Manhattan? But that's at least a two-hour drive from here. I can't drive that far at night."

"At least two hours and a half," he said, laughing. "Listen Karen, I scored a couple of seats for a Broadway musical, and I don't want to go alone, that's too depressing. But don't worry, I'm a magician."

"Of course, you're going to teleport us?"

"Nearly! I can *heliport* us! I'll pick you up in the lobby in fifteen minutes, that okay with you?"

AND WHAT AN EVENING IT WAS...

CHAPTER 47
Dazzled

WHEN PEOPLE TALK about their emotions, sometimes they use the metaphors of roller coasters, with their ups and downs, their speed, making your stomach mount up to your head or the opposite, descend down to your feet. Or sometimes you glide or soar.

When you're talking about an on-going investigation, it often seems wise to rise above the events and declarations that people make.

And talking about "rising above," I sure did rise, about 900 feet above the Long Island peninsula. The sky on the west was glowing, and the buildings in Manhattan were in the foreground, a skyline of glass and steel that reflected that incredible light of the setting ruby red sun. A poet I am not, but sitting in the interior of the helicopter, headphones on my ears to mitigate the sound of the blades, that was the image that imposed itself on me. In the headphones' embedded mic, I stammered, looking at Paul Nollington, sitting next to me, on the comfortable seats at the back of the helicopter.

"This is incredible! It's the very first time I've been in a helicopter and it's even better than flying in a plane. Thank you so much for this gift... that fell from the sky."

"Watch it! Don't say things like that, they might bring you back luck like when you say 'good luck' to actors in a play." Not even a half-hour flight to the heliport on the tip of Manhattan, in my opinion, was much better than traffic jams on Highway 27.

When we arrived, I was surprised when Paul gallantly escorted me to a limousine that was waiting for us right off the landing pad, whose chauffeur opened the doors for us.

All that luxury made my head spin as I wasn't used to things like this.

The limo set off for Manhattan, direction Broadway, and the lights in the city wearing their holiday best dazzled me. But there were questions I had to ask Paul.

"You said you had something to say to me about Laura?"

"That's right, Karen. But not now. Let's make the most out of this moment. Take advantage of it," he said, touching the back of my hand with his fingers that slowly slid along the leather seats.

Uneasy, I raised my arm pretending to push back a strand of hair behind my ear.

A quarter of an hour later, the limo dropped us off in front of the theatre where there was a huge line outside. Paul surprised me once again by leading me to a different building catering to those who had advanced tickets. I didn't dare look at the people who had been standing outside for hours in the cold weather, hoping to score a seat. I suddenly realized that none of this was free. The helicopter, the limousine, and the VIP seats for the musical. Paul, though still so young, seemed to possess a small fortune that he didn't hesitate to dent to dazzle me. Where did he get all that money from? His parents? His own successful career? Whatever, I was enjoying the moment, trying to empty my mind.

And I had to say that it did work. Musical comedies are delicious both for your eyes and for your ears. I'd always dreamed of going to a show like that, in the Mecca of musical comedies, and to boot, during Christmas vacation, something that was even better. Now, I could say I had.

When we left the theater, Paul surprised me once again.

"Karen, are you a risk-taker?"

That didn't sound good to me.

"What kind of risks?"

"Culinary ones. You're not hungry? I'm starving. Over here."

He took me by the arm and led me to the door of a small restaurant with a French name, Le Rivage, quite near the theater. It looked just like a French country house. Tempting smells instantaneously inundated my nostrils. A waiter escorted us to a table that Paul had reserved. Only when I was looking at the menu did I understand why Paul had spoken about culinary risks... Snails from Burgandy garnished with parsley and garlic, pan-fried veal liver, salted pork, frogs' legs in garlic sauce...

"French gastronomy," exulted Paul, going through the menu with his finger. "Pot-au-feu, Alsacien sauerkraut, bouillabaisse from Marseille, cassoulet, snails, maroilles cheese... And have a look at these wines from Bordeaux, Burgundy and Champagne! Ah! Why wasn't I born in Paris or in Lyon?"

"Because they don't know how to make good burgers there?" I said ironically.

"Come on! Karen, how about a little adventure? The French Discovery Menu? That's what I'm having, will you join me?"

"I would have gladly, but I'm resolutely a Pesco-Vegetarian."

Saved by the bell! He couldn't argue with that.

"But are snails considered as meat?" he insisted.

I nodded vigorously.

"That they are. A type of meat that crawls on the ground and drools to boot... Thanks, but no thanks. I'll try their French onion soup though. And their amandine trout."

"Chicken."

"We'll see whose stomach doesn't make it through the night."

To accompany our choices, Paul ordered a bottle of Chardonnay whose freshness and a tiny hint of a buttery savor won me over. Between the first and second courses, I came back to my investigation.

"So, Paul. Why'd you invite me here? Why are you being so nice to me?"

His blue eyes tenderly looked into mine. A look that destabilized me.

"Why not?"

"If you wanted to talk to me about something, we could have done it much more simply."

"Combining business with pleasure, you know the expression... Personally I've had a wonderful evening."

"I totally agree with you Paul. But could we get down to business? What did you have to tell me that could help me progress in my investigation?"

Paul Nollington, the son of the neighbors of the Vaughan family, someone still smitten with Laura, his best friend and confidant, took a deep breath before answering.

"The day that Laura and Katheline disappeared, I was at my parents' house in Montauk. From my bedroom window, you can see the dunes, and the beach beyond them... I saw them... And they weren't alone that day."

CHAPTER 48
What has been torturing my soul

MY GLASS of Chardonnay was nearly empty. I'd been sipping it slowly, listening to Paul Nollington's story. The Vaughan's neighbor came back to that key date of July 13, 2022.

"From my window, I could not only see the Vaughan's pool, that place where Laura had slit her wrists. Remember, when I'd been spying on her and saved her life. I could also see a part of the beach at the foot of our respective lots. On that July 13th, it was much too hot for me to go down to the beach, and I was in my air-conditioned room trying to finalize a complex file for one of my biggest clients, but every now and then, to take a break, I looked outside."

"You never missed an opportunity to spy on her," I said.

"No, that wasn't really the case this time. It was just a coincidence. That's what life is made of. Anyway, that afternoon, Laura was on the beach with her daughter."

"That's a fact that several others have told me. Nothing new there. Unless?"

"Yup, unless," murmured Paul, finishing his glass of white wine. "Let me tell you what I saw that day."

∽

Montauk, July 13, 2022

Below a thin veil of clouds, those that are at a really high altitude in summer, hordes of tourists and locals were crowded together on the narrow strip of sand between the dunes and the Atlantic Ocean, on miles and miles of beach, between the lighthouse and Montauk Point. Amongst those miles of sand covered by towels and tread upon by children, parents, people playing Frisbee, volleyball, or other typical beach games, Laura Vaughan and Katheline occupied a few square yards. Very few actually, as both were thin and young. The afternoon was drawing to an end, and it must have been nearly five. The mother and daughter had just returned from the ocean. Kathy was laughing loudly and asking to go back in, untiring. Wearing her little arm floatation devices and a buoy, she loved being pushed forward and backward by the waves, not being able to see over the top of them, with her mom right next to her, then rolling around in the sand that scratched her legs and got into the swimsuits, the ones that you had to rinse out in the sink so your buttocks wouldn't turn red.

Out of breath, they went back to their towels, plopping down on them while still laughing, and Laura put her arms around Kathy who was shivering a bit despite the heat. Laura smelled the sweet odor of her treasure's wavy brown hair, something she adored. They seemed to be inseparable, united by a powerful link. They'd been able to get by without Simon, the missing father. *Good riddance*, Laura often said to herself at night in her big cold bed, after having put Kathy in for the night without ever forgetting to kiss her on her forehead.

Behind his lace curtain in his room, you could make out Paul Nollington's silhouette. Squinting to see more clearly, he was following the mother and daughter on the beach. He also often thought *good riddance* late at night, those nights when sleep didn't seem to come, when he was thinking of them.

He suddenly jumped.

Just a few yards from Laura and her daughter, he thought he'd recognized the person who was taking wide strides in the sand, towards the two girls who hadn't seen him coming. There was no question at all, even at that distance, he could have identified him amongst a thousand. His muscular way of walking, his blond hair, and his bearing, as if he were royalty, or at least someone to be looked up to.

Simon Parker was back in Montauk.

Just a few months after having disappeared from the radars, leaving his wife and child to fend for themselves, after having beaten Laura, packed his bags, and run off like a thief, Simon the tough guy, was back, back where it all had started.

"Jesus, what the hell is that bastard doing here?" wondered Paul, pushing the lace curtain away to see the scene more clearly.

Now, Simon was right next to them, and visibly was berating them. Laura and Kathy, wrapped in their towels, both turned around, facing him. You could tell the discussion was heated. Paul though couldn't hear what was being said, even with his window open. There was just the confusion of a thousand undefinable voices coming up from the beach. On the other hand, the gestures they were both making proved the tone of the conversation.

Paul suddenly though saw red when Simon grabbed Laura's arm. She tried to break away from her ex-husband and little Katheline was holding on to her mother's legs for dear life. Simon began to drag Laura away.

Paul felt pure hatred rising in him. He ran across his room, took the stairs two by two, rushed through the living room and ran down to the dunes and the beach from the back of the property.

He wanted to intervene before a disaster took place.

"Unfortunately though," concluded Paul at our table in Le Rivage, "in spite of how quickly I'd run down to the beach, when I got there, all that was left of them were their towels. It must have been two or maybe three minutes at the most, but that was enough for them to disappear. I looked to the right, to the left, hoping to see them. But I didn't. I had no idea what direction they'd taken, and was afraid to choose one of them, towards the lighthouse or towards Amagansett... I asked around, but no one was able to give me any information, as if everyone couldn't have cared less about what happened to Laura and Kathy. That's people today. You can die right there in the street, people will either ignore you or they'll make a video of it was their phones and then post it on social media."

"Exactly," I jumped in on this idea. "What if someone had been filming right then?"

"Maybe, who knows? We'd have to look all over on Facebook, Instagram or TikTok, but I don't have much hope there."

"I'll try," I replied, thinking about Spider, my new resource.

"Karen, you know what has been torturing my soul ever since that day? It's knowing that this time, I didn't succeed in saving her... saving *them*."

CHAPTER 49
The truth amongst all your lies

VERSAILLES, Missouri, December 2023

Could we believe the new version of what Carrie Chastain had told us?

That was the question running through Sergeant Gallister's brain when he heard her admit that Jessy, her daughter, had been kidnapped in the summer of 2022.

"So, now you're saying that this is the truth, Mrs. Chastain? Are you sure? You're affirming something serious here. I hope you realize this."

"Yeah, that's what I told you! Kidnapped."

"By who?"

"If I only knew…"

Myra Stonehenge took over.

"Carrie, there's something bothering me in all your declarations. I can't imagine a mother being so imprecise, confused and flippant in a case like the one we're talking about. Had your daughter really been kidnapped, you wouldn't have invented all those stories about an aunt in Florida, or her running away, or even having been taken by her father or your spouse, Mumin Blasharov. How many other versions of this are you going to give?"

Carrie didn't answer that question, just lowering her head and supporting it with her callused hands. Gallister continued.

"I don't believe that version anymore. Speaking of which, we'll check that right now, but when you said your daughter was kidnapped last summer, did you notify the authorities?"

The lady, now silent, was rocking back and forth on her chair, lost in her thoughts, lost in her mental delusions.

"And how do you explain," continued the sergeant, "that we're pretty sure that we identified your Dodge pickup at the gas station in Gravois Mills on the very day that Jessy miraculously reappeared? Something that would seem to corroborate what you told us when you said that your partner had taken your daughter and disappeared with her. How can you say that they left your house whereas, according to your new version of the facts, Jessy had been kidnapped a year and a half ago? She wasn't at home, but she *still* was at home? And when your neighbor came over, she wasn't there? And no one had seen her for months with you? Or else, maybe my team and I got this all completely wrong? Who knows, maybe Jessy, your daughter, wasn't in the Dodge that the surveillance cameras got footage of. And maybe it wasn't Mumin Blasharov either. After all, black and white footage is never very clear. Plus they were wearing hoods. Jesus Christ, Mrs. Chastain, where is the truth amongst all your lies?"

Carrie raised her head, her eyes still shut and sighed loudly.

"I'm tired of all your questions Sergeant. I wanna go home."

"And I'm tired of all your contradictory statements. I've been wasting time with you for days now. And in the meanwhile, there's this little kid in the hospital that showed up from nowhere, and we don't know who she was running from or where she was going. And I'm sorry to tell you that you won't be going home for a good amount of time."

"What? But who's gonna take care of my chickens?"

"I couldn't care less about your chickens. But because I'm a nice guy, I'll ask your neighbors to feed them. I'm sure they'll say yes. For now though, I'm going to take you into provisional custody for concealment of facts and false statements and because I think that you need this, I'm going to ask the prosecutor to request an appointment with a psychiatrist for you."

Right then, someone knocked on the door. Gallister told the person to come in and Agent Bauer stuck his head in.

"Sergeant, can I see you for a minute?"

Gallister got up and walked to his agent who was in the hall. Carrie looked at them but couldn't hear what Bauer was saying to his boss. He nodded a couple of times and turned around.

"I think that's enough for today then. Myra, can you take care of this lady who's lying through her teeth, please?"

"Okay, Pete."

When Gallister and Bauer were alone in the hallway, the sergeant wanted to make sure of what he'd heard.

"You're sure of the result, Bauer?"

"Of course, Pete. Phones have very accurate geo location systems. And we found Mumin Blasharov's number without any possible errors. It was traced according to what we already discovered, in particular his stop at Happy Jack's in Gravois Mills."

"Well, at least we were right about one thing then. And what about now, do we know where this Mumin Blasharov's phone is?"

"Yup. We've got the latest data, but the location seems a bit strange. Or not... Look for yourself," said Bauer, unfolding a topographical map for Gallister.

He pointed at a spot with a red circle around it.

Mumin Blasharov's phone had been located just a few miles from there, right in the middle of Lake of the Ozarks. At the bottom.

CHAPTER 50
Thick dark waves

LAKE OF THE OZARKS, Missouri, December 2023

IN TOURIST BROCHURES, this place was often described as being idyllic. All you had to do was to imagine a lake with a rugged coastline carved out by the capricious Osage River on the west, which zigzagged just like the tail of a Chinese dragon until it flowed, on the east, into the Missouri, of which it was a tributary. When it reached Sunrise Beach, it fanned out in different directions, in the north, up to Gravois Mills. Between this northern point and Osage Beach on the south, it formed what was called Lake of the Ozarks, with a bucolic little town smack in the middle of it, called Village of Four Seasons. That was the zone in which Mumin Blasharov's cell phone had been located.

Pete Gallister and Agent Bauer were posted on the

shore with a team of divers getting ready to go in. Wearing their neoprene diving costumes, the scuba divers were getting ready to enter the nearly freezing water. Though they were used to all types of conditions, including extreme weather, diving into water that was just a bit over 32°F was still a challenge for them. Plus, at this spot in the lake and in December, the waves seemed to be dark and troubled. Today's search wouldn't be a piece of cake for them.

"What's the degree of precision for mobile geo locating?" Gallister wanted to know, fearing they'd have to dredge the entire lake.

"Round about five yards. So, we're pretty good here and it must be right about there," said Bauer, pointing at a place between the shore and fifty or so feet out.

The only problem though was that this was overlooked by a cliff where the cops were standing.

"How deep is it here?" asked Gallister to one of the divers.

"I'd say between fifteen and thirty feet. It's not a smooth bottom in this part of the lake because you've got both rocks, sand and silt. That'll be today's surprise, but we like stuff like that. Sergeant, you'll be guiding us from the cliff. Come on guys, you all ready to rumble?"

The head scuba diver joined his team a bit farther along the beach, on a sandy part where a pneumatic Zodiac was waiting for them. The divers, all with their oxygen bottles, pushed the dingy into the water and hopped in, one after the other. One of them started the motor up and the Zodiac slowly went towards the point where the GPS had pinged on Mumin Blasharov's cell phone. Sergeant Gallister, on top of the cliff, guided them with his arms.

When the divers were above the zone the software had estimated using the geo location device Agent Bauer was holding, Gallister gave them a thumbs up to confirm. The men, wearing their thermal suits, were sitting on the edge of the dingy, their backs towards the lake, let themselves fall backwards into the thick dark waves.

When they'd all disappeared below the surface of the water, Gallister mused out loud.

"What the heck is Mumin's phone doing there? Did someone throw it in, and why?"

"He probably threw it in himself," Bauer said, trying to explain. "To hide something."

"Well that didn't work," replied Pete ironically.

"Or else he went in with his phone on him. He was trying to commit suicide... After having tried to kidnap his daughter, and then she escaped... And he couldn't stand living with his crazy wife anymore... What do you think about that, Pete? Sounds plausible? You're starting to know this guy pretty good; don't you think that that's what you would have done rather than coming back home?"

"Carrie Chastain, quite the unique lady that one. I have no idea how those two could have shacked up together. Like she's no Miss America nor is she the nicest little lady either."

The two men looked towards the lake and at that very moment one of the divers came back up, his mask on his face, hooked up to his oxygen bottles. He waved his arms in a signal that Gallister understood right away. He had just found something in the lake.

"Bingo," Bauer said. "That sure was quick."

Even Gallister was astonished by the rapidity of the search. Though the zone to be investigated was relatively precise, and pinpointed by satellite localization, still, with the lake's dark waters, the sergeant had been expecting to spend much too much time up on the cliffs in the freezing weather and braving the cold wind blowing off the lake. He walked down to the diver.

"Well?"

"I think we found your phone, Sergeant. Well, not really."

"I don't get it."

"I mean that it's still really dark down there in spite of our lights. But we're sure that we're right above the zone we had targeted. On the other hand, we didn't see the cell phone. But we identified something else that I'm sure you'll be interested in. Right below the zone, we stumbled upon something we couldn't miss."

"Quit beating around the bush like that. What did you find?"

"A car."

"A wreck?"

"If when you're saying 'a wreck' you mean something like the remains of the Titanic, all rusted, something that sunk decades ago, no, not that. The vehicle we found hasn't been there for long. There's no algae, no moss, no silt. And I can even tell you the brand, Sergeant."

"Tell me then!'

"It's a Dodge pickup."

Gallister's eyes popped wide open.

"What color?"

"It's hard to say, but it's dark."

"Did you get the license plate number?"

"My guys are working on it."

A few minutes later the other divers came up. When they gave Gallister the license plate number, he nodded his head, remembering the video surveillance footage at Happy Jack gas station and the information he'd extracted from the national vehicle registration file that he'd consulted.

"No doubt, it's Blasharov's car."

CHAPTER 51
Evidence

"IS THERE A BODY INSIDE THE VEHICLE?" asked Gallister to the divers.

"We didn't see any, Sergeant."

"We'll have to fish the car out," he grumbled, grabbing his phone.

It was going to be all hands-on deck, and they'd have to use a lot of equipment. In the following hour, the blades of a helicopter were throbbing above the lake, creating circular waves on its surface. There was a steel cable hanging from the helicopter into the choppy water. Below it, the team of divers were trying to hook the pickup up so it could be extracted.

On top of the cliff overlooking the scene, Bauer and Gallister were like hound dogs, their eyes on the ground, looking for any evidence.

And they found some. Now that they knew that the Dodge had finished its trip in the lake, the policemen were easily able to see the clues it had left behind: broken branches, tracks on the grass and damaged vegetation.

Traces of tires in a straight line heading for the void, those blackish waters where they'd stop spinning forever, where the motor would drown.

The deafening noise of the helicopter's blades stopped their investigation of the site. They could see that the copter was having trouble rising, weighed down by the water-logged vehicle attached at the end of the metallic cord. Suddenly the surface of the water looked like it was about to boil, and the car emerged, pulled up by the helicopter's powerful motors.

Bauer and Gallister, on their promontory, were at the same level as the Dodge. Its windows had been opened, probably so it would sink more rapidly. Water flowed from it like a fountain.

Slowly, so the vehicle wouldn't swing, the helicopter turned towards the land and carefully lowered the car onto a woodless part of the coastline. When its harnesses had been detached, the investigators walked up to it.

As the head diver had told them, there was no one inside.

Turning towards Bauer who was holding the tablet with the geo location app, the sergeant put on a pair of gloves before trying to open the passenger-side door, a door that was quite a bit worse for the wear, as if it had been up close and personal with a tree. Gallister tried to force the handle of the distorted door.

"I hope the phone is still in there. I'd bet it's in the

glove compartment, or else it would have dropped out of the window when the helicopter was hauling it out of the water."

He opened the glove compartment and smiled when he saw the cell phone in it, imprisoned by a huge wad of wet paper, probably all the car's bills and documents. He held the object up for everyone to see.

"So, now all we gotta do is try to wake this phone up. I'm sure it's got plenty of interesting things to tell us."

Gallister ordered the Dodge to be transferred to the station for a deeper investigation of any eventual traces or clues that could help make progress in the case. He harbored no illusions though as it had spent several days immerged in that muddy water.

Gallister and Bauer went back to their police car.

"What do you think about this case? Why do you think the Dodge ended up in the water?"

Bauer thought that over.

"As the vehicle wasn't occupied by its presumed driver, meaning Blasharov, I'd imagine that for some reason or another, the most plausible reason is that someone was trying to cover up traces of some misdemeanor and they wanted to get rid of the car. The person drove it to the cliff, put it in drive and jumped out before it fell into the lake."

"Yeah, that does seem logical. Unless he drove off the cliff in the car and his body only drifted out of the wreck between the day of the accident and today, as the windows were open."

"Maybe we should continue to dredge the lake?"

"I don't think that will give us any results. In my humble opinion, Mumin must be someplace else than at the bottom of the lake. But the question is where?"

"The first question of a long series of mysteries, no?" Bauer asked.

"I'm listening."

"Well, if he's the one who drove the car into the lake, why did he leave his phone in the glove compartment?"

"To kill two birds with one stone? Maybe the cell phone had compromising data, as did the Dodge. The analyses will probably give us more info."

"But why the heck can't we find that guy? If his little lady told the truth and he actually did kidnap their daughter, and there was footage of them together – at least that what we think from the CCTV at the gas station – and she escaped him and was found in the snow on the side of the road, why didn't he respond to our call for witnesses?

"Maybe he couldn't?"

"And why couldn't he?"

"Maybe because he's dead?" Gallister concluded.

"If so, the question still remains to determine if he died *before* or *after* the pickup drove off the cliff into the lake. If he died before, that means that he wasn't the one who caused the vehicle to drive off the cliff. Which brings us to a new question: who else could have caused the truck to drive off the cliff and why?

"The eternal story of the snake biting its own tail,"

sighed Bauer, his eyes glued to the road on which the snow was beginning to fall lightly again.

Pete nodded his head, remaining lost in his thoughts for a few long seconds.

"I think I'm going to have to question that old Chastain lady once again," he said plaintively. "Not that it's something I want to do. She changes her version every five minutes. But this time I'm going to tell her we found their pickup. She'll undoubtedly have some explanation for that too. But right now, she must be in the hands of our psychiatric expert. I'm anxious to know what is going on in that head of hers..."

CHAPTER 52
A nice calm piece of heaven

MONTAUK, December 2023

RETURNING from Manhattan to Montauk in the helicopter that Paul Nollington had commissioned, the atmosphere was quite different from what it had been on the way there. Still totally enchanted by the panorama, this time at night, I silently admired the Manhattan skyline all lit up and as well as Long Island that was punctuated with thousands and thousands of twinkling stars. *Magical* was the only way I could describe it.

Yet, ever since Paul had told me what he'd seen on the day that Laura and Katheline both disappeared, about how Simon Parker disrupted them on the beach in Montauk, I could feel he was more withdrawn. I tried to reassure him.

"Paul, you can't feel guilty that you weren't able to find them in time. You did everything possible."

"No! I wasn't able to save them on that fatal day of July 13th."

"Paul, stop torturing yourself for what happened in the past, things you couldn't do. Now you have to look towards the future."

"The future?" he murmured and suddenly slid his hand over the leather seat, touching my fingers.

I turned slightly towards him. In the darkness of the night, his face was only lit up by the helicopter's lights that were yellow, red, blinking or not, making his features seem to be changing. Unsettling.

"Karen. Is it just a twist of fate that you came here, to Montauk, to shed light on the Vaughan affair?"

I didn't know how to answer his question and remained silent. Paul took off his mic-headphones and put them on his knees. He turned completely to me and took mine off. The noise of the helicopter's blades was deafening, dizzying. It surrounded us, enclosing us in a cocoon beyond the limits of time. His face neared mine while he tenderly touched my cheek with his hand. I was petrified, I was afraid to move, stuck inside that helicopter. Impossible for me to escape him... but was that something I wanted to do?

"Paul..." I said without conviction.

He put his index finger on my lips, inviting me to remain silent, then moved closer to me. I could feel his warm breath and our lips touched. I hesitated in responding to this unexpected kiss, but the sweet citrus taste of the Chardonnay came back to me, and I allowed myself to become intoxicated by his audacity.

Half an hour later we had landed and this time we traveled in Paul's car, to the parking lot in Montauk Manor. We kissed one more time, one more long and tender time. I couldn't tell you how long it had been since I'd felt such an attraction to someone. Or more exactly should I say, since I'd allowed myself to be attracted to someone. I thought I'd lost the instruction manual for men. And they'd also lost mine.

I didn't care though and allowed myself to be swept away by those novel and intoxicating sensations. I surrendered myself for a fleeting moment in his arms. Trembling from head to lips. Perhaps the moment was not the best one, but do people ever choose to experience such moments?

His hands caressed my body through my heavy winter coat, yet I could feel their warmth.

"Karen... would you invite me in for one last drink in your room? I've never been inside the Manor."

For a few seconds, I had the weakness to think of accepting his request but clearing my head and in spite of the desire I had eating away at me, I gently pushed him away, gently but firmly.

"Paul, it's still too early for me. I need more time. Time to think about what is happening to me. It would be too foolish to act like two awkward and overanxious teenagers. I hope you understand?"

Paul drew away from me, nodding, his lips pursed.

"Of course, please forgive me, Karen. It was a mistake. I'm sorry."

"No, please, don't be sorry. It's just that I'm no longer used to this and it's something that frightens me. But I had a fantastic evening with you, you spoiled me like no one has ever done before. Thank you. Sincerely. I have to go now."

"We'll stay in touch... For the Vaughan case. If you have anything new."

～

AND JUST A FEW minutes after having left Paul Nollington, I did have something new.

I went up to my room and took a hot shower, a whirlwind of thoughts spinning in my mind. Pink and black ideas, dancing around in my wet head. A merry-go-round of faces turning slowly. Paul, at first, then Melinda Vaughan, Sarah, Katheline, Simon Parker, Lieutenant Garrett, then Myrtille Fairbanks, and curiously after that, Veronika Lake, and finally the mysterious features of a young man whose eyes seemed to be absent, empty, but who I felt that I somehow knew. And it even seemed to me that I was intimately linked to that same featureless face. Someone I'd not yet met, but who I knew so very well.

I cried softly under the scorching water.

I felt like with each new investigation, I'd become more emotional, more sensitive. Especially so when my investigations concerned children. Sometimes I questioned my true motivations. As well as my resilience in dealing with such difficult cases. How long would I still be able to stand this psychologically grueling work? Shouldn't I first take care of my own quest, my own investigation, to clear my mind? Focus on what is essential?

My past, my life, my future?

When I got out of the bathroom, I had a signal on my cell phone informing me someone had tried to reach me. Spiderman!

I called him back and left a message for him to recontact me. It didn't take long and as usual, he called from a burner.

"Hey, Karen! Spida here. I got what you wanted. However, as it's the first time we've worked together – but not the last I hope –, I hope I won't offend you by asking me to pay in advance for my services?"

"No, of course not. Just tell me what to do."

"I'll send off a request to pay me in cryptocurrency, it's more discreet."

"Um, I don't know a thing about stuff like that, though."

"Don't worry. You'll get an SMS link in a couple of seconds. Just click on it and follow the instructions. It's something that only takes a sec."

And a beep announced that his message had arrived. I followed the directions and when I'd finished, I let him know while realizing that I wouldn't have an invoice to give Myrtille, my dear boss.

"It's okay, in da pocket!" said Spider. "Thanks.

Here's what I did then. I checked all my secret databases and pinpointed that infamous Simon Parker who succeeded in escaping from the cops. Either they don't want to look for him or else I'm pretty good. It must be that, don't you think?"

"For sure. Come on champ, tell me everything. How did you do it?"

"Oh no, I'm not gonna tell you that, it's my private intelligence, my secret bag of tricks. Would you ever ask a magician how he does stuff? Same with me. I've got my sources and my talents. Only the result is important, right?"

"Yup, at two hundred bucks per trick, it's true that only the result interests me. Spit it out!"

"You want the short or long version? Seven-course meal or fast food?"

Spider was laughing at his wit. I let him calm down and then asked him for the short version, an answer he wasn't expecting.

"Your guy, even since he disappeared from Montauk in the summer of 2020, abandoning his wife and daughter like you said, has travelled quite a bit around the country. I found him in the east and west, north and south. A guy on the move. You could imagine that either he was looking for something or someone, or else he was trying to *hide* from something or someone. But it's up to you to discover who or what. So anyway, the last place where I geo localized him and where he seems to have been for the past couple of days is in Missouri."

"What?" I shouted out. "Missouri?"

"Yeah, why?"

"Could you be a bit more precise?"

"Yes Ma'am! The last signal I identified pinged near a village called Village of Four Seasons. Isn't that romantic? On the map, it looks like it's a nice calm little piece of heaven…"

CHAPTER 53
Four scourges

SOME PLACE IN AMERICA...

Now and then, a window of lucidity opened in his brain fog.

Exhaustion.
Cold.
Hunger.
Thirst.

Of these four scourges, which one would be lethal and would kill him before the others?

Without even considering the wound in his shoulder that had made him lose a lot of blood, making him even weaker, literally making him suffer from anemia.

He thought he remembered that you could go without food for several days. He knew he could resist exhaustion for quite a while, by resting, not moving, not using his reserves.

But the cold? Could a human body naturally resist such torture? If only he had been wearing warm clothes. Or even had several blankets, even makeshift ones. Tough luck though. This year there had been unseasonably cold weather in Missouri. If only he could have gone under the stack of straw that was just a few yards away. That stack of straw, though rotten, nearly black, he would have welcomed it had he been able to crawl there.

But it was impossible, because his arms and legs were tied, he couldn't move, he couldn't break through them with his muscles. He'd already tried, but in vain. He'd exhausted himself for nothing, uselessly drawing on his rare and so precious resources.

What torture it was to die a slow and painful death and not be able to do anything about it.

If only he could have shouted out. But the gag covering his mouth only allowed him to diffuse an emission of muffled sounds that would have been hard to hear even at a distance of ten feet.

So he'd die here.

He now was trying to conserve what little strength he had left to survive a few days, a few more hours, in the hope that someone would find and save him. But there where he was, he was afraid no one would ever find him before... before he turned into a dried-out cadaver. Maybe next spring? When the odor of putrefaction of his body would be smelled by someone passing by? When buzzards would be flying around the shed? In the meanwhile though, the cold winter would continue to mask the smell of death. Were there any flies in winter? And what about maggots, would they come out with this cold weather?

Would he end up being eaten?

How ironic! He who could no longer feed himself. He couldn't remember the last time someone had brought him something to ease his hunger. He could feel his stomach twisting, accompanied by loud and repetitive growls. Was it retracting, eating away at itself? A physiological squeak? He never could have imagined something like that before having cruelly felt it.

The empty plate next to him was competing with the emptiness of his stomach. He no longer could compensate by food the calories he was constantly burning to try to mitigate the cold and exhaustion. The fight was now one-sided. A powerless man against omni powerful Mother Nature.

Why wasn't anyone bringing him food anymore? Had he been sentenced to death?

The worst though, he suddenly realized, was thirst.

Despite the temperature, his throat was begging him to drink something. It painfully contracted itself each time he swallowed the little saliva he had left. He thought his tongue was swelling and filling his whole mouth. The frigid wind coming through the cracks in the wood walls from the barn pricked his skin like a thousand needles. A blistering cold...

Now he was convinced that he'd die of thirst. He could even feel himself slowly slipping away. Where to? He had no idea. He felt like his body was freeing itself from a heavy weight. The weight of life. A life of suffering? Suffering that would soon end? Finally!

He closed his eyes.

And fell asleep.

Or did he die?

CHAPTER 54
Memory lapses

VERSAILLES, Missouri, December 2023

The afternoon kept on dragging on, deplored Sergeant Gallister as he came back to the Versailles police station, accompanied by Agent Bauer. Sometimes being a cop makes you have the dizzying impression that your days last between forty-eight and seventy-two hours... Cops spend more time with their colleagues than with their families. Okay, that's the case with a lot of jobs, but without trying to play the pity me card, there are way too many divorces and suicides in this profession. Because of the heavy workload, you have to add psychological strain, stress, all the horrors you meet daily, those human atrocities that become, unfortunately, your bread and butter and that you just have no other choice than to accept.

Pete plopped down on his armchair and put his

cup of coffee on his desk. Bauer was taking a day off to compensate for his overtime. Pete though, couldn't do that. Not with that case to solve. Not with that kid who was going to spend Christmas alone at the hospital. He sighed noisily, closed his eyes and put his head back on the head rest of his office chair and allowed himself a moment of relaxation, trying to clear his head. In an ideal world, he would have lied down, but he was afraid to seem ridiculous should one of his colleagues drop into his office.

Whatever. His goal was to synchronize his breathing and his body.

Sissou, his yoga professor, called this "*Pranayama*." "Pete, you must bring your mental consciousness to the activity that is usually subconscious, that of breathing, to make it more efficient and balance your oxygen, carbon dioxide and other soluble gasses in your blood. Thanks to this consciousness, you're going to use your mind to control your body. Or in other words, better mental control will bring you emotional control, a balanced life and mental clarity."

Just what the doctor ordered, thought Pete. *Thanks, Sissou.*

Mental clarity. A sharper vision of the case. Yoga, for him, had become a way of escaping everyday triviality and horrors.

He opened his eyes after a few minutes.

Back on the starting block. Wound up like a cuckoo clock.

. . .

He glanced at the time, picked up his phone and called the specialist who'd examined Carrie when he was at Lake of the Ozarks.

"Doctor Faulker? This is Sergeant Pete Gallister, from Versailles. I sent you a patient named Carrie Chastain this morning."

"A patient?" the doctor asked, cutting him off. "She sure doesn't have much."

"Much what?"

"Patience!" the psychiatrist laughed, delighted by his two-bit pun.

For a moment Pete Gallister wondered if Faulkner shouldn't consult someone himself but came back to the subject.

"Were you able to get anything out of her? What's your diagnostic?

Doctor Faulkner, head of the behavioral health department of the Jefferson City SSM Health Medical Group, was the counterpart – for adults – of Dr. Frances Cagliari, who had taken care of the little lost girl. As a legal expert, the police often asked him to testify in court cases in Missouri.

"Yes, she's really something that lady! A nice specimen. People like that, I don't see them every day. And believe me, I've seen a lot of people during my career. This lady seems to have had terrible things happen to her and her subconscious mind got terribly damaged."

"Could you tell me about your interview?" asked Gallister.

∼

Doctor Faulkner, seated in a leather armchair with wide arm rests across from a bordeaux-colored couch for his tired patients with their tortured souls, silently observed his new patient. Then he began the interview.

"Mrs. Chastain, may I call you Carrie? Is Carrie alright with you?"

"Whatever."

"Fine. Carrie, do you know why you're here today?"

"I guess you wanted to talk to me."

"Let's just say that I'm here to listen to you Carrie. You're the one who'll talk to me."

"I don't got nothing to say. No one asked me if I wanted to come. That Gallister shithead forced me."

"All right then. We can see then that you didn't come here voluntarily. In that case, do you know why that... Gallister... wanted me to see you?"

"Because he's too dumb to understand me. Maybe you'll be able to."

"You could say that it's sort of my job to understand what goes on in other people's minds. Carrie, would you say that it's a bit complicated right now in your head?"

Generally Faulkner's tone and simple sentences made people feel at ease, feel they could trust him. This is what happened with Carrie.

"With everything going on right now, yeah, it's

pretty difficult. The cops are breathing down my neck and all I want to do is get my daughter back."

"You've got a daughter?"

No answer.

"Um, yeah, I think so."

"You think so? You're not sure, Carrie?"

"I just don't know anymore. That cop made me doubt. Sometimes there's like, like holes in my memory. He's playing with that."

"What do you mean by 'holes in your memory?' That you forget things? That you can't remember, for example, why you went into a room, what you wanted to get there or do there? You've got absences?"

"Um, yeah, sometimes. Once I went out to get the eggs from my chickens and I found myself in the middle of the courtyard and didn't know what I was doing there."

"Of course. And do you think it's also possible to forget your daughter like you forgot your eggs that time?"

"No, normally no," Carrie admitted, like an ashamed little girl.

"But right now, for you it's not, let's say, not a normal time? Why? What are you feeling?"

"No, it's not normal. I'm all mixed up. I don't know what's true and what's false, you see?"

"Yes, but could you explain it with your own words, Carrie?"

The patient squirmed around on the couch, as if she was trying to get comfortable.

"Well, I don't know if I got a daughter or not."

"Continue," the psychiatrist urged her after she'd paused for a moment.

"Before, I was pretty sure I had a daughter. Before she got stolen."

"Someone stole your child? When? A long time ago?"

"I think so. Yes. Years ago."

"That's why you said you want to get her back. Where is she now?"

"Over there, not far from here. In this hospital. Doc, please let me see her."

"Maybe later," Faulkner replied. "I want to come back to something though. You said that someone stole your daughter years ago. Yet, someone else told me that you said to them that you'd sent her to live with an aunt in Florida. Do you think that you just could have, as that seems to happen often to you, forgotten that you'd sent your daughter to live with her?"

"Yeah, maybe, that's possible. Maybe like I plum forgot. I think I couldn't feed her anymore. Them hens weren't laying enough eggs."

"I understand. I was also told that your husband recently disappeared?"

Carrie jumped up from the sofa and stood straight as an I, right in the middle of the psychiatrist's office.

"Oh! Yeah, that's it! Now I remember! He's the one who stole my kid! The other day, when it was starting to snow, they left the house."

"She wasn't in Florida?"

The lady sat down again, her large posterior hanging over the edge of the sofa.

"Um, yeah, she was. I don't know anymore. Or maybe she died?"

"I'm sorry Carrie, but I can't answer this question. You're the one who knows."

"Sometimes I get everything so mixed up."

The lady remained silent for a while, her head turned to the ceiling as if trying to remember things, recollections she was striving to bring together. But she didn't say a word. The psychiatrist decided to attack again, but with a different angle.

"What kind of child were you, Carrie? Could you tell me about your childhood?"

"What do you want to know about that for? Nothing interesting happened. Plus, what's that got to do with what's happening now?"

"Are you sure? Would you say you had a happy childhood?"

"Neither more nor less happy than all the other kids placed in foster care."

"You were in foster care?"

"Yup, moved from family to family. I can't even count how many places I lived."

"Do you know why you were placed in foster care?"

"They told me. My mother, I mean the one who gave birth to me – should I call her my *real one*? –, was a young single mother and she didn't want to raise me, that's all."

"Did you ever meet your biological mother?"

"Never. Never wanted to. She didn't want me, and I don't

want her either!"

"Did you feel abandoned?"

"If you want."

"I don't want anything. I'm trying to understand you, Carrie. Do you know why you had several foster families? Do you remember?"

"They said I was too turbulent. Too angry. Sometimes I fought with the other kids in the same family. So they moved me. After that I was big enough to live alone and I met Mumin. And we started our farm."

"Is Mumin your daughter's father?"

"Yeah, the son of a bitch who stole her from me."

Faulkner nodded, without saying anything. Carrie's mental record was spinning. The doctor still had one more point to go over with his patient, who he was beginning to understand.

"Carrie, when you saw the photo that the authorities posted, what did you feel?"

"I knew right away that she was my kid."

"Which one?"

"What do ya mean, which one?"

"Which kid are you talking about now? The one your husband kidnapped? The one in Florida? The one who died a long time ago? The one that looked like your daughter? Which one? Carrie, do you even have a daughter?"

The lady remained silent faced with the series of

questions. Her lips began to twitch, her eyes filled with a glint that soon turned into tears. She sputtered an answer.

"I don't know anymore, Doctor. You're getting me all mixed up."

CHAPTER 55
Open wounds

WHEN DOCTOR FAULKNER had finished describing his interview with Carrie Chastain, Lieutenant Gallister, just as confused as all the rest of the protagonists, wanted to know the expert in behavioral psychiatry's diagnostic.

"Before I can give you a definitive diagnostic for this patient, I'll need a few more hours to get something really useful out of her. On the other hand, I can give you my first impressions now. I think this lady was extremely traumatized when she was a child. I know, I can hear you thinking that us shrinks we *always* talk about childhood, but it's a fact: the first years of your life condition all the rest of your life. Abandoned at birth by her mother, then moved from foster home to foster home, she grew up feeling excluded. Moreover, she had a very authoritarian education to which she responded by an increasing violence, firstly against herself, then against others. A mother-daughter relationship means nothing to her. I even wonder if your Carrie did have a child. I mean, maybe she was fantasizing about having a child with her Mumin Blasharov?"

"I've got the little girl's ID papers here and I had them verified. She did have a daughter."

"I trust you and that was just a working hypothesis that I imagined out loud. So, let's then admit that they did have that child together... Jessy, isn't it?"

"That's it."

"So then the hypothesis that seems the most plausible to me is this. I think the lady is internally fighting a bereavement she can't get over. Her daughter's death or disappearance. So when she saw the photo of that little girl they found on the roadside, Carrie had an emotional transfer. A type of compensation faced with her daughter's absence. The little girl looked like her daughter, and she unconsciously thought she was her mother. In her head, she was sure that the little girl was Jessy and that she herself was her mom. This is a syndrome that I've already seen in parents who tragically lost a child. They find another one, a replacement child. That's how they think they'll cauterize their open wounds."

The sergeant thanked the psychiatrist and hung up.

Pranayama. He needed to empty his mind again. But couldn't.

He tried to mentally assemble all the parts of this difficult case.

Did Carrie Chastain think she was the mother of the little girl they'd found on the roadside? Why not? Gallister mused. That would tie in with what the neighbors, Mr. and Mrs. Donovan, who hadn't seen any kids on the Chastain farm for months, maybe even years, had told him. But in that case, who was that man and that little girl who stopped to fill up their truck at the Happy Jack gas station in Gravois Mills? Weren't they Mumin and Jessy?

But the car filmed by the CCTV cameras at the gas station and the one found at the bottom of Lake Ozarks were the same one: the dark green pickup truck that belonged to Blasharov.

As was the case with the cell phone that was in the glove compartment with Mumin's number on it, according to Carrie Chastain.

But they hadn't found a body.

Rubbing his eyes, Gallister decided that this long and exhausting day was over. He thought he'd sleep on it, as the old saying goes. A muted wrath was burning inside him, smoldering like a fire. He was furious at himself for having let Carrie Chastain manipulate him: that raving lunatic had made him lose precious time. And time was priceless in police investigations.

NOW A NEW QUESTION was haunting Gallister: where was Mumin Blasharov? What happened to him?

He'd soon find out.

CHAPTER 56
A myriad of coincidences

MONTAUK, December 2023

Despite the slew of yesterday's emotions, I fell asleep quickly.

And woke up in the morning with boosted motivation, deep down inside. I thought to myself that the evening I'd spent with that charming Paul Nollington might have been the reason. Despite our difference in age – a bit over fifteen years –, I felt much younger when I was with him. I even surprised myself by smiling when combing my hair. Without going overboard, I thought for an instant that perhaps something good would finally visit my existence.

That mindset fueled me, making me ready to attack another day in my investigation surrounding the Vaughans.

What Spider told me yesterday intrigued me.

Simon Parker, who couldn't be found by the Long Island police force headed by Lieutenant Garrett, had been localized in Village of Four Seasons, in the middle of Missouri.

Missouri! Where the call for witnesses about the child discovered on the road a few days ago came from.

That little girl who Melinda Vaughan believed was her grand-daughter who'd died a year and a half ago.

The one that was Katheline Vaughan's and Simon Parker's daughter?

I began to wonder about something that bothered me: what if Melinda wasn't as crazy as she seemed? What if the elucubrations of that grieving grand-mother drowning her sorrows in alcohol had been founded?

Otherwise, how could Simon Parker's presence, right in Missouri, be explained?

A simple coincidence?

In my job, I'd often been confronted by improbable coincidences but still... How many times had the unthinkable been more consistent than the rational? Each time I'm in a situation like this, I think about Sir Arthur Conan Doyle, who, during his time, was the best author-investigator in the world.

"When you have eliminated the impossible, whatever remains, however improbable, must be the truth."

Consequently, as improbable as that seemed, perhaps the truth was someplace in Missouri?

I had to make sure. I looked on the internet to find the call for witnesses that the police force had published. I noted the number the Versailles investigators gave me for Morgan County and began to call them.

But stopped, once again, doubting. Were the cops in Missouri going to think I was nuts? Would they take me seriously? Should I call them accompanied by Melinda Vaughan who could support what I was saying? Same thing for my other sources? Would they want to know how I found where Simon Parker was? I couldn't reveal Spider...

The heck with this cowardice! I called them.

"Versailles Police Station, Agent Fitzpatrick here. How can I help you?"

"Hello. My name is Karen Blackstone. I'm a journalist for *True Crime Mysteries* and I'm currently investigating a double suicide that took place in 2022 in Montauk, Long Island. I've got good reasons to think that these events could be related, somehow or another, to the call for witnesses that you published recently about a little girl that had been found along the road.

"Oh. Okay," the agent sighed, without masking his exasperation. "A journalist for a tabloid magazine, that's all we needed."

That was what I had feared. For cops, the word 'journalist' has the same effect as a scarecrow for birds. It repels them.

"Please wait, let me explain. I admit that this could seem crazy to you, but I just need a couple of minutes."

He finally agreed to listen to me outline my story to him.

Then he asked me to wait, without hanging up. For a couple of minutes I had to listen to chamber music, a piano I think, interrupted by useful phone numbers and what to do to reach the various police stations in Missouri. I finally heard another voice than Agent Fitzpatrick's.

"Sergeant Pete Gallister here. Miss Blackstone, that's right?"

"That's right, Karen Blackstone. Thanks for taking my call, Sergeant."

"No problem. I just hope my team and I won't be wasting time with you. Because this case is seriously beginning to bother me, I guarantee. If you only had an idea about the number of crazy calls we've had. So, yours, now..."

"I do understand that what I've got to tell you could seem absurd, Sergeant. And I'm the first one to think so. But you must admit that the coincidence is too strong to be due to chance. Our country is huge, and Simon Parker could be anywhere, or even abroad. Yet, he seems to have stopped, just a couple of days ago, right near you. Right near the place where the little girl, the one that her grandma thinks she recognizes, was found."

"Yup, Agent Fitzpatrick told me all that. The poor lady thought she saw her grand-daughter, the one that died last year. Let me tell you Miss Blackstone, I don't believe in ghosts and haven't since I was a little kid."

"Me neither, Sergeant. So explain why the father of the little girl who died in the summer of 22 would be right there when she reappeared?"

"He must be chasing ghosts too? Or like the grandmother, he's still grieving?"

"It's possible. Yet you know that this same father abandoned his wife and child last year, but not without leaving a few traces of that on her face, if you see what I'm getting at. He just vanished, took his stuff, and left them both. Why? To suddenly reappear right now? No, Sergeant, there's something fishy in this scenario. There must be a logical explanation. There must be. There always is…"

"Miss Blackstone, I admire your determination. I share your desire to understand all this. You have no idea how much! If I could just spend Christmas peacefully with my family after having unraveled this can of worms, that would be fantastic."

"Just think about what I'm bringing you on a silver platter then," I insinuated. "I don't know what it's worth, but it should help. We can work together, your services and me. You in Missouri, and me in Long Island."

"We'll see. Journalism and police don't mix very well. So where was this Parker's phone localized lately?"

"In a little town with the cute name of Village of Four Seasons."

"Jesus fucking Christ!"

Underscoring Sergeant Gallister's delicate exclamation, I heard the characteristic sound of a fist beating down on a desk.

"What's going on?"

The policeman sighed noisily. I could feel he was getting ready to speak, but hesitating. He finally began.

"What's going on is that Village of Four Seasons is a little town right in the middle of a peninsula which is located smack in the center of a branch of a river that forms Lake of the Ozarks. And that is exactly where yesterday, right at the bottom, we found the car of a person named Mumin Blasharov, who is said to be the father of the little girl who was found a couple of days ago. And who has gone missing since then. And that, that sort of broadens the slew of very strange coincidences, don't you agree, Miss Blackstone?"

"Would that help you take my call seriously then?"

"Even better. What you told me just sparked a crazy question."

"Which one, Sergeant?"

Another bit of hesitation time, before the cop finally answered.

"I'm beginning to wonder if this Simon Parker and Mumin Blasharov aren't the same person..."

CHAPTER 57
On a silver platter

VERSAILLES, Missouri, December 2023

When Sergeant Gallister hung up, he could feel it in his bones that today wouldn't be a piece of cake either. As if he already didn't have enough questions without answers, she'd handed him another batch. Unless, looking on the bright side, she had brought some solutions to his headache.

Driven by an intuition undoubtedly sparked by his long professional experience, he immediately called his team in for an impromptu briefing. Myra Stonehenge and Agent Bauer were both there. Just like their boss, their faces were drawn, and they looked morose, both hoping that this case would be solved before Christmas. Gallister told them about his phone call with Karen Blackstone and asked them what they thought. They all agreed on one thing: they had to use all the resources they had to try to put their finger on that guy named Blasharov... or Parker. One or the other. Or both? Maybe that would allow them to learn more about that silent little girl.

"We're going to go over the zone around Gravois Mills and the Chastain farm. I think that that's where we'll be finding a solution to this clusterfuck. Everything seems to be pointing in that direction. I'm going to contact the prosecutor and request a perquisition mandate for their entire property, both the buildings and fields that this couple of farmers has. And we're also going to scan Village of Four Seasons and the whole peninsula. I'll ask Jefferson City for their K9 units too. And Springfield too, if we need them. We need men, resources, and freedom to investigate. So guys, let's get to work. Here's the action plan, zone by zone."

Unfolding a map on the table in the conference room, that he had already gridded, Sergeant Gallister pointed at the places where the teams, each headed by one of his men, would investigate.

Two hours later, the squads were on site, holding the precious mandate signed by the county's prosecutor.

On foot, in cars or on motorbikes, the uniformed police officers searched every street in each village, inspected all public places and questioned the inhabitants, merchants and passersby.

Other teams targeted the agricultural zones, advancing on foot in the freezing fields, going to each farm, barn or hangar. They also inspected the banks of the rivers and streams, mostly frozen now, that wound through the sector.

Precious K9 dogs, their noses to the ground, tails wagging, sniffed, growled, squealed or barked depending on the interest their canine instinct found in the field.

The men complained, grumbled, or tried to be motivated for their bosses. Ensconced in their winter coats, gloves, with warm hats on their heads instead of their usual caps, they progressed, acre by acre, in an atmosphere that was extremely acrid.

Hours went by without any results, when suddenly, as the day was drawing to an end, when the glowing sun was setting in a clear and bluish sky, a Malinois began to bark feverishly in front of a dilapidated wooden shed located on the side of a path between two parcels of cultivable fields.

The animal was pulling on its leash, dragging its holder towards the building whose rubble stones and broken roof tiles proved its age and lack of upkeep. The dog sat down in front of the door and put its front paws against the blackened wood. The door, however, was locked, with a chain. Nonetheless, by pushing it a bit, they could see a few inches inside. That was sufficient for the team leader to make out, in the shadows, a silhouette that immediately worried him.

"Break the door down," he ordered.

Several blows on the door broke through the

worm-eaten planks and when the men rushed into the shack, they were petrified by what they'd found.

Their boss immediately took out his walkie-talkie that was on his belt, connected himself to the shared frequency, and contacted Gallister.

"Sarge, you gotta come right now, I think we found what you were looking for, at least part of it."

After having given him their position, he called the rescue squad, hoping it wasn't too late.

A quarter of an hour later, Gallister arrived, noting that his instinct hadn't let him down. An ambulance quickly arrived, its sirens on and the medics rushed in to take care of the victim. The sergeant questioned the group's officer.

"When you came in, was he like that?"

"We performed first aid on him," the officer said. "We couldn't leave him like that. The poor guy must have suffered like a martyr in conditions like that. Jesus Christ, I couldn't believe my eyes! His feet and wrists were tied, he was gagged and lying on the clay floor. Worse than a dog you wanted to get rid of. He must have really pissed someone off to be tortured like that. I have no idea what he could have done, but the person who did that to him was neither a nice person nor a sentimental one."

The sergeant thanked him and walked towards the body on the ground, surrounded by the medical team.

"Is he still alive?"

The head medic turned to Gallister, his voice broken.

"As much as someone who certainly spent several days in this freezing weather without anything to eat or drink can be. But he sure didn't decide to go on a hunger strike by himself. Thank God, there's still a breath of life in him, though it's minute. His body placed itself in a type of coma, or hibernation, so he wouldn't suffer. I'm calling the helicopter from the Jefferson Hospital ER ward. He has to be taken care of right away, you could even say at this very minute."

"Thanks, Doc."

Gallister rushed out of the shack, furious against himself for not having known that such a terrible thing had unfolded not far from where he was a couple of days ago. He'd needed a turning point, a Eureka moment, to understand.

And that turning point had been brought to him on a silver platter.

By a journalist specialized in local news whose name was Karen Blackstone...

CHAPTER 58
The pedigree of the natives

MONTAUK, December 2023

I SUDDENLY NEEDED to report to Melinda Vaughan about my progress in the double tragedy of her daughter and granddaughter. Would knowing that I'd contacted the authorities in Missouri make her feel saner?

On the other hand though, learning that her ex-son-in-law had been seen in the same midwestern state certainly would spark other feelings. Like a new spectral apparition.

Ghosts from the past, those that scare you, make you anxious, and question you.

When Melinda opened the door, I noticed her teary eyes right away. I probably should have warned her I'd be stopping over, but I wanted to take advantage of the effect of surprise. You never know. I've often noticed that tongues are much freer when things haven't been planned. That way people don't have the time to prepare their speeches behind closed doors and a handsome or politically correct facade.

"It's you?" Kathy's grandmother said, surprised. "I wasn't expecting you. Please come in, I don't want to heat up the outside."

Added to her glassy eyes, when she spoke, I could smell her alcohol-filled breath. I frowned while thanking her and closed the door behind me.

"Sorry I just showed up like this, but I've got some news that will interest you."

"Please sit down. Tea? Coffee? Something stronger maybe?"

It was show and tell time for her addiction, I guess.

"A coffee would be great."

Melinda went into the kitchen and came back with a tray with two cups and a plate with cookies that seemed to be store bought on it.

"Well?" she said, impatient, sitting down next to me.

"Maybe you were right, Melinda."

"My little Kathy's alive?"

"No, that's not what I meant. But you were right when you said that you thought there was something fishy about the death of Laura, your daughter, and your grand-daughter. And as proof of this, Simon Parker, your ex-son-in-law, has recently been located in Missouri."

"That piece of scum... What's he doing in Missouri?"

Melinda's hand was trembling so much she had to put her cup of coffee down.

"At this point in my investigation, I really don't know. But that coincidence is too enormous not to be logical. But what logic? This is what I wanted to talk to you about Melinda. In your opinion, what could Simon be doing in Missouri now? Did he have any ties with that state? Is he from the Midwest? Any family members around there? Does he work there? What can you tell me about him?"

Melinda closed her eyes, recollecting her souvenirs.

"I never knew much about Simon's past. And now that you mention it, I remember that the Parkers weren't from Long Island. You know, they didn't really *fit in* here, if you see what I mean. No class, nor the *pedigree* that the natives here have, the families who have roots here in the peninsula. They moved here with the wave of *nouveaux riches*, the ones you see all over nowadays. Those who made a bundle in finance, new technologies, stuff like that. Anyway, the Parkers and Vaughans aren't from the same world. And it was easy to realize that too. All you had to do was listen to the way they spoke. Plus, now that we're on this subject, it's true that Simon had an accent from the Midwest, a twang, a way of speaking that was... how should I put this? Like a peasant. Sentences that had culture, but not the one from books, rather from the fields. I still have no idea how Laura could have fallen in love with someone like him."

I internally thought to myself that she was criticizing a way of speaking that she was herself using over and over. Undoubtedly the effects of alcoholic beverages that uninhibited her, erasing the artificial layers she must have had before the tragedy took place. Unless she herself came from that "other world," she was criticizing so loudly, "promoted" to it by wedding her husband? Leopards don't change their spots, as they say! But I kept all those thoughts to myself.

"The heart has its reasons that reason ignores. So maybe the Parker family was from the Midwest?"

"I can't be affirmative. It's merely a presumption."

"But one that could explain the coincidence. I'll try to dig into it," I said, thinking of Spider. "I also wanted to tell you that I contacted the police in Missouri, those that you were afraid to contact when you saw the call for witnesses, thinking they'd say you must be crazy. And they started off by thinking I was the one who was crazy, but I think that my call will help them make progress, on both sides, here and there."

"I hope so from the bottom of my heart," Melinda sighed. "I thought of something else since we talked last time."

"Tell me," I replied, excited.

"Have you met my neighbors? The Nollington's and the Balmer's live on the other sides of me, and they also overlook the beach where Laura and Kathy were seen for the last time."

When she mentioned the Nollington family, Paul's face immediately popped up in my mind and I had butterflies in my stomach. And I brutally realized also that ever since we had kissed in his car, I hadn't heard from him. I had to admit though in his defense that I'd told him I needed more time. But still, not even a text message, nothing... *Stop*, I said to myself, *you're not a starry-eyed young girl anymore, Karen. There's work to be done.*

"I met Paul Nollington yes, but not the Mr. and Mrs. Balmer."

"Go see them, I know they're home today. I saw them from my bedroom window this morning. I'm sure they'll have something interesting to tell you."

CHAPTER 59
Those tiny things that make something

AS I WAS in the neighborhood, I decided to follow Melinda's idea and go a-knocking on the Balmer's door, a beautiful villa right next to the Vaughan's.

A smiling lady around sixty opened the door, her dyed blond hair carefully knotted up in a chignon.

"Yes?"

"Excuse me for bothering you, Mrs. Balmer, but your neighbor, Mrs. Vaughan, advised me to speak to you. My name is Karen Blackstone," I said, handing her my press card with my photo on it, "and I'm an investigative journalist working on cases of missing persons and right now I'm working on the deaths of Laura and Katheline."

Mrs. Balmer raised her hand to her mouth, stifling a sincere "Oh."

"Good Lord! What a tragedy! The whole neighborhood was impacted. Even all of Montauk. It was awful. But how can I be of any help to you? I'm afraid that..."

"Don't be afraid, most people think they don't have anything interesting to tell me. But often they've got a tiny detail, something insignificant in appearance but that turns out to be crucial and important. My job is interpreting those tiny things that make a much bigger something. May I?"

"Please do," she said, stepping back so I could come in. "Charles? We've got a visitor. Please excuse my mess," she said, confused. "We're getting ready for Christmas. Our grandchildren are arriving tomorrow."

Charles Balmer was an elegant and sophisticated man, whose white hair and wrinkled face gave away his age of seventy plus, though he actually wasn't bad at all. He held out his hand, inviting me into their living room that was quite like the Vaughan's, with a big picture window that overlooked the back of the house, the pool and yard, as well as the dunes, beach and ocean beyond it. Like a postcard. Though today the beach was covered in a thin layer of white snow.

"Mrs. Blackstone wanted to talk about the tragedy with us," said Mrs. Balmer to her husband, warning him.

"Oh! I see. Would you like something to drink?"

"No, thanks, I just had a cup of coffee with Mrs. Vaughan."

"Poor Melinda, ever since that cursed summer, she hasn't been the same. What could we tell you? We were powerless to do anything. Just simple neighbors. You know when something as horrible as that happens right next to you, everyone feels guilty."

"What do you mean, Mr. Balmer? Guilty?"

"Yes, guilty of not having seen that coming. It's crazy, realizing that you've lived next to someone for years and you still don't know them, isn't it? You think you know everything about them, but behind their walls, their hedges, their curtains, there were secrets, things unsaid, and false pretenses."

"Please, stop torturing yourself. If you hadn't seen anything coming, maybe you'd noticed little things, even subconsciously. For example, the day they went missing, on July 13, 2022, were you at home? Did you see Laura or Katheline? Did you see them on the beach? That's where they were at the end of the afternoon."

Charles and Lucy Balmer looked at each other for a long moment, neither of them wanting to break their silent reflections. Finally Charles decided to speak.

"How can we think of memories on a precise date? You have to understand. From here, we see the shoreline every day that God gives us. And each day it's about the same thing, sometimes with the same people, but often with others. Each day seems like the previous one and announces the following one. See what I mean? It's hard to distinguish them, isolate only one day. Of course, the 13th of July marked a milestone, yet before we were informed about what happened that day, that 13th of July wasn't at all different from any other day in summer. Meaning we hadn't planned anything, and because of that we couldn't be any more precise, more aware, more attentive, in our observations. Do you understand? It's not like we hear a sentence saying: 'Please be aware that something terrible will be happening today, keep your eyes open.' No, that 13th of July began like all the other days in summer, though it ended in horror. But still..."

"Yes?"

"But still," Charles Balmer continued, "we thought back upon that day, we talked about that day so much, that we think we might have conserved a few snippets of info that you may find useful. For what, I have no idea, you'll tell us Mrs. Blackstone."

"Karen, please just call me Karen. What can you tell me?"

The Vaughan's neighbor frowned, showing how little he wanted to recall this. I remained silent, having noted that often silence sparks secrets much more than verbal pressure. He finally decided to speak.

"Lucy and I are nearly sure that we saw Laura and Katheline on the beach that afternoon. But they weren't alone. I think they were with a couple of friends of their little girl, who must have been around Katheline's age. They'd get together each day. They'd put their towels down side by side and the three adults would shoot the breeze while keeping track of their little girls who would build sandcastles together. You could see them making round trips between the ocean and their little construction site, bringing water in their pails. Stuff like that happens every day on beaches in summer."

"But that day, nothing else happened compared to the previous days?"

"At first, no. But towards the end of the day, as soon as the couple and their little girl had left, someone else came up to Laura and Katheline. As if he had been waiting for the coast to clear. He wasn't wearing a swimsuit, and I remember that because it was unusual. Then they began talking and I think arguing. Their discussion seemed to be heated and there were some nearly aggressive gestures..."

Charles Balmer shook his head. I had the feeling he didn't want to tell me what came next. This time, I invited him to continue.

"So it was a man then?"

"Yes, but I'm not sure I should be telling you this, Karen. Because I feel like I'll be gossiping here. Acting like an informant... I don't want anyone to be hurt."

"Please. That could help me understand. And allow your neighbor to grieve. Poor Melinda who's in a living hell now because she doesn't understand why her daughter and granddaughter both died so tragically."

I suddenly remembered the conversation I'd had with Paul Nollington two days ago, and to help Charles Balmer continue, I interpreted the scene he was describing.

"I think I know who it was. Simon Parker, wasn't it?"

Mr. and Mrs. Balmer's eyes both opened wide. Charles answered instantly.

"No! Not at all, Karen. We know Simon Parker, Laura's husband, and I can assure you it wasn't him that day on the beach. Not at all. And that's why I don't want to talk about it, because I don't want to cause any harm to that person who Laura seemed to be arguing with."

"Who was it?"

"Well, without any possible error, because we also know him very well, I can assure you that it was our young neighbor, Paul Nollington."

CHAPTER 60
Do you believe in ghosts?

PEOPLE ARE LYING to me in this story.

No doubt about it.

The same scene, related by different people, but with opposing versions.

One or the other of the narrators must be making a mistake.

But which one?

I left the Balmer's with an aftertaste of deception in my throat. Believe them or believe Paul? I needed to talk to Paul and called him. His phone rang six times before going to voicemail.

"Paul? This is Karen. I hope you're doing well. Could you call me back asap, I've got an important question to ask. Thanks. And I would like to see you again," I added, after a bit of hesitation.

In my car, I drove past Nollington's lot. I didn't want to disturb them and hoped that Paul would contact me quickly.

In the meantime, as I was waiting for some news from Seargeant Gallister, I went back to the hotel to write my article. Myrtille had sent me another message asking me to send it to her as quickly as possible. The January edition was nearly ready to print, and she wanted my article for ... the day before yesterday, as she put it. But I certainly had nothing against heading to my comfortable room in the Montauk Manor.

I sat down on my freshly made bed and put my laptop on my legs.

Ready to rumble. How would I attack this case? What angle should I take to narrate a story to my readers, so they'd have goosebumps on their arms? As story that would haunt their dreams, and one that could happen to them, happen to anyone... Yes, that was the way I'd grab them by their throats, prevent them from breathing, make them read my article in apnea. They'd soon close their January edition of *True Crime Mysteries* by saying: "Please Lord, don't let me be a victim of such an atrocity."

I opened a Word doc and began to write.

```
"I WANT MOMMY."
    Dear Readers, just imagine this.
Close your eyes and visualize it.
We're in the heart of the Midwest,
more precisely in Missouri. We're at
the end of December and this year, it
```

has begun to snow much earlier than usual. The roads are white and icy. It's unseasonably cold. You're driving, very slowly, because you don't have winter tires on your car, on a long and deserted straight road. Alone at the wheel. It's dark outside. Your car's windshield wipers can't completely wipe away the large snowflakes, like pure white rabbit tails, which are falling on your window.

Suddenly, in the pallid light of your headlights, your eyes are attracted by something. Right at the very last moment, you turn your steering wheel, you nearly hit... a little shape on the side of the road.

A child.

Alone.

Your car ends up in the ditch. You get out, groggy, and walk up to the little girl.

All she's wearing on her feet are slippers and she doesn't even have a coat.

She's silent.

Except for these three words she keeps repeating: "I want mommy."

I WANT MOMMY

Was she abandoned? Lost? An orphan?

The one thing that's sure is that she's freezing. Her hands and her feet are severely frostbitten. Poor kid!

These are the questions the policemen from Morgan County, in charge of the investigation, are asking.

Especially as no one has shown up to claim her.

A child from nowhere? No one's child?

They've broadcast a call for witnesses throughout the country. Tons of calls are coming on, each crazier than the other. Psychopaths, kidnappers, parents who can't have children... The authorities are bogged down in wrong tracks.

End of chapter one.

Now my dear Readers, just imagine this.

You're a lady about sixty years old. You live alone, in a huge house on the seaside, in Montauk, Long Island. Your husband passed away a few years ago and then you tragically mourned your daughter, who committed suicide, this time successfully. This time it worked!

Your daughter, who in her fatal gesture, also took her eighteen-month-old daughter to the bottom of a pond with her.

A double tragedy and your heart of a grandmother can't endure. You sink into alcohol and depression. Insanity perhaps?

Yes, insanity.

Because, my dear Readers, just imagine that you were that woman, that you had to go to the morgue to identify your daughter and your grandchild, that you had them buried in Amagansett Cemetery, Long Island, and that you could never forget this.

So wouldn't you also go crazy when you saw the Missouri police's call for witnesses, and on the photo of the little girl on the roadside who never stopped saying "I want Mommy," you thought you recognized your deceased granddaughter?

Yes, it is crazy. That's all it could be, don't you agree?

End of chapter two.

· · ·

I WANT MOMMY

A QUESTION, my dear Readers, do you believe in ghosts?

Do you believe in reincarnation? In the transmission of souls?

In the resurrection of Christ, of Lazarus?

Could this child in Missouri be the little girl who had drowned in Long Island, who had scratched the freshly hewn wood of her coffin with her nails, dug out of Amagansett Cemetery and then who had been teleported with the slippers she was wearing on the day she was buried to the snow in Gravois Mills?

THAT'S RIGHT, my dear Readers, you have no other choice than to believe in ghosts, as, for the moment, this is the only explanation I can give you.

Ghosts don't speak, do they?

Or if they do, just two or three words.

Such as "I want mommy."

DON'T MISS the next edition of *True Crime Mysteries*, my investigation is on-going...

. . .

Karen Blackstone, at your service.

∽

All that was left for me to do was to send the article off to Myrtille, who I was sure would be satisfied with my work. A tidbit of suspense, a myriad of unsettling questions, a pinch of supernatural. And an approach that goes straight to the readers' heads. She'd be eating it up, my little chickadee!

My phone was on the bed next to me. I picked it up, unlocked it and discovered sadly that Paul hadn't tried to call me back. Tough luck, I decided to call him even though that might give him false hope. I needed to clarify what the Balmer's told me about him. This time my call went directly to his voice-mail without even ringing. I didn't leave a message; he'd see that I'd tried to reach him several times.

As time went by without any news from him, I started to get worried. Had our budding relationship ended up scaring him off? Did he want to put more distance between us? Had he realized that I was much too old for him? Whatever. I left the hotel, jumped into my car and drove straight to Surfside Avenue, stopping in front of the Nollington's house.

I rang the bell, and a man opened the door. He must have been Paul's father, judging by his white hair.

He walked up to the gate, where I was standing, my hands crossed over my chest because of the cold.

I quickly introduced myself and asked him if Paul was at home or if he knew where he was. I explained that I'd been trying to contact him since the day before.

Steven Nollington, as that was his name, answered.

"Paul didn't tell you? He had to rush back to New York for his job. He unfortunately won't be able to celebrate Christmas with us, we're really sad. We were looking forward to it."

Me too, I was looking forward to it.

Maybe too much.

Am I suffering from a life sentence to relive deceiving adventures with men? That's what I thought as I drove back to Montauk Manor.

Plus wondering why Paul hadn't gotten in touch with me.

I could understand that our story was still in its infancy, quite recent, that he didn't owe me anything, but still, I would have liked to have been warned that he was leaving for New York. Especially if he was planning on staying there for several days.

I was enraged and asked myself a thousand questions about him.

Firstly, he'd lied to me about what happened on July 13th on the beach. Was that the only lie he'd told me?

Then he left Montauk and didn't even tell me.
Paul, what are you dissimulating? I wondered.
Why were you lying?
What are you running from?

CHAPTER 61
The melody of death

JEFFERSON CITY, Missouri, December 2023

While walking down the halls in Saint Mary's Hospital once again, Sergeant Gallister thought that it might be a good idea to book a room there, so he'd be able to continue his investigation more easily. That was the place where all the tips and clues seemed to merge.

First of all, the little girl, – let's call her Jessy – who was in the pediatric ward.

Then Carrie Chastain, her presumed mother – according to her anyway – who was now in the behavioral psychiatry unit.

And since a couple of hours ago, that man in a coma, found in a sordid shack, tied up, gagged, half frozen and nearly dead from hunger and thirst.

Accompanied by his deputy, Myra Stonehenge, Pete was going to the ICU where the patient had been admitted. Before they were allowed in, they had to put a paper mask, lab coat, hair cover and shoe covers on.

The sounds and smells of the ward were typical of intensive care facilities. A veil of silence seemed to have been thrown above the halls though through the large windows looking into the patients' rooms, you could still hear the sharp beeping of the monitoring devices. Pete strangely associated that electronic music with the melody of death. Or why not life? Or even better than that, with those between life and death, that no man's land where people in comas were floating, those who couldn't decide whether to remain in their carnal body or leave this lowly world and fly to ethereal heavens.

Pete remarked the odor of ether in his nostrils, even through his mask, when a nurse led him to the patient he'd asked to see.

"We're still not sure he's going to make it," she warned them. "I think he was pretty near the tipping point. The doctors give him less than a ten percent chance to recover his motor and cognitive functions should he wake up. They put him in an artificial coma so they could better monitor his vital signs – by that I mean his heart and lung functions."

"Thank you, Ma'am," said the sergeant while the nurse walked out leaving him alone with the man in his hospital bed.

Pete looked at his deputy.

"Christ, if we'd found him the day before or I don't know, even a couple of hours earlier, we could have saved him."

"He's not dead yet," replied Myra. "He could bounce back."

"Sure hope so, I'm sure that he'd have loads of stuff to tell us. He must know what the heck is going on. You know what, Myra? I've got the feeling that our investigation is hanging by a thread. And this guy is walking on it, like a tightrope walker. He's right there, between life and death, his arms spread on either side to avoid falling into emptiness and cross the deep ravine separating him from death. On the other side of the canyon, maybe he'll be able to give us the solution. But from one second to another, he could become unhooked and fall into a bottomless crater. An endless one."

"I understand what you're feeling here, Pete. I've got the same impression of trying to navigate without falling too."

"What happened to you, buddy?" asked Pete to the man in the coma. "Who did that to you? Huh? No answer?"

"Pete, stop. You're just hurting yourself."

The sergeant kept on staring at the hollowed-out face of the sleeping man with his closed eyes. His brown hair tussled. His square jaw. Under the sheets, he could tell that he was a big guy. No doubt about it, this was the man they'd been looking for.

And while he was at it, he'd have to mention this to the raving lunatic in the psychiatric ward. She'd certainly have something to say about it as she always seemed to have an opinion about everything. Though her opinions varied from one version to another.

"Okay, let's get a move on," said Gallister, turning around.

Before leaving the hospital room, he bent down to have a look at the notebook hanging on the side of the bed, with the patient's file in it. He picked it up, shook his head, and began reading it.

"Mumin Blasharov. Weight: 210 lbs. Height: 6 feet 2 inches. Estimated age: 55. Blood type: A+.

CHAPTER 62
The innermost reaches of the brain

AFTER HAVING TOSSED their paper accessories into the appropriate bin, Pete and Myra remained silent for a few moments in the stark halls of the hospital.

"Mumin Blasharov," Sergeant Gallister then repeated. "We were looking for him all over after having fished the Dodge out from the bottom of the lake and here he was, rotting like a flea-filled dog in a shack in the middle of nowhere. And now we can't get a word out of him."

"Maybe he'll come out of his coma," his deputy said, trying to calm him. "Even though the doctors aren't too optimistic, there's still a glimmer of hope."

"A tiny one. Terribly small."

Right then Agent Bauer called him.

"Sergeant, I've got the answer to the question we were asking ourselves this morning."

"Which one? There were so many of them. A fucking bushel basket full."

"The Gravois Mills Town Hall got back to me. Their land service department confirmed that the building where you found that guy is located on a parcel of agricultural land belonging to the Chastain's."

"Okay. I'm not gonna say I told you so, but I'm not surprised. That seems logical following everything that happened in the past few days. Everything leads to the Chastain farm."

He thanked him and hung up.

"Everything leads to…" Myra repeated.

"Totally. Now I know what I have to do. Even though I don't want to have another futile discussion with Carrie Chastain's sick brain, I don't think I have a choice here. We have to tell her we found her husband more dead than alive. Ah! She had no idea where he'd disappeared, huh? Ah! No, she didn't know a thing… What a pain in the ass!"

As they were already in Saint Mary's Hospital, they just changed floors to reach the Chastain lady. Gallister asked to see Doctor Faulkner. As he wasn't there, they had to wait another half an hour before he came and gave his authorization to question his patient. He warned them though.

"Sergeant, I don't know how much you'll get from here, we had to give her sedation. She was so terribly agitated, even aggressive, that we had to inject a good dose of tranquilizers. But go ahead, do your job, you'll see if she tells you anything. I personally haven't heard a word from her since last night. Total silence."

Total silence. Of course, Gallister associated that expression with the little girl. Jessy Chastain.

Faulkner walked them up to the door with a digital recognition system leading to the secure ward where the most serious cases were located. Then to Carrie Chastain's room, where he also had to key in a six-digit code. Gallister wondered if this wasn't a bit too much for Carrie, but when he thought back on the interviews he'd had with her, he decided to trust the specialists of the innermost reaches of the brain.

When they entered the dimly lit room, Carrie was sitting in an armchair with high arm rests. Sitting up straight, her head looking at them, the woman's eyes were open, but her regard seemed strangely empty, as if her brain was on strike.

Gallister pulled up the chair below a table and sat down across from her. Myra sat down too on the edge of the bed. Doctor Faulkner remained standing behind the policeman.

"Mrs. Chastain?" he asked, leaning towards her face.

She remained immobile like a wax statue, not even blinking.

"Carrie, can you hear me?" he tried again.

No reaction. The cop turned towards the psychiatrist, raising his eyebrows to mimic a question. The doctor shrugged. He'd already warned them not to expect too much from a patient who'd had a dose of tranquilizers like that.

Gallister sighed, turned again towards the woman, silent and immobile, sitting in the armchair. He put his hand in his pocket and took out his phone, his thumb moving quickly on it. Then he turned the screen to Carrie.

"Carrie, this is where you your lies led us. What can you tell me about this? What? You recognize this man, don't you?"

Carrie's eyelids blinked. Once.

"I'd like to know if you can explain how we found him: gagged, tied up, freezing and starving. Nearly dead."

She blinked again, twice. But didn't say a word.

"We're making progress here," said Gallister, ironically. "That's right, nearly dead, Mrs. Chastain. Between life and death and I can assure you that he's much closer to the second than the first. This man, you can't say you don't know him, can you? Even though his face is emaciated, his body exhausted, this man is Mumin Blasharov!"

Carrie made a muffled growing noise. Her eyes squinted slightly.

"Mumin Blasharov, your husband! And you know where we found him? In a nice little shed in the middle of a cornfield. Pretty romantic, isn't it? No comment? Look at the next picture. Do you recognize the shed?"

A new grumble, almost like an animal, accompanied by an asymmetrical twist of her mouth, only on one side. Was her shell beginning to crack?

"Of course you recognize it because it's on your farm. On the edge of your fields. Not far from your farm in Gravois Mills. Are you going to continue to affirm that you had no idea your husband was rotting away in there? I don't think so, Mrs. Chastain. I don't think so. You knew. Because you're the one who put him there, didn't you? Who else otherwise? Carrie, it's time to tell the truth now. You've been pulling our legs up to now and I'm even starting to wonder if you haven't been faking everything since the beginning. Including right now. It's easy to blame everything on pills..."

This time it wasn't a groan or growl coming from her throat, but a hearty laugh from her mouth. A lunatic's laugh. Then Carrie spoke, with a deep, raspy voice.

"That piece of shit got what he deserved! He shouldn't have run off with my Jessy!"

CHAPTER 63
Not so far from the truth

TURNING his head like a wooden puppet, Gallister glared at Doctor Faulkner.

"Numbed by sedatives, that's what you said, Doc?"

He frowned, dumbfounded, but understood when Carrie's sardonic laughter stopped, and she put her hand into the pocket of her hospital gown. She took a handful of pills out of it.

"All I had to do was keep these little suckers in a corner of my cheek while I was having a swallow of water, easy peasy. Nobody saw nothing. I don't like it when people impose chemical shit on me, got it? Only natural stuff for me. Okay, Sergeant, let's be serious now! Can you ask the doc to leave?"

Gallister nodded, looking at the psychiatrist. After a moment of hesitation, he left.

The policeman sat back down in his chair, wondering what the farmer lady would tell him this time.

"You were pretty close to the truth the other day, Sarge. Really warm when you said that I was just blabbing... It's true, sometimes I think I'm losing my marbles, but most of the time, I pretty much know what I'm doing."

"So maybe then, if that's not asking too much, you'll tell us what really happened this time?"

"Why not? But on one condition, Sergeant."

"Which is?"

"That you promise me you'll give me my Jessy back if I tell you everything."

"Mrs. Chastain, that's something I can't promise you, and you know it. I don't have the right to do that. My work consists of having people respect law and order. If you're found guilty of misdemeanors or crimes, I can't magically make them go away. And holding back key information from justice is already a crime... So, start talking and after that I'll see what I can do. Okay?"

Carrie sighed noisily.

"Looks like I don't got too much of a choice."

"Not anymore. You made lots of choices. Not always the right ones, if you look at where you are today. Tell me everything."

"Whadda you want to know?"

"For instance, what happened on the day when we found Jessy on the roadside? How she got there, only wearing slippers in all that snow."

Carrie sat up in her armchair and closed her eyes.

"That was the day when that bastard Mumin

decided to take her from me. Maybe he thought I'd let him? He sure don't know me."

~

A FEW DAYS earlier on the Chastain family farm

THE SNOW HAD STARTED to fall that afternoon, quite early for the season and much harder than it usually did in the Midwest. Mumin, who had been finetuning his escape plan for a couple of weeks, thought that those were ideal conditions. If he took the Dodge, he'd be able to put a lot of distance between Carrie and them, as she'd have problems with the car, as it wasn't really equipped for winter driving.

His wife had just put on her thick coat to go outside. Now was the time, just like every day, when she gathered the eggs in the chicken coop. She'd let everyone know that she wanted to make a lard omelet for supper tonight. So she went out, putting her hood up as soon as she'd left and disappeared into the courtyard, walking toward the chicken coop.

Mumin immediately got going in the house. He knew he didn't have a lot of wiggle room if he wanted to succeed. Carrie didn't usually take a long time to collect the eggs, just enough time to swear two or three times to the hens because they didn't lay enough eggs, they were clucking too loud or shitting on the eggshells. Sometimes, from the house, you could even see how panicked they were when she kicked them to make them get out of the way. She always had a very good reason to take out her frustration and bad temper out on those feathered little animals. Anyway, it was better than beating her daughter, wasn't it? That was something Mumin couldn't stand. He was sick and tired of his shrew of a wife's viciousness. She'd forced him to do terrible things. How could he have followed her in her insanity? And how could he even have fallen in love with such a woman? He'd been asking himself the same question for years now. As the years went by, she must have changed. She undoubtedly wasn't as crazy as that when they'd first met.

Mumin had opened the padlocked door and rushed downstairs. Jessy was still sleeping. As the room didn't have any windows, the child could no longer distinguish night from day. She often lost the notion of time and slept or dozed off. Her fragile little body was all curled up on the mattress and Mumin picked her up, lifting her like a tiny bale of hay in his muscular arms. He also took the woolen cover with him. That should be enough, he didn't have time to get her dressed. He saw that she was still wearing her purple slippers with the pompoms on them and smiled tenderly. She was holding her little stuffed lion in her arms, the one that never left her.

Quick, up the stairs, through the hall and kitchen, out the front door, ready to run across the yard to the Dodge that he'd parked facing the path leading to the road. When he opened the back door, Mumin heard a new slew of swear words coming from the chicken coop as well as the noise the panicked hens were making. Then the characteristic noise of the wooden gate that was closing, the one that Carrie always slammed when she was leaving.

He quickly put the half-asleep little girl down on the back seat of the pickup truck. He got in and turned the key. The motor coughed once or twice and started. This time he wouldn't be able to sneak out without Carrie seeing him. He put it into first gear and stepped on it, making the tires squeal on the dusting of snow that covered the clay driveway.

He didn't want to turn his head but couldn't help but glancing out of the rear-view mirror. And he saw his wife, her arms dangling, the basket of eggs in her left hand and a chicken in her right, that she was holding by its legs. She'd slit the throat of the animal and blood was dropping out on the immaculate white snow. When she understood what was happening after having glimpsed her daughter's curly hair from the back window, Carrie opened her mouth, stupefied, and dropped everything. The dead animal dropped to the snow and the basket tipped over, its eggs rolling around on the ground just like oval tennis balls.

"You bastard!" screamed the hysterical woman, running up to the Dodge, her work shoes slipping on the fresh snow, her fist raised in anger. "My daughter!"

∼

Mumin accelerated, nearly losing control of the vehicle that had begun to skid. In the rear-view mirror he saw Carrie slip on the fresh snow, falling down, gesticulating in their direction. He could well imagine what she was yelling. The man regretted that he'd not taken the keys of their car to prevent his wife from following them. He hadn't sufficiently worked on his escape plan. He was reacting more by instinct than by using his brain. Otherwise he would have filled the Dodge up before fleeing.

At the end of their driveway, right before the road, Mumin glanced one last time behind him. He could see Carrie's silhouette lurching towards the kitchen.

~

"See Sergeant what a bastard that Mumin is! A kidnapper! Stealing my own daughter behind my back! Something like that, he'll go to jail for, won't he? Kidnapping of a child from her marital home, something like that, doncha think? Me, the only thing I did wrong was to try to get her back. I'm as white as snow, huh?"

Carrie began to laugh loudly, proud of her pun. She was sure of herself and believed she had the right to do what she did.

"You still have to prove your innocence, Mrs. Chastain," replied Gallister. "Please continue."

"But I told you, I'm innocent! Mumin's the guilty one! He's the one you gotta arrest, not me. All you gotta do is let me and my daughter go and close the case. I'll take her back home, and we'll do fine without that son of a bitch, believe me."

"Did you follow them with your car that day?"

"Ha! Ha! Let me tell you, that was quite the race, Sergeant. Lots of fun... I must say that I was lucky though to catch up with them because I couldn't find my keys and it took me a while to start the car. So I was lagging behind. But I was able to track them because of the snow. Listen up."

CHAPTER 64
A normal family

GRAVOIS MILLS, a few days earlier

Carrie Chastain, though she was several minutes and a few miles behind them, had no intention of allowing her husband and their daughter to escape. No need to go downstairs to her special room to know that Jessy was no longer there.

Mumin had been strange, not as usual, for the past couple of days. He'd hinted several times that he wanted their little girl to come upstairs, to go outside and play, to see other people. But she'd always refused, saying that they couldn't do that, that it was still too early, that she wasn't quite ready yet. Mumin had replied that for months now all danger was behind them. That they could live like a normal family now. Each time they had a discussion like this, Carrie categorically vetoed the idea, swearing and threatening her husband who she said was too weak, too sentimental, too naive! Who was it that wore the pants in that home, she always asked him, knowing that it was her, not him.

Yet this time, he'd dared take the lead, show his determination, cross the Rubicon. No longer with words, but with actions. He'd taken her.

When Carrie left the farm, she was able to follow the tracks from the pickup in the snow. They'd headed to Gravois Mills, taking the main road. She drove through the little town slowly, peering at the intersections and parking lots, when suddenly she saw the Dodge leaving the Happy Jack gas station.

"He ain't got no smarts," Carrie sneered. "You wanna beat it and you forget to fill the truck up… What an amateur!"

She sped up to catch up with them. The tires of her car were having trouble finding purchase on the fresh snow, the back was weaving, the front was struggling, but Carrie couldn't have cared less, she wasn't scared. Never! She made out the back lights of the Dodge intermittently, through the waltz of the windshield wipers and heavy snowflakes. Mumin, not as brave as her despite the more reliable tires on the pickup truck, was going slowly, probably afraid of sliding off into a ditch with his daughter, something that would have axed his projects of evasion.

"What a limp dick," Carrie swore between her clenched teeth. "You're too afraid to leave like that. Just wait till I catch you."

She stepped on the gas, nearly flooring it, turning the steering wheel right and left.

She was catching up with the fugitives. Now they were driving down the road from Gravois Mills to Sunrise Beach, heading south. It was getting dark and with all the trees along Route 5, Mumin had to turn his headlights on. The weather had taken a turn for the worse and they were the only people out that night. Not weather fit for man nor beast.

"Even less so for a little kid," complained Carrie, holding firmly onto the steering wheel.

Paying no attention to her car skidding right and left, she was nearing Mumin. Suddenly little Jessy's head popped up when she sat up in the back seat. Then she turned and she could see her face in the yellowish halo of the headlights. Carrie flashed her brights several times, as if telling her daughter she was there, she'd deliver her from her stupid father's hands. Soon there was only about three hundred feet separating the two vehicles and she was gaining on them.

The Dodge suddenly braked and swerved to the left, taking a path in the forest.

"What the hell is he doing now? That path don't go nowhere. Except to the lake."

Carrie's car skidded, but she controlled it, when she also turned in the same direction, determined not to let the pickup get away from her. There, in the middle of the forest, the path had less snow on it, but was also less suitable, as it was full of potholes and ruts.

They continued until there were only about a

dozen feet between the two vehicles. Now she could see Jessy's little face clearly in her headlights. The little girl put one of her hands on the back window. Carrie didn't know what she meant by this, was it "Hi Mommy, I recognized you," or "Mommy, come get me, I'm scared," or on the contrary, a sign meaning "Stop! Leave Daddy and me alone. We don't want you anymore..."

To her surprise, Carrie felt tears welling up in her eyes. She wiped them away with the back of her hand and accelerated a bit more.

Suddenly, right in front of her, an atrocious spectacle shocked her. She watched it unfold, as if it had been filmed in slowmo.

She saw the back wheels jump out of a big rut, then slowly, the Dodge started to tip to the driver's side while the right part began to rise. Carrie saw her daughter's frightened face. Her eyes wide open with fear, her mouth twisted in incomprehension, and a scream that she couldn't hear from her own car coming from her throat.

A few seconds later, the Dodge recovered its four-wheel drive but this time, its nose gear began to spin at the edge of the ruts, and it started to turn, like a wooden top. Carrie had to slow down so she wouldn't run into the now incontrollable vehicle and stopped while it continued its infernal spirals. The farmer saw Jessy's frightened eyes, then Mumin's frantic face. Jessy, Mumin, Jessy, Mumin.

Then there was a brutal shock when the pickup hit

the trunk of an oak tree that must have been there for decades, perhaps even centuries. Carrie heard the deafening noise of the truck's sheeting against the bark and saw it buckle and warp on the entire right side.

"Jesus Christ!" she shouted. "If you killed my little girl, you bastard, I'll finish you off right now!"

She rattled the door handle a couple of seconds before opening it, without forgetting her late father's shotgun, the one that usually was placed on the fireplace mantle in the kitchen, and that she'd taken when she found the car keys. In one of her pockets, she took the only two cartridges that she'd found.

She got out of the car and walked towards them, her arm aimed at the Dodge hugging the tree. While walking, she opened the shotgun to put the two cartridges in and closed it with a metallic clicking sound that echoed in the muffled silence of the forest. She walked up carefully, keeping an eye on the driver's door to see any movement. For her vast satisfaction, nothing happened and when she was able to see inside the vehicle, she saw Mumin lying against the steering wheel, his face stuck on the horn, a stream of blood coming from one of his ears.

"You out for the count, you son of a bitch?"

Just as carefully, she put a hand on the handle of the back door.

"My little baby," she whispered, discovering Jessy, unconscious, on the back seat. "My sweetie!"

At first, she thought she was dead. If that was the case, she knew what she had to do. Two cartridges in the shotgun. One for Mumin, the second one for herself. She didn't want to survive if her treasure was no longer with her.

But she saw a tiny movement. Jessy was trying to sit up, wincing and crying.

"You're alive! Come on, honey, we're going home. It's cold and it's dark outside. You shouldn't be outside in the forest."

Carrie held her hand out to her daughter to help her get up, but the little girl just looked at her, frightened.

"No!" she said, shaking her brown curly hair. No!"

"Come on, you're not the one giving orders here. We're going home."

The mother took her child's arm and yanked her out of the car to take her to hers, parked about thirty feet in back. The little girl was clutching her stuffed animal with the other. You could hear their footsteps on the thin layer of snow and the soles of their shoes were full of fallen leaves. They got to the door of Carrie's car.

"Let her go immediately, you crazy old bag!"

Carrie turned around, still holding her daughter's hand with her left hand and the shotgun with her right one.

Mumin, his face covered with blood, was walking fearlessly towards them.

"All this is over now," he said to her. "You understand me? Let her go right now and let me take her away. This is something I should have done much earlier, I was a coward, I admit it. But it's not too late. I have to take her away. She doesn't have a life here with you polluting the atmosphere."

"Shut your fucking face up Mumin!" shouted Carrie, pointing the gun at him. "Back up. Let me go."

"No way."

The gun went off. The detonation echoed through the forest before being snuffed out by the snow.

Mumin collapsed with a throaty shout, almost like a buck that hunters had cornered.

CHAPTER 65
Going sour

IN THE ROOM in the psychiatric ward of Saint Mary's Hospital, Sergeant Gallister was listening intently to Carrie Chastain's tale, now that she seemed to be wanting to spill the beans. Could the policeman however believe this version, knowing the woman's propensity to distort the facts and exaggerate? He nonetheless thought he heard notes of sincerity in her voice this time, something he hadn't felt during their previous confrontations. She'd been faking before, but now she seemed to be wanting to get everything off her chest.

Of course, as soon as possible Gallister would have to check her declarations with tangible elements, ballistic analyses and other tests, such as the wound that he remembered having seen on Mumin when he found him in the abandoned shed. He did however have her repeat.

"So, you are the one who shot Mumin Blasharov? You shot your own husband?"

"That's what I said," she replied, as if boasting about it. "Didn't have no choice, he wanted my kid."

The officer nodded.

"But the *kid*, as you said, he didn't end up with her finally, did he? Neither did you. So, after you shot him, then what happened?"

"You cops, you wanna know everything, don't you?" Carrie said with a smirk. "But I'm in a good mood today, I'll tell you what happened next. After that I socked him one in the face and he collapsed…"

∽

Gravois Mills Forest, a few days earlier

THE SITUATION brutally had gone sour in the Chastain family. The echo of the detonation was weaker and weaker in the ears of the little girl, who, stupefied, opened her eyes to see her mother shooting her father with a shotgun. She began to scream.

"Shut up, will ya?" shouted Carrie, shaking her. "And get in here right now."

Instead of obeying Carrie, the child tried to free herself from the powerful grip of the hand on her arm. She struggled as much as she could, trying to kick her mother in her tibias. Her little legs though were too short, shorter than the arms of the lady holding her back and who finally pushed her into the back seat.

Right then Carrie loosened her grip and that was when Jessy turned her head and bit her hand.

She didn't have a huge jaw of course, but she did have those pointed little baby teeth that entered deeply into her flesh. Carrie shouted sharply and let her go.

As fast as lightning while she was shaking her bloody and painful hand, the little girl slipped under her arm and ran away as fast as she could.

"Come back here right now!"

Carrie started running after her. The little girl was running as fast as her tiny legs would carry her but wasn't much of a challenge for her more powerful though much heavier mother. She was only forty or fifty feet ahead.

Jessy had no idea where she was nor where she was going. She simply followed her instinct, running straight ahead, trying to avoid traps like ruts, potholes, roots and branches. The light slippers on her feet didn't help her in her absurd attempt to escape. Her mother was shouting out behind her, now nearly out of breath.

"You idiot, you're gonna get lost! It's getting dark out, it's freezing! Think of all the wild animals in the forest: Wolves, Jessy, you'll be eaten alive by wolves if you're alone! Come back!"

But the little girl, used to a harsh environment during her short but intense life as a child, still preferred wolves to Carrie...

She accelerated as much as she could, increasing the distance between them, without however dropping her little stuffed lion.

Right then, her mother's exhaustion, as she wasn't used to any physical exercise, was what saved her.

CARRIE CHASTAIN, completely out of breath, had to stop, incapable of going even two more steps. She slowly saw her daughter, her only treasure, her sweetie, her princess, disappear. Into the forest. Escaping from her. She had to decide before it was too late. She closed her eyes for a fleeting moment, took a deep breath, then opened them again and raised her late father's shotgun.

Visibility was nearly zero at that time of day, and it was dark under the foliage. Jessy's tiny silhouette was shrinking quickly.

Carrie pointed her double-barreled shotgun towards the moving target of her daughter and the little stuffed animal she was holding.

A second detonation broke through the silence of the forest.

A sharp scream echoed.

CHAPTER 66
Dead or alive

INCREDULOUS, horrified, Gallister listened to Chastain's tale.

"You actually shot at your daughter…"

That wasn't a question, he could see the truth in Carrie's dark eyes.

"Yeah, I shot at her 'cuz she was running away. I was gonna lose her!"

"Had you killed her, you would also have lost her!"

"It wouldn't have been the same, Sergeant. I didn't want anyone else to have her. Other parents, see what I mean?"

"No I don't! And I'll never understand that anyone could try to kill a child, for whatever reason. If there's a crime that's more serious than any others, it's infanticide, Mrs. Chastain. And you were just this far from being guilty," he added, showing a tiny distance between his thumb and index finger. "Luckily you missed."

Carrie Chastain shrugged her shoulders.

"Yeah, it was too dark, and she was too far. Otherwise I would have got her. I don't wanna boast, but I've often shot chickens at thirty feet, just for practice. So, one more, one less..."

"You're despicable," Myra Stonehenge who had been completely disgusted when listening to the tale of that lunatic said, her instinct as a woman having forced her to speak. "You're horrible! You make me sick!"

"So, she got away," continued Gallister, so she'd continue. "What did you do then?"

"At first, I tried to follow her footprints, but the snow in the woods wasn't thick enough for that. So I went back to my car, thinking that maybe I'd find her using my headlights, when I turned around. But when I got back to my car, the other bastard was still moving.

∾

Gravois Mills Forest, a few days earlier

Mumin heard another gunshot when he regained consciousness, after he'd collapsed, shot in the shoulder. An inch or so lower and the bullet would have gone through his subclavian artery, meaning he wouldn't have been around to hear the second detonation.

That one was even worse than the first one, as it

meant that she'd tried to shoot their daughter. That made him furious.

He tried to get back up, avoiding putting any pressure on his injured shoulder. A wave of searing pain ripped through him, making him clench his teeth and cry out when he tried to stand up. The Dodge was just fifteen feet from him, as was the second car. She hadn't left. She was still in the woods. Come on, you can do this! Jump in behind the steering wheel of the pickup. Thank the Lord for automatic transmission. He had to find Jessy. Dead or alive, he didn't want to leave her in the woods.

Just as he managed to get up, a voice behind his back froze him.

"You're as tough as nails, aren't ya!"

His adorably sweet wife was back.

"I'm bleeding," Mumin moaned.

"Let me laugh. I couldn't care less! Now you did it! Everything that happened, well it's all your fault! You tried to outwit me. You wanted to kill me by taking me kid from me. So what happened? She ran away and I couldn't catch up with her. The Dodge hit a tree, and I don't know if we'll be able to get it out. And you, you big asshole! You're bleeding out like a stuck pig... You ain't gonna be here much longer! You won't suffer for a long time. Less than me, as long as we're talking about that. Can you imagine my life now? My life without my daughter? How much I'll suffer as of today?"

"Carrie, take me to the ER. Please."

"Tsk, tsk, tsk. You make me laugh. I've got other projects for you. You're lucky that my two cartridges didn't do their job. The first one didn't kill you and the second one ended up in a tree trunk. If not, you can believe me, I would have loved to shorten your fucking life. But all's well that ends well as they say, and I'm glad you're suffering. Glad you got time to brood about the situation you got us in. So I'm gonna keep you alive for a while, just for fun…"

"Carrie, you really are a raving lunatic. I never should have agreed to everything you wanted. I should have told the cops everything when I still had time. Now, things have gone too far!"

"Just zip it!"

Her eyes reddened by hatred and bitterness, Carrie Chastain turned the shotgun in her hands, gripping it by its double barrel and raised it over Mumin's head.

In a well-adjusted circular movement, she brought it down with all her strength on her husband's head.

CHAPTER 67
Thinking and acting quickly

"TALK ABOUT TOUGH LOVE," Sergeant Gallister said ironically. "Smashing in your husband's head with a rifle butt... Congrats! The epitome of a delicate lady, Mrs. Chastain. I can't wait to know what's coming next. What did you do with him? Are you the one who drove him to the shed?"

"I got brains up here, maybe you didn't notice," she said pointing to her head. "Once again, I didn't have a choice. I knew that sooner or later, someone, a driver, a cop, someone like you, would end up finding the kid. Dead or alive, I had no idea. And then, sooner or later, you'd find us. Me. I had to delete all traces of our nocturnal outing as two lovebirds."

Carrie's laugh exasperated the sergeant and his deputy, but they didn't say anything and let her continue.

I WANT MOMMY

A FEW DAYS EARLIER, somewhere near Gravois Mills

LUCKILY FOR HER, Carrie Chastain had the corpulence and physical strength of her genitor. Her father was as strong as a bull and Carrie could easily compete with him. She put her hands under Mumin's armpits and dragged him towards the Dodge, but he was heavier than she'd imagined and dropped him on the ground like a bag of garbage.

Time for plan B. She had to think and act rapidly. She had an idea what to do. She knew this area well. She knew that they weren't too far from Lake of the Ozarks. If they had kept on going down that trail through the forest, they'd end up there. Perhaps, if luck was on her side, the path would even lead them right to the cliffs. And from there...

"Don't you move," she said to the body lying in the fallen leaves. "I gotta do the work all alone to save us. Um, save *me*, actually. 'Coz you're pretty worthless..."

Carrie walked around the Dodge, noting the damage on the passenger side and thought that she could probably still drive it and get it out of there. She got in, found Mumin's cell phone on the seat and threw it into the glove compartment. She turned the key, and the engine immediately started up.

"These old clunkers got good motors," she said, putting it in reverse and using the four-wheel drive.

The wheels spun a bit when the pickup was

pulling away from the big oak tree in a grim creaking sound. Then slowly the car began its way to the lake, which was only about half a mile away. A distance that only took her a few minutes of careful driving, though she was in a hurry.

When Carrie got to the grassy plateau leading to the cliffs, she stopped the car. This wasn't a place where tourists came and there weren't any fences. And ideal spot to make the Dodge disappear. She turned the wheels in the direction of the lake, the lights from its headlights disappearing above the calm water. Then she opened the windows and door and put the gear into neutral. She got out, picked up a large stone, put the pickup in first gear and put the stone on the accelerator.

She just had enough time to jump out before the Dodge started off in the direction of the cliffs and continued into the lake. She went right up to the end to hear a loud *plouf* when the car hit the lake and looked at it slowly but surely sinking. She knew that it was from fifteen to thirty feet deep here.

Then she turned around.

99 bottles of beer on the wall, 99 bottles of beer. If one of the bottles should happen to fall, 98 bottles of beer on the wall, she sang to herself to keep her mind off the cold. Carrie had never been a girl scout, but with the snow that was still falling in the dark forest, it was nice to keep herself company. Her plan wasn't totally finished.

All that was left though was to get rid of Mumin...

CHAPTER 68
A slow and foreseeable death

MYRA STONEHENGE TURNED the light on in Carrie Chastain's room, because the darkness of the room was resonating with the darkness of the woman's story, making it even more frightening.

"You weren't just talking about killing him?" asked Gallister. "You wanted to make him suffer, right?"

This time the woman laughed, if you could call it that, silently, simply by raising her lips just like a wolf who growled to show its domination. At least that was what the sergeant thought.

"A little of that, yeah," confirmed Carrie. "He screwed everything up, that he did, yup ! Hey look, I'm a poet and I didn't even know it, Sergeant ! I had to make him understand how serious all that was. When I got back to my car, he was still there, unconscious, lying on the ground in a pile of fallen leaves. His coat was covered with blood from his shoulder. At first, I thought he'd emptied out, like a stuck pig, and I was a little disappointed, you understand, don't you? But then I took his pulse, and he was still alive, that Old Man Mumin. So here's what I did."

∽

The Gravois Mills Forest, a few days earlier

She couldn't just leave him there in the middle of the woods without the risk that someone walking by or a lumberjack would find him, which would fatally lead the cops right up to her door. You didn't need too much smarts to understand that. So the only solution she had was to haul him away and hide him elsewhere. The blood on the white snow could easily pass for that of a wounded animal. But she still had to get him into the car, something she hadn't been able to do with the pickup. The advantage of the car was that it was lower than the Dodge. She was sure that if she called upon all her strength, she'd be able to haul him onto the back seat. She grabbed her husband below his armpits, took a deep breath, and pulled him like a workhorse.

"Jesus fucking Christ!" she grumbled. "You weigh more than a sack of wheat, you pig. Heave ho!"

After ten or so minutes, she had finally crammed

him into the back seat of the car. She sat down in the driver's seat and turned the key.

Where to? She'd had enough time to think that over in the half-mile or so walk back from the cliff. She'd thought of several options. The first would be to go back to the farm. She'd briefly thought that Jessy would have gone back there for shelter, because that was one of the rare places she was used to and it would have reassured her, but then Carrie quickly chased that idea from her mind. Jessy, go back to the farm? Never! That would be like asking a rabbit to obediently return to its cage.

Though Carrie had abandoned all hope of finding Jessie at home, she still had to stop there to pick up a few things she'd be needing. She thus drove carefully to the empty farm, and got out of the car, checking that Mumin was still out for the count. She rushed to the workshop where she picked up a roll of Duct tape, a pair of scissors, a chain, a padlock and an old rag they used to clean tools with.

She got back in the car, put it in reverse, and rushed down the gravel driveway to the path that went into the fields that had been left fallow for this season. There, near the path, between two fields, was an old shack in need of repair, though still standing, that hadn't been used for ages. All that was left inside was a bit of filthy straw, probably a home for rats.

No one would ever think of looking for Mumin there. First of all they'd have to fish the Dodge out of the lake, and that could take time, thought Carrie, pulling as hard as she could on her unconscious husband's body.

She dropped him on the floor of the shed while he was slowly coming to.

"So you're back with us, you bastard? How's that little shoulder doing? Don't worry, it'll heal itself. So, I got better stuff to do like trying to find the kid. I'm going to give you time to think things over. Put your arms behind your back."

As the man didn't obey, she repeated herself, an order accompanied by a few choice swear words and a heavy blow to his head, twisting it, which made him do what she'd said. Carrie put a few layers of Duct tape around his wrists. When she thought it was tight enough, she guided him to the straw so he could sit down and told him to put his legs out. Another couple of Duct tape layers, nice and tight, around his two ankles.

"Now you'll be able to gallop as fast as a stallion. And as I don't want you inviting everyone over here..."

Turning talk into action, while Mumin was trying to struggle by shaking his head, right up to when a new blow to it made him understand that he wouldn't be winning here, Carrie stuffed a handkerchief into his mouth and then gagged him with the rag she'd taken from their workshop and tied it in a double knot behind his head.

"Perfect!" the shrew gloated, backing up to admire her work.

She turned around before leaving.

"See you soon, my dear!" she said, mocking him. "Maybe..."

She closed the door of the shack, put the chain in the rings and locked it, putting the key underneath a big rock next to the door.

Mumin heard the motor of the car driving away in the night and closed his tear-filled eyes, powerless, abandoning himself to a slow and foreseeable death.

CHAPTER 69
Accelerating

GALLISTER LOOKED DOWN at Carrie's hands joined together on her thighs, just like a nun who was praying. He noticed there was a bandage on one of them, the one that Jessy had bitten into before running away in the forest.

"Looks like your daughter left you a little souvenir before running away," insinuated the officer.

"Just like her mother, she knows how to affirm herself!"

"Enough with your stupid sentences, Mrs. Chastain," Gallister said angrily. "You're tiring me."

"You gotta accept me like I am, Sergeant. With my qualities and my imperfections, just like everyone. Just like you, right?"

Gallister clenched his fists, as if curbing the urge to get rid of that infernal, cynical and destructive harpy. Make her change her attitude, give her a taste of all the violence she'd inflicted on her family.

"Tell the judge that for your trial," he warned her. "In the meanwhile, could you please explain to me why, after your nocturnal joy ride, it took you three days before you came here looking for your daughter? Why you faked insanity?"

Carrie slowly shook her head several times. Gallister thought of those little dogs shaking their heads or wagging their tails you see in cars.

"I couldn't show up at the cop's just like that. I was stuck. I weighed the pros and the cons I don't know how many times. Like I thought that you'd never believe that my daughter ran away from the farm all by herself on a night like that. Not without complicity, like you say. Mine or her father's. So I needed some time to disguise all that, all that stuff I just told you. Wrap it all up and pretend that she had been kidnapped. But then once again, it wasn't easy because you learned pretty quickly when you questioned the neighbors, hard to make you think that Jessy was kidnapped when apparently there hadn't been any kids at home for a while. Hard to explain that!"

Pete Gallister agreed. That was exactly the question that had been eating away at him for a while, since Carrie's tale this time supported what the investigators had found. Mumin in the abandoned shed, a bullet wound in his shoulder, the little girl with blood on her chin – blood from Carrie's hand, the analyses would soon prove that – and the Dodge that had been fished out from the bottom of the lake. That version would also explain why the little girl was so frightened when her mom showed up in her room in the hospital. This time, the tale the woman had spun matched their theories: Jessy, with the complicity of Mumin, had escaped from the Chastain farm. Yet, and all the witnesses said the same thing, it had been months since there was a child in that farm. There was still an element missing.

"So, where was your daughter all that time?" asked the sergeant, anticipating the answer.

"Let's say, let's just say that we were protecting her!"

Those were the last words Carrie Chastain said that evening in her room in the psychiatric ward of Saint Mary's Hospital. She refused to say anymore.

∼

THE NEXT MORNING, Gallister accelerated the investigation, tackling the verification of all the key points Carrie had mentioned when explaining how her daughter had run away and reappeared.

He ordered a comparison of blood samples. Firstly the old Chastain lady's blood, as it had been taken on the day when she showed up drunk at the police station. And then the sample that Dr. Johnson had taken when she cleaned up the blood on the little girl's chin when examining her. No brainer, both samples of blood were the same. The blood on the child's chin was the blood from her mother's hand she'd bitten.

He also put out a new call for witnesses to check what now seemed evident to him, that the Chastain family had locked their own daughter away for months. Where? Why? And how? Those were the questions that Gallister needed to answer. And sooner rather than later. He also asked Dr. Frances Cagliari to try to talk to the child now that he had additional data on what could have taken place. Would Jessy finally speak to ease her aching, imprisoned heart?

There were several witnesses who seemed to support the hypothesis of a sequestration. Gallister was particularly interested in one of them.

It was a plumber from Gravois Mills who had come to the Chastain farm last winter to repair a water pipe that had frozen and then burst, flooding the basement.

"I'd say it must have been in January and February last year," declared Max Powell, the plumber. "If you want, I can check my agenda and give you the exact date. Plus, they still haven't paid me..."

"That won't be necessary, Mr. Powell. Just tell me what you saw at the Chastain's."

"Well, the owners were pretty icy themselves. It was winter, you might say. Especially the lady, a farmer lady with character, if you see what I mean."

"I do."

"So anyway, they let me in because like I said, they were flooded, and they needed me. But they stood right behind my back the whole time I was there. The lady guided me around the house. And when I wanted to go to the basement, that's where things got complicated. I had to access each room where the water pipes went through, I was just doing my job!"

"I understand."

"So right then she wouldn't let me go into one of the rooms downstairs. She said the pipework didn't go through there, there wasn't anything to see down there, that it didn't leak there, etc. I insisted because I could see a water pipe going along the ceiling and I knew it went into that room through the stone wall. But even though I insisted, she wouldn't let me in. She stood in front of the door, her arms crossed. And then I thought I heard some noise coming from behind the door. I asked her if there was someone in there and she said, no, it was a dog, and a nasty one and I shouldn't try to approach it. So I gave up and the man showed me the room where the leak was. And the whole time I was working he was right there next to me. He escorted me each time I went back to my truck to get some tools or material. And each time the lady was standing in front of that forbidden room, like a Cerberus. Except one time, I came back down, and the door was slightly ajar. Oh! Not for a long time, I saw that she was just closing it behind her, but in the corner of my eye I noticed something that looked like curly brown hair. So I said to myself that must be their dog. Curly hair like a poodle. You think poodles bite though? So I started to doubt her story. Anyway, I must have been there for a good hour. While I was working, I thought I heard the woman's loud voice a couple of times scolding the dog. Except when I'd finished and I'd gone past that forbidden door that wasn't guarded by her because she was inside, I heard something. I thought I must be going nuts: it was words, but not very understandable ones. Something like "Mommy, I want mommy," but with an accent or not very well articulated. But the guy following me had an explanation. 'Darn dog yapping again.' But I forgot about that pretty quick, I left and went to my next job. But today, with what we know about this case, I sort of think that a dog wouldn't have asked for 'Mommy' like that..."

CHAPTER 70
We're real good

SOMEONE'S IN THE HOUSE, *I'm sure of that. I hear a voice I don't know. That doesn't happen very often.*

I don't think anyone ever comes here. That's 'cuz the people who live here aren't nice. We don't want to live with them.

Except for him, the one named Mumin. He's nicer than her, Carrie. Not too hard!

Even though he looks scary like a bear, his voice is soft when he talks to me. She always talks loud, she swears all the time, she scares me and her breath stinks like she just ate a dead rat. Like the one that was all stiff in the corner of the room and that Mumin picked up after my story.

'Cuz Mumin reads me stories. She never does. She puts my meal tray down and tells me "Time for bed now," and turns off the lamp. Never even a "Good night."

He lets me sit on his lap and reads me a story and shows me the pictures. And I can even hold my little Leo, my stuffed lion, then. That way he can listen to the story too. We're real good, my little stuffed lion and me.

And before leaving Mumin always kisses me on the forehead and tells me to sleep tight. And he never turns off the light until I'm fast asleep. Unless that mean lady comes before him.

The other day, I thought I heard a voice upstairs. An old lady's voice. She was talking about sugar and candy I think. I wanted to shout to tell her I was here. I would have liked some candy... But I got scared and I didn't make any noise. They always said I should never talk to strangers.

Today someone's here too. A man. I hear him talking about a leak and I hear booms in the pipes. I think they're just behind my door. Can I do it now? I'm going to yell so someone will get me out of here.

But the wicked witch comes in right away and closes the door behind her. I make a little noise, like a puppy that's yelping. She makes a face and says "You better close that mouth right now, or..." She didn't say mouth though, she said another word, something I don't like. And she raised her hand, I know what that means... I don't say anything.

But I still want someone to hear me. The man who is pounding on the pipes is going now. I can't stand it here all alone anymore.

"I want Mumin" I say, a little louder than usual.

She slaps me on the cheek, it hurts.

I don't say anything else, and I sob, silently.

CHAPTER 71
Up to... an obsession

MONTAUK, December 2023

My investigation wasn't making any progress. I was afraid I wouldn't be solving this case. At the same time my relationship – would I dare call it a *love story*? – with Paul had also crashed right into a wall and that even before it really began. What an idiot I was! *Forty years old and still believing in fairy tales just like when you were a kid... And plus that, falling in love with a youngster. And you're surprised he split? Don't be so naive, Karen Blackstone!*

I was ready to give up on that investigation that my dear Myrtille Fairbanks, my boss and tabloid investigation magazines queen, had assigned to me. For the very first time in my career, I was ready to hang up my gloves before having solved the enigma. Or did I just need more time? Maybe I'd find the solution later.

Twenty-four hours had gone by since I had gone to Nollington's and I still hadn't had any news from Paul, though I'd asked him to call me back several times. Each time I was redirected to his voicemail. I left messages, I couldn't help myself, but to no avail.

I still had an ace up my sleeve though before checking out from Montauk Manor and going back to Portland. I wanted to understand what could be happening with Paul, understand his attitude. His sudden behavior didn't seem to match what he'd led me to glimpse of him in the previous days. There had to be an explanation, and I was going to get it.

I jumped into my Ranchero and drove to Nollington's place. Paul's father, with a metallic and throaty voice, asked me who I was and what I wanted.

"Mr. Nollington, I'm really worried. Could I please come in, I'd like to speak to you. It's important. Please."

I heard the gate being unlocked and walked up to their front door.

"Please sit down. Some coffee?"

"A tea please, if that's not too much trouble."

"None at all," Mrs. Nollington replied. "Black, green, white?"

"A green tea would be perfect, thanks."

While Paul's mother was in the kitchen, his father and I spoke about this and that, their ocean view, the weather that was unusually cold for the season, how lucky they were to live in Montauk full-time, especially outside of the tourist season when the peninsula belonged only to its residents. When the hot drinks were served, I told them the reason I'd come.

"Have you had any news from Paul since he left?"

"Of course, why?" asked Mrs. Nollington, quite astonished.

That was what I had feared. Paul was avoiding me. I didn't know what words to use to talk about the relationship I had with Paul, – did I actually have one though? – without shocking them. A forty-year-old in love with their twenty-five-year-old son...

"Paul and I..." I hesitated. "We had an edifying discussion about the disappearance of Laura and Katheline," I said, pointing that their neighbor's villa with my chin. He told me a host of interesting things during a dinner we had together in New York, then he dropped me off at my hotel, and I haven't heard a word from him since. He doesn't answer my phone calls or my messages. But seeing as how you've spoken to him, there's nothing to worry about, so..."

I could see a smile on Mrs. Nollington's lips.

"We know that you two talked about that. And I think that it was something that must have stirred up a bunch of things inside him and that he wanted to put a bit of distance from all those terrible memories. These places," she said with a large gesture of her arm towards the villa, dunes, and the beach, "these cursed places still affect him."

"I'm sorry."

"It's not your fault, don't be. It's just that our son, well, our son is someone who's hypersensitive. I'm sure that bringing all those atrocities back up to the surface again was something that really shook him up. Those were such intense moments for him, if you only knew."

"I think I did understand that."

"Plus he had front row seats at that time. He must have told you how much Laura Vaughan counted for him."

"He did. I'm sure he was secretly in love with her, am I right?"

Mrs. Nollington smiled blissfully, like a mother who was overjoyed to see that her child was happy.

"That's right, *secretly*. And that's what makes him sad. When love isn't reciprocal, it's something that generates a terrible frustration. Then jealousy, bitterness, unsatisfied longing, so many toxic feelings."

"Toxic?"

"For him, I meant. Because of his hypersensitivity, each feeling is multiplied by a hundredfold, so you can just imagine how he felt on the day that he learned that the person he secretly was in love with had died... To be truthful, I still don't think he's over that. And when I say that he loved her, it's still not strong enough. He idolized her, he was intensely and profoundly crazy about her. He worshipped her. Up to... an obsession..."

That word petrified me and neither Paul's parents nor I said anything, a silence that nourished itself with everything that the word implied.

"Obsessional love is a pathology," I said.

Both Mr. and Mrs. Nollington nodded. He was the one who interrupted the embarrassing silence between us.

"You're right, Karen, a pathology that could lead to committing many a foolish act…"

CHAPTER 72
Be a man

OBSESSION, lies, manipulation, foolish acts... a multitude of words about Paul Nollington were dancing around in my mind.

Who was he really?

What did he do?

"What do you mean by 'a foolish act?'"

Mrs. Nollington shook her head, embarrassed. Her husband put a comforting hand on her arm. He sighed and answered my question.

"I'm not convinced that we should be telling you this. Paul is the one who should confess what he did. Now he's an adult."

"But as he never answers my calls, how can I..."

Steven Nollington raised a hand to stop me in the middle of my sentence.

"Wait a sec. Elia, give me the phone please."

I looked at him unlock the screen and then tap on

it several times before putting it up to his ear. I heard it ring three times.

"Paul? Dad here. How are you? (...) Listen, we're here at home with Miss Blackstone (...) Yes, Karen (...) Listen Paul, don't interrupt me. I know why you left Montauk so quickly, but this person needs to know, to understand. You have to talk to her. You have to tell her everything. Everything you know and everything you did or couldn't do (...) No, don't hang up, Paul. It's time to turn the page on all that... Be a man, okay? Stop running away. (...) If you want, if you'll feel better like that. (...) I'll tell her. See you soon, son. Love you, your mom too."

Then he turned to me.

"He's expecting you. He's at our house in New York. That's where he goes when Montauk is too heavy for him. I'll write the address down for you."

Ripping off a sheet of paper from an office block, Steven Nollington jotted down a few indications and handed it to me.

"I'd suggest taking the train to go there, the apartment is near Grand Central."

∽

My brain was overloaded with questions in the train to New York, once again reminding me of Jim Carrey in *Eternal Sunshine of the Spotless Mind*. Scenes he saw from the train in Long Island when he met Kate Winslet. I felt as lost as the hero of this movie.

What would I find in New York?

While the white-coated landscapes were rushing by, my phone rang. Hmm, a guy named Pete Gallister...

"Miss Blackstone, Sergeant Gallister from Missouri here. Am I bothering you?"

"Only in my reflections. What can I do for you, Sergeant?"

"Help me clarify mine."

"Do you mean we'll work together and share our info?"

"First of all I want to tell you that you have to give me your sources about Simon Parker. I want to collar that man as soon as possible, as, like you also thought, he didn't just happen to go to Missouri."

I rolled my eyes.

"Sergeant, I can't give you my sources. But what I can do is try to help you localize him more precisely. And in consideration, you'll tell me where your investigation took you."

A laugh as thick as a slice of ham was my response.

"That's not the way it works, Miss Blackstone. Remember the difference between us is that you're a journalist and I'm a cop. I got a slight advantage on you; don't you think so?"

"Okay. I'll call you back in half an hour."

I quickly called Spider and asked him to situate the exact place where Simon Parker was, using his secret hacker tools. For a handful of extra bucks on his unofficial bill, he agreed and said he'd get back to me in a couple of minutes. The professional and nonetheless clandestine hacker lived up to his word and efficiency and sent me a geo location file using encrypted Proton Mail. I made a screen shot of it and transferred it to Sergeant Gallister, who called me right back. And I did all that in the train taking me to the Big Apple.

"Thank you, Miss Blackstone. So, all I can tell you on my side is that the little girl who was found on the side of the road, the one who looked like the Vaughan old lady's grand-daughter, had probably been forcibly confined for months, if not longer, on a farm in Missouri. And I'm wondering if Simon Parker had anything to do with that. And thanks to your help, that's what I hope to discover pretty soon."

He hung up, leaving me stunned by this new twist.

Suddenly, when the train had nearly reached New York, I remembered what Steven Nollington had told me about his own son.

"You're right, Karen, a pathology that could lead to committing many a foolish act…"

Good Lord! Paul, what did you do?

CHAPTER 73
A Christmas story

VERSAILLES, Missouri, December 2023

THE FIVE POLICE cars from Morgan County, their lights still flashing, pulled to a stop at the entrance of the industrial zone in Versailles. Gallister was the first to rush out of the patrol car, immediately followed by Myra Stonehenge and Agent Bauer. All three had their guns in their hands.

Surrounding the parking lot of the Days Inn Motel, a lower class one with cheap rooms, they were trying to prevent any eventual attempts at escaping. One squad went to the back of the building and the other, including Gallister, surrounded the main entrance right when the motel's manager rushed up to the front desk.

"Hey! What's going on?"

"Sir, could you give us Simon Parker's room number please?"

"Easy," replied the man, pointing at the parking lot where most places were vacant. "We don't have a lot of tourists at this time of the year. Parker is in Room 23, right over there, on the second floor."

And Gallister did see the curtain move in that room.

"This way guys!"

Two by two the policemen climbed the metallic stairs and Gallister knocked on the door of Room 23.

"Police! Open up, Parker, we know you're here. Don't do anything dumb. Just open up, hands in the air."

Myra Stonehenge had unhooked the pair of handcuffs attached to her belt, ready to react if needed.

Silence followed Gallister's traditional welcome speech, but they could hear footsteps behind the door, followed by a click, unlocking it.

A man between twenty-five and thirty, blond hair down to his shoulders and a thin mustache, opened the door, wearing a pair of jeans and a white t-shirt that clung to his pecs and showed off his well-maintained biceps. Hands raised above his head, he looked Gallister straight in the eyes, a slight snicker on his lips.

"Hey hey! Sure took you long enough, Sergeant. I've been expecting you."

Half an hour after he'd been arrested, Simon Parker was seated on an uncomfortable chair in one of the interview rooms at the Versailles police station. Sergeant Pete Gallister and his deputy Myra Stonehenge were sitting side by side across from him, flipping through a large file. One of their colleagues came into the room with three cups of hot coffee and a box of cookies.

Gallister pushed one of the goblets on the Formica table towards Parker. The man nodded to thank him and waited until the cops were ready to begin questioning him. Because he'd been fully cooperative, they'd taken him to the station without handcuffing him.

"Mr. Parker," began Gallister, "do you know why you're here?"

"It's got something to do with the little kid that was found around here a couple of days ago."

"That's right. And you seemed to be expecting us. Could you tell us how you fit into this story?"

"It's a long story, Sergeant."

"Ever since I was little, I've always loved long stories. Plus, considering what time of year it is, I must say that I prefer nice Christmas stories. Are you going to tell us a Christmas story?"

"Not so sure of that. Unless you like evil characters like the Grinch[1]? Because, believe me, we're going to have a lot of them in this tale."

"We'll try to proceed methodically to understand everything. Okay with you?"

Parker nodded. Gallister began his interview.

"What ties do you have with the State of Missouri, Mr. Parker?"

"Not a one."

"Well then, what brings you to this beautiful neck of the woods at this time of the year, if you're not on vacation?"

"You know why."

"I have to hear you say it for the recording."

"As did many American citizens, I saw your call for witnesses with the photo of the little girl."

"And?"

"And I must say that it shook me up."

"How come?"

"Because the little girl looked really familiar to me, in the literal sense of that term."

"Can you be more precise, Mr. Parker?"

"When I saw her face, her brown curly hair, her eyes, I hallucinated. For a split second I thought it was my daughter… But I know that's impossible. My Katheline died last summer in Montauk, where she lived with her mother, Laura Vaughan. We'd been separated for several months, her and me. Things didn't end well between us."

"What happened?" Myra Stonehenge wanted to know.

"At that time, I had a little problem with alcoholic beverages, and that made me a bit… violent at time. I had several unfortunate gestures. I hit my wife once or twice."

"Only your wife?"

Simon nodded his head.

"If you're insinuating I also hit my daughter, you can stop right there. I never struck Kathy. Never!"

"What did your daughter die from?" Gallister asked innocently, as Karen Blackstone, the investigative journalist who had handed Parker to him on a silver platter, had already given him the answer.

The man hesitated, moving his lips and tongue inside his cheeks, as if ruminating the best answer to give them.

"As I wasn't in Montauk then, I only know what I know through hearsay. My ex-wife filed a complaint on me, and I had a restraining order and couldn't be in Montauk. I'd become a *persona non grata*. But... Jesus Christ... what happened there, it was so terrible..."

Parker's voice broke. It looked as if he was about to cry, sincerely touched by that painful souvenir. The two investigators gave him some time.

"I can't believe that Laura killed our daughter!" he said with a smothered sob.

Gallister continued his innocent questions.

"You said that your ex-wife killed your daughter? And how?"

"Laura was always a psychologically fragile person. She was depressive and had tried to commit suicide several times. But that time she succeeded, and brought Kathy with her to the bottom of the pond... I can't believe a mother would do that! It's abject!"

Gallister was surprised by the words Simon had used.

"As you knew that your ex-wife and daughter died last summer in Montauk, why did you rush over to Missouri when you saw the photo of a little girl who looked vaguely like yours?"

"I must say that I hesitated. I ran all the theories through my mind, including the most outlandish ones. Sergeant, you can believe me when I say that I don't believe in ghosts, in ghouls, in reincarnation and all that crap. But she looked so much like her, such a coincidence that I couldn't help myself. I wanted to understand, decide for myself. Know for sure. That's why I jumped in my car. I live in Pittsburgh, Pennsylvania. I drove all night in terrible weather. All that snow that never stopped falling. And as it said on the call for witnesses that you were heading the investigation in Versailles, I went directly here."

"You were here?" Gallister asked, astonished. "In our police station?"

Parker smiled again, a smirk that annoyed the policeman.

"You could say that you waltz in and waltz out of here pretty easy," said Katheline's father while Gallister frowned. "Okay, I was teasing you here. But yes, I wanted to testify because it did concern me. While I was waiting in your lobby with other people, I hesitated though. You had a whole dedicated team to take testimonials. I hesitated because I was afraid you'd think I was crazy. And you would have, am I right?"

Now it was Gallister's turn to smile, thinking back on the myriad of nonsensical depositions he had to process, including the ones a certain Carrie Chastain gave him, the most ridiculous of them all.

"You could say, Mr. Parker, that we listen to crazy people day in and day out. One more or one less... So finally, you didn't testify then? How come?"

After thinking it over for a moment and wincing after he'd downed the rest of his now cold coffee, Simon Parker surprised the two investigators.

"Because I suddenly had like an impression of *déjà-vu*. You know what that is? A lady came into the lobby shouting like her life depended on it. She looked like she was half-drunk, if I could say that, or under the influence of some drugs. And that lady, it seemed to me that I'd already seen her. I couldn't remember where or when, but deep down inside, I was sure that I'd already run across her. She was yelling out that she wanted her kid back..."

1 The Grinch is a fictional character invented by Theodor Seuss Geisel, known as Dr. Seuss, for his children's book published in 1957 *How the Grinch Stole Christmas*! A movie directed by Ron Howard with Jim Carrey (once again!) in the main role, had the same title.

CHAPTER 74

A vague souvenir

SERGEANT GALLISTER and Deputy Stonehenge looked at one another, gaping, with their cups of cold coffee in their hands, after Simon Parker's latest revelation, like a bomb that had dropped.

"You're telling us that first of all, you were here, in our premises, and then that you thought you recognized a lady who came in about the same time?"

"That's it, Sergeant," confirmed Parker.

"But you can't remember when nor where you two met. You think it's a simple impression of *déjà-vu*, like when you try to put your finger on something, but nothing registers in your brain."

"Exactly. At least, it was exactly that at that precise moment. And what finally convinced me to step back. And not come forward to you with my ghost story. I preferred to discreetly wait a bit longer and to learn more about that hysterical lady who I thought I'd seen somewhere. A typical type of person that you maybe see only once in your life and someone you never forget, even if that memory is stored someplace in the back of your mind. An extraordinary character, I could say. But now I know..."

"What do you know?"

"I know who she is. I mean, I know her name."

"Yes?" Myra encouraged him to continue.

"It's Carrie Chastain, isn't it?"

That time the two investigators were less surprised, as they'd already foreseen he'd been referring to Jessy's mother.

"How did you find out? Did you have a lightbulb moment?"

"No. I actually had no idea of her name before I came here to Missouri. I learned it here."

"At the police station?"

"Not exactly. Let me continue."

"Please do, Mr. Parker, please do," murmured Gallister.

"So, here I go. I could feel something fishy was taking place around here with the photo of that little girl you found on the road. My intuition told me to stay in the shadows to try to understand who that woman I thought I'd recognized was, so I left the police station and patiently waited in my car on the corner of the road. I can tell you I nearly froze my butt off, but I didn't want to give up. So I just sucked it up, wrapped a thick blanket around me and waited in the front seat. Long minutes went by, soon becoming long hours. I must have dozed off every once in a while, because I can't remember seeing each and every hour on my watch. I deduced that you must have offered hospitality to that drunken lady, if you see what I mean. And let her sleep it off in the drunk tank."

"You're very perceptive, Mr. Parker. You should be a cop."

"With my antecedents, I'm not sure I'd be accepted," joked Simon, "but I'm delighted to know that I was right. So the next morning, when she'd slept it off and when I was still waiting near the police station, I saw you leave with her, escort her to her car and you set off in a line, a police car in front of her and one behind. I followed you, but not too closely, still guided by my curiosity and that little feeling I had in my gut. Funny, isn't it? It's usually the opposite with cops following suspects! Anyway it wasn't too hard to follow you guys as there weren't a lot of people out on the roads because of the weather."

Simon could read a glint of anger tinted with shame in the eyes of the cops who realized that they'd been tailed by an ordinary dude without even knowing it. In their defense though, they had other fish to fry at that time and neither of them commented, letting Parker continue.

"I followed you to Gravois Mills, then up to the intersection with a path leading to the farm. I drove on a bit farther and parked on the side of the road. I got out of my car, and from where I was standing, I could see you through the trees. You were waiting for a while in her front yard and then you left without her. When you left the farm, I hid so you wouldn't see me and when you disappeared down the road, I walked up a little closer to spy on her. And found her name on the mailbox: Carrie Chastain. And the name of her husband or partner probably, a guy named Mumin Blasharov. Neither of these two names rang a bell, yet I could feel I was getting nearer to that vague souvenir, but I still didn't know where or when it could have taken place. I'd find out later, but at that moment, I was still in a deep fog. I went up to their yard where I could see her walking in front of the windows in their house but didn't learn anything else. And then a bit later she went out, with a winter coat on, and started walking down a path in their backyard. I followed her but stayed in the distance. I'd say that we walked in the snow that day a good mile, mile and a half maybe. My shoes weren't the best for that, but once again, I continued. And luckily so, as at the end of that path, you could say that I was finally rewarded for all my efforts since the day before. That was where I confirmed my intuition. And where I was able to make the link to the place where I'd already seen that lady... And that man too! To the person she'd unknowingly led me to, that Mumin Blasharov that she'd sequestered in an old shed."

CHAPTER 75
Privileged witness

ONCE AGAIN, Simon Parker's tale had the two investigators hanging on every word. Gallister was both furious but wanted him to continue.

"You should be a private detective, not a cop," he said ironically. "You're good at tailing people, Mr. Parker. Could you continue please? You followed Carrie Chastain to the shed in the field. After that?"

"After that? I kept watch outside, with my ear glued to the wooden planks falling apart and peaked in quickly. I couldn't make out much to tell the truth, but it was enough to get an idea of what was going on inside. And what I heard and saw there chilled my blood, I swear. That lady is a heartless harpy! Like I said, the Grinch compared to her is an angel!"

"Well, you could also say you are an eminent psychologist, Mr. Parker," added the sergeant.

"Hey! If you came and got me from the hotel just

to make fun of me, I'm just gonna shut up! I'm bringing you answers and that's how you're thanking me!"

Gallister raised both arms, showing him he'd finished.

"Sorry, Mr. Parker, please continue. A little break maybe before? Another cup of coffee maybe?"

"With pleasure."

The sergeant left the room, leaving Myra with Parker who had shifted from potential suspect to the status of privileged witness. Gallister came back into the room with the coffee, eager to hear what Simon would now tell them. He was hoping, thanks to his statement, to learn more about Mumin Blasharov. And when Parker continued, he wasn't disappointed.

"Like I said before, that Carrie Chastain is a total harpy. Plus she's nuts. I remember, almost word for word, her incorrigible smoker's voice when she said 'Jesus Christ! What the hell did you do with the kid, huh? Why did you have to screw things up again?'"

Gallister nodded, imagining the scene: Carrie balling out her husband, not without previously having shot him in the shoulder with her gun. He let Simon Parker continue.

"So she kept on yelling at him with a terrible acidity: 'So what are we gonna do now? What am I going to do? How am I going get us out of this shithole one more time? You're strong as a bull. Excuse me but I'm not going to undo you. You'll eat like the dogs do, with your teeth.' And that's when I heard his voice, yelling at her when she took his gag off so he could eat. He started to yell 'You damn...' but couldn't finish his sentence because I heard her clock him a good one, followed by: 'Shut up, or I won't let you eat! And one more word and I'll use this. And you already know that I'm capable of it, don't you?'"

"But then Mr. Parker," Myra asked, "you didn't try to intervene, to help that more visibly threatened man?

Simon shrugged, showing he was helpless.

"That lady was not only crazy, but she was also armed. And I personally never carry a gun. So you see, I could never be a cop... To answer your question, no, I'm sorry, but I didn't come in bare-handedly like John Wayne."

"What did you do then?"

"I stepped back a couple of feet from the shack, behind a hedge that hid me pretty well. And waited there till the woman left. She probably only stayed inside for about fifteen minutes. And then she closed the door and locked it with a chain and a padlock. I don't know why she didn't put the key to the padlock in her pocket, but she put it beneath a stone next to the door. I don't know if fate was helping me along here, but thanks to that key, I was able to obtain the *key to the mystery* of my *déjà-vu* syndrome."

Gallister leaned over the table as if reducing the distance between his questions and Parker's elements of response he was about to give.

"Please give us that symbolic key, Mr. Parker. We can't wait. What did you do?"

"I waited until she had gone all the way down that path, the one going to their farm, and I got out of my hideout. I lifted up the stone, took the padlock key and went inside the old shed. It was starting to get dark already. But that didn't stop me from discovering what was inside. A man who was gagged, his hands and feet tied together by duct tape, and dried blood on his chest. When he saw the door reopen, he instinctively pulled back, trying to get as far away from me as he could. He must have thought that it was his wife coming back to clock him again, but he quickly understood that it was someone else. But he wasn't reassured at all. Quite the opposite! His eyes popped wide open like a kid who'd seen the Grinch coming towards them. No, worse than the Grinch, the Grim Reaper! Anyway, he must have thought that I'd come to finish up what his wife had started and that she'd hired me so she wouldn't get her hands dirty. He was shaking his head back and forth, making little noises under his gag, his eyes were bulging. I slowly went up to him, raising my hands to calm him. And when I got close enough to distinguish his face, once again I had that feeling of *déjà-vu*... and that was when I started to understand.

"Understand what?" Gallister asked, irritated by the plethora of details in Parker's story.

He would have liked the man to tell him directly what had happened, though at the same time he did need those details.

"I began to understand the breadth of their unimaginable conspiracy… All the pieces of the puzzle finally fit together perfectly. Totally unspeakable horror…"

CHAPTER 76
That's life

"I TOLD HIM, to reassure him, that I didn't want to hurt him, that I hadn't come to finish him off or torture him. The closer I got, the more he shook his head. But then when I'd promised I wouldn't do anything, little by little he calmed down. I told him I wanted to talk to him. But especially listen to him because I had loads of questions I wanted the answers to."

"Questions? So you knew him then?" asked Gallister.

"I wouldn't say that I knew him, but I'd run across him someplace."

"Where?" asked the officer, impatiently.

"You'll find out soon enough, Sergeant. And I think you'll be surprised. But let me tell you what we talked about, him and me, in that freezing little shed."

A few days earlier, not too far from Gravois Mills

Simon Parker walked up to Mumin Blasharov's tied feet. Looking at his chest cavity that was going up and down difficultly, he could tell that Mumin was having trouble breathing behind the rag rolled up in his mouth. Fear had also probably accelerated his heartbeat.

"Don't we know each other?"

Mumin shook his head back and forth, in incomprehension and denegation.

"Yeah, I'm pretty sure we do. Funny things happen, that's life, isn't it? Crossed destinies, coincidences. Had someone told me that one day we'd see each other again, with you tied up like a roast beef and me free to do whatever I wanted with you…"

Mumin groaned, furious.

"If I untie you, will you stay put?"

Carrie's prisoner's eyes narrowed, a sign he was weighing the pros and the cons. He finally agreed, moving his chin.

"I'm thirsty!" were the first words he pronounced with difficulty when Simon took his gag off."

"It's not very hot. Would his Honor like a cup of tea with a cloud of milk?"

"Water… please…"

Simon touched the bowl with the tip of his foot that Carrie had left on the ground.

"Maybe I'll give you some when you'll have confessed to me."

"Hurts. Dry throat. Can't talk."

Kathy's father sighed and brought the bowl to Mumin's lips. He took several long gulps of the water that, though half-frozen and dirty, seemed to quench the thirst of the wounded giant.

"Now it's time to talk," said Simon. "If you cooperate, you'll get more. I'm pretty generous."

"I don't know you!" Mumin shouted this time. "I never saw you before!"

"That's possible. Well, I've got the distinct impression that I've already seen you somewhere, but it's probable that where I was standing that day, you couldn't see me."

"Quit your mysteries and please untie me. Can't you see I'm dying here?"

"Ahh, you're not going to die now, you look pretty good to me."

"Shit! I'm wounded! I was shot, just look at my shoulder! I'm losing blood! Do something! What's it to you if I'm attached or not?"

"Sorry 'bout that, I just feel more reassured that way. When you find out who I am, you'll understand right away why I'm taking my precautions."

"Jesus, who are you then?"

"No, neither Jesus nor one of his saints. Nor are you. Nor your shrew of a wife. If I trust my intuition, both of you have had quite an interesting past... something you're gonna explain to me in detail. I've got all the time in the world," concluded Simon Parker sitting down on a wooden stump in the corner of the shack.

Before sitting down though, he had to take out the axe in the middle of it. He weighed it in his hand, flipping it around like a wannabe Bruce Lee with his nunchaku, while continuing to keep an eye out on Mumin. Then he put the tool down next to the wooden stump.

"Details about what? I don't even know what you're talking about here."

"I'm talking about a nice vacation that you had with your wife and your daughter."

"What vacation? I don't understand, we never go on vacation. We got too much work at the farm."

"Don't try to get out of answering my questions. Summer vacation, at the beach. In the north-eastern part of the country, next to New York. Long Island to be exact. And to be even more precise, at a beach at the foot of the dunes, by Surfside Avenue. In Montauk... Only the best, right? Does Montauk ring a bell?"

CHAPTER 77

How much your actions can hurt

NEW YORK CITY, December 2023

When the train got to the Grand Central terminal, I was still lost in my thoughts about the Vaughan affair. Paul Nollington seemed to have played a more important role than he'd let on. Anyway, according to his parents, he had made a huge mistake, one that he still hadn't gotten over, to the point of severing all links with me and my investigation into what had taken place in Montauk.

There was still a thin layer of snow in front of the Manhattan station. New York like you see it on postcards! Except I wasn't here as a tourist. I unfolded the piece of paper where Steven Nollington had jotted the address of his son's apartment. On Park Avenue and 57th, not even a quarter of a mile from here. I could easily walk there while appreciating the brightly lit shop windows. Though they were all decorated for Christmas, my heart wasn't celebrating. I walked slowly to Paul's place, oppressed by the fear of what he would reveal to me.

Paul had come into my life by surprise, he'd rushed into it, if I could put it that way.

Paul who was able to see what I'd been dissimulating beneath my armor.

Paul, in whom I'd undoubtedly believed in a bit naively, something I had never in my life done.

Paul the liar, hypersensitive up to obsessional.

Those were the thoughts spinning around in my brain when I reached the building I'd been looking for. I spotted his name on the interphone and pressed the button.

"I'm opening," Paul's voice resonated. "Thirty-sixth floor, on your left, door 365 on the Park side."

He'd been waiting for me, not even asking who'd rung.

I walked into the huge lobby with its very classy marble-colored walls and floor. The elevator quickly took me to the thirty-sixth floor where I saw Paul standing in front of his door. The hall seemed like it would never end. He moved aside when I'd joined him.

"Come in, please."

The inside of his apartment was just as sophisticated as the building itself, with beautiful furniture that seemed to date back to the thirties.

"A New York getaway that's been in the family for several generations," said Paul, almost apologetically.

"What would you like to drink? I prepared a pitcher of gin tonic. I think we'll need it."

"Sure, thanks."

He invited me to sit on the sofa facing the picture window. The view overlooked the south-eastern angle of Central Park and The Pond, one that sadly reminded me of Oyster Pond in Montauk, where Laura and Katheline both drowned. Paul seemed to want to talk but no words came out of his mouth.

"Why didn't you ever answer any of my messages," I began to encourage him. "I'd hoped that... you and I..."

"Shhhh, Karen. Don't say anything that could damage what we share. I got scared, that's all."

"Scared of what?"

"Scared of myself... I'm sure my parents explained my hypersensitivity and everything that goes with it?"

"Not everything, no. I was hoping you could enlighten me. Why did you lie to me?"

"I lied to you?"

"Yes, you did, Paul. When you told me that you'd seen Simon Parker, on that tragic day, on Montauk Beach, shouting at Laura. Remember that?"

Paul lowered his head in shame after having taken a good swallow of his gin. But remained silent.

"Mr. and Mrs. Balmer gave me a completely different version of that story. They told me that it wasn't Simon Parker who was yelling at Laura... It was you, Paul! They were categorical. So? Who should I believe?"

Paul sighed loudly.

"The Balmer's told you the truth, Karen. On July 13, 2022, I did go down to the beach to see Laura and Kathy."

I frowned.

"And you got in a fight?"

"That's right. But it was completely my fault. I'm so terribly sorry now. What if my obsession, my jealousy, my possessiveness and my behavior that day were at the origin of her suicide?"

Paul's question hit me like an uppercut. I couldn't say a word. Turning the question around in my mind, I tried to quell his fears.

"Was that the big mistake you were talking about? You feel guilty to have caused her to commit suicide with her daughter? Paul, seriously, you can't inflict a horrible weight like that on your conscience!"

"Yes, I can. Because it's sadly the truth."

"What kind of proof do you have? None!"

"It's true, I don't have any proof. Except for my intimate, terrible and painful convictions."

I shook my head, dumbfounded by his expiratory explanation.

"Paul, it's your hypersensitivity that makes you see everything in black. You're not responsible for what Laura did. On the contrary, you always tried to help her, you were always there when she needed someone. You saved her Paul; you didn't kill her..."

"Who knows?" he sighed sadly. "You never really realize how much your actions can hurt, even those that are insignificant apparently. The same thing is true for what you say, or what you write. How many crimes were committed for one too many words? How many suicides were caused by a single damning statement? Verbal harassment, social networking, all that. Karen, you're a journalist, you must believe in the weight and importance of words. You can't say that you don't. Words, sentences, that's your job."

He was right. Completely right. One too many words, an insinuation, all of those things can kill.

"What did you and Laura say to each other that day on the beach?"

"I exploded with jealousy."

"But why? Jealous of what?"

"I was jealous because of her relationships at that time and those of... her daughter... Kathy. They'd been spending days with a couple of tourists. They were together all the time, and they had a daughter who was nearly as beautiful as Kathy. The girls played together in the sand, jumped in the waves, were totally inseparable. And their parents and Laura only had eyes for them. And me, I was behind my curtains in my room, moping and miserable all alone, looking down on all of them having fun. So yes, that day, when the other couple left, probably saying that they'd see them again tomorrow, I went down to the beach and yes, I did make a scene. Good Lord, Karen, if you only knew how much I've hated myself since that day! That was the last time I saw them alive. The last words I had with Laura were spiteful, atrocious, unnecessarily evil.

And all that because I couldn't seem to manage my jealousy of her and them. I was jealous because she was so happy! Jealous of not having been the one she spent her joy and days with! The words I said that day weighed down so much on her poor soul that she wanted to end it all. I killed her, I told you so!"

CHAPTER 78
How kids are

VERSAILLES, Missouri, December 2023

Sergeant Gallister didn't believe his ears. The man sitting across from him in the interview room, the man from Pittsburg, Pennsylvania, was both a witness and a stakeholder in the affair of the little girl who had been found. It was now clear that both affairs, the current one that was open, and that he was heading here in Missouri, and the one that was closed but that Karen Blackstone had reopened in Long Island, were somehow linked. But how? That was what Simon Parker would now tell the investigators.

"In that dark shed, the guy dying from cold, hunger and thirst told me everything. And I finally understood."

I WANT MOMMY

A few days earlier, not too far from Gravois Mills

Mumin Blasharov remained silent for quite a while, weighing his chances of survival. Pretty thin. He tried to negotiate with Simon Parker.

"If I tell you everything from A to Z, will you untie me and let me go?"

Katheline's father just smiled.

"I don't know yet, that's going to depend on what you tell me, if it's bullshit or the truth."

"I swear I'll tell the truth. Please."

"You know what? Let's make a deal. We'll do this in stages. First of all, I promise to give you something to drink and a little bit to eat, I've got a sandwich in my car, it's not too far from here. After that, if your whole story suits me, either I'll free you or I'll call the cops, and they'll take care of you. Okay with you?"

"I don't got much choice here."

"So go ahead. I'm waiting. What were you and your wife doing in Montauk last summer?"

The man took a deep breath and started to explain.

"You can tell we don't got much money. A vacation in Long Island is something we'd never be able to pay for ourselves, and even less in Montauk. One day my wife and me found a coupon for a contest in a sack of fertilizer that we always buy. It was a scratch ticket. And the prize was a vacation. We uncovered three ears of corn meaning we'd won the first prize: We didn't believe it; we'd never won a thing in our lives. A whole week all expenses paid in Montauk Manor. I'd never even heard of it. But it was true. We called the number on the coupon and decided together on the dates. And a couple days later we got the hotel voucher and left for Montauk on July 8, 2022. That was a Friday, and our stay there started on a Saturday. As we had pretty far to drive, we stayed in a hotel, and we got there the next afternoon. We were completely dazzled! The ocean, the dunes, the blue skey and New York's skyline that we could see in the distance!"

"You can skip all the details for tourists, I know the place. And then? What did you do for your week of a free vacation?"

"We mostly went to the beach. It was so nice. We'd never been to the sea. Quite a difference from Missouri's lakes."

"That it is!" said Parker, patronizing him. "A beach where you met nice people, didn't you?"

"What are you insinuating?"

"Calm down, Mumin. I'm just referring to when you met a single mother with her curly brown-haired daughter..."

"How do you know that?"

"Heard it through the grapevine! So how did you and your family get close to them?"

Blasharov looked anxiously at his inquisitor.

"It just happened, how come?"

"I'm the one asking the questions here. Answer!"

"We left the Manor, and as we didn't know our way around, we walked up and down the streets in

Montauk and ended up following the signs leading to the beach, and that's how we decided to go to Surfside Avenue, just because we liked the name. We put our towels down, unpacked Jessy's toys and relaxed. For us it was like we died and went to heaven! Plus you know how kids are, they started playing together really quickly, they're not like us adults who never dare make the first move. Our daughter got close to another little girl of her age, they shared toys, they both wanted to do the same things. Make little sandcastles, jump over the waves, roll around in the sand. You know, stuff that kids do. It was really sweet watching them. They even looked like each other, it was crazy. Luckily, they weren't wearing the same swimsuits, otherwise we might have taken the wrong one home with us! And that's how the mother of the other little girl started to talk to us, about how much those two looked alike. And then as time went by, we moved our towels closer to theirs and started talking."

At that moment Parker felt a twinge of sorrow hearing how his ex-wife had made friends with strangers. Same thing with their daughter, playing with another little girl.

"What did you talk about?" demanded Simon angrily.

"That's not important."

"What did you talk about?" reiterated Parker loudly.

"Anything and everything. The weather, our kids, the peninsula. The lady told us she spent her childhood there, in a house above the dunes. And I don't know what else. It was a while ago."

"Some things you never forget."

"Well, I forgot. All I can say is that the next day we met at the same place, then the day after and that our two daughters got along as if they were two sisters, and they had loads of fun. And we got on well too with the mother, though it was only too evident that we didn't weren't in the same universe, the same class. But having kids made us closer, I guess. And one day, after the beach, she even invited us over."

Simon Parker clenched his jaws and fists simultaneously.

"You went to my... to her house?"

"We did, but that evening, on the other hand, is one I'll never forget..."

CHAPTER 79
It was pounding pretty hard

"THAT WAS the night that everything changed in our lives. The life of that lady, Laura, and her daughter, Katheline, the one she always called Kathy. And our lives, too, my wife Carrie, my daughter Jessy and mine. Laura had invited us over for a barbecue. Something simple and no fuss. She asked me if I could take care of it, 'cuz ever since her husband split, apparently some good-for-nothing loser, she said..."

Parker clenched his fists even tighter, ready to pounce on that son of a bitch Blasharov who was speaking of him as if he wasn't even present. Of course, he couldn't have known. Not yet...

"... that she'd never even touched the barbecue because she was afraid she wouldn't know how to use it, and she'd burn the hot dogs and burgers. I of course said I'd be glad to take care of it and I cooked the meat while both women went into the kitchen to prepare some salads. The girls were playing in the yard and on the swing. It was perfect. While checking the charcoal and burgers and listening to the kids laughing, I internally thanked that fertilizer brand for that unforgettable moment. Nothing nice like that ever happened at the farm. But that's a whole 'nother story."

"Yeah, get back on track here, Blasharov," said Parker impatiently. "The facts: that evening!"

Groaning and wincing with the effort, Mumin tried to sit straighter against the shed's wooden walls. His arms were still tied behind his back, causing stabbing pain in his shoulders and arms.

"Can you at least untie my hands?" he begged. "I can't take it anymore."

His guardian just shook his head slowly.

"That evening, dammit, that evening!"

"What the hell do you care about what we did on our vacation? Okay, I'll continue," said Blasharov looking Parker in the eyes. "To sum it up, it was a really great evening between new friends. It was nice and warm, so we ate outside on the patio. The girls played in the yard until it got dark. As the evening went by, they both got really tired and we said that we'd better be going back to the hotel to put Jessy to bed, but Laura insisted that we stay a bit longer. We hadn't yet finished eating, so we did. I remember Laura telling us that she was glad to be having people over, that she felt alone, that she thought we were friendly and that she'd like to talk a little longer. She suggested putting Jessy to bed in her room and at the same time putting Kathy to bed in her bedroom, next to it. Once the two girls were sleeping, we'd be between adults and could finish the evening peacefully. That was the expression she used: 'Peacefully.' I gotta tell you though that we all had quite a bit to drink that night. Laura wanted to open a couple of good bottles of wine that her husband had bought a couple of years ago from a vineyard in Long Island, when they got married, and that he hadn't taken when he left her. I never drink wine, and I didn't even know that there were grapes in this part of the country. For me wine is made in California and in Oregon, that's all. But let me tell you, that was damn good stuff!"

Parker was furious but allowed him to continue.

"And as she wanted us to try several different kinds of wine, we finished a bottle of Chardonnay to begin with, then we opened a Merlot and a Cabernet-Sauvignon, and I can't remember what else. Little by little those names began to bounce around in my head, it was pounding pretty hard in my forehead, like I said, I'm not used to drinking wine. Same thing for my wife, it wasn't a good idea for her to have so much to drink that night."

"How come?"

"You'll see. Before I talk about her, I just want to digress a bit about Laura, our charming hostess. Jesus, if only you'd seen her, such a classy woman, the complete opposite of my old lady, that's for sure! And one of those beauties that you don't see too many of around, with eyes that would make your fly buttons pop off, a mouth that... and the ass she had..."

"Okay, hey! Enough of that! Why are you insisting on that, you bastard? You had quite an eyeful, that's it? Or did you two screw that night?"

Parker got up from the stump where he was sitting, getting dangerously close to Mumin, with his fists clenched. He bent down so they were face to face.

"Okay, calm down, what's the problem?" Mumin asked. "Do you know the lady?"

"What the fuck is it to you? Huh? Quit beating around the bush with your stupid insinuations. Let's get to the point: did you fuck her or not? Or rape her, maybe as she was intoxicated, is that it? You raped her and you killed her you bastard! Or maybe it was your wife..."

"No! No! No! We didn't kill Laura!" Mumin said, sobbing. "No! The opposite, we listened to her. We paid attention to what she was saying. She needed to get stuff off her chest, Laura, that night. She was really upset... That poor lady had suffered so much, she was so uncomfortable, so insecure. I don't know if the alcohol was the reason that she reacted like that, but what's sure is that she really got everything off her chest that night in July last year..."

CHAPTER 80
Shooting blanks

SIMON PARKER WAS furious listening to Mumin Blasharov. The poor tied up guy was getting ready to spit out truths that he undoubtedly didn't want to hear. But he had to listen. If only in memory of Laura and Kathy. Simon was pretty sure that the next couple of minutes would be something he wouldn't like, and he was wondering if he had the capacity to stand them. What would he do with what he heard? And what would he do with that man?

"So what did she have to get off her chest then?" he asked.

"Like I said," continued Mumin, trying to hold his sobs back, "all of us had had a lot to drink that night, I can't even remember how many bottles we finished off. Probably, as Laura was really drunk, all her emotional seawalls broke. And also probably as we had been total strangers just a couple of days ago, she felt that she was freer to confess her flaws to us. And she had a lot to confess! Starting with the scars on both of her wrists. She wasn't embarrassed to tell us about how she tried to commit suicide when she was a teen. She was a young fragile lady, out of her element, and she must have scared her skin like that to engrave her unhappiness forever. Those are the words she used. And she even went upstairs and read us a letter that she always had in her purse. A letter that she'd written when she was completely down and out addressed to her mother. A letter of explanations and excuses that she'd leave her the day that... that she would decide to end it all! And she added that no one understood her, except her best friend, her confidant. A neighbor, I think his name was Paul."

When he heard that name Simon jumped and unconsciously grabbed the axe that he'd put down next to the stump. Another wedge in his soul. When all was said and done, Paul Nollington had always been his worst enemy. He'd always jealously protected Laura from other men, just like a watchdog. An aggressive little dachshund that only knew how to bark and that trembled in front of a bulldog! Yet Simon didn't say a word.

Mumin continued.

"Laura told us about an entire era of her life, when she was younger, with tears in her eyes. We knew everything that happened in an hour or two. Her schooling, her hobbies, what she wanted to do, her regrets, what made her sad, her remorse, her love life. Ah! Her love life, what a story! She kept on repeating that her married life was a failure, that she'd made a huge mistake, that she should have thought twice before saying 'I do,' to that loser. We got all the gory details. And then to underscore what she said, she followed by saying that it was a miracle that her daughter had been born."

"Huh? What did she say about that?"

"I don't know if it was the truth or the ravings and ramblings of a too sensitive and too drunk lady, but we sure got too much information about her husband…"

"So what was the problem with her husband?"

"She complained that as time went by, he'd become aggressive with her, even violent. That sometimes he even hit her and that was why they separated, when their kid was still little, three or four months I think. The straw that broke the camel's back. She told us how he became violent, because of her."

"Because of their daughter? What the hell did she have to do with it?"

"Gimme a break! It's been a year and a half! Even me, I was two sheets to the wind, though not as much as the two ladies, who were both really out of it. Both were laying on the planks of the patio, leaning against a wall, a half-empty glass of wine in their hands, that I do remember. And that was when Laura told us about the… the intimate problems her husband had."

"What the fuck? Old wives' tales! Okay, continue. What was wrong with her husband?"

"You don't get it?"

"I want to hear it from your own mouth, you bastard."

"Jesus Christ, what did I do to you? What do you want?"

"I want to understand everything. So spill the beans!"

"Well, Laura told us that her husband was good-looking, muscular, with everything that you needed in the right place, well hung you could even say. But that didn't prevent him from... Hell, his nuts were dry! There you go! He could get it up, he could screw, but he was just shooting blanks..."

Parker could no longer contain himself. He picked up the axe and descended upon Mumin Blasharov, a miserable prey who couldn't defend himself.

CHAPTER 81
Setting our fates ablaze

"YOU SON OF A BITCH, I'm gonna split your head in two!"

Mumin, tied up, tried to hunch back into himself in a paltry gesture of self-defense, something that wouldn't prevent the axe from coming straight down on his head. He began to sputter.

"Why are you doing this? Who are you?"

A purely rhetorical question as Mumin had instinctively understood who Simon was, yet Simon, furious and uncontrollable, answered the question.

"I'm her fucking ex-husband who was incapable of getting her pregnant, that's who I am dammit! And now I'm going to split you right in two."

And he raised the axe a bit higher, ready to strike him dead.

"Stop!" Blasharov begged. "You don't wanna know what came next?"

Parker's arm stopped mid-air. His eyes were crazy,

his lips drooling, and for a few long seconds he remained silent, breathing in and out heavily like a bull ready to race towards its opponent in the ring. Then the need to know won over the instinct to kill. He furiously threw the axe to the other side of the shed. It noisily hit the wooden walls before falling onto the blackened pile of hay.

"Okay. Continue your story and then I'll decide what to do with you."

"No, that's not the way it works! I want you to swear to me that you'll let me go if I tell you everything!"

"Yeah, sure, you think you're able to negotiate things, here and now? Get on with it. Spit it out."

Mumin signed and conceded.

"That night, between two sobs, Laura insinuated that her daughter wasn't her ex-husband's daughter... I mean yours. And that you knew it. And that's why you were violent with her because you knew she'd cheated on you."

"Total bullshit! Okay, maybe it was possible that I was sterile, something I'd accepted. But we never did any tests to be sure. And it finally worked!"

"It must have because you had a daughter. And that's why she said that Kathy was a miracle child. But also that you never wanted to believe her, that you'd accused her of cheating, that Kathy wasn't your daughter, stuff like that. She couldn't stand all those doubts anymore, all those insinuations, your wrath, couldn't stand living with you anymore. And that night, she told us she wanted to end it all, like she said in the letter... We tried to talk her out of it, tried to console her, but nothing worked, she was at the end of her rope. We kept on telling her that she had to live for her beautiful little girl, but she continued, she was stubborn, plus like I said, she'd had a lot to drink, way too much. Exhaustion, alcohol, and we found out after, that she also had been taking medication, antidepressants, all that was a dangerous cocktail. And that was the precise moment when everything exploded... The spark that set all our fates ablaze..."

CHAPTER 82
Being a mother

MONTAUK, July 13, 2022

OUTSIDE, the immaculate night sky was cloudless and above Long Island showed a twinkling lace of stars. Amongst that multitude of stars, the red harvest moon shone brightly, like an evil sphere of fate.

And at Laura Vaughan's house, the atmosphere was full of electricity, full of black and threatening cumulonimbus clouds and lightning flashing in the minds of all those present. A storm was coming in and lightning would soon strike the group of individuals that destiny had united at that precise date and place. Destiny, or fate, whatever you call it, it couldn't care less about people or their souls.

That night in Montauk, destiny had decided to play dirty.

Laura, unreasonable, had belted down glass after glass, despite the risk of incompatibility with the antidepressants that she took. For months now she'd needed them. Every single evening. When the sun had set and Kathy was sleeping in her little crib, with her stuffed animal snuggled tightly against her, she was alone in that empty house, in that empty bed and spent her nights listening to the symphony playing in her head, the one that reminded her how much she now hated life, her life.. Laura fell into a deep sleep, knocked out by that mind-numbing cocktail.

Mumin, who hadn't refused his share of cocktails and wine, was also groggy. Still awake, though resting on a patch of dry grass next to the wooden patio. A glass in his hand, gazing up at the stars, he was appreciating that unhoped-for break for a week in their hard existence as farm-laborers and for the first time in his life, had enjoyed the sun. The sun on the beach, a relaxing one, contrary to the sun in Missouri, which was too hot and shiny over their fields.

Katheline, innocently sleeping, was probably dreaming improbable dreams that only the mind of a two-year-old child could imagine. Her large and innocent smile radiated in the shadows of her room, just lit up by the beams of the harvest moon and a dim nightlight.

Jessy, the poor child who'd never known the joys of vacations, a victim of parents who were never available for her, of a mother lacking all maternal instincts, of a father who was too submissive to his cantankerous wife and who was too docile to contest her power. Jessy, who must have been awakened suddenly by a terrible nightmare in her deep sleep in the middle of that big bed she didn't recognize, in a room she'd never seen before, popped up like a jack-in-the-box, and began to scream in the light of that harvest moon with its evil and smirking aura. Her eyes popping wide open, filled with tears, saliva dripping from her mouth and running down her chin and tiny neck, Jessy was screaming and couldn't seem to stop.

Carrie had also had much more to drink than she should have. She was used to drinking alone at the farm, but that night, she'd had much more than her usual dose. A drum was beating in the middle of her forehead, like a blacksmith pounding on a reddish horseshoe. And it was pounding, pounding, hurting, and deafening her. Resonating and confusing her. And now that kid, that *screaming kid* who just added to it, who was crying in her bed. "Jesus! She's gonna wake up Laura's kid too," grumbled Carried, awkwardly moving her hefty body out of the chair and zigzagging to the bedroom where her daughter was.

Carrie went into the bedroom, her eyes half-closed, knocked out by alcohol and fatigue, and yelled at Jessy, sitting in the middle of the bed, distraught.

"You gonna shut up now, dammit! You're gonna wake up your little friend! Is that what you want? You calm down right now!"

Does shouting at a two-year-old child help them to

calm down? Not so sure, but Carrie had neither the codes nor the instincts of a mother. Jessy sobbed even louder.

"What the hell's wrong? Tell me, now! Did you have a nightmare? What are you afraid of?"

Did Carrie know how to speak softly, how to whisper to calm her down? No, of course not, that was something that no one had ever used with her when she was a child. Being a mother is neither hereditary nor innate! It's something you learn, use and get better at, day after day, night after night, with patience and abnegation. But patience and abnegation were not Carrie's best features, if you could have said that she had others.

The lady with her plump but nonetheless powerful arms leaned over the child to pick her up. Do you believe that such a mother would be capable of tenderly rocking her crying daughter, her daughter who had been terrorized by a nightmare and an unfamiliar environment? Not Carrie. Still very inebriated, infuriated by Jessy's shrieks and tears, she picked her up by the shoulders and shook her to make her react.

Not unsurprisingly, the child didn't calm down. Quite the opposite, she cried even louder, still screaming. Snot was running from her nose down to her mouth, greenish drops of saliva were projected onto the furious face of the mother, who saw this smelly spray as an insult.

Carrie was furious, uncontrollable.

She slapped her in the face.

Her large famer's hand, calloused and rough, landed on Jessy's pink cheek. Her little head bent over to the left, like a spring, in an improbable angle of her nape. Her eyes opened with surprise. She hadn't been expecting something like that. The first consequence of that slap in the face was a sudden silence in the room, the child's mouth wide open with incomprehension.

The second consequence was that she began to holler even louder, shrill screams, almost like a bird.

And the third consequence took place in the neighboring room, where Katheline was sleeping and where there were now a second concert of frantic tears.

"Congratulations, you won!" seethed Carrie. "You woke the other kid up. You don't think of anyone but yourself! You're impossible!"

Mad as hell, Carrie Chastain continued to verbally accuse her daughter, but now punctuating each of her sentences with a new blow. One slap in the face, then another, then again another... The ring she was wearing on her finger lacerated her fragile skin. Each slap gradually reduced the volume of the child's cries.

Until there was silence in the room.

Until Jessy Chastain couldn't cry anymore...

The next day, her swollen and distorted face would be black and blue, red, yellow, scarred, unrecognizable.

In the next room, Kathy had fallen back to sleep, despite the noise. Children are magical that way, capable of sleeping anywhere, anytime. Even when a tragedy is taking place.

Mumin, slowly emerging from his contemplative lethargy, ran in.

But it was too late.

When he entered the bedroom, Carrie Chastain was holding the cadaver of her daughter in her arms and humming a lullaby.

CHAPTER 83
No more stars

ON THE DOORSTEP, Mumin remained stupefied. He saw Jessy, lifeless, her head dangling, in Carrie's arms. Her neck had an improbable angle, her face was tumefied, her open eyes were empty. Stars would no longer shine in them.

"Jesus Christ Carrie, what did you do?"

The haggard woman was still humming that indecent lullaby and rocking her now dead daughter, something that Mumin had never even suspected that she was capable of doing. But she didn't answer his question. Which wasn't actually a question as her husband knew what he saw. He understood, he felt everything.

He suddenly became lucid, as if he hadn't had a drop to drink.

"Carrie, put her down. Give her to me, slowly."

He tiptoed up to her, putting his arms out towards his daughter.

"Let her go," he repeated calmly. "It'll be okay, just relax your arms."

But her arms were like a vice squeezing the lifeless body of the little girl.

"You have to let her go now. I'll take care of it."

Carrie turned her head towards her husband, lightning in her eyes.

"Don't you touch my daughter!"

"Our daughter," Mumin added calmly. "She's not feeling well, you have to trust me."

"I know she's not feeling well, you fucking asshole! She's dead, you get it? She couldn't be any worse…"

Without any warning Carrie howled like a wolf looking up at the moon, that round and reddish moon that was overlooking the drama taking place down there. She looked at her child and shouted at her, shaking her once again.

"You're gonna live! You're gonna wake up now! It's an order! Come back! Why did you do that? Why? What did you do that to me?"

Unfortunately the child would never be able to answer her unseemly and indecent questions.

"Carrie, please. Stop it. We have to go to the police. It was an accident."

"No! And then what'll happen? They'll take my daughter, and I'll never see her again? I need her! Can't you understand that Mumin? I need a child. If not, I'm gonna die too. Is that what you want? For me to die? Ah! Yeah, maybe that's your fucking project… You want me to die."

"No, nobody wants anyone to die, Carrie. Calm down."

"Don't you get any closer to me. Leave me alone. Go see what that Laura is doing."

Sighing noisily, but docile, Mumin left and went to see their host, lying down on the swinging chair on the patio. She had passed out and was probably in an ethylic coma due to the mixture of antidepressants and alcohol. Mumin curiously thought that she wouldn't be a problem.

Then he went to Kathy's room, finding her fast asleep, luckily totally ignorant of the tragedy that had taken place right next to her. After that he came back to his wife.

Carrie had put Jessy down on the bed. She'd closed her daughter's eyes. If you hadn't seen her face, you would have thought she was serenely sleeping.

Carrie's face was serious, *dark and murky*, as they described it in horror novels in the 19th century. Behind her melancholic eyes you could feel intense underhandedness. In the woman's mind a diabolic plan was beginning to shape itself and she would implicate her stupid sheep of a husband in it.

"Listen," she said with her scratchy voice, "here's what we're gonna do. You listen and you do everything I say, okay? Because if we gotta count on your pea-sized brain, it's not gonna work. Ready, you concentrating, Mumin? So, here's what…"

For several long minutes Carrie Chastain detailed what her diabolically evil brain had contrived.

And in the following hour, it would be showtime for them.

CHAPTER 84
A terrible silence

NEAR GRAVOIS MILLS, Missouri, December 2023

IN THE SHED trying to shelter himself from December's unfurling and frigid wind, Simon Parker didn't know how to react to what Mumin Blasharov had told him. He was hesitating between anger, compassion and relief. Though he had just learned that his daughter was still alive, he still wanted to hear the details from the mouth of that tied up man.

"So what was your crazy wife's plan?"

Mumin, that big docile baby, was now openly crying after having told his jailer about the painful evening at Laura Vaughan's. But the hardest part was yet to come. Looking at the axe in Parker's hand though, he had to continue.

"I wasn't brave enough to go against her, she

controlled me. So I obeyed her and helped her with her plan. She was pretty quick in imagining the stratagem, and with hindsight, it *was* horrible, but so easy for her with her morbid reflections. Carrie wasn't wrong when she said that the two girls, Jessy and Kathy, nearly looked like twins. Same age, same height, almost the same features and twinkles in their eyes, same hair color, everything matched, she couldn't let an opportunity like that pass by. She'd decided that Jessy would continue to live! Laura was completely out of it, drunk and doped up by too many pills. We could do what we wanted with her. Carrie convinced me, she told me she had a perfect plan, that the circumstances were good for us. Laura was having a depression, she'd already tried to kill herself several times, and that meant that she could easily try again. And take her daughter with her, just like she'd written in the letter to her mother... Carrie had thought of all that in just a few minutes, inspired by that letter that gave us a miraculous *modus operandi*. Her brain wasn't that crazy when she was designing such a Machiavellian plan. She ordered me to carry Laura, still unconscious, and she followed me with Jessy's body. We put both of them in our trunk. Before closing it, Carrie took the ring off her hand, the one that had wounded Jessy's face, and put it on Laura's right hand. On her middle finger, because that was her largest finger, and the only one that the ring would fit on, as Carrie's fingers were much fatter. That was supposed to be a detail that would confirm the hypothesis in which the suicidal mother, completely inebriated, had beaten her daughter until she died. Which wasn't far from the truth, if you want to know. But a different mother though. Then she told me to go get Kathy who was still sleeping, and to put her in the back seat. We got all our stuff and tried our best to wipe down any traces of our passage in her house that night. Before leaving, I went back into Kathy's room and picked up her favorite little stuffed animal, the one she never left the house without."

"Her little stuffed lion," Simon replied pensively.

"That's right. I thought that would be something she'd remember, a reference in the midst of chaos that was waiting for her. So anyway, we left, Carrie sitting in the passenger seat, and she told me to drive off. Luckily, I'd sobered up. She was like a copilot, and she had a precise place in her head. Oyster Pond, an isolated pond on the left bank of Montauk, a place we'd hiked to all three of us, the day before in the morning. A little hike from the hotel, before meeting Laura and Kathy back on the beach. There, using our headlights, we lugged the still unconscious Laura and our dead daughter Jessy to the banks of the pond. We put them together in a macabre hug and pushed them in. They sunk rapidly. I'm thirsty, give me something to drink..."

"You two are monsters!" sputtered Simon Parker without considering Mumin's request. "Psychopathic weirdos, both of you, you and your wife! Do you realize that you drowned my wife in cold blood, and you threw your own daughter into the water?"

"Your ex-wife."

"What the fuck do you care if it was my wife or my ex-wife? You killed a human being, trying to disguise her disappearance as a suicide, cowardly taking advantage of her ethylic coma. And you added a third crime to that double one. You kidnapped and sequestrated a child! Monsters!"

Furious, Simon Parker threw the axe towards the tied-up man. It circled, just missing horrified Mumin's head by a few mere inches, and hit the wooden wall of the shed in a muffled noise.

"You're crazy!" shouted Mumin.

"I'm crazy? You're saying I'm the one who's crazy? You gotta be kidding! I'm standing in front of a man guilty of three crimes and I'm the one who's crazy? You're damn lucky you haven't told me everything yet, otherwise I would have aimed right between your two eyes."

"You gonna kill me?"

Simon thought this question over.

"I'm not an assassin," he finally sighed. "When I was younger, maybe I was a fighter, but I'm not a killer. Hurry up, tell me the rest!"

Blasharov hesitated for a while, looking his adversary straight in the eyes. Then he began to speak.

"Okay. Anyway, I already told you too much, you might as well know everything. So anyway after having left Oyster Pond, we drove back to Montauk Manor to pack our bags and start driving back to Missouri. We wanted to leave as soon as possible, put some distance between what we'd just done. Kathy was sleeping in the back seat. We drove all night, Carrie and me, just stopping for gas or to have a coffee. Then as day was breaking, when we were going through the Appalachians, Kathy woke up, rubbing her eyes with her little hands. I saw her in the rear-view mirror, and for a fleeting moment, it was like it was our Jessy. Crazy, I know. Except at that precise moment she started to look around, frantic, looking for Laura. Carrie turned around. "You slept well, my little Jessy. Now we're going back home." Kathy started to cry and all she could say was: "I want mommy, I want mommy." And that was when Carrie and me, we both understood that we'd made a huge mistake and now we were up shit creek without a paddle. That's what I told Carrie. Plus I gave her some advice. 'We gotta get rid of her as fast as we can.' And then I turned off onto Route 70."

CHAPTER 85
All traces of life

SIMON PARKER WAS NOW PUZZLED and suddenly feared what else Blasharov could tell him. They'd kidnapped Kathy, using her to *replace* their dead daughter. As if you could say that you owned a human being and wanted to exchange them just like a car that you had an accident with!

"We drove to the exit, and I parked in on the side of a little road," Mumin continued. "Kathy stayed in the car, she had calmed down and was dozing off, with her stuffed animal in her arms, probably tired of saying the same thing over and over. Carrie and I were outside wondering what to do next. I wanted to go to the police, give them the little girl back and confess everything. Of course, that solution didn't suit Carrie at all. We argued there, on the side of the road, and once again my wife's point of view won. This was what she decided to do. We would have to be very careful with the little girl and especially with our neighbors, the authorities, and so on. Kathy would never accept that she had been suddenly and violently separated from her mother without even having said goodbye. Luckily, she'd known us for the past couple of days and in her little head, we were good friends of her mom. So we told her that we'd be taking her on vacation for a couple of weeks at our house in Missouri because her mommy had a lot of work to do. And we added that she'd asked us to take good care of her until she came back. And later when she asked us where her friend Jessy was, we told her that she was on vacation at her aunt's house in Florida. When they're young like that, little kids never contest explanations like that, they just believe everything adults tell them. She was disappointed that they wouldn't be travelling together. Up until then, our lie was working. The hardest thing, like I said before, would be to prevent her from talking! In her innocent little mind, she would have told anyone and everyone where she was born, who she was, who her mother was, etc. But for Carrie, she was no longer *Kathy*, she had become *Jessy II*... We would have to format her to delete all traces of her former life from her memory, up until her own identity. So from that moment on we only called her Jessy. At the beginning it was pretty strange for her, she would shake her head, contest, saying: 'No, no, Kathy.' And Carrie quickly understood that that wouldn't be enough, that we'd have to brainwash her. When they're that little, their brains are like sponges, they absorb everything you put into them. And luckily for us, not sufficiently developed to remember things. It's pretty rare to have any souvenirs before you're two or three. That was our lucky point in this sad story. Just a year later and our plan would never have succeeded. So to give us enough time to shape Kathy's memory - our *Jessy II*, - we had to isolate her from everyone else. Lock her up. Prevent her from talking. So we locked her down in the basement in a windowless room. I know what you're thinking. She stayed in there from July 2022, when we got back from Montauk, up till the other day, when both of us escaped. A year and a half in that room! Each day I went down to feed her, wash her, and read her stories. She loved stories! I think that was the best moment of the day for her, during that long formatting time when she *became Jessy*. As time went by, Carrie, who never actually had any maternal feelings, but - and I know it's ironic - couldn't live without her daughter, gradually lost interest in her. I sort of became her second *mommy*..."

"But not her second daddy," added Simon Parker. "I'm still here. I'm back."

"I'm not trying to replace anyone. Like I said, before I found myself here, beaten up and tied up by my own wife, I was trying to make things right, or at least better. I didn't know how, and I knew that it wouldn't be easy and that I'd never forget the crimes I'd committed... but I could no longer live with myself in peace after having done such horrible things."

Simon Parker walked up to Mumin Blasharov. Now that the man had given him his version of the story, Kathy-Jessy's true father was going to have to make a serious decision. Mumin could undoubtedly read in his eyes the dilemma he was facing.

"What are you going to do to me now? Kill me?"

Parker didn't answer, he was thinking things over and picked up the axe. Mumin thought his last hour had come. He closed his eyes, felt the man moving around him and mentally prepared himself to die. He suddenly heard the characteristic noise of the axe in the air... landing on the wooden stump. He opened his eyes. Parker was standing, staring at him. He pronounced his sentence.

CHAPTER 86
On the brink

"I'VE GOT a couple of different options," stated Parker calmly to Mumin. "I could kill you right here and now. Easy in your situation. I could also let you go because, in a way, you expressed remorse for what you'd done and even tried to give a new and better life to my daughter by leaving that living hell where you and your wife put her. But for me, it's a no deal for either of these options. You're not the guiltiest person here. It's your wife, and by far. You're mostly guilty of cowardice and blindly complying with her delusions. A partner-in-crime. So here's what I'm going to do. I'm going to put your life in the hands of fate. I'm just going to give fate a helping hand, putting everything back where I found it."

When saying that, Parker kneeled down next to Mumin and picked up the rag that had been used to gag him.

"No!" he begged. "Please, not that!"

Any other words he had were smothered behind the rolled-up rag stuffed into his mouth and taped using the roll of duct tape that Carrie had left behind.

Simon got back up, rubbing the handle of the axe when he passed it and left the shed, without looking back. He locked the door with the padlock and put the key back under the stone where he'd seen Carrie put it.

THREE DAYS LATER, Sergeant Gallister and his team found Mumin Blasharov, unconscious, on the brink of death.

~

AT THE VERSAILLES POLICE STATION, December 2023

"IF WHAT YOU just told us is true, Mr. Parker, that would explain a lot of our questions about this case. Or should I say, in *these* cases, because I have to include one that was closed in the past, in Montauk, and that a journalist specializing in cold cases has recently reopened. We'll try to set up a meeting between you and your daughter, Kathy. After that, I'll have to decide on what will come of you, Mr. Parker."

"Meaning?"

"Though today we heard you as a witness, you still

are guilty of failure to assist a person in danger for Mumin Blasharov, who is now in a coma."

"I must be dreaming," objected Parker. "They killed my wife, kidnapped and sequestered my daughter for a year and a half... and there's no mitigating circumstances for me?"

"I'm legally bound to comply with this procedure. Nonetheless, considering the circumstances, I'll take my time before informing the prosecutor. I'm going to call Dr. Cagliari so we can set up a meeting with Katheline as soon as possible. Are you capable of that, Mr. Parker?"

"I've been waiting for this for years now, Sergeant," replied Simon, his voice broken by a sudden emotion.

"I've still got a question though," added Myra Stonehenge. "Why didn't you try to see your daughter earlier?"

"After Laura and I separated, things were pretty tense, and she'd filed a complaint against me, and I had a restraining order prohibiting me from getting near her house and even Long Island. And that was why, on the day that I saw that couple on the beach with Laura and Kathy, I couldn't come down to talk to them. It would have caused me problems. But had I known, I would have been able to prevent even worse ones..."

"You've always got 20/20 hindsight," said Gallister philosophically, "don't get all worked up about it, Mr. Parker. Tell yourself that thanks to your intervention in the shed and your testimonial, we were able to learn more about the whys and wherefores of this case."

"You think that's what the prosecutor will say too?"

"I haven't contacted him yet. Could you wait here a couple of minutes?"

He left the interview room, leaving Myra with Parker, picked up his phone and called Dr. Cagliari.

"Frances? Pete Gallister here. I'd like to organize a visit with the little girl. With her real father. Do you think she'd be up to it?"

"If it ends up like the last time with her mother, I'd say no," the child psychiatrist warned him. "She's still very psychologically fragile."

"To tell you the truth," the officer continued, "her *mother* isn't really her *mother*. I'll explain all that to you when I see you.

"And her *father* isn't really her *father*?" asked Frances Cagliari ironically.

"It all depends on who you're talking about!"

"Usually at Christmas, there's a child who was born. Not their parents! Okay then Sarge, bring him in."

CHAPTER 87
She's looking down on you

JEFFERSON, Missouri, December 2023

Sergeant Gallister, walking Simon Parker, escorted by Myra Stonehenge and Dr. Frances Cagliari, down the long halls of Saint Mary's Hospital, was getting fed up with being there one more time. He'd end up getting to know each and every corner of the place! Pediatrics, psychiatry, ICU, he was getting sick and tired of those sanitized odors and white tiles! What he was dreaming of was spending time with his family around a table filled with a Christmas sized turkey, mashed sweet potatoes, and of course, cranberry sauce, even if the turkey was overdone, he wanted to close this case before Jesus's birthday.

Gallister had updated the doctor about the latest developments in his investigation.

A cop, seated in front of the little girl's room got up, respectfully greeting his colleagues.

"Let me go in first," the child psychiatrist said. "I'll prepare her for what's coming and call you in after."

The child was sitting up in her bed, her back resting against the pillow. She'd pulled the bedside table used for meals next to her and there was a pile of white sheets of paper and a box of crayons on it.

"Hello. What are you drawing, sweetie?"

As usual, the little girl didn't answer. But she did smile at Frances and showed her the drawing she was doing. This time, it wasn't a scary one. It looked like she was trying to draw her favorite stuffed animal, that little lion that never left her side.

"What a good job!" the psychiatrist said. "You're really gifted. Are you feeling well today?"

The child's eyes seemed to reply that she was.

"There's someone who wants to see you. He's waiting in the hall. But before I let him in, I want to tell you a couple of really important things."

The doctor put her hand on the little girl's.

"I know you've been through a really hard time. I know that you've suffered a lot because of what happened in the past few days and even... in the last few months. If you agree to talk to me, and I think that you can, that will really help me make you better you know. I need you. Just like your little lion needs you and you need it. I'm sure that you tell your stuffed animal lots of secrets. I'm right, aren't I?"

She nodded her head, making Dr. Cagliari understand that it was true.

"Your little lion lived through the same things as you. It never left your side. Never. It was always there for you, and it loves you. It's always been there for you, ever since... since you left Montauk. Does Montauk ring a bell? Long Island? The sandy beach, the ocean, the dunes? Your grandma Melinda's big house?"

The child's eyes squinted, as if she were trying to remember. The places and names the doctor had mentioned seemed to resonate someplace inside her, you could tell.

"That's where you are from, honey. You've forgotten all that now. Like you forgot your mommy's name. Not the lady who came here the other day, the one that you didn't want to see. She wasn't your real mommy. Your real mommy's name was Laura. Laura, do you remember that name?"

This time, there was another different kind of spark in the child's pupils.

"Now mommy Laura is in heaven, but she can see you, she looks down on you every single day. She cares about her darling daughter, Katheline. Her dear Kathy. Because that's your real name. Your name is Katheline, and you were born in Long Island. Kathy, that's a pretty name. It's the nicest one in the whole world. Do you like it?"

The little girl nodded, accompanied by a huge smile on her chubby little face.

"That's good! I can see that you like it. You like it

because you heard it often, that's why. Mommy Laura called you that. Grandma Melinda also did. And both of them love you, you know that, Kathy?"

Now she was nodding her head quickly, her features were sparking, and finally the miracle happened.

"Ka-thy," the child said slowly. "Ka-thy." Kathy! Ka-the-line... Katheline! I'm Kathy."

The doctor shared Kathy's enthusiasm, still holding her hand smiling at these words that finally came out of her throat.

"That is marvelous sweetie, fantastic. Now, would you like to see your real daddy? Huh? Because he's right here, right on the other side of the door, and if you say yes, I'll go get him."

"Okay."

A conversation! Just a few words, but so much more than before, Frances thought to herself, overjoyed. She got up from the chair next to the bed and went to the door to let Simon Parker in. Gallister and Stonehenge followed him but stayed respectfully behind.

The room was completely silent. No one dared break this stirring and emotional silence.

Kathy, her eyes wide open now, stared at that unknown man – she hadn't seen him since she was only four months old, and even then, after nearly two years, would never have been able to recognize him.

Simon walked slowly up to the bed, his eyes humid, his hands trembling, his jaw locked by emotion. She'd grown up so much, but there was no way he couldn't recognize that oval face, those bright eyes, her brown curly hair. His daughter! At that precise moment he measured how much he regretted those years gone by; those years he'd lost. He wanted to catch up as quickly as possible... and the best he could.

Dr. Cagliari, who had also stood back, contemplated with compassion that father and his daughter finally reunited after so many trials: separation, the death of Laura, sequestration, and loss of memory. As a professional she knew all too well that both of them would require long psychological work.

Sergeant Gallister, standing at the door, could feel the tension in the hospital room. He was hoping that the child would succeed in overcoming this new trauma.

Parker was now standing at the bedside, and he held his hand out to his daughter. Docile, she took it, but the smile that she'd had on her face before had disappeared. She began to pant.

"My Kathy," said Simon, his voice broken by the emotion. "I'm so terribly sorry. You probably can't even remember me. You were so little when your mommy – Laura – and me... It doesn't matter. Today I'm here for you and I'll never leave you again. Okay with you? You want to keep me as your daddy?"

The little girl swallowed, gave him a timid smile, but didn't answer. How could she answer a question like that at this stage? Perhaps she'd have to ask her little stuffed lion before? Yet, she let her father hold her hand. Then she turned her head towards the window.

"I want Mumin," she said.

"What did she say?" asked Gallister, too far away to understand those words she'd whispered with her little accent or problem of articulation.

"She said, "I want mommy," supposed Dr. Cagliari.

"No," Simon cut her off painfully. "She said '*I want Mumin*... He's the one she considers as being her real father as he's the only one she remembers."

CHAPTER 88
Breaking my heart

NEW YORK, December 2023

While sitting next to me on the couch in his large Manhattan apartment, Paul Nollington kept on repeating, like a mantra, that he felt he was responsible for the death of both Laura and Katheline, I suddenly felt my cell phone vibrate in my pocket. Darn it! Never a moment of peace! Mechanically, as the gesture had become a habit and the phone a passive addiction, I looked at the screen to see who was calling. Pete Gallister.

"Excuse me Paul, this is a call I have to take."

"Don't worry Karen. I'll pour us another round of gin tonics. Okay with you?"

I nodded while picking up.

"Hello."

"Miss Blackstone, this is Sergeant Gallister from Versailles. Could I have five minutes of your time?"

"Of course, no problem. What's new?"

"Well, I've got some recent information about your investigation and I'm sure you'll want to hear this. You can tell Melinda Vaughan that she's not as crazy as she thinks."

"And? What are you insinuating?"

"I'm not insinuating anything; I'm *affirming* that the little girl we found is Mrs. Vaughan's grand-daughter. Her conviction as a grandmother was right when she said she thought she recognized Katheline on the photo we broadcast in our call for witnesses."

I needed a couple of seconds to assimilate what the words the sergeant had just uttered meant.

"But how is that possible? She's not dead and buried in Long Island?"

"According to what Simon Parker, her father, just told me, she's not. I'll be reopening the investigation with my colleague there, – it's Lieutenant Garrett, isn't it? – to exhume the body in Amagansett Cemetery. And I'll bet you anything you want that the analyses will identify the child as being Jessica Chastain, who was born in Missouri."

I didn't believe it. All the characters were dancing around in my mind while the police officer was giving me his progress in the case. For several minutes, I religiously listened to him, nodding or repeating names, both of people and places. I glanced over at Paul walking around in the large room overlooking Central

Park, as he served our cocktails, pensively admiring the brightly lit-up avenue before turning around to look at me, with haggard and inquisitive eyes. When I finally had hung up, overwhelmed by the terrible things Gallister had just told me, Paul was anxious to know more.

"Well? Did they solve the case?"

"They did, Paul. It's almost over now. And down there in Missouri they found what really happened."

"You're sure of that?"

"I am, why? They proved that the little girl that was found actually is Katheline Vaughan-Parker. She was kidnapped in Montauk, at her house, on July 13, 2022, the day she disappeared, by a couple of farmers from Missouri."

Then it was my turn to relate to Paul how everything took place and what Sergeant Gallister had told me.

Paul, the hypersensitive person, fell apart. When I'd finally finished, he threw me another curveball, one that I'd have to – or not – inform the police investigators of later.

"That is all so atrocious, it makes me sick," he sputtered. "You have no idea how this is breaking my heart, destroying my soul. It's so incredible yet so plausible. Karen, you know that general news in a little town is always terrible. But there's one little detail – or is it really a detail? – that could change everything and that the cops don't know about."

"One that you are sure of?"

"Totally. I know from a trustworthy source that Simon Parker is *not* Katheline's father."

"Who's your source?" I asked, captivated.

"The most involved person in this whole story told me so. I was the one Laura told all her secrets to, and she told me…"

CHAPTER 89
Folly of wanting to die

"LAURA EXPLICITLY TOLD you that Simon was *not* Katheline's biological father?"

Paul looked me in the eye before answering.

"She confirmed to me that there was no way in hell that he was. Like I told you before, Laura considered me as her best friend, and it was a role I'd always accepted. Reluctantly, of course, because I dreamed of playing another role, one that in my opinion was much more important. One evening, she called me, crying. She wanted us to see each other in private. I was right here, in this apartment. She said she'd come over, she needed to see me, to talk, to cuddle against me, to tell me about what was bothering her, like a brother and a sister. Of course, that was something I couldn't say no to. I knew I was important to her, and I was proud of that. I couldn't wait till she came, impatiently walking around in circles like a caged lion. When she came, she rushed to my arms and cried on my shoulder for a long time. I must admit that I also shed some tears. Then we sat down on the couch, and she confessed that Simon was sterile, that he'd never be able to give her what she was dreaming of. What she wanted the most in life: giving birth. Taking care of a little flesh and blood doll, a mini-Laura. She said that helping a child to grow up would make her forget her own demons, her desires to kill herself. Raising a daughter would give her a reason to live, erasing her folly of wanting to die. '*Folly of wanting to die.*' Those were her exact words. And as I'm sure you can imagine, I was terribly touched by them. After that, when she'd calmed down, I asked her why she didn't just leave Simon, as he couldn't satisfy her dream of becoming a mother. I was hoping she'd read between the lines... But no, she didn't jump on my invitation to love her, to make her happy. Once again, I had no idea what he had that was better than me. So I suggested thinking about assisted reproduction or adoption. But Simon refused . He was too proud and too full of himself to, first of all, accept his inability to procreate and then, accept a child that wouldn't be his. So you see Karen, it was an extremely complicated and fragile situation. We spent the whole evening talking about this, trying to find a way out while drinking champagne, as I had two bottles in the fridge. We said that their bubbles would help us rise towards better horizons, lighter ones. And then, when day was about to break, after having talked the entire night, we both slid down on the sofa and... and we tenderly and violently made love. It was a rage of emotions, a storm of silences, a hurricane of feelings and sensations. That night here in Manhattan, took place exactly nine months before Kathy was born…"

CHAPTER 90
Pluck up my courage

RIGHT UP TO the very end, when I was mentally rewinding everything I'd learned since coming to Montauk a few days ago, right up to the very end I had doubted everything. From uncertainty to convictions, doubts to suspicions, suspicions to confessions, confessions to finally understanding the whole affair. Like a puzzle you put together, piece after piece, until you get to the penultimate one.

Or the next to last piece of the puzzle, as concerning the last one, Paul still had things to add.

"Laura and I never talked about our crazy night in Manhattan. It was our secret. A secret she took with her to her tomb. The big mistake that my parents talked about was that. I'm Katheline Parker's biological father and I never did a thing to become her putative father, legally her father. And she never said a word about it, of course never confessed that to her husband.

Simon must have felt as proud as a rooster in a coop when he learned that he finally could father a child. But it's evident when you look at Kathy that she doesn't look like him at all."

Paul shook his head, a lump in his throat. I respected his silence.

"On that terrible day of July 13th, I couldn't take it any longer looking down at how happy my daughter was on Montauk Beach, hidden behind the curtain in my bedroom. I plucked up my courage and went down. To tell you the truth, that scene that the Balmer's saw concerned my paternity. That day I threatened Laura to reveal our secret. I wanted to be a real father! But she didn't agree. She said that she could raise Kathy alone. That drove me crazy. I swear to God, if I hadn't been such a reasonable person, maybe it would have been me who killed Laura that day and taken Kathy with me. But fate is fickle and that was what happened that very night…"

I took Paul's hand in mine.

"And what are you going to do with that info now?"

"I don't know. Maybe it's time that I assume my responsibilities… A simple DNA test would be enough to confirm my declarations. But Kathy is alive and that's what's the most important. Though she lost everything. She was raised with a false father who locked her up. She doesn't even remember her genitor, as he never assumed his role. She's got one left…"

"Paul, there's no way I can tell you what to do. But I think, that in Laura's memory…"

Paul cut me off in the middle of my sentence.

"Let's call Sergeant Gallister."

CHAPTER 91
So very fragile

JEFFERSON, Missouri, December 2023

An odor of antiseptics filled Katheline's nostrils while she was walking down the ICU hall with Dr. Frances Cagliari, followed by Gallister. Kathy had said she wanted to see Mumin, despite everything. That man, the one she considered – or tolerated – as her adoptive father, was the only one she'd ever known. The doctor had explained to her that he was very sick, and he was sleeping, and that maybe he wouldn't see her or wouldn't even hear her.

"I want Mumin," Kathy had said. That was what she had been saying from day one, ever since the day she'd escaped from Carrie Chastain in the forest and was miraculously found on the side of a snow-filled road, before Rebecca Stern picked her up. Those three words she'd been repeating over and over to the driver who nearly ran her over. She'd been asking for *Mumin*, not for *Mommy*, a lady she'd forgotten.

The child psychiatrist had spoken with the nurses and the intern on call, and they were allowed to enter Mumin Blasharov's room, though he was still in a coma.

Lying on the medialized bed, hooked up to various machines, Blasharov's body was imposing. The little girl was in awe when she saw that strong man who now seemed so very fragile. The beeps of the monitors chirred in the child's ears, though she didn't seem too bothered by them.

She walked up to the bed and held out her hand, putting it through the bars and grabbed one of Mumin's hairy hands.

The monitor suddenly peaked. Was he coming to?

"Mumin..." she said softly. "Mumin? Are you sleeping? Mumin?"

But the man in a coma seemed to be in an inaccessible limbo.

"Mumin gonna die?" Kathy asked Dr. Cagliari.

"We don't know, honey. I think he's trying to resist."

"Don't want that. Don't die, Mumin."

Suddenly, to everyone's surprise, the heart monitor went crazy. Blasharov groaned and weakly moved. Then he opened an eye... and the other.

He turned to Kathy and looked at her. In a scratchy voice he awkwardly tried to speak.

"Jessy?"

"No, not Jessy. Kathy."

"You're right. Kathy. Kathy. My darling little Kathy."

The man's eyes closed.

His head dropped to the side.

The monitor had flatlined.

Then there was silence.

Epilogue

I SPENT Christmas in Manhattan with Paul. As neither of us had any obligations, we decided to spend two days, two whole days together just for us, to consolidate our budding couple.

Then I went back to Montauk, left the Manor, and sent my expense slip to Myrtille Fairbanks accompanied by a long article for the February edition of *True Crime Mysteries*. In that article, I wrote about all the secrets of the various protagonists of the Vaughan-Chastain case though sugar-coating a couple of events that could hurt or harm those surviving. Though I do work for a tabloid magazine that highlights the back and local pages in papers, I hate voyeurism and over-dramatizing them. And for that Myrtille always lets me do my thing.

After Mumin Blasharov's death, Carrie was arrested and placed in pre-trial custody in a jail that had a psychiatric ward. She was facing a sentence of a hundred and twenty-four years of prison.

The grave with Katheline Vaughan-Parker's name on it was opened and the remains of Jessy Chastain were exhumed and then transferred down to Missouri to a grave next to her father, Mumin Blasharov. They were reunited in death, waiting for Carrie, someone who would only leave jail feet first in a wooden box.

In Long Island, the copper plate on the tomb in Amagansett Cemetery was modified: only the name of Laura Vaughan Parker was now mentioned on it.

Paul took a DNA test to confirm his paternity. He was hoping that he'd be awarded custody of Kathy, his biological child, conceived with Laura that one crazy night in Manhattan.

Simon Parker, at first opposed to Paul's undertaking, could only note the weaknesses in his file as well as his lack of assuming his role as a father.

∽

Paul and I promised to see each other as soon as possible. For the very first time I was able to open up to someone. I didn't want to count my chickens before they'd hatched, but had decided to just let myself live, finally. I went back to my little house, where I found my antique and failproof Ford Ranchero that my late father had given me. I had so missed that hunk of junk when I was in Long Island!

. . .

Before going farther with Paul, and Katheline, I needed to take care of myself.

Work on myself, my wounds and other gray areas from my past. To accomplish this, everything had to start with a phone call from here at home, looking out the window over the magnificent Casco Bay, in Portland, Maine.

"Spider?"

"Hey! What's up with Miss Karen Blackstone? My little tips work out for you?"

"You were totally perfect," I conceded. "Just goes to say that giving fate a little helping hand or sneaking into a database, those are things that can help. Thank you again."

"My pleasure. You calling to congratulate me and thank me? That's nice. I like having grateful clients, it's pretty rare."

"I'm going to need your occult services once again."

"Okay. What can I do for you this time?"

"I'd like to have the list of births in Cambridge Massachusetts on February 28, 1999. Think you could get that for me?"

"Wow! I'm not promising anything, that goes way the heck back!"

"Thanks, you're too nice! I was eighteen then and I'm not a dinosaur..."

"Whoops! So, when do you need it for?"

"The day before yesterday if you can do it."

"I can do anything when I'm paid for it, you know."

"Name your price. It's really important to me, do you understand? Very personnel, if you see what I'm getting at."

"I do, don't sweat it. I'll get back to you."

∽

Three days after, I got that oh so important information that I'd been lacking for years. A male child named Luke Virgil Matthews, born from an anonymous mother on February 28, 1999, first name, Luke, middle name, Virgil, and last name Matthews, was registered. According to Spider's sources, he now lived in California, somewhere near Los Angeles.

I thanked him warmly, paid for his service in bitcoins, and dialed another number.

"Hello, Myrtille? I need you to send me on an investigation in the roundabouts of Los Angeles…"

"Honey, do I look like I'm running a travel agency? You're hoping to go on an all-inclusive vacation? Let me have a look. Just because it's you!"

THE END

Acknowledgments

You, my dear readers, the ones holding this book in your hands, will you read these couple of extra sentences or would you prefer, like many people do, to ignore them, thinking to yourself that they don't concern you? You'd be wrong, I affirm that, as here I'd like to pay homage to you.

What would an author be without his readers? Like a pen without ink, a keyboard without keys, a book without words... Inconceivable!

These words are directly addressed to you as warm and sincere thanks. There were so many of you who loved the first book of this *trilogy* – that's right, you'll soon find Karen Blackstone investigating a new cold case – or this *series*, with the inspiration of yours truly and your interest to continue reading about this new character I'd imagined. Without your enthusiastic comments, I'm sure I wouldn't have continued with Karen as quickly. Now we can't leave each other. And I hope you don't want to leave her either.

Once again, thank you, thank you so very much!

I'd also like to thank Natacha, my wife, who this time had preferred to distance herself from the building of my scenario and writing of my novel, so she'd be able to discover it just like all my other readers. I hope I surprised her and brought her on-board in this suspense-filled story.

As always, I'd like to thank my beta-readers, Nadine, Sonia, Marie-Chantal, la Fée, Isabelle, Nanouchka, Cindy and Magali. Each of them, strangely I only have women in my team, has contributed to forcing me to progress, more and always, with the only goal of helping me to improve myself and give my future readers a pleasure filled experience.

And I can't forget Jacquie Bridonneau, my French to English translator, without whom you wouldn't have been able to read this book!

Ah! *Erratum*, Eric joined my beta team not too long ago. I'd like to thank him too for the same reasons.

I don't want to forget Ludo, my favorite graphic artist, especially for this series. Thank you for your patience in my numerous requests for modifications, for the hours spent on the phone talking about this and that, often about not much at all, but which ended up by creating the design of this book cover which, as always, is awesome.

Last but not least, thank you Sophie, my eagle-eyed and loyal proofreader, one who is also a fantastic pastry chef!

My dear Readers, I'm looking forward to seeing you again soon!

Also by Nino S. Theveny

DISCOVER « THE LOST SON », A KAREN BLACKSTONE THRILLER, VOLUME III

The young lady was running desperately, as if fleeing Death itself.

Which actually was the case.

Nikki was running as fast as her legs could carry her. As fast as her lungs would allow. She could feel them tearing apart, burning. Her irregular panting betrayed how close she was to abandoning.

She soon would no longer be able to escape the person pursuing her.

She didn't even know where she was running to. Just why she was fleeing. The young lady had no idea where she was heading in that dense and moist forest. A rainforest. Trees and gigantic vines towered towards the jet-black sky, one that barely let beams from the reddish harvest moon that could have belonged in a horror movie come through.

Surrounding her, Nikki could hear the terrifying noises of the Amazonian jungle mixed in with her own throaty, dry breathing. Wild animals growling in the shadows, reptiles she couldn't even see hissing eerily, constantly fearing to put one of her feet down on the cold and sticky skin of a snake with a deadly venin. Shrill shrieks from nocturnal birds with yellow eyes cut through the darkness between the huge bleeding leaves from the myriad of poisonous plants in the region.

Her pulse was pounding in her head like the bass notes of drums in the Bronx, where she had been born twenty-eight years ago and lived until that fatal day when she decided to go to Brazil with Jason. What had brought her here, lost and alone in the middle of the Amazon?

Why was she fleeing, her bloody bare feet full of wounds, attacked by deadly roots in the arch of each foot, fearing she'd twist an ankle because she was running so fast, that she'd bump into one of those roots, slip and fall on the muddy, spongy and hostile ground in that hostile forest.

Nikki knew that should she trip and fall, that would be the end. The man would pounce on her just like a vulture on its prey, and she would be a goner.

While drawing on the last bit of her resources left, the young lady thought once again of Jason.

Her boyfriend hadn't been able to escape their aggressor a bit earlier in the cabin they'd rented. What an idiot he was, such a dumb idea! "A long weekend for us two lovebirds, far from everything," was what he'd proudly told her, showing her the reservation he'd made in the isolated cabin in the middle of the rainforest. Just the two of them, making love day and night, with no one to bother them, no one to prevent them from joining together.

Just the two of them?

Too alone, too isolated... faced with that surprise guest who broke into the cabin in the middle of the night, a brightly colored wrestler's mask on his face, without a shirt, just his oversized muscles, pecs, biceps, and deltoids tight with wrath and fury. And above all, that curved machete he was waving in front of them. The ideal wilderness survival tool. Advancing through the forest, cutting vines, cutting down leaves that were just as long as hammocks.

As well as being the perfect instrument to cut Jason into bits.

Nikki had succeeded in escaping the blind wrath of their aggressor by jumping out of the back window of their cabin, scratching her thighs through the nearly transparent nightgown that barely covered her intimacy. It was so hot and humid in the rainforest that Jason and she had spent most of their time as wannabe Robinsons, nearly nude. Now the silk was stuck to her skin, almost like a snake that was molting.

Her nightie, from fleeing that horrible, hooded man, was now in shreds, and you could now easily imagine Nikki's generous and firm shapes, her ebony color standing out in the cold and pale moonlight.

She suddenly heard the footsteps more distinctly of the evil man hunting her down. She was exhausted. Her legs could no longer hold her up, her feet were bloody stumps, her lungs had been ripped open, her eyes were filled with tears.

She collapsed, panting, her face against the spongy, muddy ground.

Her heart was pounding. Nikki thought for a fleeting moment that maybe she'd die right then from a heart attack.

A death that would probably be preferable to the one she'd have.

Above her, she could feel the heavy presence of the assailant.

"Turn around," hissed the man through his rubber mask. "Look at the face of Death."

The young lady mentally refused to obey that atrocious order. Nonetheless, her head turned slightly.

Behind the round holes of the mask, two yellow eyes were shining, just like those of the caiman lizards here in South America's brownish waters.

The man raised his machete above her head, Jason's fresh red blood still dripping from it.

Nikki's eyes opened with horror, and she screamed, breaking the noisy silence of the Amazon rain forest.

Moonlight reflected itself on the curved blade right before it reached her neck.

"Cut!" shouted Brad Purcell, the movie director, with satisfaction. "We're rolling with this one. Thanks guys, it was just perfect."

Bibliography

THE KAREN BLACKSTONE SERIES
Sugar Island (2022) *(Winner of the Cuxac d'Aude Favorite Novel, 2023 / Finalist in the Loiret Crime Award, 2023)*
I Want Mommy (2023) *(N°1 in Amazon Storyteller France sales 2023)*
The Lost Son (2023)
Alone (2024)
Volume 5 to be published in 2025

THE BASTERO SERIES
French Riviera (2017) *(Winner of the Indie Ilestbiencelivre Award 2017)*
Perfect crime (2020)
Bloody Bonds (2022)

OTHER NOVELS
True Blood Never Lies (2022)
Thirty Seconds Before Dying (2021)
Eight more Minutes of Sunshine (2020)

Printed in Dunstable, United Kingdom